D1498465

The Hyperion Library of World Literature

Little John
of Saintré

PLATE I

ANTOINE DE LA SALE PRESENTS A BOOK TO PHILIP THE GOOD,
DUKE OF BURGUNDY

Little John of Saintré

LE PETIT JEHAN DE SAINTRÉ

BY

ANTOINE DE LA SALE

c. 1386-1462

Translated for the first time into English with an Introduction by

IRVINE GRAY

Late Scholar of Jesus College, Cambridge

HYPERION PRESS, INC.

Westport, Connecticut

Published in 1931 by George Routledge & Sons, Ltd., London
Hyperion reprint edition 1978
Library of Congress Catalog Number 76-48432
ISBN 0-88355-560-3 (cloth ed.)
Printed in the United States of America

Library of Congress Cataloging in Publication Data
La Sale, Antoine de, b. 1388?
    Little John of Saintre = Le petit Jehan de Saintre.

    (The Hyperion library of world literature)
    Translation of L'hystoyre et plaisante cronicque.
    Reprint of the 1931 ed. published by G. Routledge,
London, in series: Broadway medieval library.
    Bibliography: p. 29
    1. Saintre, Jean de 1320 (ca.) - 1368 — Fiction.
I. Gray, Irvine Egerton. II. Title. III. Series.
IV. Series: Broadway medieval library.
PQ1567.H3G7   1977   843'.2   76-48432
ISBN 0-88355-560-3

CONTENTS

TRANSLATOR'S PREFACE

SELECTIONS from *Le Petit Jehan de Saintré* were translated into English by Alexander Vance in 1862—based, no doubt, on the Guichard text of Saintré (see Introduction, p. 27). For the present version the splendid Champion-Desonay edition has been used, so that the translation, whatever excuse there may be for its shortcomings, cannot plead the want of a reliable French text. Louis Haugmard's transliteration of *Saintré* into modern French, though highly untrustworthy, has also been helpful. No apology is needed, I think, for attempting to give the English an archaic flavour, or for not attempting to produce fifteenth century English.

Not one of the editions of *Saintré* is furnished with adequate notes, and there are passages in the French of which the exact meaning is doubtful, though the general sense can be gathered. Difficulties occur in the descriptions of jousts and tournaments, which are as technical as a modern newspaper account of a boxing match or a golf championship. It seemed better as a rule to make a readable English version than to dig out obscure terms for clothes and armour and explain them in notes. Some notes were needed, however, and will be found at the end of the book.

The only cuts which have been made are : two or three pages of theological doctrine in Chapter 9, the greater part of the long list of names and arms in Chapter 58, and a catalogue of Dutch and German knights in Chapter 59.

Six of the eight illustrations (of which some details are given on the next page) are taken from early La Sale manuscripts and are reproduced here by courtesy of *Les Éditions du Trianon*, publishers of the Champion-Desonay edition referred to above and on page 27.

Thanks are due to M. Oscar Grojean, Librarian of the Egyptian University, for allowing me to cull dates and other fruit from his oasis in an otherwise bookless desert; likewise to my editor, Dr Eileen Power, for permission to quote from several of the excellent notes to her translation of *Le Ménagier de Paris*.

I.E.G.

Cairo, 1930.

LIST OF ILLUSTRATIONS

LIST OF ILLUSTRATIONS

*Plates I, IV, V, VI, VII, and VIII are reproduced by
permission of Les Editions du Trianon, Publishers of
the French text*

INTRODUCTION

THE TIME

Mr G. K. Chesterton, in one of his essays, laments that the Middle Ages are remembered only by the odour of their ultimate decay. This has certainly been true of France, and in particular of French literature. The fifteenth century is always shunned or damned by the critics. Histories of 'modern' literature begin with the Renaissance; the classic work on the medieval period, by Gaston Paris, stops short at the early thirteen-hundreds. General histories for the most part label fifteenth century letters as decadent, and leave it at that; or restrict their attention to one or two writers who, for no very evident reason, are declared to be 'apart from their age'.

It would be juster to say that the fifteenth century, politically and socially rotten, incapable of producing a healthy crop of literature, was none the less full of interest and full of promise whenever some flower managed to struggle through the weeds. It goes almost without saying that for the student, curious of literary cause and effect, the eve of a great epoch often holds a keener fascination than the epoch itself: but the age which preceded the Renaissance can claim more than mere signs and portents. Say what you will of its innumerable pedants and doggerel-mongers, it still produced Villon, the first modern lyric poet, Commines, the founder of modern history, and

I

Chriſtine de Piſan, the earlieſt of that long line of *femmes de lettres* which is not leaſt among the glories of France.

The later ſtages of the Hundred Years War, apart from the Joan of Arc episode, are not as a rule given a prominent place in English hiſtory books ; and indeed they do us no honour. They left a great part of France in a ſtate of devaſtation which only the twentieth century has succeeded in outdoing. Death, the plundering English and Burgundians, and the payment of fantaſtic sums in ransom of prisoners taken at Agincourt and elsewhere, had ruined many noble houses. Numbers of penniless knights and squires turned *routier* (or freelance), giving mercenary service to any great lord who might be in need of it, living on the country and dealing ungently with the wretched peasants. The worſt of these warriors— some of them were fairly reputable—earned for themselves the siniſter nickname of 'The Flayers'. They ravaged the land with nameless atrocities, until at laſt Charles VII put an end to their profession by founding the rudiments of a ſtanding army, using some of the ' free companies ' for the purpose, and suppressing the reſt, where need was, by force of arms.

The less enterprising vegetated in their tumbledown manors, or set to work to earn an honeſt living. Records of the time show us many of the lesser nobility taking to trade, and ſtill more intermarrying with the comparatively prosperous bourgeoisie of the larger towns, some of which, thanks to their ſtout walls, had escaped the general deſtruction. The minor gentry of Frankish descent and the Gallic *Tiers Etat*, separate caſtes for centuries, are fusing into a single middle class, the feudal pyramid is crumbling, and the end of the Middle Ages is in sight.

2

In the midst of all this wreckage there remained a few isolated spots where literature was cultivated, zealously if not always with success. Charles VII of France, whenever his domestic and foreign enemies allowed him any leisure, was himself a patron of letters. But the more notable centres of culture were the provincial courts of his nominal vassals the great feudal lords. It was the fashion of the time to play Maecenas, but some of them had genuine taste and even talent. Of such was the Duke Charles of Orleans, returned from long captivity in England to spend his later years writing cynical verse in the company of a few dilettante friends. At the court of Philip the Good, Duke of Burgundy, we find a different scene. The wealth of the Low Countries, the future sinews of the Habsburgs' power, was lavished on extravagant display of luxury in a last gaudy artificial revival of Chivalry. All the cults which had hitherto existed chiefly in romance—knight-errantry, Courts of Love, and the rest of it—were here practised with infinite elaboration, to the tune of dreadful ' rhetorical ' verse, trumpeted forth by an orchestra of very minor poets. These versifiers enjoyed a prodigious repute among their contemporaries and have been amply reviled by every succeeding generation of critics. There is no need for us to dwell on their demerits, which are great. It is fair, however, to add, as a rider to the common verdict, that some of them did good work for the beginnings of modern history and science ; and that Philip, who employed a whole army of copyists and illuminators, founded a library which was one of the marvels of Europe.[1]

Further South, in that Provence where, three centuries earlier, the rich poetry of the Troubadours

---

[1] The Bibliothèque de Bourgogne was the nucleus of the existing Bibliothèque Royale in Brussels, which incidentally possesses several MSS of La Sale's works.

had flowered and died, 'Good King René' held his court. René—King of Naples, Sicily, and Jerusalem, Duke of Anjou, Bar and Lorraine, and Count of Provence—is among the most picturesque and attractive figures of the time. Though his sister Marie was Charles VII's queen, René, a younger son, started life with no great expectations. None of his titles, except the last and least, brought him anything but misfortune and war. The kingship of Jerusalem was strictly a courtesy title. To the dukedoms of Bar and Lorraine he succeeded when scarcely more than a boy. His right to the succession was disputed by the Comte de Vaudemont, who fought with him and eventually took him prisoner. René was still a prisoner when his elder brother, Louis III of Anjou, died and left him the duchy of Anjou and another small war, arising out of a disputed claim to the Kingdom of Naples. Our king-in-exile, having purchased his freedom, presently set out for Italy and manfully strove to make good his family's pretensions.

When, after several years of varying fortune, the tide turned definitely against him, he retired to Provence and Anjou (the latter had been ravaged by the English while Louis III and René were chasing wild geese beyond the Alps) to devote the rest of his life to gentler pursuits. "René", says Lavisse (*Histoire de France*), "lacked Philip the Good's wealth. But he had a livelier and a keener mind than the Duke of Burgundy, an insatiable curiosity, an ardent passion for art, letters, everything which appeals to the intellect." French poets and Flemish painters gathered at his Court. The king himself had some skill in painting.[1] He rhymed in rondeaux and pastoral verse. He loved the pageantry which was already growing a little old-fashioned; delighted in tournaments and

[1] There are still extant several paintings attributed to him, probably in error.

4

PLATE II

KING RENÉ OF ANJOU

A portrait taken from his " Book of Hours "

wrote a treatise on them. His domains were governed with fatherly care, and one of his hobbies was the improvement of agriculture. He was the soul of courtesy, honour, and generosity.

René's misfortunes followed him into his retirement, and in later life came thickly upon him. His son and his brother died, his daughter—Margaret, Queen of England—sought his protection, dethroned and a refugee. He bore all with a resignation which became proverbial. The last blow fell when the unscrupulous Louis XI invented a pretext for annexing René's beloved Anjou. The best-known tradition about ' Le bon roi René ' relates that he was painting a partridge when the news of the annexation was brought to him. He went on painting.

This chivalrous gentleman was the patron and friend of our author, Antoine de la Sale.

THE WRITER

(I)

Mr Richard Aldington, in the introduction to his admirable translation of *Les XV Joies de Mariage*[1], has set out briefly the known facts about Antoine de la Sale and his writings. I am indebted to this sketch, and at the same time embarrassed by the task of trying to repeat without plagiarizing. Readers who wish to make closer acquaintance with the scanty data are referred to M. Nève's short biography.[2] What follows here is simply a rough account of La Sale's career, punctuated with as few references as possible. It may be taken that anything which is stated as a fact has documentary evidence to confirm it.

---

[1] *The XV Joys of Marriage*; translated by Richard Aldington, with an Introduction. (Broadway Translations) 1926.

[2] *Antoine de La Salle, Sa Vie et ses Ouvrages*, by Joseph Nève (Paris, 1903).

Among the free-lance captains whom we have already had occasion to mention there was one Bernard de la Salle or Sale, a gentleman of good family[1] who towards the end of the fourteenth century had gained a reputation for enterprise and agility in scaling the walls of other people's castles. ("Subtil eschelleur comme un chat", says Froissart.) He served many masters, including Du Guesclin and the Black Prince, but the last years of his adventurous life were spent in the service of the princely House of Anjou, which at this time and for long afterwards was defending a claim to the throne of Naples.

Bernard had a son Antoine, born very likely near Arles-en-Provence. The exact date of his birth is disputable, and I shall mention later on my reasons for supposing it to have been 1386, and not 1388, the year generally accepted. Of his mother, Périnète Damendel, we have practically no knowledge beyond her name and the fact that she was not married to Bernard, who already had a wife in Italy. A baton sinister was not a serious handicap then, and did not bar Antoine's way to an honourable and distinguished career.

Bernard de la Sale met his death in 1391, in an unsuccessful military expedition. His orphan was taken at the age of fourteen into the service of Louis II of Anjou, and doubtless had personal experience of the page's life which he describes in *Saintré*. Antoine's youth we can only reconstruct sketchily from scattered allusions. In 1406 we find him at Messina (the Angevin princes were Kings of Sicily); he tells us of trips to the Liparian Islands and to Stromboli. A year later his name appears among those present at two tournaments in Flanders. He is tasting for the first time the splendours of the Burgundian Court.

[1] See Note II, page 324.

By 1409 he was back in Italy, at Pisa. After another appearance in the Low Countries, he took part (1415) in a toy crusade organized by John I of Portugal to take Ceuta from the Moors. An incident of which he was an eyewitness during this expedition forms part of his small work known as *Le Réconfort de Madame du Fresne*.

Returning to the service of Anjou, Antoine followed Louis III (Louis II's successor) to Italy in 1420, fought in his wars against Alphonse of Aragon, lived for a while at Rome, visited the 'sybil's grotto' near Norcia. He may have been writing at this period, but anything which he published has been lost. There is nothing in his extant works which would lead us to suppose that he absorbed any of the new learning or was appreciably affected by the humanist spirit which had already taken possession of Italy. He is still soldier and courtier.

We do not know exactly when he went back to France, but in 1429 he was '*viguier*' (or chief magistrate of Arles). From his own references and from official documents we gather that he took an intelligent personal interest in his duties, at a time when a good many officials were content to fulfil their functions by proxy.

Now begins the part of La Sale's life which chiefly interests us. In 1438, after recovering his freedom, the young King René set out to conquer his kingdom of Naples.[1] With him to Italy fared Antoine de la Sale, though he was fifty and had lately married; and shared his master's vicissitudes. René did not finally abandon the struggle until 1442, but in August, 1440, his wife Isabel of Lorraine, with his children, had been sent back to France. His son Jean, Duke of Calabria, was of age to need a tutor; and who more apt to the task

---

[1] See page 4.

than the faithful Antoine de la Sale, upright, cultured, erudite in everything pertaining to courtly breeding? The king chose well. Before his early death, Jean of Calabria was reputed as no less brilliant and high-minded than his father. I have not seen it suggested anywhere, but it seems very possible that La Sale also had a hand in the education of René's daughter, our own gifted, unhappy Queen Margaret of Anjou. Beyond doubt she must have known him intimately.

La Sale wrote for his pupil a pedagogical hotch-potch, which he called *La Salade* because, as he explains, it contained " plusiers bonnes herbes ". They are herbs which the modern reader will find, with one or two exceptions, pretty indigestible, and the book has no value save as a curiosity, and for certain personal reminiscences of the author's.

These were the happiest years of René's reign. In 1445 his daughter was married to Henry VI of England; Antoine de la Sale journeyed to the great tournament which was held at Nancy in honour of the event. A year later René organized, and himself fought in, another tourney, this time at Saumur. The judges were two knights and " two esquires well versed in every sort of combat ". One of the latter was La Sale.

This pleasant existence lasted until 1448. By then the Duke of Calabria was a grown man, Governor of Lorraine, and his tutor was over sixty—an old man as things went in those days. He had earned, one would think, an honourable retirement among old friends, in his native Provence. Instead of that, he leaves his friends, leaves Provence, and becomes tutor to the three sons of the Comte de St Pol, in a remote country-house in the north of France. None of La Sale's biographers express any surprise at the sudden severance of ties, nearly fifty years old, with the House of Anjou.

Yet it *is* surprising. La Sale was not, as far as one can judge, a poor man. The Angevin princes had been generous in their recognition of his services. He had a fief near Tarascon, a house at Arles, the usufruct of the château of Séderon; and his wife's dowry was a thousand crowns. By his will, made in 1438 before he embarked for Italy, he left, besides other bequests, enough to endow a hospital, provide pensions for four poor orphan girls, and found a Mass for the repose of his soul. He had not quarrelled with King René, who gave him a hundred florins as a parting present, describing him in the deed of gift as " our esquire and companion "; nor with the Duke of Calabria, to whom he later on affectionately dedicated *Saintré*. Why, then, should he suddenly uproot himself from his native soil ?

In the preface to his work called *La Salle*, written three years after this, there occurs a curious passage in which the author explains his reasons for compiling the book. First of all, " to escape the passing perilous sin of idleness ". And he adds : " aussi pour passer de mon triste cœur la tres-deplaisante merencolie par infortune tumbé ou LXIIIme an de ma vie et ou XLIXe de mon premier service : jour et nuyt il avoit tant a souffrir seullement pour tresloyaument amer et suivre que dieux par nature mavoit ordonné ". [also to drive from my sad heart the passing grievous melancholy wherein it fell by ill-fortune in the 63rd year of my life and 49th of my first service : day and night it (his heart) had so sorely to suffer, and all for right loyally loving and following that which God had by nature bid me.] Now I take this to mean (and I cannot see what other meaning can be extracted from it) that *before* quitting the service of Anjou, La Sale had suffered some misfortune which had affected him deeply. What it was we have no means of telling, but it seems at least likely that it was the reason for his leaving René's court.

This passage is important also because it contains our only direct indication of the date of La Sale's birth. But M. Gossart,[1] who first called attention to the passage, has, I think, misinterpreted the evidence, and everybody else appears to have acquiesced in his reading without taking the trouble to verify it. He assumes that the year to which La Sale alludes—the 63rd of his life and the 49th of his first service—was the actual year in which he wrote this preface to *La Salle*. This is absurd, because we know the preface in question to have been written in 1451—three years after he left his " first service ". So, to find La Sale's year of birth, Gossart reckoned back 62 years from 1451, whereas he should have reckoned from 1448 at the latest. It follows that La Sale, unless he made a mistake about his age, was born in 1386, or earlier. There has always been some difficulty about accepting the year 1388, because his father was absent from France from June, 1386, until 1390.

Whatever the cause of La Sale's joining the house-hold of the Comte de St Pol, his subsequent efforts to avoid the sin of idleness won him such fame as he possesses. To be sure, the first result of his labours was unpromising. It was the work already referred to, *La Salle*; another collection of moral fragments, historical anecdotes, and notes on genealogy, all framed in a dull elaborate allegory. *La Salle* is even less readable than *La Salade*, and of so little general interest that it has never been printed, and in all likelihood never will be.[2]

[1] E. Gossart, *Antoine de la Salle : sa vie et ses œuvres.*

[2] Two MSS exist in the Bibliothèque Royale, in Brussels, one of them very beautifully illustrated, for Philip the Good, by Lyédet, a well-known miniaturist. The miniatures include one which we have used as our frontispiece.

It was finished in October, 1451, at Châtelet-sur-Oise. In 1458 La Sale wrote his short *Réconfort de Madame du Fresne*, and in 1459 a treatise on tournaments and feats of arms. But meanwhile he had produced the work on which his literary reputation rests. At nearly seventy years of age, this pedagogue publishes a romance, loaded, it is true, with a great deal of didactic matter, but yet possessing enough freshness and originality to keep it sweet for five centuries. This is *Le Petit Jehan de Saintré*, the story of a page at the Court of France who becomes the protégé and eventually the lover of a young widow " of the royal kin ", rising through her patronage and good counsel to be a knight of high renown. We shall consider *Saintré* in more detail presently.

For ten years or more (c. 1448-59) La Sale lived and wrote in the peaceful obscurity of St Pol's country-seats at Chatelet-sur-Oise and Vendeuil; but he was not destined to spend all his last years in this retirement. In September, 1459, we suddenly find him at Genappe, in the south of what is now Belgium. The château of Genappe was at this epoch tenanted by a small but lively Court.[1] Thither, three years before, Louis the Dauphin—the future Louis Onze—had fled in panic from a justly enraged father ; and there he had remained, soothing an exile's grief with the good wine of Burgundy, supplied at the cost of his " fair uncle ", Duke Philip. Some of Louis's old associates had joined him, and the gayer spirits of the Burgundian Court used to ride over from Brussels to make merry. What, we may well ask, was our elderly tutor doing *dans cette galère* ?

There are those who believe that he was employed in writing ribald tales to amuse the Dauphin : with this theory we shall deal later. With any due respect

[1] Vide Baron Kervyn de Lettenhove, *La Flandre sous les Ducs de Bourgogne.*

11

for its adherents, I am inclined to think that the true explanation is simpler, and more creditable to La Sale. Our evidence of his presence at Genappe is contained in the dedication of a copy of *Saintré* to the Duke of Calabria. The original 'author's manuscript' of *Saintré*, which is still in existence, was finished and signed by La Sale as early as 1455, but probably he had no means at Châtelet-sur-Oise of having a manuscript prepared fit for presentation to the dedicatee. There is nothing more likely than that in 1459 he should have taken the opportunity to travel with his employer— St Pol was at this period intriguing with Burgundy and the Dauphin—to Brabant, where Philip the Good had collected the best scribes and illuminators in Europe. The probability of this is strengthened by another dedication, this time of a copy of *La Salle*, presented to Philip in Brussels.

This, in June, 1461, is the last we hear of Antoine de la Sale. A month later Charles VII of France died and the Dauphin Louis succeeded as Louis XI. If La Sale was really attached in any capacity to the Court at Genappe, he may conceivably have followed Louis to Paris. It is much more likely that he returned to Châtelet-sur-Oise and died there.

(II)

An author of repute, belonging to an age which produced anonymous books in large numbers, is almost inevitably credited, sooner or later, with the paternity of one or other of these foundlings. La Sale has been peculiarly unlucky (or lucky, if you like to think so) in this respect. In 1830, through a palpably inadequate solution of a rebus attached to a manuscript of *Les XV Joies de Mariage*, that coarse though clever satire was labelled as his work. No satisfactory explanation of this curious riddle has ever been found, but Mr Aldington[1] mentions some of the difficulties which stand in the way of our believing that La Sale wrote *Les XV Joies*. To my own mind, La Sale's life-history and the character of his authentic works, apart from anything else, make it utterly incredible that he could have written this book. Study La Sale's life and writings ; you are left with a picture of a simple, pious, scholarly man, rather old-fashioned, fond of heraldry, in request as a referee of tournaments, and living from first to last, as soldier, magistrate, tutor, and friend, in the society of the higher aristocracy. The nearest approach to humour in his books is the vein of gentle wit which runs through *Saintré* and crops up occasionally amid the aridity of his other works : *esprit français* but not ' *esprit gaulois* '. There is no suggestion of dramatic talent. Then read the *XV Joies* and ask yourself by what miracle of unholy inspiration he could have compiled such a shrewd, amusing, scandalous comedy of bourgeois manners.

Attempts have likewise been made to father on to La Sale the *Cent Nouvelles Nouvelles*, a collection of Boccacian tales composed, according to tradition, for the edification of Louis the Dauphin. One of the *Nouvelles* is ascribed in the original to " Monseigneur de la Salle, premier maistre d'ostel de Monseigneur le Duc ". This is not necessarily Antoine, and, even if it is, there is no evidence to make him responsible for the whole collection. More recent and careful exam-ination of this theory of authorship has brushed away most of its flimsy foundations[2], and it is probably no

---

[1] *The XV Joys of Marriage :* Introduction, pp. 1-7.

[2] M. Pierre Champion, who has recently (1928) re-edited the *C Nouvelles Nouvelles*, does not believe that La Sale either wrote or edited them, though M. Gustave Cohen of the Sorbonne, in *Les Nouvelles Littéraires* of the 24th August, 1929, re-asserts, not very convincingly, the opposite view.

more warranted than the notion, which was for a time entertained, that the anonymous farce of *Maître Patelin* is La Sale's. This celebrated play has at one time or another been attributed to various contemporary authors, including François Villon, who was certainly more capable than La Sale of producing it. M. Nève, writing in 1903, strongly contests the idea that La Sale was responsible for any of these works, and it is significant that in M. Pierre Champion's sketch of La Sale's life, in the 1926 ' *édition définitive* ' of the *Petit Jehan de Saintré*, neither the *XV Joies* nor the *Cent Nouvelles Nouvelles* is so much as mentioned. Standard literary historians, however, Faguet and Lanson among them, still appear to take it for granted that the theory of La Sale's authorship is generally accepted. It does not, after all, matter much who wrote these books, but it does seem of some importance that we should not get a totally wrong impression of La Sale's character by crediting them to him.

Perhaps it is as well to dispel here a misconception which might be created by a casual reading of the *Petit Jehan de Saintré* in the mind of anyone unfamiliar with Fifteenth Century ethics. *Saintré* is definitely a moral book, though its morality is not ours. *Autre temps autres mœurs :* the fifteenth century was not shocked by the idea of a hero whose mistress supplied him with financial backing. So long as the knight and his lady-love were faithful to one another, little else mattered, according to the chivalrous code. Again, although we know La Sale to have been a devout Catholic, the episode in which the Abbot " confesses " My Lady mingles the religious with the suggestive in a way which strikes a present-day mind as simply blasphemous. Evidently the author and his contemporaries thought nothing of it. Their religion was so much part of their normal daily life that sacred and profane could be mentioned in the same breath without any sense of incongruity. " . . . and there on his knees, with head bared and hands joined, did devoutly make his prayers and oblations unto God and unto Our Lady. And afterward they went thence to dinner." In spite of the somewhat equivocal passage to which I have alluded, there is not a coarse word in the whole of La Sale's romance. Not many authors of the time could boast as much.

It has been suggested by M. Raynaud, and the suggestion is perhaps worthy of mention, that the *Chronique de Jacques de Lalaing* was by La Sale. This biography is at any rate the sort of thing which he might have written, and there are curious resemblances between Saintré's fictitious career and Lalaing's real one.[1] There is, however, no direct evidence to prove that La Sale was the author.

THE BOOK

(I)

Medieval people of the governing classes took, as we should say nowadays, an interest in education—not in the narrow curriculum of the early grammar-schools, but in the breeding of their sons to the duties which their feudal status demanded of them. Their educational system was admirably suited to its purpose. The boy of gentle birth was sent to be a page in the household of some great man, usually the feudal overlord. With his fellow-pages, he was taught by the tutor or chaplain, learned to acquit himself creditably in manly sports, to wait on his elders, to carve at table. This apprenticeship to knighthood

[1] See page 18.

must have passed pleasantly enough. If ſtudiously inclined, the page might browse at will on the household library ; if otherwise—as we may suppose to have been more usual—book-learning made no excessive demands upon his time. Reading, writing, a smattering of aſtrology, a little hiſtory in the form of improving anecdotes, a grain or two of scholaſtic philosophy—such was about the sum of it. Other ſtudies were more exaċting. The seven knightly accomplishments, according to one English version, were : to ride, to swim, to shoot with the bow, to box, to hawk, to play chess, and to make verses. The laſt item need not surprise us ; it was a legacy from the troubadours and minnesinger, and formed part of the code of gallantry which saturates our romance of Saintré and the whole social life of the time.[1]

Altogether, with its insiſtence on physical development and the training of charaċter rather than intelleċt, pagehood is suggeſtive, *mutatis mutandis*, of a modern public-school education. In addition, conſtant attendance on people, especially women, of breeding and refinement, supplied an education in good manners which nothing else could have given. At its beſt the syſtem was brilliantly successful. In the later fifteenth and sixteenth century promising boys of the middle or lower classes were taken up by enlightened patrons and bred as pages with their own sons. This happened to Wolsey, to Drayton, very possibly to Shakespeare.[2]

The decadent and debauched courts of France, in the early fifteenth century, were not nurseries of

[1] For some discussion and bibliography of 'la courtoisie', and the medieval attitude towards women, see Aldington's introduċtion to *The XV Joys of Marriage* ; cf. also Ch. Gidel, *Hiſt. de la Litt. Franç.*, I, 153.

[2] In " A Chapter in the Early Life of Shakespeare ", the Maſter of Jesus College, Cambridge, gives a liſt of Tudor worthies who had their early or their only education as pages in the houses of wealthy patrons.

virtue, and it may be supposed that moſt of the pages who had their breeding in them might have ſtayed at home with advantage to their morals. Were things really as black as some hiſtorians have painted them ? Careers of monſtrous vice, aᴄts of revolting cruelty, were possible because of the lawless ſtate of the country. It would be rash to assume that they were the rule, or if they were the rule, to imagine that there were no exceptions. Nearly all our information comes from legal records, in which vice and crime inevitably have the biggeſt place. What will hiſtorians a thousand years hence have to say about twentieth century morals if their only sources are the Divorce Court proceedings or the files of the Sunday papers ?

At leaſt honourable conduᴄt could ſtili command respeᴄt. The pride and flower of Philip the Good's knights was Jacques de Lalaing, and his education was after this wise : "When the father, that was wise and prudent, perceived that he was of ripe age to be endoᴄtrined and taught, the child was put to a clerk for schooling ; who in a passing short space, made him expert and able well to speak, underſtand, and write, in Latin and in French ; in skill how to devise of hunting and hawking, there was none that excelled him ; in playing at chess, at tables (*backgammon*) and in all other disports a gentleman ought to know, he was schooled and taught better than any man of his age ; for, truth to tell, God and Nature had forgot nothing in the making of him".[1] His father gave him good advice when sending him to Court. "Know", said Guillaume de Lalaing, "that few gentle men come to high eſtate of prowess and good renown, save if they have some lady or damosel of whom they are amorous ; but take heed, my son, that it be not light love, for so should ye be for ever held in great villainy and reproach."[1]

[1] From the *Chronique de Jacques de Lalaing.*

Jacques did not disappoint his teachers. " He was a gentle knight, kind and courteous, bounteous in almsgiving and pitiful ; all his days he succoured the poor, the widow and the orphan. God had given him five gifts : and firstly, he was the flower of knighthood, he was fair like Paris, he was pious like Aeneas, he was wise like Ulysses the Greek. Whenas he was in battle against his enemies he had the ire of Hector the Trojan, but when he beheld that he had the mastery over his foes, there was never man found more clement, nor humbler."[1]

This Bayard roamed through all Europe seeking tourneys and adventures. That he was killed, aged 32, by a mangonel shot fired by a boy, in a petty siege during an ignoble civil war, sums up almost adequately the whole period with which we are concerned.

I have translated these extracts partly for their own sake, partly because the *Petit Jehan* was written when de Lalaing was at the height of his fame. La Sale must have heard all about him, and not improbably used him as a model for his hero.[2]

Such were the ideals of 'pagehood' education, seldom realized in the Fifteenth Century, but not unworthy. Though some of its best success was attained after the decline of feudalism, the system was closely bound up with the feudal scheme. From the prince's point of view, it was policy to persuade his vassals to send their sons to his court. The court became a second home to them, and their loyalty was assured. "It is fitting", quotes Gidel (*Littérature Française*, p. 38) from an old book on chivalry, "that a knight's son be subject to his lord . . . and to this end, every knight ought to put his son in the household of another knight, that he may learn in his

[1] From the *Chronique de Jacques de Lalaing.*
[2] cf. page 15.

18

youth to carve at table and to serve, and to arm and attire a knight. Thus, as it is fitting for a man that would learn to be a tailor or a carpenter, that he have a master that is a tailor or carpenter, even so is it meet that any gentle man, that loveth the order of chivalry and desireth to become and be a good knight, should have first of all a master that is a knight."

(II)

The Page and his Tutor, then, were familiar figures in a medieval Court. Add the Knight and the Lady, the Prince himself, counsellors and ecclesiastics, assorted esquires and varlets; and the cast of our little *commedia dell'arte* is almost complete.

To call the *Petit Jehan de Saintré*, as some enthusiasts have called it, a 'roman de caractère' would be to give the reader extravagant anticipations. Like Molière, La Sale draws types rather than true character, and he draws them from a very narrow world. 'Little John' himself is a conventional figure. The only personages who are really alive are My Lady " des Belles Cousines " and the Abbot[1], the coquette and the wordly cleric, both typical products of the time and no doubt thoroughly well known to La Sale's readers, who may have amused themselves by identifying them with actual people. To us, five centuries away, the romance is chiefly interesting because of the naïve and intimate fashion in which it describes the manners of a society to which manners were almost a religion. We must look for nothing profound nor prophetic. But a better picture of late medieval Court life, and the folk who lived it, would be far to seek. Their child-like love of fine clothes and ceremony, their tournaments and heraldry, their decadent

[1] Perhaps we ought to add the Court Physician; but we get no more than glimpse of him.

Church, their complete disregard of conventions which we nowadays look on as moral principles, and their elaborate observance of their own code of conventions; all is gracefully painted. The world outside, the middle-class life of the towns, the sordid misery of the peasants, the devastated country, are not so much as hinted at. They might never have existed.

The last part of the book is so different from what precedes it that some people have invented theories of double authorship, while others have evolved an ingenious tale of La Sale's having altered the original ending in order to substitute a salacious climax calculated to tickle the palate of Louis the Dauphin. Unfortunately for the latter hypothesis, we now know that *Saintré* was finished before either La Sale or Louis had arrived at Genappe. Without subscribing to either of these heresies, we may admit that an explanation is needed. A reasonable one is not difficult to find. The first part of *Saintré* was probably written in the days when La Sale was tutor in the Court of Anjou. Years afterwards, at his old pupil's request (as the dedication tells us) he patches up the original didactic story[1], with its pious admonitions and quotations from the Saints, and finds that it needs an ending. The ending which he writes for the grown-up Duke of Calabria is naturally not quite the same as the ending which he would have written for Calabria aged fourteen; in fact, La Sale is for once able to forget, to a certain extent, that he is a schoolmaster responsible for a young prince's morals.

For the earlier part of the book—it is as well to warn the reader at once—is far less a romance than a book of good manners, a treatise on the Court etiquette of

---

[1] This would account for the fact that the alterations and additions in La Sale's writing in the original MS (see Introduction, page 26) are practically confined to the first two-fifths of the text.

PLATE III

JEAN D'ANJOU, DUKE OF CALABRIA
(La Sale's Pupil)

From a portrait in his "Book of Hours"

the period, a ' Theory and Practice of Chivalry '. My
Lady's charming lips expound to her pupil all that a
Page should know, but the voice is the voice of La Sale
the tutor ; and when she gives Saintré a list of books
to read it is almost word for word the list which La Sale
had commended to the young Duke of Calabria, years
before, in his other work *La Salade*. Before Saintré
sets out for the Wars, he describes to My Lady his
liveries and his coat-of-arms, with a wealth of detail
but in language heraldically inaccurate. Whose voice
but the tutor's is it that remonstrates patiently and
gravely : " I pray you, fair son, blazon them after
another fashion " ?

Saintré grows up, goes forth to seek adventures in
" arms courteous and arms armigerous ", covers
himself with glory, slays the Grand Turk. Then he
comes back to find that his Lady, tired of waiting, is
indulging in a vulgar amour with an unscrupulous
young Abbot. The rest of the book describes the
rivalry between Petit Jehan and the Abbot, and the
latter's final discomfiture. Some writers see in these
last chapters of *Saintré* an attempt on La Sale's part
to mock at chivalry and its trappings. Actually,
everything that La Sale ever did or wrote bears
evidence that he had an intense admiration for the
chivalrous institutions of the Middle Ages, and
nothing but regret for their passing. When Little
John accepts the Abbot's challenge to a wrestling
match, he is behaving like a varlet and deserves to be
beaten—as he is. When he dons armour and fights
like a gentleman, he is victorious. That Saintré is
tricked and deserted by his Lady is merely a final
test of his virtues. He shows his knightly valour by
worsting his rival, his magnanimity by sparing his life,
his courteous breeding by his polite exposure of
My Lady's infidelity. From beginning to end the

pedagogue never neglects to point a moral. Whether by so doing he adorns his tale, the reader must judge for himself.

(III)

Even apart from its didactic purpose, the *Petit Jehan de Saintré* is not a work of pure fiction. Pure fiction indeed, in the form of the novel as we know it, had not been invented, and the public for whom La Sale wrote, while prepared to swallow any quantity of supernatural happenings, insisted on a hero of flesh and blood.[1] Accordingly the hero chosen by La Sale had an historical existence[2] (though we may be excused for doubting whether he really slew the Grand Turk), and the inscription quoted from his tombstone may well be genuine.

What is really interesting is that our author, however much he may draw the long bow, never draws Excalibur. He respects the bounds of human possibility. As Guichard, the editor of the 1843 edition, pointed out, there is not in the whole book a single giant, dwarf, dragon, wizard, or any one of the prodigies and enchantments which were the common stage decorations of Arthurian and other contemporary romance. We have, therefore, a definite break with tradition, or rather, a return to the older tradition of the Chansons de Geste, which an invasion of Celtic myths had interrupted. If the *Petit Jehan de Saintré* is not big enough to be a landmark in French literature, it is at least a milestone.

What is its value as a work of art ? What is its place in literary history ? Neither question is easily answered. The book, as we have seen, falls into no very

[1] Caxton, in his preface to the *Morte d'Arthur*, is at immense pains to demonstrate that Arthur was not an imaginary person.

[2] See Note I, page 323.

definite category : it blends the novel and the didactic treatise.   On the latter side its pedigree is not so hard to trace.   All through the later Middle Ages one of the most characteristic forms of literature had been the ' *Castoiement* ', a moral homily of one sort or another. Books on chivalry and good manners had abounded too, but to coat the pill with a romance was perhaps a new idea.

Considered as a romance, had *Saintré* any ancestry ? I am not disposed to enumerate all the works which La Sale *may* have read, and which *may* have reacted upon his subconscious mind.   Of course he was familiar with the romances of the Table Round, and no doubt with many of the *fableaux*, the minstrels' tales.   Everybody in his world knew the *Roman de la Rose*.   The endless rehearsals of names and armorial bearings before each battle or tournament are an epic touch, linking *Saintré* with the Chansons de Geste. But there is nothing to suggest direct borrowing from any of these sources, or even conscious imitation. Within the modest limits of his subject, we may allow the author the quality of originality, except, obviously, for his undisguised quotations from Holy Writ and the Philosophers.

Although the *Petit Jehan* was a popular book, I cannot find that it was imitated ; yet there was no lack of educational literature in the succeeding century.   Rabelais and Montaigne are the names which occur to one most readily ; but the Rabelaisian scheme of education most certainly had nothing in common with La Sale's mild curriculum, and Montaigne's ideas, if akin to the aims of the pagehood system, were his own.   Nor do the romances which served later generations as hand-books of etiquette show indebtedness to *Saintré*.   *Amadis de Gaule*, the most popular courtly romance of the sixteenth century, is a translation from the Spanish, while its seventeenth century successor, d'Urfé's *l'Astrée*, is a euphuistic pastoral, entirely lacking in La Sale's matter-of-fact realism.

Another royal tutor, in a later and more polished age, wrote a didactic novel for his pupil. Comparison would be not so much odious as ludicrous between the simple-minded old pedagogue who wrote *Saintré* and the saintly Fénelon, the Swan of Cambrai, " of whom one enemy says that his cleverness was enough to strike terror, and another, that genius poured in torrents from his eyes ". Yet I am not sure that *Saintré* is not a more readable tale, as a tale, than *Télémaque*, which is too full of political allusions and cumbered with classical garb to attract many modern readers.

The *Petit Jehan de Saintré* has never aroused much excitement. The murmurs following its tranquil progress through the centuries have been on the whole approving. A strange diversity of opinion about the general qualities of the book suggests that we are on perilous ground in seeking to penetrate the medieval mind. *Saintré* has been variously styled a novel of character, a novel of manners, a satire, a burlesque, an historical novel. It has received high praise from literary writers of consequence. Faguet, with his usual uncompromising frankness, observes that everybody seems to find it exquisite, and for his part, he can only say that it strikes him as fatuous. Still, the fifteenth century is not Faguet's period.

To this mixture of views, I can only add my own impressions: that *Saintré* contains precious little history, not much true character-drawing, no satire[1].

---

[1] The Abbot's satirical remarks on the subject of knight-errantry are no doubt the expression of opinions current among the bourgeoisie or the ecclesiastics but certainly not shared by La Sale.

The author was not a genius; he displays little imagination and no feeling for Nature. But his observation is accurate, and his mind seldom ſtrays from its purpose—remember, the moralizing digressions are all part of the plan. His little world is at his fingers' ends. There is charm, too, in the dialogue. There is art (or is it perfeſtion of artlessness?) in the description of intimate detail at every ſtep.

La Sale ſtands in the doorway that opens on the Renaissance, with his back to the light, and his gaze bent, a little wiſtfully perhaps, on the splendours of ' le bon vieux temps '. On the tapeſtried walls there are battles and feats of arms ; are they indeed fading, or is it his old eyes that grow dim ? We!l, his book of *Saintré* shall do something to bring back the glories of other days, when all knights were " men of worship ", and all ladies true. Alas, alas, good Antoine,

> " n'enquerez de sepmaine
> Ou elles sont, ni de ceſt an ;
> Que ce reffrain ne vous remaine :—
> Mais où sont les neiges d'antan ? "

If La Sale's outlook is purely medieval, his ſtyle is in some respeſts modern. We have already considered his quite un-medieval realism. Secondly, he writes in prose, and this in itself was almoſt an innovation, for we muſt remember that printing had not yet found its way to France, and nearly all fiſtion was ſtill written in verse, to be recited by minſtrels. Finally, his prose is, in spite of occasional tangles, graceful, and far clearer than much French prose that followed it, as well as moſt that went before. A hundred years after, prose writers were ſtill ſtruggling with impossible Latin conſtruſtions, and later yet Descartes, who apologized for writing in French at all, might better have apologized for the classical unwieldiness of his style. Fortunately La Sale was not very learned, except in heraldry and chivalrous etiquette: " moy, qui suis ", as he says in his epilogue, " et ay toujours esté rude et de tres gros engin ".[1]

(IV)

Ten MSS of *Le Petit Jehan de Saintré* are known: two at the British Museum, five in the Bibliothèque Nationale in Paris, one in Florence, one in the Vatican library, and one in Brussels (the Bibliothèque Royale). Until quite recently, apart from a summary examination by the late G. Raynaud, the collation of these manuscripts had never attracted any competent medievalist; however, the work has now been done with more than ordinary thoroughness. Each manuscript is minutely described in M. Fernand Desonay's critical notes appended to the Champion-Desonay edition of *Saintré*. Further, M. Pierre Champion[2] has identified the Bibliothèque Nationale MS (Nouv. acq. fr. 10057), beyond reasonable doubt, as the actual author's manuscript, bearing notes and corrections in La Sale's own handwriting: a rarity indeed.

The modest Antoine would probably have been surprised to learn that his breviary of chivalrous conduct was to become a popular favourite. It was certainly no less. The survival of so many as ten manuscripts testifies to its early vogue. It was printed in 1517, and by 1523 had reached a third edition. A fourth appeared in 1553; then no more for a hundred and seventy years. The eighteenth century rediscovered *Saintré* with the help of a new edition, published in 1724, which gave rise to much

[1] engin = mind (*ingenium*).
[2] P. Champion, *Le manuscrit d'auteur du Petit Jehan de Saintré avec les notes autographes d'Antoine de La Sale.*

theorizing and some little controversy about the historical foundations of the romance. In 1780 a version of the story, abridged and altered almost beyond recognition by a certain Comte de Tressan, met with enough success to take it into several editions. After an appearance on the Parisian stage as an inferior one-act play (1823) and a reprinting by Firmin Didot (1830), we come, in 1843, to the first serious attempt to collate the available manuscripts and establish an accurate text. All the earlier printed editions had been copied, with varying degrees of inaccuracy, from one another; their common ancestor was a corrupt MS dating probably from the end of the fifteenth century. Guichard, who edited the 1843 edition, used only three manuscripts, but his work, so far as it went, was carefully done, and made a notable advance. More recent editions (Hellény, 1890, and one in the 'Renaissance du Livre' series) merely reproduce Guichard's text. It was not until 1926 that MM. Pierre Champion and Fernand Desonay published an authoritative *Saintré*, based on La Sale's original manuscript, recording variant readings from others, and equipped with proper critical notes on the manuscripts, though not, unfortunately and unaccountably, with notes to the text.[1]

[1] See Translator's Preface.

BIBLIOGRAPHY

Le Petit Jehan de Saintré : texte nouveau publié d'après le manuscrit de l'auteur avec des Variantes et une Introduction par Pierre Champion et Fernand Desonay. Editions du Trianon, Paris, 1926.

Le Petit Jehan de Saintré : ed. J. M. Guichard, Paris, 1843.

Le Petit Jehan de Saintré : pubd. by Jean Gillequin & Cie., Paris. ('La Renaissance du Livre' Series.)

Le Petit Jehan de Saintré : transposée littéralement en français moderne par Louis Haugmard. E. Sansot & Cie., Paris.

Antoine de la Salle : sa vie et ses ouvrages : by Joseph Nève, Paris, 1903.

Antoine de la Salle : sa vie et ses œuvres inédites : by Ernest Gossart, 2nd edn., Brussels, 1902.

The Fifteen Joys of Marriage : translated by Richard Aldington, with an Introduction. (Broadway Translations) Geo. Routledge & Sons.

La Salade : "Nouvellement imprimé à Paris" (16th century).

René d'Anjou, *Œuvres Complètes*, 2 vols., Paris, 1845-6.

To You, most excellent and most puissant prince, My Lord John of Anjou, Duke of Calabria and of Lorraine, Margrave and Marquis du Pont, and my most honoured lord.

As by me most humbly and obediently propounded, and to fulfil your desires, which are to me no less than commandments, it hath been my pleasure to make for you four fair histories[1], in two books, that they may the more easily be carried; whereof this former treateth of the loves of a Lady of the Royal Kin of France[2], whom I name by none other name, and the passing valiant knight the Lord of Saintré.

FIRST CHAPTER

How John of Saintré served in the Court of King John of France as page of honour, riding in the King's train

In the time of King John of France³, that was eldest son to King Philip of Valois, there was at his Court the lord of Pouilly in Touraine, who in his household had a passing gentle and courteous lad, called John, and first-born son to the lord of Saintré, in Touraine likewise. And this lad, by his gracious bearing, found so great favour with the King, that he was fain to have him in his Court, and ordained him (for he was yet full young) to be his page, but only to ride in his train and beside to serve in hall with his other pages of honour. The same John of Saintré, above all the other pages of honour, served every man at table, on this hand and on that, right diligently, and some-deal more so than any of the rest; and in especial the ladies, in all pleasures and services which they required of him, as best he might. Moreover, for his age, which was XIII years, he was a skilful youth and an hardy, whether for riding a full rough courser⁴, for singing, dancing, or playing at tennis, for running, for leaping, and for all other exercises and disports which he saw the men do; in all things he sought to share joyously, albeit he was but frail and slender of stature, and ever so remained. But his heart, when he was among his fellows, was all iron and steel. For this his skill and graciousness, gentleness and courtesy, he was so well loved and bespoke of the King, the Queen, lords, ladies, and every man, that all esteemed and declared he would surely be, an he should live, one of the most worshipful gentlemen of France. And truly so he was, for at his passing from this world he was accounted the most valiant of knights; and as for a part of his deeds, this history shall hereafter relate them.

SECOND CHAPTER

How there was in the Court of the Queen of France a young Dame that would not marry again, notwithstanding that she was thereto much entreated. And of the answer that she made concerning the ladies of ancient times

In those days, at the Court of Queen Bonne of Bohemia, wife of the aforesaid King John, there was a young lady, a widow, that was of the Royal Kin of France; but her name and seigneury the history telleth not, by reason of a matter which ye shall hereafter know. And this lady, ever after my lord her first husband's death, would not wed a second time, whatsoever occasion offered; perchance in the intent to be like to the faithful widows of aforetime, whereof the Roman histories, which are the worthiest of all, make such glorious mention; but of these I now forbear to speak, that I may shortly come to my purpose and tell of this lady, who since that she was widowed would never take an husband. And meseemeth, *prima facie*, that she was minded to follow the ancient widows of aforetime, as the histories relate; to wit, how the Romans had a right commendable custom of greatly praising and exalting such widow women as after the death of their first husbands would never more assent to marry again, but because

34

of the very great and loyal love they bore them did chose rather to keep honourable and perfect chastity.

Of this the Apostle saith, in his first Epistle *ad Timotheum*, in the fifth chapter : " Honour widows ". They are no true widows, that abstain from second marriage because they find none to espouse ; that is to say, because they are ruled by their pleasure, or else by their profit, or by some other cause, and do it not for the love of God, nor for the love that they bore their first husbands, like those others that would take no man, neither worse nor better. Even as Virgil saith in the fourth book of Eneas, which Eneas so loved Dido that he was like to die of it; yet Dido recked nothing of his love, for so had she loved her husband and yet did love him being dead, that she might not forget him : and to Anne her sister, when she spake unto her of marrying, she made answer as followeth :

> " Ille meos primus, qui me junxit, amores abstulit ;
> ille habeat secum, servetque sepulcro,"

of which verse the interpretation is this : " He that first joined me to him, alas, the same won my true love, which it is my will he should have ever, and keep it with him even in his grave ".

The Romans were wont to honour with crowns them that did great feats of arms ; as that he who first passed the moat or the rampart of the enemy's host was crowned with the Crown Valerian, and he who first mounted upon the scaling-ladder or upon the walls, at the assault of a city or a castle or a town, was crowned with the Crown Mural, and so also was their custom for other deeds of valiance ; and in like wise they crowned right solemnly, with the Crown of Chastity, such widow women as for the love and honour of their first husbands would not assent to marry again, but would honourably keep their virtue ; and these were held in much more honour than other widows were.

Whereof Saint Jerome telleth, in his second book, speaking unto Juvinian of such widows, and sheweth ensamples of divers widows that never would take second husbands.

Like as of Marcia, that was Cato's daughter ; who made dole unceasing for her husband ; her friends, seeking to comfort her, asked her : " Well-a-day, when shall your mourning cease ? " and she answering said that it should cease on the most blessed day of her life, the last.

He telleth also of another, called Lucia, which day and night ceased not from weeping and making moan for her goodman dead ; and her father, to turn her from her dolour, spake unto her of taking a new husband. " Alas ", said she, " for God's love, Sir, speak to me never more of this." And when her father chided her, for that she stayed widow, and she so young, she made answer to him at length : " Sir, I so love that one, that I could never love any other the least whit ; and if in my foolish simpleness I were to take one that were good to me, never could my heart have any joy of him, for fear of losing him : and if he were proud or hard of heart, certes my unhappy life should end full soon ". So did she resolve to remain in that estate of widowhood all her life long.

And the same blessed saint shewed sundry other fair ensamples, whereof I make no rehearsal, for he that listeth may there read them. .

Among these ensamples of marriage, he giveth in the Fourscore-and-sixteenth of his Epistle, one other, the which is ludicrous. It is of a woman at Rome, that was not one of these passing faithful widows, for she espoused XXII husbands. Now there was, as it

36

chanced, a man of that city, which had espoused XX
wives ; and these two were married with great feaſting
and merriment, for the people of Rome had great
disport and joy thereat, being curious to know which
of the two should outlive the other. And it came to
pass that the wife died firſt. Then came all the young
gallants of Rome, and put into the husband's hand a
laurel branch, in token of his victory over her that had
discomfited XXII husbands. And on his head, in
token of great rejoicing, they set a cap of green twigs,
and so led him through the city with tabors and with
trumpets, crying on every side : " Long live Palmo,
who hath discomfited the woman of twenty-two
husbands ".

And now will I make an end of these ensamples, to
turn again to the tale of My Lady and little Saintré.

THIRD CHAPTER

*How this aforesaid Lady was minded to make a worshipful
knight out of little Saintré, and calling him to her
chamber asked him who was his lady-love ; whereat
little Saintré was all shamefaſt, and answered never a
word, save to say at the laſt that he had none*

THIS lady, as hath been said, was resolved never more
to marry, for no occasion whatsoever ; but notwithſtanding, her mind was taken up with divers imaginings ;
among others she pondered many a time how she
would gladly make of some young knight or squire a
man of renown ; and on this design she fixed. And
for the space of a few days, she took note everywhere
of the manners and bearing of all the young gentle men
and pages at Court, to choose the one that should be

37

moſt to her liking ; and at the laſt her choice fell upon
little Saintré. So it came about that in the intent
to observe his manner of bearing him and of speaking,
she parlied with him divers times of sundry matters,
and that publicly ; and ever the more she spake with
him, the more found she him to her liking. But
concerning love she neither ventured nor desired to
avow aught.

And it befell, as fortune and love willed it, that My
Lady, having attended the queen's Retiring, was
returning unto her chamber ; and as she passed
through the galleries with her esquires, her gentlewomen and her damosels following, she found there
little Saintré watching the players that played at
tennis⁵ in the court below. And when he saw My
Lady's esquires passing by, he ſtraightway bent his
knee and did obeisance. Now when My Lady espied
him she was passing glad, and as she went by, said
unto him :

" Saintré, what do you here ? Is that the way of
a gentle squire, not to bear ladies company ? Fie, Sir,
come ; go you on afore us."

So little Saintré, all abashed, his countenance afire
with shame, bowed low and set himself before her,
with the others. And when My Lady saw him going
before, she said laughing to her gentlewomen, as she
passed on : " Do you but wait until we are in my
chamber ; then shall we have mirth ".—" Why,
Madam," said Dame Joan, " Whereof ? " " Whereof ? " said My Lady ; " ye shall see a battle anon
betwixt little Saintré and me ". " Alack, Madam,"
said Dame Katherine, " what hath he done amiss :
'tis so good a lad."

And by the time that this was done saying, My Lady
was come into her chamber. Then said she to all
her esquires : " Begone, all ye men, to your own kind,

38

and leave us here ". With that they departed all, and little Saintré took his leave on bended knee. And when My Lady saw him kneel, she said to him : " You shall abide, Sir, you are not numbered with the grown men : I would have speech with you here ".

Then was the door shut ; My Lady, sitting upon the foot of the bed, made him to ſtand betwixt her and her gentlewomen, and then took an oath of him, that he should faithfully answer all that she might ask. And so did the poor page promise her, not guessing what was her intent ; and thus doing, " Alack ", thought he, " what have I done ? and what shall become of me ? "

And as he thus wondered, said My Lady, smiling to her gentlewomen :

" Come now, maſter, by the faith that you have pledged me, tell me firſt of all, when 'twas you saw laſt your lady-love ? "

And when he heard speak of a lady-love, he that never had thought on one, his eyes were filled with tears and his heart with trembling, and he grew wan of face, so that no word could he utter.

Then said My Lady unto him : " Why, maſter, what is this ? and what meaneth this sorry cheer ? " " Now, Saintré, fair son," said the other ladies thaτ, ſtood round about, laughing, " wherefore will you not tell My Lady when 'twas you saw laſt your lady-love ? 'tis no great matter to ask " ; and so urged him, until he said : " Ma'am, I have none ". " Have you none ? " quoth My Lady ; " forsooth, she would be lucky that had such a lover. It may well be that you have won no lady's favour. But she that you moſt love, and would that she were your lady, when saw you her laſt ? "

Little Saintré, who never yet, as hath been said, had known nor taſted of amorous delights in any wise,

39

and by this time had loſt all countenance, ſtood long
a-twiſting the tassel of his girdle round his fingers,
and speaking never a word. And My Lady, perceiving
that he made no answer, said to him : " Well, fair
sir, what countenance is this ? Speak you no word ?
If I do ask of you when 'twas you saw laſt her whose
servant you moſt desire to be, I do you no disworship ".
Then Dame Joan, Dame Katharine, Isabel, and the
reſt, that all were laughing at this, took pity of him.
So they said unto My Lady : " He is not at this time
ready to make you such an answer ; but an it please
you to excuse him now, he shall make it you tomorrow".
" Tomorrow ? " quoth My Lady, " nay, 'tis my will
to know it ere he depart hence." Then said they
every one unto him—one : " Fair son ", another
" Friend ", and another " Little Saintré "—" tell My
Lady soothly when you laſt beheld your lady-love ;
else are you her prisoner ".

And being hard beset of them all, he said at laſt :
" What would ye that I should say unto you, when I
have none ? An I had, I would tell you willingly ".
—" Do but tell ", said they " her name, that you love
beſt."—" She that I love beſt ? 'Tis my lady mother,
and next her my siſter Jacqueline."

Then said My Lady unto him : " Sir Simpleton,
I mean not your mother nor your siſter, for the love of
mother, of siſter, and of kinsfolk is in no wise like that
of a lady *par amours* ; but I ask concerning them that
are nothing sib to you ". " Them that are nothing
sib to me ? " said he, " by my faith, Ma'am, I love
none."

" You love none ? " said My Lady, " O recreant
knight ! Say you that you love none ? By this I
know well that you shall never be a man of worship.
Why, faint-heart that ye be ! whence are come the
high prowess, the mighty enterprises and knightly

deeds of Lancelot, of Gawain, of Triſtram, of Giron the courteous, and the other warriors of the Table Round, and likewise those of Ponthus and so many other passing valiant knights and squires of this kingdom and others beyond number (that I could well rehearse an I had time) if it were not from seeking to serve Love and to uphold them in the favour of their moſt beloved ladies; and I wot of some that by being true lovers and right loyally serving their ladies, are come to such high honour that men shall ever tell of their deeds; and save they had been so, they would be of no more account than a simple commoner. And you, messire, say then that you have no lady, nor ever desired to have. Now, sith thus it is, get you gone, moſt craven of them all!"

My Lady smiling as she spake these words, her gentlewomen well perceived that they were but in jeſt, albeit they were true. But when poor Saintré heard his cruel dismissal, from My Lady; alack! he deemed him no less than dead, or for ever dishonoured, and anon fell to weeping full sore. Then took Dame Joan, Dame Katharine, Isabel, and the other damosels great pity of him, and laughing knelt all before My Lady, beseeching her that she would deign to forgive him for that one time, and vowing for him that by the morrow he should have found and chosen a lady for to serve. "Nay," said My Lady, "ye err an ye eſteem that such a faint-heart shall ever do aught so worthy."—"Madam," said they, "that shall he." "And what say you, messire?" quoth My Lady. "Are you asleep? Shall ever there be in you as much good as they say?"

Then the poor discomfited lad took heart and said: "Yea, Madam, sith it is pleasing to you".—"And do you so promise me?"—"Ay, Madam, by my faith!" —"Well," said My Lady, "go your ways, and look

41

to it, whatever befall, that tomorrow, at the same hour as today, you be in the galleries, where I shall seek you ; or else count yourself no more friend of mine."

Thus delivered, the poor captive taketh his leave of My Lady, on his knees, and thereafter of the rest, and so goeth thence. And at his leave-taking, they say unto him : " Remember the promise ; for we are surety for you ".

And when he was out of the chamber, he fled away as fast as he might, as he were hunted of fifty wolves. My Lady and her gentlewomen, whose intent had been to sleep that day, ceased not all day from laughing and devising of the sore affright that he had had in her lodging, and thereof such mirth had they that it rang to vespers and they must needs arise without sleeping.

Now when he found the other pages, his fellows, he told them, God wot, his new adventures. Anon, well content to have escaped, little by little he forgot his promise, save that whensoever he saw My Lady and her gentlewomen, he fled them as they were the Fiend ; whereat they laughed right merrily. But at one of these occasions, at dinner, the two gentlewomen sitting at meat beheld him where he went back and forth among the tables, serving all other ladies and damosels, as was his wont, save them only. So they caused him to come unto them, and said to him : " Why, fair Messire Saintré, at what game have we lost you ? You were wont to serve us like the rest, and now you shun us ".—" Ladies," quoth he, casting down his eyes for shame, " by your leave . . . " and so saying, fled. Then was there much mirth between them. By chance My Lady, who was seated at the nether end of the King's and Queen's table, saw little Saintré before them and also how they laughed after him. And she demanded of them, after

42

the tables were removed, what little Saintré might have said unto them, whereat they thus laughed. Then said they unto her how that he served all the ladies save them only, and what answer he had made to their questions as he passed by.

" Now let be," said My Lady, " let but My Lady the Queen go to rest ; then shall we make disport of him again."

And when they came to the Parting-Cup,[6] My Lady, seeing little Saintré bearing a cup and serving, called him unto her, and said to him : " Saintré, get you to the galleries and there abide until I come, and fail not, for I would send you into the town to do me a pleasure, and so shall you be truly my friend ". Little Saintré, at hearing My Lady speak so gently, was passing glad, and weened she had quite forgot his promise ; and answered her : " Madam, right gladly will I ".

Anon the King withdrew and the Queen also. Then fareth little John to the galleries. And it was not long before the King went to rest, and My Lady, returning again to her chamber, found little Saintré as she had bid him. Then said she unto him : " Go you before with the rest ".

And when she was come into her chamber and seated upon the foot of the couch, she bade all her esquires and other folk to go forth. Then called she little Saintré, and said unto him : " Now, Messire, I have you here. Where is your faith that you twice pledged me ? These four days past have you fled me. What vengeance and what punishment shall be taken of a man that hath broke faith ? " At these hard words and so cruel, he deemed him as good as dead. Then fell he all suddenly upon his knees, with hands clasped, craving mercy of My Lady, and saying that truly he had had much to do.

43

My Lady, who saw her gentlewomen laughing behind him, herself kept from laughing as well as she was able, and said unto him : "Well, now, Messire, supposing it be as you aver : in these four days have you chosen a Lady ? "

And when he heard speak of choosing a lady, he prized life no more than death. He began to weep, his face all wan and sweating, by cause that he had utterly forgot all his promise ; and wist not what to do nor say, nor what excuse to make. My Lady, seeing him in such case, said all smiling unto her gentlewomen : "What say ye of a recreant squire, that twice hath pledged his faith to a lady, as ye know, and hath broke it for so small cause ? What punishment shall he have ? You, Dame Joan, I ask first of all ".

And when the poor gentle lad heard My Lady thus missay him, he weened no less this time than to be undone and for ever dishonoured. Anon with hands clasped, on his knees yet, again he begged mercy of My Lady, for God's sake ; then turned he him unto the others, to beg them entreat for him. My Lady, well pleased with all this and loving him the better when she beheld him so humble and so innocent, thought that could she by some means win him to her service, she might well shape him to her design ; but before Dame Joan and the rest she must keep up her teasing of him. Dame Joan, quite moved to pity, and not perceiving (nor any of the others) whereto My Lady intended, answered her : "Marry, Madam, if he hath broke his promise, you have heard his excuse— that he hath been about much business ; and he sueth right meekly for pardon, on his knees and with hands clasped ; and so do we all on his behalf ".—" And you, Dame Katherine, what say you ? "—" Alack, Madam, I know not what to say, save that it repenteth him of his misdoing, and that shall you find sooth; wherefore I do entreat of you pardon for him."— "And Ysabel, you that are the oldest, what say you?"— "Madam, I say as the others do; and, moreover, you know that the poor prisoner honestly avowed to you, that he had chosen no lady to serve, wherefore I think him worthier than if he had done otherwise. By your leave, Madam, the heart of a young lover (that is resolved, as he is, loyally to serve) hath much perplexity in choosing well and in obeying in all things his Lady's behest, if he be not well acquainted with Love. But by my faith, Madam, I ween that Saintré hath never beheld Love nor had speech of him; is't not so, fair son?" said Isabel.—"Yea, on my faith, Mother Isabel, I never spake with him nor did behold him."—"Come now, Madam, see this poor lad, that ne'er yet beheld nor knew nor spake with Love; how should he so soon have chosen him a lady, when they that are already acquaint with Love, ponder the matter long enough, fearing refusal? Wherefore I say, Madam, that verily he ought to be forgiven this once."—"And what say ye, Margaret, Alice, and ye others? I will that each say her say." Then with one accord they abode by Isabel's counsel, as being the eldest, and she that had most seen and heard.

FOURTH CHAPTER

How little Saintré made answer to My Lady (all abashed and as one that never yet had felt the flames of Love) that his lady-love was Maudelyn de Courcy, that was but ten years old

"WELL," said My Lady, "I have heard all your opinions, and touching the breaking of faith and

forgiveness, ye be all of one mind. And as for me,
for the love of you all I do forgive him this once ; but
I let you wit that he is to blame in one thing, inasmuch
as he was to have chosen him a Lady, and that hath
he not done."—"Why, Madam," said they, laughing,
"but he hath!"—"But nay!" said My Lady.—
"What!" said they, "how think you, Madam, that
he hath spent these four days, save in choosing her
that he will serve ?"—"But nay!" said My Lady.
"Forsooth yea!" said they; "we will be his surety
therefor." Then said they unto him: "Is't not
true, fair son ?" The poor lad, all bewildered and
thus tormented, needs muſt say yea. And when her
had said yea, quoth My Lady unto him: "Now are
you a man of worship! May it so prove! Tell us
now who she may be, and you shall be verily my
friend". At that, needs muſt he name some one;
wherefore his eyes fell a-weeping and his fair countenance to lose its hue, because he had never before
undertaken any such thing. Then said My Lady to
her gentlewomen: "Did I not tell you truly that he
hath said this but in the intent to escape ?" "Alack!"
said they all, "Saintré, tell My Lady soothly; and
you, Madam, withdraw you with him apart, then shall
he tell it you : think you that any true lover will thus
publish abroad his Lady's name, that he so dearly
loveth ?" Then said My Lady unto him: "Come,
draw hither aside", and then "Come now Saintré,
fair son, here are but you and I that can hear : now
tell me truly". And when poor Saintré perceived
that he might by no other means be delivered, he
said unto her: "Alas, Ma'am, may't please you to
forgive me! Since you are so wishful to know it,
. . . . " and weighing what he should say, he
bethought him (thus Nature maketh hearts to desire
and draw unto like hearts) to name a little maid of the

court, of the age of ten years. And he said : " Ma'am, 'tis Maudelyn de Courcy ". And when My Lady heard him name Maudelyn de Courcy, she knew verily that 'twas but childish love and innocent. Nathless she made great to-do in her chamber, more than before, saying unto him : " Now indeed do I see that you are truly a right sorry squire, to have chosen Maudelyn to serve. I say not that Maudelyn be not a passing fair maid and of good lineage, and better lineage, messire, than befitteth you. But what good is there in her, what profit, what honour, what sustenance, what advantage, what comfort, help or counsel to raise you up and make you a valiant knight ? What good can you have of Maudelyn, that is yet but a child ? It behoveth you, messire, to choose you a lady that is come of high and noble blood ; wise, and able to help you and supply your needs, and her so to serve and loyally to love, whatsoever pains you suffer for her cause, that she may know the perfect love that in all honour you do bear her. And if you so do, doubt not that in time, whosoever she be (an she be not crueller than all other that I ever heard tell of) she shall take cognizance and pity and mercy and compassion of you and shall look kindly upon you ; and therewith shall you become a man of worship. But otherwise I give not a straw for you nor your deeds. Even as the Poet[7] saith in his ballade which here followeth :—

> The seal of love is loyalty
> And in a single path to tread ;
> Who knows not this for verity
> Is of well-doing wearièd
> And all his nobleness is dead ;
> For heart that roveth everywhere
> And by a thousand stars is led
> In true love hath but little share.

If share he hath, 'tis shamefully,
In places all dishonourèd ;
And this I tell you certainly,
When he that with such meat is fed
Hath after well considerèd,
God knoweth, he is then aware
How he, where tables rich are spread,
In true love hath but little share.

Such love is soilèd woefully
Where many have adventurèd,
And never any charity
Hath such a lover merited,
But all to his disfame is said ;
For heart that roveth everywhere
And by a thousand ſtars is led
In true love hath but little share.

FIFTH CHAPTER

*How My Lady taught little Saintré many good things
and salutary doctrines, concerning the manner of escaping
from the Seven Deadly Sins*[3]

"Moreover concerning this I tell you also, that
whoso ſtriveth loyally to serve his Lady, the same, I
say, may be saved, both soul and body : and behold
this is the reason thereof. In regard to the soul, we
muſt know that whoso avoideth mortal sin, the same
is saved ; for the other venial sins are forgiven through
true confession, and effaced with but small penance.
Now, as for keeping from mortal sin, if a man love as
here followeth, he is saved.

"And firſtly, touching the sin of Pride, the lover,
that he may win his Lady's moſt desirèd favour, shall
ſtrive to be gentle, humble, courteous and gracious,
to the end that naught may be said to his dishonour ;

48

remembering the words of the learned Thales of
Miletus, who thus saith :

> ' *Si tibi copia, si sapientia formaque detur ;*
> *Sola superbia destruit omnia, si comitetur.*'

"That is to say, fair son :' 'Though thou have
abundance of riches, though thou have wisdom, though
thou have nobleness and all perfection of body, pride
alone, if it be in thee, destroyeth all thy virtues'.
And to this purpose Socrates saith :

> ' *Quantumcumque bonus fueris, essendo superbus,*
> *totum depravat, te sola superbia dampnat.*'

"That is to say, fair son : 'Howsoever virtuous
thou be, yet is all marred if thou be proud ; thy pride
alone doth damn thee '. And in this regard also
saith Trimides, the philosopher :

> ' *Ut non infleris, memor esto quod morieris ; unde venis*
> *cerne, quo vadis, te quoque sperne.*'

" ' Lest thou be puffed up with pride, remember
that thou must die ; consider whence thou camest and
whither thou goest ; so shalt thou hold thyself in
contempt.'

"And many other authorities also, that it would be a
full long matter to rehearse, which for the present
I leave, and turn to my purpose, which is that the true
lover, as I conceive him, shall obey them all, in the
intent to win the most desirable favour of his most
fair lady, and so shall he cast from him this very
hateful' and abominable sin of Pride, with all the
appurtenances thereof, and shall take for his companion
the lovely virtue of humility ; whereby he shall be
quit and saved from this sin.

"As for the second sin, which is Choler, certes
no true Lover was ever choleric. I have indeed heard
say that love hath at some times caused lovers certain

displeasures, for to make trial of them ; yet were they never moved to wrath, save if they were smitten with other ill than love. And forasmuch, fair son, as this sin is hateful to God, so is it likewise hurtful to the honour and to the body of him that committeth it ; therefore ſtrive with all thy might to shun it and to follow the teaching of the philosopher that saith :

> ' *Triſticiam mentis caveas plusquam mala dentis ; ſeniciem*
> *fugias, nunquam piger ad bona fias.*'

"That is to say, fair son : Flee from vexation of mind more than from the toothache ; and, to drive dolour from thy heart, shun idleness and do ever that which is good.

"And as to this saith Pittacus of Mitylene :

> ' *Effugias iram, ne peſtem det tibi diram ;*
> *Juris delira, nutrix eſt schismatis ira.*'

"That is to say, fair son : Shun choler and wrath, leſt they give thee their cruel peſtilence ; for these are the ways that shall lead thee aſtray out of the true path, and they are nurses of all schisms and dissensions. And of this the Gospel saith :—

> ' *Non odias aliquem, sed eum pocius tibi placa ; quisquis*
> *odit fratrem, censetur ob hoc homicida.*'

"That is to say, fair son : Bear no anger nor hatred to any man, be at peace with all ; for whosoever hateth his neighbour, is a murderer, as the Gospel saith. And of this matter Saint Auguſtine saith, in one of his Epiſtles, that even as bad wine marreth and corrupteth the vessel wherein it is, if it long remain there, so doth anger mar and corrupt hearts wherein it dwelleth. And this the Apoſtle also confirmeth, saying :

> ' *Sol non occidat super iracondiam veſtram.*'

50

" That is to say, fair son : Let not the sun go down
upon your wrath or choler.   And again touching this
Cato saith :

'Impedit ira animum, ne possit cernere verum.'

" That is to say, fair son, that anger and wrath do
hinder and blind the spirit of man in such wise that
he cannot perceive that which is true.   Wherefore,
fair son, the true Lover, as I conceive him, is and ought
to be ever joyous, trusting that by good and loyal
service he shall find true joy in love and in his Lady
most desirable.   And so he singeth, danseth, and is
merry, following the counsel of Solomon, who at the
end of his last book saith in conclusion :

" Bene vivere et laetari."

" That is to say, fair son : live well and merrily ; but
this well living doth not only signify eating rich meats,
drinking good wines, sleeping long o'mornings and in
fair beds, and in brief dwelling amid all manner of
pleasures, but it signifieth : first, to live well toward
God, to dwell with honour and truth, and therewith
merrily.   Wherefore I say, let all true lovers, to win
their fair Ladies' most desired favour, flee with all
their might from this sin of Choler, which is most
hateful to God and to Man, and take for their companion the very lovely virtue of Patience ; whereby
they shall be quit and saved from this passing hateful
and envious sin of Choler.

" Now as to the third sin, which is Envy, this true
Lover, as I do conceive him, shall never be envious
of any man ; for an it should come to his Lady's
knowledge, he should surely lose her.   For never may
honourable lady love one that is envious, unless he be
envious of good virtues, to win therein the most
worship ; as, to be at church the most devout, at

table the best-mannered, in company of ladies the most courteous and the most gay, in arms armigerous and arms courteous the most valiant ; in these things may he be envious to win most worship, but in no other wise. And Seneca saith, touching this :

> '*Quid auro melius ? jaspis. Quid jaspide ? sensus.*
> *Quid sensu ? racio. Quid racione ? modus. Omnibus*
> *adde modum : modus est pulcherrima virtus.*'

"That is to say, fair son : 'What thing is better than gold ? Jasper. What better than jasper ? Feeling. What better than feeling ? Reason. What better than reason ? Conduct ; for conduct is the crown of all virtues'. And further concerning this the philosopher saith :

> '*Filius ancillae morosus plus valet ille quam regis natus, sy non*
> *sit moriginatus.*'

"That is to say, fair son, that the serving-wench's son well nurtured is of more worth than the king's son that is ill bred. And in this regard also, for the better observance of good conduct, I put you in remembrance, fair son, of the wise Solon's saying, of Athens, who thus saith :

> '*Per vinum miser, per talos et mulieres ; haec tria sy sequeris,*
> *semper egenus eris.*'

"That is to say, fair son, that through wine, through dicing, and the company of light women, if such things you do follow after, you shall be ever poor, evil and wretched, and hated of all good men.

"And moreover, of this vile sin of Envy Plato saith :

> '*Invidiam fugere studeas et amore carere, quae reddit siccum*
> *corpus, faciens cor iniquum.*'

"'Study to eschew Envy ; for Envy is loveless and withereth up the body and maketh the heart unjust and evil.' And therefore, fair son, shun all sin and all sinful folk; for love and honourable ladies do require this of all true lovers, following the words of the philosopher, which saith :

' *Malo mori fame quam nomen perdere fame.*'

" That is to say, fair son : ' I had liefer die of hunger than lose the name of good repute '. Now, laſtly, be mindful of this saying : ' I had liefer die of hunger than be willing to lose my good name '. And again concerning this saying of the philosopher, the wise Thilon of Lacedemonia saith :

' *Nobilis es genere, debes nobilis magis esse ; nobilitas morum plus eſt quam progenitorum ; nobilitas generis mortem superare nequibit.*'

" That is to say, fair son : ' If thou art noble of birth, then oughteſt thou to be nobler of virtues ; for nobleness of conduct is of much more worth than nobleness of lineage ; nor can that nobleness, howsoever great it be and mighty, overcome Death '. Wherefore, that you may be that true lover whereof I speak, you shall eschew the moſt dishonourable sin of Envy, and dwell with the glorious virtue of Charity, which is the daughter of God and which he hath so much commended unto us, as it is written.

" Then shall you be clean, quit, and saved in regard of this sin.

" As for the fourth sin, which is Avarice, certainly Avarice and true love cannot lodge together in one heart. And if a miser by some chance fall amorous, never doubt but that it is of some vile and sorry thing, so that he shall have no occasion to spend aught. But the true and loyal Lover shall ſtrive ever to serve Love and his Lady with honour and all largesse, keeping himself well clad, well horsed, and all his people likewise, according to his eſtate. And he that spendeth more than he hath is foolish and shall have

53

ill comfort thereby, for Love and ladies of honour love not spendthrift wooers, nor such folk; but they love such as do bear themselves honourably according to their estate, that is to wit: by making such show as properly they may, at jousts, tourneys, passages-at-arms, and in all noble company, without foolish spending; and such as give of their goods to the most needy, for the love of God, following the Gospel of Our Lord, wherein he saith:

'Beati misericordes, quoniam ipsi misericordiam consequentur.'
Matthew, the V Chapter.

"That is to say, fair son: 'Blessed are they that are merciful for they shall find mercy'. And thus saith Periandus of Corinth:

'Ut sis praeclarus, non sis cupidus nec avarus; vix ut ulli carus cupidus cunctis fit avarus.'

"That is to say, fair son: 'To the end that thou win good renown, be not covetous nor miserly, even though thou have great riches; for one of such condition cannot be loved by any man, but is hated of all'. And to this opinion holdeth also the philosopher that saith:

'Furtum, rappina, fenus, fraudem, simoniam, causat avaritia, ludum, periuria, bella; radix cunctorum fit nempe cupido malorum.'

"That is to say, fair son, that avarice is the cause of theft, of ravishment, of usury, of fraud, of simony, of barratry[10], of perjury, of battles, and in fine, of all evils. And in this opinion agreeth Bias of Prienne, thus saying:

'Plus flet perdendo cupidus quam gaudet habendo; et magis est servus, cum plus sibi crescit acervus.'

"That is to say, fair son: 'The covetous grieveth more in losing than he rejoiceth in having, and the

54

more he hath gathered, the more is he a slave and wretched '. And of this Saint Augustine saith : that the miser's heart is like unto Hell, for Hell swalloweth up many souls, yet never crieth : ' Hold ! enough ! ' And thus it is with the avaricious man, for though all the treasures of the world were in his power, never would he say : ' Hold ! enough ! '

" And in this regard the Scriptures say :

' *Insaciabilis oculus cupidi in partem iniquitatis non saciabitur.*'
Ecclesiasticus, the XIV Chapter.

" That is to say, fair son : ' The eye of the covetous is insatiable ; he shall never be surfeited with iniquity '.

" And so many more authorities, fair son, that it would be a full long matter to rehearse, and to make an end I needs must leave them. So in this wise the true Lover, as I do conceive him, to win his fair Lady's most desired favour, shall obey them all, eschewing this passing hateful sin of Avarice and abiding with the very sweet and lovely virtue of Munificence, which is beloved of God and honoured of the world, and thereby shall he be saved.

" As for the fifth sin, which is Idleness ; certes, fair son, never was true Lover idle ; for the passing sweet and amorous thoughts that he hath, both day and night, of winning his fair Lady's most desired favour, could not assent thereunto. For he is above all others the most diligent and the most joyous, whether in singing, in dancing, rising betimes, saying his Hours, hearing Mass devoutly, going a-hunting or a-hawking, whiles sluggard lovers are yet asleep ; and thus avoideth he this sin, and followeth after the saying of the philosopher Epicturus, which thus saith :

' *Otia, vina, dapes caveas, ne sit tibi labes ;*
Vix homo sit castus requiescens et bene pastus.'

" That is to say, fair son : ' Shun idleness, excess of

55

wine and of meats, lest thou be defiled by lust; for an idle man and a well-fed cannot easily abide in chastity'. Saint Bernard also saith, concerning this same wicked sin of Idleness:

' *Vidi stultos se excusantes sub fortuna ; vix autem dilligenciam cum in fortunio sociabis ; sed minus infortunium a pigracia separabis.*'

"That is to say, fair son: 'I have seen fools cast blame on Fortune; ye shall seldom find a diligent man that is misfortunate; but ye shall ever behold that idleness and ill-fortune are companions'.

"And in this regard Saint Bernard saith moreover:

' *Revidere quae sua sunt, quomodo sunt, summa prudencia est.*'

"That is to say, fair son, that for a man to review his affairs, what they be and in what condition, is sovereign prudence. And he doth not only say: 'to view his affairs', but 'to review'; and this word review signifieth that no man can too oft view them. And concerning this Atheus also, the poet, saith:

' *Otia sunt juvenium menty plerumque venenum ; est juvenum pausa vixiorum maxima causa.*'

"That is to say, fair son, that slothfulness is full oft a poison for young men's minds; for idleness is in the young an especial cause of vice. And in this regard Seneca saith:

' *Accidiam linque, quae dat mala tedia vitae ; tedia virtutis fuge, nam sunt dampna salutis.*'

"That is to say, fair son: 'Forsake idleness, which giveth to life an evil lethargy, and shun the enemies of virtuous living'. And forasmuch, fair son, as true Lovers (such as I do conceive them) are saved by such virtues, forsaking this very vile and miserable sin of Idleness to dwell in company with the glorious virtue of Industry, therefore I pray you that you be of their number ; and so shall you be quit and saved from this passing shameful sin of Idleness.

"And as for the sixth sin, which is Gutting or Gluttony, assuredly the true Lover hath none of it. For he eateth and drinketh but to live ; even as the philosopher saith, that men ought only to eat and drink to live, and not to live for eating and drinking, as swinish folk do. And of this the learned Thales of Miletus saith :

' *Pone gulle frenum, ne sumas inde venenum ;*
Nam male digestus cibus exta saepe molestus.'

"That is to say, fair son : 'Put a bridle on thy mouth, lest thou take poison thereby ; for abundance of victuals ill digested is to the body a passing hurtful venom'. And moreover concerning this the wise Solon of Athens saith :

' *Ne confonderis, nunquam vino replearis ; vili diceris, nisi vino to modereris.*'

"That is to say, fair son : 'Be never full of wine, lest thou be put to confusion, for thou wilt be accounted a knave an thou moderate not thyself in respect to wine and wine in respect to thee'. Moreover, concerning this matter of gluttony, Saint Gregory saith in his Morals, that when the vice of gluttony getteth the mastery over a man's body, he undoeth all good that he hath ever done, and if the belly be not checked by the ordinances of sobriety, all virtues are drowned therein. And touching this, Saint Paul saith :

' *Quorum finis interitus, quorum Deus venter est ; et gloria in confusione eorum, qui terrena sapiunt.*'
Ad Phillipenses, IV° Capitulo.

"That is to say, fair son, that the end of such as rejoice in earthly things is death ; of them also which

57

make their belly their God; and all their glory in arms, in honours, and in strength, shall be turned to confusion.

"Therefore I pray you that you be not numbered with these, but that you follow the teaching of Avicenes, to eschew all this; who thus saith:

> '*Sic semper comedas, ut surgas esuriendo;*
> *Sic eciam sumas moderate vina bibendo.*'

"That is to say, fair son: 'Eat ever in such fashion that, when thou risest from table, thine appetite be not sated; and let thy drinking likewise be temperate'. Thus shall you live long in course of nature, and in regard to this sin you shall find favour with God; with Love also and with your Lady; and so shall you forsake this knavish and dishonourable sin of Gluttony, and shall dwell with the sweet virtue of Temperance, the flower of all virtues, and then shall you be quit and saved from this sin. And here will I make an end concerning the salvation of true and faithful lovers from the sixth deadly sin, which is Gluttony.

"And as for the seventh sin, which is Lechery; verily, fair son, that sin is altogether dead in the true Lover's heart. For so great his fear is lest his Lady should take displeasure thereat, that there is never any dishonourable thought in him. Thus doth he follow the teaching of Saint Augustine, who thus saith:

> '*Luxuriam fugito, ne vili nomine fias; carni non credas, ne Christum crimine ledas.*'

"That is to say, fair son: 'Flee from lechery, lest thou be brought into ill-repute; neither believe in the flesh, lest thou offend Christ Jesus by this sin'. And this Saint Peter the Apostle also affirmeth, in his first Epistle, wherein he saith:—

> '*Obsecro vos, tanquam advenas et perigrinos, abstinere vos a carnalibus desideriis, quae militant adversus animam.*'
>
> *Prima Petri, II° Capitulo.*

"That is to say, fair son: 'I adjure you, as a stranger and a pilgrim, that ye abstain from carnal pleasures, for they war day and night against the soul'. And in this regard the philosopher also saith :—

> *Sex perdunt vere homines in muliere: animam, ingenium, mores, vim, lumina, voces.*

"That is to say, fair son, that he that consorteth with light women loseth six things ; whereof the first is that he loseth his soul, the second his understanding, the third his virtue, the fourth his strength, the fifth his sight and the sixth his voice.

"And therefore, fair son, shun this sin and all that thereto appertaineth, as Cassiodorus saith, writing of the Psalter : that vanity caused the angels to become devils, and brought death to the first man, and dispossessed him of the bliss that had been assigned him ; and that vanity is the wet-nurse of all evils, the fount of all vices, and the path of iniquity which leadeth men away from the grace of God.

"And in this regard David saith, in his Psalter, speaking unto God :

> *Odisti observantes vanitates, supervacue.*
>
> *Psalmus XXX°.*

"That is to say, fair son : 'Thou, mine only God, hast hated and hatest all such as respect vanities'. And so many more testimonies have the virtuous doctors of Holy Church recorded, and moreover the philosophers also, the poets, and other learned heathen (which had not been touched, in true conscience, by the most blessed and lovely grace of our true God the Holy Spirit) have so oft condemned this sin that their writings would be full long to rehearse ; which therefore I purpose to pass over, and come to the rest of my matter ; save only for the saying which Boethius saith thereof :

' Luxuria est ardor in accessu, fector in recessu, brevis delectatio corporis, et animae destructio.'

" That is to say, fair son, that lust is a passion in its coming, foulness in its going, a brief delectation of the body, and the destruction of the soul. And forasmuch as this sin, fair son, is so very dishonourable, the true Lover, as I have said, fleeth it with all his might, for fear lest his Lady take displeasure thereat, and to win her favour. And if by sore constraint of love, he falleth in any wise into this sin, so great and so very great are his grievous pains and tribulations, by reason of the great perils which therefrom may ensue, which the anxious hearts of true lovers must suffer, that it ought not to be accounted unto them as mortal sin; and if indeed there be any sin, assuredly it ought to be utterly atoned by the aforesaid pains which they must so sorely suffer." Therefore may I well affirm that the true Lover, as I do conceive him, is quit, free, and saved, as well from this deadly sin as from all others."

SIXTH CHAPTER

How My Lady gave little Saintré other instruction, concerning the virtues and the estate and means of nobility

" And as for the salvation of the body (forasmuch as I have said that the true Lover may be saved both in soul and in body), now after the salvation from the Seven Deadly Sins, which assail the soul, I shall tell you of the salvation of the body, and by divers means, whereof the first hath to do with Love itself.

" This true and faithful Lover, that is of gentle birth, whole and sound in mind and in body, pursueth day and night his amorous quest for the favour of his fair Lady, and in fashion contrary to the Seven Deadly Sins, as hath been said ; the which gentle Lady shall be above all others (I call them ladies all, for in love all are ladies) : suppose now that she is nowise minded to love either him or any other : yet nature, justice, love and reason do demand that she esteem, prize and honour him the better therefor ; and so much so that she shall be rejoiced at his welfare, at his honour, and his every advancement, and contrariwise shall be afflicted at his displeasure, whatsoever lady she be. And he, what gentle man soever he be, as I have said, it shall never fail him of her favours according to his need ; else were she by nature base and thankless, and worthy to be banished by all people of honour, and then cast into the great foul pit of the sin of Ingratitude, both soul and body ; howbeit, I never yet heard tell of any lady that was such as this. And so in this wise the true Lover, that is saved as to the soul, may be saved likewise as to the body.

" For the rest, touching the further salvation of the body, the true gentleman and Lover, that is neither ordained nor disposed to the study of the right virtuous and blessed sciences of theology, of Canon Law nor of Civil Law, nor any other study of science, saving only the most noble and illustrious science and profession of arms, doth therein shew and advance himself forwardly, for to win worship and the most dear favour of his fair Lady ; and so beareth him, that there is good report of him among the rest. And when he is at church, he is the most devout ; at table the best-mannered ; in company with lords and ladies the most courteous ; his ears hearken unto no base word ; in his eyes there is no false look, nor in his mouth any foul speech ; his hands take no false oath, and his feet fare not in places of ill fame." What

shall I say more ?   He shall be ever the beſt arrayed,
and in feats of arms, as far as he may be, the beſt and
newlieſt armed, horsed, and bedight ; and for love of
his Lady he shall jouſt a-horseback and afoot ; though
indeed men might say that his deeds of arms are
compounded of vanity and by Holy Church forbidden,[13]
as it is written in the canons, which thus say, as
I have heard recorded : firſtly, in the canon that
saith :

' Et alibi non temptabis Dominum Deum tuum.'

because men seek to know whether God doth help him
that is in the right.

"Item : ' Predeſtinaciones' : vicesima tertia : ques-
tione quarta : thereas experience nor law suffer not
such aɛts.   Again they would shew that it is a tempting
of God ; for the clerks hold that to ask a thing contrary
to nature is to ask a miracle or to tempt God.

"And further : ' De purgatione Vulgari'.

"And other canons beyond number, forbidding all
gages of battle and the deeds of arms whereof I speak.

"Nathless by emperors, kings, and other lords
temporal, following their laws and cuſtoms of temporal
lordship, such combats are ordained and approved
when the case requireth it.   And concerning this
matter there was great disputation between the Holy
Father Pope Urban, the Vth of that name, and the
good king John of France, touching a gage of battle
that the king held between two knights, the one
French and the other English, in the Newtown of
Avignon.   And forasmuch as the Pope sought to
uphold the canon law, he commanded and let affix
bills on all the church doors, that no man, on pain of
excommunication, should go to see that jouſting.
But notwithſtanding, the Moſt Chriſtian King, to
maintain his royal privileges, would not be turned

therefrom, but chose to do according to the laws of princes temporal, which thus say : *Lege, etc.*

" And many more also, touching this matter of trial by battle ; and the laws which are called Lombard do suffer it largely and in sundry fashion. Yet is it at this present time in great part forbidden by the ordinances of the Most Christian King, the good King Philip, which laws we now use ; to wit, it is allowed for four cases only and no more.

" The first case is, if it be a notorious, certain and evident thing that felony hath been done : and this is the clause which saith that there must be murder, treason, or other felony beyond doubt apparent.

" The second case is, if the matter be such that it must of necessity be punishable by death, save for the case of larceny, wherein trial by battle is not suffered to be made : and this is the clause which saith that pain of death must ensue therefrom.

" The third case is, if there may be no punishment other than by way of battle : and this is the clause which speaketh of secret murder or treason ; so that he that had committed the same should have no defence save by his body.

" The fourth is, when he that is challenged to battle is commonly reported guilty, by evidence or likely presumption ; and this is the clause which speaketh of presumption.

" But notwithstanding that these challenges of battle be thus forbidden or reserved for such cases as the Church and the Canon Law have ordained, both because of the sin of tempting God and for that of Vanity, yet the true Lover (turning again to my purpose) doeth this same, not for either of these two sins, but only for to win worship, and without quarrel, hatred, or prejudice to any man. For I will answer for him, that whensoever he entereth into the lists, he shall wish his adversary neither harm nor dishonour, no more than himself; and he ought to call God to witness and help therein; therefore for his part, and that God may the more favourably hear him, he goeth confest and repentant, by reason of the perils that may ensue. Of the oaths that they swear, and of the ceremonies, I make no present rehearsal, for the sake of brevity. But when the true Lover issueth forth out of his pavilion, armed at all points as he ought to be, furnished with his shield and all weapons that he is to bear, he maketh a great sign of the Cross, and then lowereth his banner. And anon they give him into his left hand his spear or his sword, for assault and defence to the best of his power. And he abideth there upon a stool, or upon his feet, until the judge or marshal of the lists summoneth or calleth upon him. Then doth this true and loyal Lover bestir him, and cometh on hardily and fiercely, as though he should devour all; yet dealeth the first strokes warily and in measure, upon his guard; even as Valerius Maximus saith in his Sixth Book, wherein he saith that it is great blame to the captain of an army or to any warrior, if he should say: ' I foresaw not that it should have been thus '; for so it is in all matters which conclude and end by force of arms (as battles do, which are most perilous things) that no man can do them over again, for to amend them : and likewise in all feats of war, which must be both conceived and also executed with good and ripe and sane counsel. And this doth Vegecius confirm in his first book of the Art of Chivalry,[14] where he saith :

" ' For such as do fare without prudence in every matter, all may be amended, save only the mistakes of ill-ordered wars and battles, which no man may amend, for the punishment followeth straightway upon the fault.'

"Wherefore, fair son, the prudent, true, and loyal Lover is and muſt ever be governed by order and moderation, in all his deeds and words : and such men it is commonly which, though they be not ſtrongeſt nor moſt puissant of body nor in the number of their soldiers, yet discomfit great hoſts and win the maſtery in wars armigerous, and subdue their enemies ; and all by following the words of the sage that saith, as hath already been recorded :

Malo mori fame, quam nomen perdere famae.

"That is to say, fair son : ' I had liefer by far die of famine, than lose my good fame '. And moreover, in respect to all that have done him or do him good service, whether by counsel, by reproof or by gifts, this perfect Lover shall all his days obey the words of Ariſtotle, who saith : *Diis, parentibus et doctoribus non possumus reddere equivalens.* That is to say, fair son, that to the gods and to parents (which signifieth ' to God, to fathers, mothers, and others of our blood ') and to men of learning, we are not ever able to make equal return for the benefits that they have done us."

SEVENTH CHAPTER

How My Lady sought to know little Saintré's mind concerning the matter of Love

"Now, fair son, I have shewn and declared unto you many things, and I pray God that he grant you thoroughly to have underſtood and remembered all, or the moſt part thereof. What say you ? Doth your heart feel valiant now to achieve these things, in time to come ? Come, tell me your intent."

And when My Lady had made an end of speaking, Saintré, young that he was and much admiring all this fair doctrine, answered nothing. Then said she unto him : " Well, fair Sir, what say you ? Will you have courage so to do ? " Then answered the poor tormented lad, lifting up his eyes unto her, and speaking low : " Ay, Madam, right willingly ".— " You will do this, fair son ? "—" Madam, ay, and with a good will. Yet what Lady such as you say would accept my service, or love such as I ? "—" And wherefore not ? " quoth My Lady. " Are you not of gentle birth ? Are you not a comely youth ? Have you not eyes to see with ? ears to hear with ? mouth and tongue to talk with ? arms and hands to serve with ? legs and feet to walk with ? heart and body to use and loyally to employ in whatsoever she may be pleased to command you ? "—" Madam, that have I."—" Well, then," said she, " wherefore should you not adventure yourself ? Ween you that, for such worth as is in you, there is any lady that so little prizeth her honour as to *ask* service of you ?—though some there be, so constrained by love, that needs must they gently reveal their willingness, and so point the way to be followed. Wherefore then should you not adventure yourself ? For the more honourable the lady, the more shall she esteem you, even though she refuse you."

" Madam, I had as lief die as proffer me and be refused, and then be made a mock and a jape of, as others are, as I have heard tell. And therefore, Ma'am, 'twere better for me to abide as I am."

And when My Lady heard him so say, and with reason, and perceived that he understood not her intent, then was she no more able to keep from discovering her heart unto him, and she said :

66

EIGHTH CHAPTER

How My Lady opened her heart unto little Saintré, discovering unto him that she was minded to love him

"WELL, now, good Christian and gentleman that you are, you shall make me this vow, by God, by your faith as a Christian, and by your honour, here where there is none but you and I can hear; to wit: that concerning anything that I shall say unto you, you shall in no wise tell, discover, nor make known unto any man living or dead, that which I say unto you presently or at another time; and this shall you promise me, your hand in mine."—"Yea Madam," answered he, "on my faith!"

Then said My Lady unto him: "Now Saintré, suppose that I were she whereof I have spoken, and suppose that I were minded, in recompense for loyal service, to do you much good and bring you to high honour; would you serve me?"

Little Saintré, who never had thought to serve such a lady for love's sake, wist not what to do, save to kneel upon his knee, saying: "Madam, I would do all that you might be pleased to command me". "And do you pledge me your faith on this, your hand in mine?" "Yea, by my faith and by my loyalty, Ma'am, so do I pledge you; and I will do all that you may be pleased to command me."—"Well, arise then; hear these my words and remember them: "

67

NINTH CHAPTER

How My Lady admonished the lad Saintré concerning the ten commandments of the Law, and the estate of virtue and nobility

" First of all, I desire and bid you that above all things you love God with all your heart, according to his ordinances and the commandments of Holy Church, as best you may and are able.

" Moreover, I desire and bid you that, after God, you love and serve, above all else, the blessed Virgin Mary, as best you may and are able.

" Moreover, I desire and bid you that you love and commend yourself unto the most blessed true Cross, whereon for our salvation Our Lord died and suffered ; the which is our true sign and defence against all our enemies and evil spirits.

" Moreover, I desire and bid you that every day you use some Paternoster or other orison and commend you unto your good angel, unto whom Our Lord hath given the guidance and the keeping of your soul and of you ; praying that he guide, keep, and defend you, if your own strength fail, and abide with you in life and in death.

" Moreover, I desire and bid you that you keep alway in your heart Saint Michael, Saint Gabriel, or some other angel or saint of Paradise, to the end that they may be your advocates, procurators and ambassadors with Our Lord and Our Lady ; such as men commonly have at the courts of Kings and other great lords, when they cannot see nor have speech of them.

68

" Moreover, I desire and bid you that you fulfil and keep, as best you may, the X Commandments of the Law, to wit :

> First, Thou shalt worship no idols, nor any false gods.
> Thou shalt not swear the name of God in vain.
> . Thou shalt keep the sabbaths and feasts ordained.
> Thou shalt honour father and mother.
> Thou shalt do no murder.
> Thou shalt do no adultery.
> Thou shalt do no larceny.
> Thou shalt bear no false witness.
> Thou shalt not covet thy neighbour's wife.
> And thou shalt not covet another man's goods.

" Moreover, I desire and bid you that you believe wholly the XII articles of the Faith, which are theological virtues, the mothers of good conscience, even as Cassiodorus saith, in his expoundment of the Creed, that Faith is the light of the soul, the gate of Paradise, the window of life and the fundament of eternal Salvation : for without Faith can no man find favour with God. And touching this Saint Peter, the Apostle, saith :

> ' *Sine fide est impossibile placere Deo.*'
>
> *The XI Chapter.*

" That is to say, fair son, that unless he have Faith, it is not possible for any man to be acceptable to God."[15]

" Moreover, I desire and bid you that when you are come to man's estate and achieve noble feats of arms, as men of worship do, which are in battles by sea and by land, in single combat or in companies, in encounters, in petards, in sallies, in scalings, in barricadoes, in skirmishes, or in other wise—that you forget not this holy benison, which Our Lord spake unto Moses to tell Aaron his brother, that was High Priest of the Law,

for to bless the Children of Israel therewithal; even
as the Bible saith, in the Book of Numbers and in the
XIIII Chapter, where it is written:

> '*Benedicat tibi Dominus et cuſtodiat te. Oſtendat faciem suam
> tibi Dominus et misereatur tui. Convertat Dominus vultum
> suum ad te et det tibi pacem.*'

"For meseemeth this benison, issuing from the
very mouth of Our Lord, is more commendable and
more profitable than any other that I wot of. And
therefore I commend it unto you, to say at your
uprising and at your going to bed. But meseemeth
that saying it in this fashion, you bless others and not
yourself. Wherefore meseemeth that you ought,
making the sign of the Cross, to say thus:

> '*Benedicat mihi Dominus et cuſtodiat me. Oſtendat faciem
> suam mihi Dominus et misereatur mei. Convertat Dominus
> vultum suum ad me et det mihi pacem.*'

"And thereafter do joyfully all that you have to
do, for there shall no evil befall you.

"This benison did my lord Saint Francis give unto
Friar Leo, his companion, that was tempted of some
diabolical temptation; the which never after assailed
him.

"Moreover I desire and bid you that when you
are come to man's eſtate and go forth to deeds of arms
and to battles, and when you have overcome your
enemies and then are tempted to vengeance or cruel
wrath, that you remember the words which God
spake in the firſt book of the Bible, in Deuteronomy:

> '*Quicumque fuderit sanguinem humanum fondetur et sanguis
> illius.*'

"He said also in his Passion:

> '*Qui gladio percussit gladio peribit.*'

70

" That is to say, fair son : ' Whoso slayeth with the sword, with the sword shall he be slain '.

" Moreover he said unto David :

' Non edifficabis mihi domum, quia vir sanguinum es.'

He saith moreover by the mouth of David :

' Virum sanguinum et dolosum non dimidiabunt dies suos.'

That is to say, fair son : ' Men of blood shall never see fulness of days '.

" He saith also in the same place :

' Virum sanguinum et dolosum abbominabitur Dominus.'

That is to say, fair son, that the bloody and malicious man is an abomination to Our Lord.

" He saith further, by the mouth of David :

' Sy occideris, Deus, peccatores, viri sanguinum declinate a me.'

That is to say, fair son : ' If thou slayest sinners, O God, far from me be the blood of men '.

" And so many more injunctions of pity and mercy hath he commanded and shewn unto us, in his own person (wherewith all the Scriptures are filled) that for the most learned of clerks it were too long a matter to rehearse them all.

" And therefore, fair son, I desire and command you that with all your might you strive to keep from offending God, Our Lady, and the Court of Heaven by this most barbarous sin, as by all others, and that you take ensample by the right goodly words of Seneca, that was a paynim, and thus saith :

' Sy scirem deos ignoscituros et homines ignoraturos, non tamen dignarer peccare propter vilitatem ipsius peccati."

" That is to say, fair son : ' Though I knew that the gods held it no blame and that no man had knowledge thereof, yet would I not deign to sin, by cause

71

of the great vileness that is in sinning'. Now therefore behold, fair son, this Seneca that was but a paynim, yet did so greatly abhor the vileness of sin : how greatly then ought we to abhor it, that are of the most holy faith of Chrisl Jesus, by true baptism.

"All these things I desire and bid you that you do your utmosl to accomplish.

"And for the resl, concerning your person, I desire and bid you that every morning when you arise, and every night when you go to resl, you shall bless yourself, making the sign of the Cross aright ; neither let it be awke nor askew, as I have aforetime told you, for these are diabolical signs. And you shall commend you unto God, unto Our Lady, unto the True Cross, unto your good angel, and unto all your saints and holy advocates : and you shall arise betimes and do on your raiment fairly and joyously as you may, and without great noise. And when you are well laced in your doublet, and your hose neat and drawn well up, and your shoes well cleaned and well laced, then comb your hair and wash well your hands and your face, and thereafter clean your finger-nails and if need be trim them ; and then do on your girdle and gather up your cloak. And when you are fully arrayed, as you go forth from your chamber make the sign of the Cross, and commend you unto Our Lord, Our Lady, your good angel, and all the saints, and do the bidding of Saint Augusline, who saith : ' *Primo querite regnum Dei* ' : that is, before you do any work, whatsoever it be, go to church and take of holy water, and then hear Mass, if there be any. And if not, go down upon your knees before the image and memorial of Our Lord and likewise of Our Lady, and with hands together, casling not your eyes either to this side or to that, say your prayers and orisons (not unto the images but for the sake of Him that is in Heaven) with all your heart, to the best you may. And then get you to the Antechamber, and there, with the other knights and squires, abide until My Lord the King and My Lady the Queen, or either one of them, goeth to hear Mass, and thither attend them. And if you have not heard Mass, then kneel down and look not to either side, save to be sure that you are not before any lord or lady, knight or esquire, that by honourable rank hath precedence of you. Neither sit among the varlets, for of all estates the middle is the best, as the philosopher saith in his Ethicks, wherein he saith: '*Virtus consistit in medio*'.

"That is to say, fair son, that virtue consisteth in the middle course of things. And the versifier saith, touching this: '*Medium tenuere beati*'. That is to say, fair son, that those folk are blessed which seek not to rise over-high but are content with moderation.

"And there hear Mass honestly and with a good will, and say your Hours, and anon worshipfully attend My Lord and My Lady back again; and if you are hungry or thirsty go break your fast decently and soberly, to tide you until dinner; not with gluttonous lust of eating or of drinking, but only as I have told you, as a philosopher saith: that men ought to eat and drink only to live, and not to live for eating and drinking, as swinish folk do. And the common saying of the leeches is most true: that gluttony slayeth more than swords do.

"Moreover I charge you that you be not a brawler, neither a liar, nor a bearer of lying tales whereof evil may come. Of such folk Cassiodorus saith in his book *Of the Praises of Saint Paul*, as I have told you already: that the quality of Falsehood is such that of itself it falleth down and is manifest to all men, though none raise his voice against it; whereas the quality of Truth is contrariwise, for so passing steadfast

73

and firm is it that the more gainsayers it hath, the more
doth it flourish and wax great.

" And concerning this, Holy Writ saith :

' *Super omnia veritas.*'
Secundum Esdrae, III° Capitulo.

" That is to say, that Truth is above all else. Wherefore, fair son, be ever steadfast and truthful, shunning
the fellowship of liars and slanderers, for they are full
perilous folk.

" Likewise be loyal of hands and of mouth, and
serve every man as best you may, doing no despite nor
rejecting any good service. Seek the fellowship of
good men ; hearken to their words and remember
them. Be humble and courteous wheresoever you go,
boasting not nor talking overmuch, neither be dumb
altogether. For the proverb saith that for talking
overmuch or for being ever silent, a man is held
witless. Look to it that no lady nor damosel be in
reproach through your default, nor any woman, of
whatsoever quality she be. And if you fall into
company where men speak disworshipfully of any
woman, show by gracious words that it pleaseth you
not, and depart thence.

" Moreover I desire and bid you that you be pitiful
toward the poor, neither make mock of another's
poverty ; and give unto them of your goods according to your means. And be mindful of the words
of Albertus, who saith :

' *Non tua claudatur ad vocem pauperis auris.*'

" That is to say, fair son : ' Let not your ears be
shut to the voice of the poor '.

" Moreover I desire and bid you, if God raise you
to any high estate by gifts of fortune, that you take
heed not to forget the most glorious and everlasting

74

riches of Heaven for the sake of the riches of this dark and transitory life. Even as I have before told you concerning the words of the versifier which thus saith :

> ' Quando dives moritur,
> In tres partes dividitur ;
> Caro datur vermibus,
> Peccuniam parentibus,
> Animam demonibus,
> Nisi Deus miseretur.'

"That is to say, fair son, that when a rich man dieth, he and his goods shall be parted into three parts : and firstly, his flesh shall be given to the worms ; his gold, his silver, and his rings and all that he hath, to his kin ; and his soul to all the fiends of Hell, unless God in his grace have mercy of him. And in this regard, fair son, remember the profitable words of Aristotle, who saith :

> ' Vir bone, que curas rex ville et rex perituras, nil proffituras,
> dampno quandoque futuras ; nemo diu manssit in crimine, sed
> cito transsit : et brevis atque levis in mundo gloria que vis.'

"That is to say, fair son, that Aristotle saith, in general teaching : ' O thou Man, that by adventurous might strivest to rise to high estate of glory and riches, take heed lest by thy very might thou be brought low ; for never was any toilsome height without great peril : and what is worse, when all is done, Death cometh '.

"Moreover, I desire and bid you, for better remembrance, that in time of prosperity you be mindful of Seneca's words, in his VIth book of *Benefits*, and in the XXIst Chapter, wherein he saith, of them that are raised to high estate, that they have no greater need of anything, than that men should tell them truth. And there followeth his opinion concerning the enviousness and great rivalries which are in the courts

75

of great lords : who best shall please them and most subtly flatter. Whereof it is written in his *Politics*, in the third book and in the ninth Chapter, that the flatterer is an enemy of all truth ; and that he sticketh as it were a nail into his lord's eye, when he hearkeneth to his flattery ; whereby are princes blinded, so that they lose the love of God and honour, and know not themselves ; nor can they tell, among several things, which to choose and which to leave ; and think to be much praised for that which is accounted much blame to them, and blamed for that wherefor they would be much praised ; and all this because men will not tell them truth.

"Wherefore, fair son, above all things which I have told you and shall tell you, eschew and flee the perilous company of such flatterers, whereof, if you have estate and substance, you shall find no lack.

"These things have I told you that you may be a true friend of God, and a man of renown in this realm, nay, among all that be now living in the world. And so, following these precepts in your Lady's service and in Love's, you shall not fail of true salvation, not in body only, but in soul and body. And let this much suffice you for this present time.

"And when I see that you do so govern you, or at the least as well as you are able, in all these matters, then shall I love you and incline unto you, and you shall be verily my friend. What say you ? Are you minded to do as I bid you ? "

At that fell little Saintré upon his knees and said : "Madam, for all this I thank you well, and I will indeed perform it, God willing ".

"You shall perform it," quoth My Lady, "and I shall see that you do perform it. And now be of good cheer, come what may, and be not dismayed at aught that I shall say unto you now ; yet do I not desire that you should seem to make light thereof, lest my gentlewomen suspect what is between us; but when they are by, do as though you were still all affrighted, as you were before. And abide here, for I shall shortly return."

With that My Lady rose up and said out loud to her gentlewomen : "What think ye of this false fellow ? I have confessed him a full long space, and am not able to discover who is his Lady ". Then said she unto him, as she were wroth : "Get you gone, fellow, you shall never be worth a straw ". And as she was entering into her robing-room, she turning about her said unto him on a sudden, as if in anger : "Abide until I come, master, abide ; for I have more to say unto you ! "

Then well assured, yet feigning somewhat as he were affrighted, as she had bid him, he abode still. And it was not long until My Lady returned back. Then called she him and said, so loud that all might hear : " Come now, master, say, may I know who is your Lady ? Or if I should guess aright, would you tell me, on your faith ? Is't not she, or she, or she ? " " Nay, Madam." " Such an one, or such, or such ? " " Nay, Madam." " Oh," quoth Isabel, " now are we perplexed truly, for we had vowed for him that this time soothly he should have chosen a Lady ; and you see well that it is none of them which you have named : yet it must be that he hath one. Now since the case is thus, draw you apart with him, and if he is such as he ought to be, he shall surely tell you her name, and so be quit of his oath."

Then My Lady, all laughing and as in sport, drew with him apart, and said unto him softly :

TENTH CHAPTER

How My Lady, being enamoured of little Saintré, gave him XII Crowns to accoutre and array him worthily

" Fair son, I give unto you this little purse, such as it is, and XII crowns that are therein. And I desire you from henceforth, for love of me, to wear the colours whereof it is made and these letters interlaced : and as for the XII crowns, you shall buy you a doublet of crimson damask or satin therewithal, and two pair of good hose, the one of fine Scarlet[16] and the other of fine Saint-Lô brunet,[17] which shall be broidered all down the outward side with the colours and device of the purse ; and you shall have also four pair of fine linen shirts, and four seemly kerchiefs ; shoes likewise, and pattens, fairly made ; and next Sunday let me see you in goodly array. And if you do wisely and honestly in this matter, I shall, God willing, soon do more for you."

Little Saintré, like a young lad shamefast and innocent, would have refused the purse, saying : " Ma'am, I thank you, but may't please you, I had liever not take it, for I have in no wise earned it ".

" Earned ? " quoth My Lady, " I wot well that you have not earned it ; but with God's grace earn it you shall. 'Tis my will and commandment that you take it ". And so saying, she wrapped it in a scarf and laid it softly and secretly in his sleeve, and then said unto him : " Now go hence and set your mind on well-doing, that I may hear good report of you ; and God be with you ! But come no more unto the gallery until you are arrayed. And for the present I say naught else unto you, save only that I pray God that all the virtues whereof I have told you, or the moſt part thereof, may be in you ".

Then My Lady, feigning as she were wroth, said unto him out loud : " Come, get you gone, Sir faint-heart and faint-wit : away with you for now ! But you are not yet quit ; we shall have more to say unto you at another time ".

And when he was out of her chamber and had taken his leave full piteously, she said unto her gentle-women, laughing : " I ween we lose our labour, and that he hath not yet wit enow to know how to choose him a Lady, nor hath ever thought of love ; but at the leaſt we have had good sport with him, and shall have more ".

Anon My Lady bade unrobe her, and laid her down to sleep, and so did they all ; for My Lady's long parleying with Saintré had wearied some among them mightily. And now for a space will I leave speaking of My Lady and of her gentlewomen, that I may turn to little Saintré.

ELEVENTH CHAPTER

How little Saintré arrayed him honourably, as My Lady had bid him, and how, finding him in the galleries, she caused him to come unto her chamber and queſtioned him concerning the devices that he bore ; all to the intent that her damosels should not be aware of her love : and how she gave him sixty crowns more, in a purse

LITTLE SAINTRÉ, when he was a great way from My Lady's chamber, sought a place apart, and looked to one side and the other to be sure that none could espy him. Then drew he the purse out of his sleeve

79

and unwrapped it. And when he saw how fair it was, and the twelve crowns therein, doubt not but he was well content. Such joy was there in his heart that he deemed himself no poorer than the King.

Now, to fulfil My Lady's bidding, and to be thus worthily arrayed on the next Sunday, he thought within himself many joyous imaginings. Then went he thence unto Perkin de Solle, that was the King's tailor, and said unto him: "Friend Perkin, for how much might I have by next Sunday a doublet for myself, all made of good crimson damask?" Perkin, perceiving that he was but small, took his measure, and said unto him: "Have you money?"—"Ay, Perkin; only let it not be too dear!" At that Perkin, who was ever gracious to all men, said unto him: "By my faith, Saintré, fair son, for less than six crowns I cannot: but it shall be of the finest". So Saintré, being young and eager, drew out his purse, and gave him the six crowns. And after he had paid for his doublet, he went thence to John de Busse, that was purveyor of hose to the King, and made covenant that two pair of hose should cost together, two crowns; the which, to be the better served, he paid then and there. Then went he unto Francis de Nantes, the King's broiderer, and shewed him the purse to be broidered, in such fashion as My Lady had said; whereof the price was covenanted at two crowns. And so he had now but two crowns remaining. Then went he unto a goodwife of Paris, unto whom his father, the Seigneur de Saintré, had divers times commended him, and said unto her: "Mary de Lisle, good mother, should I have two pair of fine linen shirts for a crown?" "Son," said she, "I know not; have you that crown?"—"Yea."—"'Tis well", quoth Mary. "Now, mother, see here it is; and let me have one pair to wear on Sunday." With that he drew out from his bosom the purse, all enwrapped, and shewed her the two crowns. " Why, fair son," said she, " who hath given them you ? "—" Mother," said he, " my lady mother hath sent me twelve ; and prayeth you that one be employed in linen and that I may keep the other with the purse." And when Mary saw that fair purse, she was right glad for his sake, and said : " God's blessing on my lady, that so careth for her good son ! " Then said she unto him : " And where be the other ten crowns ? "—" Good mother," said he, " they are already spent."—" Alack, fair son !" quoth she, " I ween you have lost them, or spent them but ill."—" Mother," quoth he, " truly I have not ; and that shall you see on Sunday."

And so all that week passed until the Sunday morning, when to the chamber of Jacques Martel, the King's first groom of the stables (wherein little Saintré and the King's other pages were wont to sleep) there came all together Perkin de Solle, the tailor, John de Busse, the hosier, Francis de Nantes, the broiderer, and William Soldam, the cordwainer, all purveyors to the King ; bearing one the doublet, another the broidered hose, another the shoes and pattens. And when Jacques Martel was aware how they were all assembled at his chamber door, he bade open it. Then entered they in all together, and he saw how that they bore the doublet, the scarlet broidered hose, the shoes and the pattens ; he asked of them, for whom all this might be. " For our master," said they laughing; " 'tis for our master, little Saintré : we be all his men." Then Jacques turned toward little Saintré, and smiling said unto him : " Saintré, I doubt you have told your creditors a fine tale ! "—" Master," answered he, " 'tis my lady mother hath told it, for she hath sent me money for my pleasuring and for my needs ; and meseemeth there

81

is little I can do with money, save to array myself honourably." "Truly", said the Esquire, "I ever loved you well, but now I love you more than ever I did." Then turning toward the other gentlemen pages, he said unto them : "Ah, naughty knaves that ye are, 'twill be long ere ye do the like! Ye had rather go spend them in dicing, in ale-houses, in taverns, and in other knavery, than so to do! And therefore have I well beaten you, for chaſtisement". And then said he unto the craftsmen : "Come now, array me him ſtraightway, and make him goodly to look upon". And when he was all arrayed and attired, little Saintré, having before paid them all, gave unto the apprentices the half of his laſt crown, and the other half unto the Esquire's varlets, who loved him already more than any other of the pages, because he gave them freely of his old garments.

And when the Esquire and all of them were arrayed, they followed him to Mass, and afterward to the ante-chamber to wait upon the King ; but all this was not without much enviousness and talk of the other pages concerning him. And when the King issued forth out of his bedchamber and beheld little Saintré thus arrayed, he fell to laughing, and asked the Esquire whence this came, that he was so comely. "Sire," said he, "I was this morning mightily aſtonied, when Perkin de Solle, John de Busse, Francis de Nantes, and William Soldam, with their varlets, came unto my chamber bearing his raiment ; verily I weened they were come to take me prisoner."

At that, the King and all the lords which were with him, fell to praising Saintré greatly. "I would he had three or four of my years," said the King ; "he should be my carving squire." And with these words the King entered into the Chapel, and the Queen following. And when Mass was said, as they returned,

My Lady perceived little Saintré a short way off, thus gracefully arrayed. Anon as they passed by she drew near and said unto the Queen: "O Madam, see the little lad Saintré, how fairly he is clad!"—"Why, Fair Cousin," said the Queen, "you say sooth; verily is he goodly to look upon." With that they went into Hall for dinner. My Lady, whose eyes could not keep from looking at him, called other ladies (the more covertly to see him and be able to speak with him) and said unto them: "Shall we look what badges are these that little Saintré beareth on his hose? Truly", said she, "we are come to a pretty pass when such as he take upon them to wear emblems and play the lover!"—"Why, Madam, 'tis of good intent he doth so." Then quoth one: "Perdy, Madam, let us see what 'tis"; and another: "Madam, let us make sport of him!" Anon My Lady and the rest drew apart to a window, and called him unto them. And My Lady said unto him, as though she wist nothing of it: "Now, master, now, we would fain know and behold what badge it is you bear upon your hose". Then little Saintré, upon his knees, let them importune him a little. "Certes", said they, "we are resolved to know; and let us make haste, for the King goeth to dinner." Then one took him by the arm, another by the shoulder and the rest by the middle, and so lifted him to his feet. So My Lady and all the rest, and sundry that were not asked, beheld those badges, which were, by all that were there, much admired; and as for the great joy which My Lady had thereof, it solaced her both heart and body.

Now, to be short, when all the tables were cleared, and grace said, then began the minstrels to play, and joyous hearts[18] to dance and to sing, until the King, desiring to depart, called for the spices and the Parting Cup. And while they danced, My Lady's eyes dwelt ever upon little Saintré, so well did he dance and sing. Then she bethought her that she would gladly see his badges and speak with him more at leisure; for the more she beheld him, the more did he please her; and there was none in the Court but esteemed him worthy.

So as he passed by, bearing the Parting Cup, My Lady said unto him: " Do as you did the other day, little Saintré "; the which words he well understood. And it was not long until the King withdrew and the Queen went to her bed. Anon went My Lady thence to her chamber, and found little Saintré in the gallery, as she had bid him; and said unto him, as she were half astonied: " What, master popinjay, are you here? Go you on before us! You have fled us these five or six days; we have a reckoning to make with you ". Then turned she her about toward her gentlewomen, and said unto them: " We must see this lad's badges, and know, an we may, whence he hath them, and to what intent; I cannot believe that he hath found wit or sense enough to be fallen in love ". And so devising she came unto her chamber. Then bade she all the men withdraw, save him only, and let shut the door. And there, in the midst of all her gentlewomen, My Lady was pleased to behold his badges, and then said unto him: " What, master, master! You say you have no Lady-love, and yet array you so gaily! " " Madam," answered he, " I thank you, 'tis God and my lady mother have so gaily arrayed me." " How now! " quoth My Lady, " hath she so fairly arrayed you, that is in Touraine and I ween was never here? "—" Ma'am, 'tis twelve crowns she hath sent me in a fair purse all of gold and silk, that have so fairly arrayed me."—" Verily? " said My Lady, " we must see this purse and know what is become of the XII crowns; and an they be not well spent, I shall write and bid her to send you no more."

84

Then little Saintré drew the purse from his bosom, all wrapped in a fair little kerchief : and My Lady, being well assured that none among her women would know it, took the purse and examined it before them all, as though she had never before beheld it ; and she saw then the badges upon his hose, how that they were the same.   Then said she unto him : " Well now, maſter, firſt of all, what hath this doublet coſt you ? " " Madam, I paid Perkin de Solle six crowns for it, juſt as it is."   " And the hose," quoth My Lady ; " who hath made them and what coſt they you ? "— " Madam, these scarlet hose, and another pair of fine Saint-Lô brunet, I had from John de Busse for two crowns ; and the broidering of these hose coſt me two crowns more to Francis de Nantes."—" Well, messire, that is ten crowns.   And what have you done with the other two ? "—" Ma'am, with one, I had for three pence two pair of fine linen shirts, and for twenty pence, I had three pair of shoes and two pair of pattens ; and the reſt I gave for wine to the maſter craftsmen's apprentices and to our maſter the Esquire his varlets."

My Lady, well content at all this, and perceiving that his graciousness toward the maſter craftsmen had ſtood him in good ſtead, and likewise his largesse well spent, said unto her gentlewomen, laughing : " He hath squandered the half of it ".   " Nay, by my faith, Madam," said he, " may't please you, I had not a penny over."   Then said My Lady, " this time I will know who is your Lady-love !   Come hither now and speak with me ".   " Perdy, Ma'am," said her gentle-women, " you plague him overmuch, seeking to know so many things of him."—" Fret you not," said My Lady ; " but withdraw, all of you, for I am resolved to know it."   And when all were a little withdrawn, My Lady said unto him : " Well now, fair son, thus

85

far am I well pleased with you. Be ever mindful of well-doing, for you shall be ever the better thereby. Above all else I command you that you suffer no man, nay, not your most friend, to know aught of what is between us ".—" That shall he not, Madam, for on mine oath, I had liefer die."—" Well now, fair son, I desire you to have two more gowns, whereof one shall be of fine Saint-Lô brunet, and the same trimmed with sable ; and the other shall be of good Monti-villiers grey, lined with fine white lambswool, to wear every day, except when you ride behind my lord the King. And you shall have also two hoods, the one scarlet and the other black. And likewise shall you have a doublet of blue satin and two pair more of good hose ; kerchiefs also and shirts, shoes, pattens, points, and laces. Play now and then at tennis ; and get you bows and arrows ; these are honourable disports whereby, in a measure, the body hath benefit. And for all this, and for your sustenance, I shall give you sixty crowns : and I shall watch how you rule your spending. And sith you have as yet no varlet of your own, I desire you to give every month a wage of VIII pence to Gillet de Corps, who is a good and faithful serving-man of the Esquire's, and let him have charge of your gowns, your hose, and your other raiment. And if you do rule yourself honourably and well, you shall have a collar, a chain, a Bohemian girdle, a damask gown and other things enow ; only be loyal, discreet, and a man of honour."—" Madam," said he, " an't please God, I will."—" Now, fair son, hearken unto me : whatsoever menaces and harsh words I shall say unto you before my gentlewomen and elsewhere, be never dismayed."—" That will I not, Madam," said he, " sith it is your good pleasure."

Then My Lady, as she were very ill-content with him, spake chidingly unto him before her women ;

and anon entering into her closet, opened the casket and put sixty crowns in a little silken purse; then came she again and called unto him: " Come, master, come, are you not yet resolved? Will you not trust me? Or, if you are not minded to tell me, tell Dame Joan, or Dame Katharine, or Ysabel, or whomsoever you please ".--" What can I tell you, Ma'am, when I have no Lady? "—" And you wear badges and letters interlaced, and play the lover, Sir Greenhorn! "— " Ma'am, on my oath, I have told you her that I most love in this world, and that biddeth me wear these devices."—" Ah, master, master, you think to persuade us that 'tis your mother: I well believe that you love your mother and that 'tis she that cherisheth you; but 'tis not for her you wear that device. Come hither now; I have bethought me of another Lady that I have not yet named."

Then called she him apart, and said unto him: " Take this little purse, and take heed that you lose it not: there are LX crowns therein! Now I shall watch well how you rule your spending. And I desire that you come no more unto the galleries at the hour when I pass through, nor tarry too oft before me; but when you see me pick my teeth with a pin, that shall be for a sign that I would speak with you; and then shall you rub your right eye, and by that I shall know that you have understood me; and then shall you come hither. Now, have you well understood all that I have said unto you? "—" Ay, Madam, right well."—" Then be mindful of well-doing; and I shall love you. And when I shall see that you govern yourself well, I shall take you for my Lover and give you fair raiment." " Madam," said he, " that will I do, please God."—" Now get you gone, for I would sleep. And as I have bid you, when I chide you before my people, be not dismayed."

87

TWELFTH CHAPTER

How My Lady feigned to threaten little Saintré, telling him before her gentlewomen that he would never be of any worth. And afterward how the aforesaid Saintré went thence to have more raiment made with the moneys which My Lady had given him ; and then how My Lady spake with him and he told her that his mother had sent him the moneys wherewith he was arrayed

Then said My Lady unto him, as though wroth : " Get you gone, boy ; away with you ! for you shall never be of any worth ".—" Alack, Madam," said they all, " let not his banishment be for ever. If it be thus, Saintré, 'twere better you should tell My Lady the truth." But Saintré, who had learnt his lesson of My Lady, feigned as he were angered, and kneeling took his leave, saying never a word. Then fell they all a-laughing at My Lady's plaguing of him, saying : " Alack, now have we lost him and shall no more have our sport of him ! " For they knew naught of the gentle covenant between My Lady and him. " Hold your peace," quoth My Lady ; " he is not yet quit ; the best of the game is yet to come ! "—" Alack and welladay ! " quoth Ysabel ; " this poor lad is sore tormented among us."

And with that I shall leave for a space to speak of the mirth and disport which My Lady and her gentlewomen had of him ; and I come to tell how he spent his sixty crowns.

When little Saintré was departed from My Lady, he went straightway to count his treasure. And beholding such a fortune of crowns in his hand, he was so passing glad that he wist not what to do nor what to think. All that day he pondered where he might hide them,

for he durst not give them into the Esquire's keeping,
nor any other man's, because My Lady had straitly
charged him that none should know aught thereof.
So he resolved to hide them in his pockets until the
morrow, when he might spend them ; and so he did.
And that night seemed to him longer than any he ever
knew. But in the morning early, when he had arisen
and heard Mass, he sought out Perkin de Solle, the
King's tailor, and bade him make the three gowns as
My Lady had commanded, and to trim the same with
fur ; whereof he wore one the Sunday after, with the
doublet of blue damask ; for he found money enow
to accomplish all this, and a plenty yet remaining.

Now when My Lady beheld little Saintré clad in his
black gown trimmed with ermine, she was passing
glad, more than before. Anon, winking at him, she
made their signal with the tooth-pick ; whereto he
answered. And as My Lady returned into her
chamber, she found him in the gallery ; and espying
him from afar off, she said unto her gentlewomen :
" Lo, yonder is our jesting-stock ; let us parley with
him ! " And when he perceived her, he made
semblance to turn away and take another road. Then
commanded My Lady to call him, and said unto him :
" What, master, master ! Do you flee thus from
ladies ? It shall not avail you. Come, go before
us ! " And when My Lady was come into her
chamber, she sent thence all the men, excepting only
John de Soussy, a squire of the Queen's, and Tybalt
de Roussy, a squire of her own (the two that had the
best mouths for telling what they should keep secret)
and said unto them : " I have kept you here that you
may make merry with us ".

Then began My Lady to say unto little Saintré :
" Now, master, now, sith we have all of us so oft
entreated you to tell us who is your Lady-love, yet

might never come to know it, neither by prayers, by entreaties, by menaces, nor by hard words; and sith the case is that you have not been pleased to confide in any one among us; now at leaſt tell John de Soussy or Tybalt de Roussy, which are your friends, or either one of them".—"Why, Madam," said John de Soussy, "why should he rather tell it us, when he hath been unwilling to tell it you?" Little Saintré, who was now well assured and well underſtood My Lady's words, said naught, but feigned as he were altogether dismayed. And My Lady, perceiving how he kept silence, said unto John de Soussy and unto Tybalt: "This lording, whom you here see wearing an ermine gown, a silk doublet, and broidered hose, so gay, would have us believe that he hath no Lady, and what is worse, that he loveth none! And i'faith, when I well consider him, she would be doting indeed that would take him for a lover". And so saying she looked very ſternly on him, and then said unto him: "Well, sir, you that are yet but a page, albeit of a good household: whence had you this ermine gown and this doublet?"—"Ma'am," said he, "sith it pleaseth my lady mother, who desireth me thus to be arrayed, she hath sent and bid me have them."— "And how much hath she sent you?"—"Sixty crowns, Ma'am."—"Sixty crowns!" quoth My Lady, "I trow you have squandered the half of them."— "That have I not, Ma'am, on my oath!"—"And this gown, this hood, this doublet, and these hose; have these coſt you sixty crowns, I would fain know?" —"Nenni, Madam; I have bought, beside all that you see upon me, another gown of fine blue ſtuff, trimmed with fine Romany[19] lambswool, and another gown of good grey Montivilliers lined with fair white wool, two pair of good hose, whereof one is of Scarlet; and there are four crowns over."—"And who hath

90

been your counsellor in doing all these things ? "—
" Madam, no man, save Perkin de Solle, and myself."
—" Perkin de Solle ? " said My Lady ; " I wit well
he is a man of prudence, and that hath he shewn indeed
in your affairs ; for your money is to my thinking well
spent. And said you not of late that your mother
had sent you X or XII crowns, whereby you were so
fairly arrayed ? "—" Yea, Madam."—" Now God
preserve you such a mother and grant that you be a
good son to her. Come now, get you hence all, for
'tis time for us to sleep."

With that they went every man thence, and as they
went, John de Soussy and Tybalt de Roussy praised
little Saintré greatly, telling him he need not be vexed
at My Lady's rigorous words. And on the other hand
they cried shame on My Lady, that she should so
unmercifully plague him, seeking to know matters that
in no wise concerned her. " Truly ", said Saintré,
" who should take pleasure in all the ungracious
words which she saith unto me, because that I tell
not her, nor her gentlewomen, who is my Lady ? and
she will not believe that I neither have any, nor desire
to have. Why, by my faith, an I had a Lady, never
would I tell them, they have so plagued me ! " At
that they fell all to laughing, and anon went their
several ways : and all this they told afterward to My
Lady and to them all ; and had great merriment
thereat among them. And it was not long before
My Lady's converse, and her gentlewomen's, with
little Saintré, were reported by the squires in divers
quarters, as My Lady had intended, and there was
much merriment thereat. And so had it been with
other matters, an they had had knowledge thereof.
And thus was this true love kept a secret, until that
Fortune in her fickleness turned her back upon them,
as shall afterward appear.

This loyal and secret love endured XVI years. And when My Lady desired to speak with little Saintré, she said unto him (that it might be more secret) :— " Fair son, 'tis not enough to join in the dance, but we muſt come out of it also with honour. I have made you to come hither from the galleries too oft ; and though you say your mother hath thus fairly arrayed you, yet there are those about us that may think many things, and one is enough to devine and discover all. Therefore am I resolved that I will no more meet you in the galleries ; but when I desire to speak unto you, or you unto me, let us make our two signals, as we have devised. And then shall you come and open my garden-gate, when you do perceive that I am returned into my chamber at nightfall : and behold here is the key. And there will we talk together and devise our pleasures ".

THIRTEENTH CHAPTER

How My Lady prevailed with the Queen to speak unto the King, that he should make little Saintré his Carving Squire

Now when the third year of their love was come, and he was in his sixteenth year, My Lady bethought her that he was now old enough to be free of page's service, for he knew well how to carve,[20] and was proper to be Carving Squire to the King, or the Queen, whichever might take him. Then she took thought how beſt she might bring this to pass, saying within herself : " An thou speak unto the Esquire that hath charge of him, he may surmise, because of the twelve crowns and the reſt, how that it was all thy doing ; an

THE KING'S CARVING SQUIRE

thou speak unto this lord, or that, or that other, one among them may guess the cause thereof; and yet, he muſt be holpen and taken out of pagehood ". And she resolved that she would herself, in his behalf, ask of the Queen that she should make his suit unto the King. Then made she the signal with the tooth-pick, whereunto he answered.

And when they were together in the Pleasance, she said unto him, kissing him full lovingly: " My moſt true desire, you are now of the age of XVI years, and are henceforth too old to be a page. I have bethought me that, for your advancement, I will make petition unto My Lady the Queen in your behalf, that My Lord the King may take you out of page's service, and that you may be Carving Squire to one or the other of them; for the firſt time that he saw you so fairly arrayed, he said in jeſt that he would you had four or five of his years, that he might ordain you to carve before him. Wherefore I pray you, if My Lady the Queen speak unto you in any wise thereof, thank her right dutifully, leſt I be accounted untruthful ".

At these words little Saintré was passing joyful, and thanked My Lady humbly; who anon, kissing him full tenderly, bade him depart. Then went Saintré forth, and My Lady shut the door all quietly after him, and thereafter went to reſt.

On the morrow, at the Queen's arising, My Lady (who ceased not day or night from seeking the advancement of her humble servant) said unto her, smiling: " Madam, I muſt acquit me of a promise that I had forgot for some days: 'tis to make of you a requeſt in the behalf of a young bashful squire that is so timorous he durſt not make it of himself ".—" And who is he ? " asked the Queen. " Madam, 'tis little Saintré."—" And what would he ? "—" Madam, he saith that it shameth him to be any longer a page, and that he is already XVI years old, or XVII; may it please you to make petition unto My Lord the King, that he might be his Carving Squire; and he will write unto his father and to his mother, who will find him horses and help array him worshipfully."—" In sooth ", said the Queen, " his petition is but rightful and honourable, and I will right gladly prefer it, for I wot that My Lord loveth him well; and 'tis moreover a full courteous youth, and I have hope, Fair Lady, that he shall one day be a man of much worship." And it was not long before that petition was made unto the King. The King, for Saintré's worthiness and the good report he had of him, granted it right willingly. And that the thing might no longer be delayed, the firſt time that the Queen saw the seneschal with the King, she put him in mind thereof. Then the King commanded that little Saintré should serve him as Carving Squire, beginning at that day's dinner; and that he should have three horses and two varlets at livery. The seneschal, being informed of the King's will and the Queen's petition, when he perceived little Saintré among the other gentle pages, called him and said unto him : " Saintré, fair son, what is your name?" " My lord Seneschal," said he, " they call me John."— " John," quoth he, " from henceforth you are no more a page; the King hath ordained you his Carving Squire, with three horses at livery, and two varlets. Therefore, fair son, if thou didſt ever well, do better from now on; for by the report of your courteous service, doing despite to no man, the King loveth you well. Be not vainglorious on that account; for I hope that he may advance you yet more. Keep your hands and your nails clean, and the reſt of your body, to the moſt of your power; for that doth your office require more than any other in serving at a lord's table." And all they that were in the hall, and heard those words, were every one passing glad of little Saintré's advancement.

Thus is it a right fair and profitable thing for all young esquires to serve without doing any man disservice, to be gentle, lowly, and patient, that they may win favour of God and of all men; even as the common proverb saith :—

> " Who cannot suffer good and ill
> Shall never place of honour fill." [21]

FOURTEENTH CHAPTER

How little Saintré thanked the King, the Queen, and My Lady, for that he had been made Squire. And how he carved before the King, and performed his office very worthily

THEN John of Saintré, humble, gentle, and courteous that he was, fell straightway on his knees before the King, and thanked him for the great honour that he did him. The King, like a wise, gentle and gracious prince, said unto him : " Saintré, only do worthily, and we shall requite it you ". Then turned Saintré toward the seneschal, and there in presence of the King and all men, he thanked him for the good counsel which he had given him, nor was he ashamed, as some might have been, to thank him publicly. And anon he departed and came unto the Queen, who was in her chamber; and openly, making no sign to My Lady, he gave her thanks, right humbly kneeling on his knees, before all the lords and ladies that were there. And the Queen said unto him : " Saintré, the services and courtesies which you have done unto all, and in especial unto ladies, have hastened the time for you to be taken out of pagehood, and made My

95

Lord's squire and mine. Wherefore, fair son, think ever on well-doing and on rendering every man service ; for there shall come one that shall pay for all ".

Then were the tables set and the seneschal came to seek the Queen for dinner. My Lady, feigning herself ignorant of all these matters, while that the other ladies and damosels all spake of Saintré, did but say : " In sooth, 'tis a worthy young squire ".

When the King and the Queen were seated, and My Lady also at the foot of the table, the seneschal took the napkin from the bread-basket and laid it upon John of Saintré's shoulder. Then began he to perform his office of Carving Squire, and so courteously that he well pleased the King, the Queen, and every man. My Lady, who sat at the nether end of the table, looked ever and again upon him ; and anon she bethought her that truly he ought to have the three horses which were assigned him, and his two varlets. Then took she the pin from her breast amd made her signal, feigning to pick her teeth, and so oft that John of Saintré was at length aware of it, and answered her signal as well as he might.

FIFTEENTH CHAPTER

How little Saintré went to speak with My Lady in the Pleasance ; how she kissed him lovingly and gave him an hundred and sixty crowns to get him an horse and other things needful

AND when the evening was come, he opened the Pleasance gate and there awaited My Lady, who was not long in coming. Then was such greeting between them as no man nor woman can conceive of, unless Love have taught it them. Anon she said unto him :

" Mine only love and moſt sweet thought, you cannot long tarry here : kiss me for true love's sake. And take here in this little purse an hundred and sixty crowns, the which I give you to buy a fair, nimble and spirited riding-horse, that shall be full lively and brisk ; whatsoever it coſt you, up to fourscore crowns ; and another upſtanding one, for your every day riding, up to XX crowns ; and another pair, for XXX crowns, to bear your box and a varlet : and that is an hundred and thirty crowns. With the XXX crowns that remain over, you shall let make fair raiment of cloth, and you shall clothe both yourself and your serving-men in your livery when you go riding. And the remnant you shall have for your spending so long as any remaineth, and when it faileth, you have but to make our signal ". And after those words she said : " Farewell, dear love ! farewell mine only hope and weal ! "— " And fare you well, Lady ! farewell, my treasure ! farewell, you that may moſt command me and that I muſt and will the moſt obey ! " And this saying, they departed.

John of Saintré went thence and lay that night in the Esquire's chamber ; who said unto him : " Saintré, fair son, right sorry am I that you do leave us, but passing glad of your good fortune ". Then said he unto the King's other pages, that ſtood round about Saintré : " Consider now, my sons, is't not a fair thing to do well and to be humble, gentle, peaceable, and courteous to every man ? Lo here is your fellow, who for being such hath won the King's favour, the Queen's, and all men's. But ye, that are brawlers, card-players and dicers, and consort with knaves in taverns and ale-houses, 'tis in vain I have you whipped, I cannot amend you ; and so, though ye be of noble eſtate, yet an ye mend not your ways, ye shall be ever unworthier as ye grow older ".

And while he spake these words, they had all unclad them and went now to their beds.

Little Saintré, who durst not discover to any man the place wherein his hundred and sixty crowns were hid, let them lie that night in his pockets, for fear lest he should be robbed of them. (God knoweth, that night seemed long to him, for the desire that he had to buy the horses.) But when the day was come, and he was ready and attired, he went straightway, after he had heard Mass, unto that goodwife Mary de Lisle, whereof I have spoken, and said unto her: "Mary, good mother, I bring you news".—"What news, fair son?" "The King, of his bounty, hath taken me out of page's service, and caused me to carve before him yesterday, and hath assigned me three horses and two varlets; and afterward, all privily, hath sent me by one of his chamberlains an hundred and sixty crowns, to mount and array me and my varlets, and to keep me in good point; charging me to tell no man, by cause of the envy that some might have. So I pray you, good mother, keep it for me, and let no man in the world know aught of it."—"Now God be praised, fair son!" quoth Mary; "Nay, tell no man; and for my part, there shall be never a word spoken. But how will you do? It behoveth you to find one that hath skill of horses, and can seek you out good serving-men."—"Good friend and mother, I have bethought me to write unto My Lord,[22] praying him send me one or two; and as for the horses, our master the Esquire will right gladly help me, and others a-plenty an I chose to ask them; but I would not be over-hasty, lest folk suspect." What more shall I say? Ere that a month was passed, he had varlets and was well horsed; and he and his varlets well bedight. And the King loved him and cherished him more than ever before, and the Queen also, so that there was much

98

talk thereof. And when My Lady beheld what
favour the King shewed him, she took her tooth-pick
and made their signal until Saintré espied it and anon
answered her. And when they were together at
evening, in the Pleasance, My Lady said unto him :
" My love and my heart, I do perceive how My Lord
and My Lady also, God be thanked, hold you in high
favour. Now muſt we consider how beſt you may
keep it, which is a passing hard thing at Court by
reason of the slanderous talk of the envious, unless
you make friends among them that be neareſt to the
King : some by presents and others by promises,
since we cannot give unto all ; the which promises
muſt be fulfilled as time and occasion serve ; to one
an horse or an hackney, to another a gown. For gifts
and promises, when they can be fulfilled, with honours
and good cheer to every man according to his ſtation,
do so bind, beguile, and make captive men's hearts,
that all are yours.

" To officers of the Household, suits of livery, that
they may be all for you ; to My Lady the Queen, at
one time a fair hackney, at another a good horse for
her litter or for her coach ; to other ladies according
who they be : to some, fair ornaments, to others
girdles of silver finely gilded ; to some, fine ſtuffs
only, to others fair jewels ; to some, goodly diamonds
and rubies, and to others, gold rings cunningly
enamelled ; and to damosels of lesser degree, purses,
gloves, laces and brooches, according to their ſtation.
And thus, by reason of your largesse, there shall follow
you every man's honour, favour, and love. And if
you ask of me whence all these things shall come unto
you, I make answer : So long as you shall loyally
serve me, I will furnish you therewithal. And when
you are a little ſtouter of body, then I desire you to
undertake some notable deeds of arms, wherein you

shall wear the Emprise[23] which I shall give you : and thereby shall you rise yet higher in the King's love and favour, in the Queen's, and in every man's. And for to make a beginning in these matters, behold here in this purse are three hundred crowns, whereof one hundred shall be for a good hackney or horse which you shall give presently unto the Queen, thanking her for the honour that My Lord the King hath done you at her request. And another hundred crowns to make distribution of raiment unto the varlets of their Bedchamber, all of cloth of one colour, bearing the royal device ; and for greater courtesy, you shall wear one at this coming feast of All Hallows. And when we come to the feast of Christmas, you shall cause to be made for all the other officers of the Household, each one a gown bearing the royal device, and of cloth of another colour. And the other hundred crowns shall be to buy such things as I have told you for the ladies, damosels and others, for presents next New Year's Day ; for raiment also which you shall give unto the Kings-of-arms, heralds, trumpeters and minstrels. And now, for we may no longer abide here together, my Heart, my Love, and my most loyal servant, kiss me and God be with you ".

John of Saintré, when he heard and understood what great benefits and honours My Lady gave and procured him, young as he was, did on his knees full humbly thank her, saying : " O my most honoured Lady, most perfect in the world in all virtue and honour ; alas ! how shall I ever requite you the thousandth part of that I owe you ? Yet, my most true Lady, I shall do as much as I am able ; and God, who knoweth my true mind and my desire, shall acquit me of the rest ". Then My Lady bade him arise, and kissed him ; and " God be with you ! "

100

SIXTEENTH CHAPTER

*How little Saintré furnished him with horses, as My
Lady had bid him, and came then to thank her, and how
she again admonished him and taught him how he ought
to bear himself at Court and in war, and in all other
occasions*

Now when the morrow came, after Mass was heard,
John of Saintré rested not until he had found the
King's and the Queen's grooms and equerries. And
he made them a good breakfast in his chamber, and
afterward said unto them: " I would fain lay out
fourscore or an hundred crowns on a fair good hackney :
which among you can find me one ? " Then sent they
to inquire of the most proficient and the trustworthiest
horse-dealers, to know the fairest hackneys that were
to be had in Paris, and went to see them ; and they
bought one, which he gave for his present to the
Queen, saying privily unto her : " My sovereign Lady,
as well and as humbly as I am able, I thank you for all
the benefits and honours which both the King at
your request, and yourself also, have done me. And in
remembrance of these things, if it please you, Ma'am,
to draw some whit nearer the window, you shall see
a little hackney, which I bring you as a gift ; and I
pray that you take it not amiss, for I must cut my coat
according to my cloth ".[24] The Queen excused herself
courteously, but she came at length unto the window to
behold the hackney, which was a passing fair and good
one, caparisoned in trappings of silk of the Queen's
colours and emblems ; whereat she was well pleased,
and he much praised of all that were there. And
after he was departed, the Queen fell to saying much

good of him, whereby My Lady's heart, for the praise that all spake of him, was greatly rejoiced ; yet spake she herself but coldly of him.

And when the Feaſt of Chriſtmas was come, all the varlets of the Household, and likewise the officers, Kings-of-arms, heralds, trumpeters, and minſtrels, as hath been said, were all arrayed, and the ladies also had their gifts, and My Lady, for hers, chose the leaſt of all the rubies. Henceforth, throughout the Court and all the Kingdom the renown of his largesse flourished ; howbeit, not without much enviousness, as the way is in all Courts. Nathless, the good praised him, and so greatly that the King and the Queen held him in more eſteem than ever before. And thus he so bore him that the King loved him every day better. And he won many favours of the King and found many good friends. Yet for all the King's good will toward him, and for all favour that he won, his pride grew not by a finger's breadth, and he sought ever to be gracious unto them that were his covert enemies. In such condition he abode for the space of three or four years.

My Lady perceiving and knowing all these things, it was not long before she desired to have speech with him, and she made her signal with the tooth-pick, whereto he replied. And when they were in the Pleasance together, she said unto him : " Mine only Love, God be thanked, there is neither King nor Queen, duke, lord, lady, nor damosel, even to the very leaſt, but speaketh good of you, because that you both have been and are humble and courteous ; and now, by your largesse, your renown flourisheth. And without any foolish or prodigal spending, which redoundeth far more to shame than to honour, to hurt than to profit, I pray and exhort you that largesse well employed be commended unto you, for it hath in it these virtues: firſt, it crowneth the soul with eternal glory; it holdeth faſt men's affections and winneth new friends; it causeth good renown of you to flourish; it extinguisheth anger in men's hearts; it is a bringer of all surety, for it maketh enemies friends. Therefore, dear Love, I do commend it unto you. And if, by God's will, Fortune come to your aid, employ your time either in deeds of arms, or in serving lords or being by them served. Let your intent be to win the love of God and of many friends; and though Fortune hath given you already some share of her transitory favours, truſt not so well in her love that you forget that which Alanus saith in *Anti Claudiano*, wherein he saith :—

> *Tempore felici*
> *Multi numerantur amici ;*
> *Cum fortuna perit*
> *Nullus amicus evit.*

" That is to say, dear Love, that so long as Fortune is a friend to any man and hath set him in some high eſtate, then shall he find false friends beyond number ; but when she turneth her back upon him, he shall find none of them. And therefore is he that putteth his truſt in her worse than a fool."

SEVENTEENTH CHAPTER

How My Lady counselled little Saintré to read books and romances, that he might know the deeds of noble men in times paſt[25]

" MOREOVER, I desire and beseech you that your pleasure be oftentimes to read fair hiſtories, in especial the true and marvellous feats of arms which the

Romans did upon all the monarchies of the world : read Livy and Orosius.

" If you would know of the XII Cæsars or Cæsarians, read Suetonius.

" And if you would know of the deeds of Catilina and of the conspiracy or conjuration, read Salluſt.

" And if you would know of the passing fierce war between Julius Cæsar and Pompey, likewise of the sovereign battle between their powers in Thessaly, wherein the aforesaid Pompey was discomfited : read Lucan.

" And if you would know of the Kings of Egypt, read Mathaſtrius.

" And if you wouid know of the Trojans, read Dares the Phrygian.

" And if you would know of Ptolemy, read Polybius.

" And if you would know of the diversity of tongues, read Arnobius.

" And if you would know of the Jews and of the deſtruction of Jerusalem, read Josephus.

" And if you would know of the hiſtory of Africa, read Victor.

" But Pompeius Trogus, so Valerius writeth, is he that hath the moſt writ concerning the times before his own, for he treateth as it were of the beginning of all regions and of the situation of lands.

" And here make I an end of ancient hiſtories, desiring and enjoining you to take pleasure in hearing and reading them, seeing that, to inſtruct your mind in all noble and illuſtrious acts, you cannot better employ your time ; even as the versifier saith :—

' Ut ver dat florem,
Flos fructum, fructus odorem ;
Sicut ſtudium mores,
Mos sensus, sensus honorem.'

"That is to say, dear Love:—'As Spring giveth the flower, the flower the fruit, and the fruit the savour; even so doth ftudy give morals, morals wisdom, and wisdom honour'. So, by thus reading, hearkening to and remembering noble hiftories, ensamples and teachings, you may acquire the everlafting joys of Paradise, honour in arms, honour in wisdom and honour in riches, and live worshipfully and cheerfully. And whensoever your lord or any other shall ask of you loyal counsel, follow the words of Claudian the poet, when he exhorted the Emperor Honorius, in his second Book, where he saith unto him:

> *Te patrem civemque geras: tu consule cunctis.*
> *Non tibi, nec tua removeant, sed publica vota.*'

"That is to say:—

"'Be thou as a father and as a friend: ftrengthen them with good counsel; think not of thyself only, but love God and the common weal.'

"For so did the good Romans, and thereby held the dominion over all the world; and made laws which we yet do use. And touching this, Saint Auguftine, in the fourth Book of the *City of God,* and in the twelfth chapter, citeth a passage of Salluft recording the words of Cato, who said: 'Those things which made our Romans so mighty were good sense, induftry, and honeft counsel in our Courts and council-chambers'. Wherefore, dear Love, I do commend these ftudies unto you, to the end that you keep loyally and hold secret the counsel of your lord and of all others that shall confide in you; for thereby hangeth in great measure your honour, and the honour of them that do otherwise.

"Now dear Love, I have said enow unto you for this present time; and I pray God that he grant you worthily to perform all this, or the moft part thereof."

EIGHTEENTH CHAPTER

How little Saintré kneeled before My Lady, thanking her ; further, how the King and the Queen gave him moneys for his advancement ; and lastly, how My Lady told him her desire that he should on the First day of May procure him a bracelet enamelled with her device, and should wear it for the space of a whole year, in the intent to contend in arms against some knight

WHEN My Lady had made an end of speaking, John of Saintré kneeled down and thanked her full humbly, saying : "My most honoured Lady, that mayest command me more than all the rest of the world, I thank you as humbly as I may". At that, for the lateness of the hour, she kissed him and said then unto him : "Get you gone : I know well what you would say ; and trust the rest to me".

On the morrow, as soon as the day was light, Saintré arose ; and after matins, as soon as he was able, he went before any other unto the King's ante-chamber. And it was not long before the other knights and esquires came thither. Now as the King went on his way to Mass, he beheld Saintré so well and gaily arrayed ; and seeing the Lord of Ivry, said unto him : "I shall be much in error if Saintré is not some day a notable man. But whence hath he the means to be thus arrayed ?"—"Sir," said the Lord of Ivry, "I have heard say that his lady mother purveyeth for him thus ; and I doubt not that it is by the will of his father, who doeth him this honour."

The King said at that time no more, but resolved within himself that he would help him. And when

106

he was returned into his chamber, he let summon his treasurer, and commanded that Saintré be given five hundred crowns. And the Queen, when she heard of it, bade give him three hundred, and a piece of damask. And in such favour was Saintré of the King and the Queen, that there was none other esquire in greater ; and all this through My Lady's good counsel and bounty, who for the space of seven years had cherished him. And he was now of the age of twenty or twenty-one years, at which time the King shewed him many favours.

As for the other times that My Lady had converse with him, I pass them over, for it were too long a matter to rehearse.

When Saintré was of the age that I have said, My Lady, whose whole mind was bent to make him a man of worship and renown, bethought her that verily he now had courage and strength of body enough to make a name for himself. And when they were together, after their amorous greetings, My Lady said unto him, with a passing glad countenance : " My true Love, my heart, and my most joyous thought : sith by God's pleasure you are in such good favour of my lord the King, and my lady the Queen, and of all the rest also, methinketh you are henceforth man enow to do some notable deed in arms, by challenge, that there may be good report of you, as well in this realm as beyond it. And this to do, I desire that, this first day of May next ensuing, you wear for love of me a bracelet of gold enamelled with our devices, bordered with six good diamonds, six good rubies, and six good large pearls, each one of four or five carats ; the which you shall find here wrapped in a little purse in this satchel, wherein are also two thousand gold crowns to put you in good array. And for the rest of your costs, in going, sojourning, and

107

returning, have no fear; for I will undertake that the King, the Queen, and my fair uncles of Anjou, of Berry, and of Burgundy, and other lords of our blood, shall every one aid you; and if they did not so, my dear Love, have no care for so long as ten thousand crowns may laſt!"

And when Saintré heard the great benefits, honours and love that My Lady gave him, he could not speak for joy. Nathless, he fell on his knees and rendered her the beſt thanks that he might. My Lady, who well knew what he would have said, answered him: "My dear Love, I that have chosen you above all other for to serve me, do again beseech you that you have no care save to be gay and joyful and to make everywhere good cheer; as for gold, silver, and jewels, to put you in good array at this your firſt beginning, I shall furnish you well enough. And when your bracelet is made, the night of the firſt day of May that shortly cometh, you shall come hither unto me, and I will set it upon your arm for the firſt time. And from the day following, you shall wear it for the space of a twelvemonth, unless before that time you find some knight or squire of gentle birth and coat-armour, without reproach, who to fulfil your challenge, ahorse and afoot, shall free you of the bracelet, under covenant to deliver it again unto you unless, in the jouſting that he shall do againſt you, he have the advantage and so win it. The said jouſting shall be: firſt, a spear-running on horseback, one againſt the other, in full harness and war-saddles, until one of you hath well and truly broken three lances; that is to wit, an half-foot at leaſt below the casing of the point and a foot in front of the roundel.[26] And he that shall firſt break three lances, his adversary, mounted and in the judge's presence, shall give unto him a diamond, set in gold, of the price of three hundred crowns or upwards, to give unto his fair Lady. And the day following, if God hath preserved your bodies from honourable scathe, or otherwise the eighth day after, at the time by the judge appointed you shall both combat afoot one against the other, with your two pole-axes[27] only; wherewith you shall make play until one or other of you is borne to the earth or hath let go his weapon with both hands. And if at the conclusion of these jousts, your adversary shall have had the advantage, I desire and bid you that you give unto him your aforesaid bracelet, there and at that same time. And if God give you the advantage over your adversary, he shall be quit by delivering up to you his axe, there and at that same time; and after he hath unarmed him, his harness also, for the whole of that day.

"And though, dear Love, you are but young in years and not of the stoutest in body, yet for all that you have no need to fear any man; for it hath oftentime befallen that the weaker hath discomfited the stronger, and in battle the fewer by far have discomfited the more, when they have stood well with God; for in such case it is men that fight but God that giveth the victory to whom he listeth. Do you therefore ask of Him counsel, strength, and help, with all your heart, and you shall never come to an ill end. And if Fortune were contrary to you, which I pray God may not be, be not cast down, for never shall my good will toward you fail on that account, but rather shall I love you the better, for by the laws of honour and of arms you shall be all the more estimable. And thus, whatsoever you do, you cannot but do well; only God preserve your body from hurt! as he will do, if you commend yourself unto him with a faithful heart. And I had liefer you should have ado with a man of renown than with one young like yourself.

And for that reason I propose and desire that before they have beheld you, a month before your setting forth, you shall send a King-of-Arms or herald unto these Courts :—first, unto the King of Aragon's, then unto the King of Navarre's (which are the first in Spain), and after to the King of Castile's, and then to the King of Portugal's, which are the four Christian Kings of that land,—for to present your letters of challenge ; if indeed they find not, in one of the two former Courts, some knight or squire, as hath been said who will undertake to deliver you ; and if they find one, they shall return and meet you on your way, bearing his letter and his seal. And if God, as I do hope, is with you in all or in part, my Love and my dear heart, you shall be a squire of renown. And God wot how my lord the King and my lady the Queen and every one shall love and esteem you ; that thought alone is enough to overcome a giant. And therefore, dear Love, strive to be valiant and ask of God counsel and help ; so shall you never fail. And this said, we must part ; I say no more unto you at this time".

NINETEENTH CHAPTER

How little Saintré thanked My Lady and thereafter caused the bracelet to be made as she had bid him ; and how he came and shewed it unto her, whereat she was well pleased

Then fell Saintré on his knees and said : " My most honoured Lady, my goddess and mine only weal, I thank you for all this as humbly as I may ; and as for the combats which you do command me to undertake, 'fore God, Our Lady and my lord Saint Michael the Angel, I was never more glad of anything, save of your love; and by God's grace you shall hear such news that you and my lords shall be all well content".

Thereafter he took leave of her, with most loving kisses, given and given again, ten, fifteen and twenty times; and so "God be with you".

All that night Saintré thought upon these new designs. And when the day was come, and he had heard his matins, he sent for Gilbert Lorin, the King's goldsmith, who was reputed a worthy man, and said privily unto him: "Friend Gilbert, I would have a bracelet of gold, enamelled with my colours and my badge, and bordered on the two sides with six diamonds, six rubies, and six pearls, which you here do see". With that he shewed them unto Gilbert, and they pleased him well. And to be brief, within a few days the bracelet was made. And when Saintré was next in My Lady's presence, he rubbed his right eye, for their signal that was agreed between them, and My Lady answered with her tooth-pick. And when they were in the Pleasance that evening, to talk together, Saintré shewed her the bracelet by the light of the moon, but they could not well see it. My Lady said unto him: "I shall see it by torch-light, and tomorrow also; then in the evening I shall give it you again, when we return hither to take our pleasures together".

And then My Lady bade him take his leave, as she was wont to do.

TWENTIETH CHAPTER

*How My Lady counselled Saintré that he should cause
his enterprise to be published forth by an herald-of-arms,
giving out that the best dancer, whether squire or lady,
should have a seemly prize; and how she put him the
bracelet upon his arm. Also how Saintré made a feast
to all the lords and ladies; and after, at eventide,
returned unto the Pleasance to My Lady, who told him
that he must let proclaim his letters of challenge at the
Courts of four Kings*

Now on the day following, when My Lady beheld
that right fair and rich bracelet, she was passing glad.
Anon she made Saintré her signal, whereto he straightway replied. And when they were together, My Lady
said unto him : " Dear Love, behold here is your
bracelet, which seemeth to me so fair that it might
scarce be fairer. And while we sat at meat, I have
bethought me that tomorrow, which will be the eve
of the first day of May, you shall give a goodly supper
unto divers lords, knights, ladies, and damosels of the
Court, and others : whereat I will not be present,
though you shall invite me. And then, the more
honourably to make known your enterprise, you shall
let cry by a King-of-Arms or herald : that the lady
or damosel, knight or squire, who at the dancing
before that feast shall sing the best, the lady or damosel
shall from you receive a fine diamond, and the knight
or squire shall have a fine ruby ; and in like manner
the lady or damosel and knight or squire that shall
dance the best.

" And after the dancing and singing, you shall have
ready a fair and noble banquet, with entremets and

many other new fashions of viands; and at the laſt you shall fetch in the peacock. Then shall the lords, ladies and damosels, knights and squires make every one their vows, and when all are made, then shall you vow unto the ladies and unto the peacock,[130] and unto your Lady eleét or thereafter to be chosen, that this firſt day of May, that is, on the morrow, you will put a certain bracelet of gold upon your left arm, for the space of a twelvemonth, unless within the year you shall have found a knight or esquire of blood and coat-armour, without reproach, and the reſt as hath . been said; subjeét always to the King's good will and pleasure. And when you have done all this and attended forth the ladies, bring hither with you the bracelet, hidden in your bosom, that I may that night put it upon you for the firſt time ".

" Lady," said Saintré, " the true God, who requiteth all good deeds, requite this to you, and give me grace to deserve it of you; my heart and my mind have none other desire ! " And these words said, My Lady, according to her use and wont, bade him take his leave.

The next day after, which was the laſt day of April, as soon as it was day, Saintré sought him out cooks, and viands of diver sorts ; and, to be brief, he made ready the supper and the feaſt as My Lady had said. Then bade he to the feaſt lords, ladies and damosels, knights, esquires, burgesses of Paris and their wives, and others a-plenty. And when the supper, the feaſt, the dances and the vows were all done, and Saintré with the others had attended forth the ladies of the Court, and the King and Queen had taken their Parting-Cup, and all were departed, then went Saintré thence unto the Pleasance, as My Lady had bid him. And it was not long before My Lady came thither. Then, kissing him, she set the bracelet upon his left arm for the first time, and because the hour was late, they were there but a brief space before they needs must part. But putting it upon him, she said : " My Love and my true desire, I pray God and Our Lady that I put this upon you at such favourable time and season that you may return with all honour. And if so it be, I vow unto them that every Friday and Saturday I will wear no linen next my naked body, for as many Fridays and Saturdays as you shall be gone ".—" Ah, Lady ! " quoth he, " how have I merited, ne how shall I ever merit, that such a Lady should make such vows for me ? "—" Why, dear Love," said she, " 'tis because you are such as I would have you be. Now I counsel you, with the King's good will and leave, to send forth your letters of challenge as soon as may be, unto the Courts of the four Kings aforesaid, by some herald or pursuivant who shall bring back answer to you as you go thitherward." And so saying, My Lady bade him depart, and so parted they one from the other, their hearts filled with sighing and their eyes with tears.

ONE-AND-TWENTIETH CHAPTER

How Saintré went to present his letter of challenge before the King and Queen, and to ask leave to uphold it ; and how the King was constrained to grant him his desire

THE day following, which was the first day of May, Saintré was all newly clad and his servants well arrayed ; and put on his bracelet. Then went he forth to hear Mass, causing the Office of the Holy Ghost to be said ; and there called together all his friends, as My Lady had told him. And all with a

114

good will accompanied him unto the King, and there were many that proffered themselves to attend him on his journey. And at the King's issuing forth out of his bedchamber, where were that day the Dukes his brothers and sundry others of his blood, Saintré with all his friends kneeled before him. Then began he joyously to speak, and said: "Our Sovereign Lord, it is the usage of all gentlemen to win increase to their honour by the most noble profession of arms, and that in divers fashions; wherefore I, desirous to be as one of them, and trusting to have leave and license by your good favour, and not otherwise, did yesterday vow at my little feast, in presence of my most honoured lords and ladies, damosels, knights and squires, so-and-so; and many more, that I would this morning wear upon my left arm a bracelet of gold (which you here may see), and the rest of my vow you may here read written, an it be your good pleasure". Then took the King that letter of challenge and bade read it publicly before him; and after was long in making answer, thinking of the peril of jousting and of Saintré's youth, because of the great love he bore him. And when Saintré perceived how the King was long in answering, he doubted much to be denied, and said unto him: "O Sire, this is the first petition of arms that ever I made you; vouchsafe to grant it me, for God's love!" At that my lords the King's brothers and all that were there present, beholding his great eagerness besought the King on his behalf, and all so entreated him that at the last he assented. Then went the King forth for to hear Matins. And Saintré, when he had thanked him full humbly, went to seek the Queen, who came after. And she passed forth and all her train following. Then fell Saintré upon his knees, and his companions also, and said unto her: "Sovereign Lady, it hath pleased the King

115

to give me leave to accomplish my enterprise at arms, (in token whereof you here behold this bracelet) with the help of God, Our Lady, and my lord Saint Michael the Angel, even as it is set forth in this letter of challenge ; and I beseech you, my Sovereign Lady, that it may be your good pleasure also ".—" Why, fair son," said the Queen, " would you undertake deeds of arms already ? Who hath counselled you this ? " " Madam," said he, " God and mine honour have been my counsellors." " Nay, then, sith they have thus counselled you, I shall pray and entreat them to give you joy thereof."

" O Madam," said many that were there, " let read the letter, that we may know the tenour thereof." " That will We not, until We be returned from Mass." At this there drew near My Lady, who looked full lovingly upon him, and all the rest likewise, for to hear what he said. Then said the Queen unto him : " Saintré, what pleaseth my lord must please me also : if the thing stand thus, I pray God, Our Lady, and my lord Saint Julian that they grant you all such good success as you shall desire ". Then went the Queen thence to Mass. And upon her returning, she asked for the letter of challenge, and bade read it ; then said she : " Good lack, how hath this young man, that is yet but a child, had courage to take upon him such deeds of arms ? It must be that this cometh from a great and high heart ; and if God bring him safe back, meseemeth he shall have no need to do aught else, sith he goeth thus young to adventure himself ". And so saying, the Queen went thence to table, for dinner.

TWO-AND-TWENTIETH CHAPTER

How Saintré entered into the lists, well and sumptuously arrayed, and bore him valiantly, so that he was by all men praised and honoured

AND when the tables were removed, the King, the Queen, the ladies and everyman went up into the galleries to behold the jousts that were that day to begin. Then came Saintré, he and his courser trapped in white damask, broidered all with forget-me-nots. And anon began the joust, they without against them within[28]; but for shortness' sake their names I rehearse not, neither the names of any that were at that jousting, excepting only Saintré, who brake lances, smote one to earth from the saddle of his courser, and smote down two more with their coursers; and so long endured in his helm that of all the jousters he was the first and the last in the lists. No need to ask whether My Lady was joyful, and truly so were also the King, the Queen, and all they of the Court, marvelling much at his fortune in the jousting. And for the first time he received from them of the assailants' party a goodly diamond, which he gave unto My Lady.

The day following he came again unto the jousts, trapped he and his courser in other new raiment, all of green satin flowered with pansies. What shall I say more? He did again so well, that all men marvelled thereat: but by reason of the enterprise that he had undertaken, the King bade him withdraw for fear of some mischief; and therefore during those jousts he jousted no more.

THREE-AND-TWENTIETH CHAPTER

*How Saintré betook him to the Pleasance for to speak with
My Lady, and declared unto her in every point how he
was accoutred, and what people and officers he had for
the performance of his enterprise ; and how My Lady
asked to know of his liveries and his arms. And then
how they parted one from the other with many tears and
lamentations*

Now when the first Feasts were past, Saintré busied
him with seeking out stout coursers, and sought him
also knights and squires, of his kin and his friends,
Kings-of-Arms, heralds, trumpeters, minstrels and
two taborers ; and let make gowns, ornaments,
armour, habiliments, plumes, and other things needful,
that he might shortly go forth upon his journey and
perform his jousts. And when he was well furnished
with all things, he made My Lady his signal. And
that evening, in the Pleasance, he told her all that
he had done : how that he had three knights, such
an one and such and such, with XIII horses ; IX
squires with XXIII horses ; a chaplain with two
horses ; Anjou King-of-arms with two horses ; the
heralds Touraine and Lusignan, with IV horses ;
IV trumpeters with VI horses ; two taborers with
two horses ; "and four passing fair and puissant
coursers, whereon four comely young pages shall ride
all the way, led by two varlets on horseback, who
shall lead and tend them ; two cooks with III horses ;
a forager, a smith, and an armourer ; VIII sumpter-
beasts, IV for me and IV for my company ; and XII
more serving-men on horseback for my household and
body-service ; and one with three horses to be master

of the household; in all fourscore and nine horses, which shall be all trapped in your colours and bear your device ". And this sum of men and horses he spake all shyly, as though it were too great a number for him to ordain at his pleasure.

But when My Lady, who was right glad to hear it, perceived how he spake fearfully, doubting lest the cost be too great, she said unto him : " Dear Love, meseemeth you have so well done that none might have done better. And as for the cost, I desire that you have no care therefor ; for I hope that my lord the King, my lady the Queen, and my lords my fair uncles in especial, shall help you in this matter ; and if indeed they did not so, verily dear Love, for your costs for the space of a year I shall not suffer you to be shamed. Now, dear Love, what apparel have you ? " " Lady, I have three caparisons,[29] and passing rich ; whereof one is of crimson damask very richly woven with silver, and bordured with sable marten ; and I have another of blue satin, bespangled with our device lozengewise in gold, and bordured with white fur ; and another also of black damask, whereof the edge is all purfled with silver thread and the middle sewn with flat clusters of ostrich feathers of your colours, green, purple, and grey, bordured with tufts of white ostrich feathers, beflecked with black tufts, as it were ermine ; and on this I purpose to do my jousting a-horseback, so it be your good pleasure. The which all men do say are rich and most fair to see. And I have another also and my surcoat likewise (wherein I shall enter the lists to perform my jousts on foot) which is of crimson satin, all besewn with gold spangles tinctured with bright red ; with a great band of white satin all bespangled with silver, with three ribbons of yellow satin bespangled with fair glistering gold ; which are my arms." " Now, dear Love, I pray you blazon them after another fashion." "Lady, my arms are gules, a bend argent; three labels or."[30] "O Jesu," said My Lady, "how fair a thing to see! And in truth, I would fain see them, were it not for the fear of people's tongues; yet will I find the means without loss of honour, for I shall speak subtly unto My Lady the Queen, and she shall ask you." "Well, Lady," said Saintré, "now am I all prepared to go forth when it shall be your good pleasure; for meseemeth that the sooner is the better. Lusignan my herald is by this time arrived, I ween; and if peradventure he shall have found one to deliver me of my vow, I shall meet him on the road." Then appointed they for his setting forth the fifteenth day of July following. And with that they parted one from the other, with great sighs and most loving kisses.

FOUR-AND-TWENTIETH CHAPTER

How My Lady told the Queen how that Saintré was marvellous well accoutred with horses and other things; whereupon the Queen bade Saintré bring his horses into the court-yard, for her to see; which he did. And how the King and the Queen beheld them and praised him mightily

ON the morning of the next day, at the Queen's attiring, My Lady had not forgot her intent to see his fair caparisons; and said unto the Queen softly: "Madam, I have heard tell that the young squire Saintré hath had made marvellous fine horse-trappings; truly I cannot believe it. Yet if it be your good pleasure, Madam, to behold them, among us women, with none other present,—for, as I understand, he keepeth them most secretly—and if you should ask it of him, he would do it right willingly ". " Say you soothly, Fair Cousin, that these trappings are so fine ? " " Madam, fairer by far, so they do say, than I could ever tell you." " Why then," said the Queen, " if we be not denied, we will see them." " Madam," said she, " sith he doth so privily keep them, bid him let bring his four coursers hither unto the small court below, and let bear hither the trappings all covered up, and here put them upon the coursers, and you shall let shut the doors and guard them.". " Now by my faith ", quoth the Queen, " you say well ; do you call it to my mind when you shall next see him." And these words spoken, the Queen went thence to Mass ; and in the ante-chamber she beheld Saintré, who was there. Then drew near My Lady, and said softly unto the Queen : " Lo, Madam, yonder is Saintré ". Then called the Queen her usher-at-arms, William de Lurs, and let summon Saintré. " Saintré," said the Queen, " God give you joy of that thing which you most desire. We pray you that we may behold your caparisons for the jousting, upon your coursers ; the which men say are so fine." " Why, Madam," answered he, " with no disworship to them that so say, they are but trappings for a simple squire ; I should shame me to have you behold so poor a thing." " Well, fair sir, such as they be, we pray you that we may see them in this court below, after dinner ; and we will let shut and keep the doors ; and to do it the more covertly, if you so desire, let your men bear hither the trappings, all covered up, and then let them lead hither all your coursers ; and after, when they are arrayed, send privily to call us." " Madam," answered Saintré, " sith such is your pleasure, your desires are to me even as commandments."

After the King and the Queen had dined, and all the tables were removed, Saintré sent seek his trappings, and anon, one courser after another, he caused them to be led in all four; the doors were shut, as it had been commanded; and then were the trappings put upon the coursers.

Then went Saintré unto the Queen, as she had bid him. And the Queen, thereto moved by My Lady and by her own desire also, was not able to keep from telling the King of the coming of the horses with their caparisons. "What?" said the King, "are they so fine?" "My Lord, an it please you, you shall behold them." "That will I, in sooth," said the King, "let us bid bring the Parting-Cup." "O My Lord," quoth the Queen, "let there be but few there present."

After the Parting-Cup, the King and Queen went thence, and from the galleries above they looked upon the coursers with their trappings, which seemed passing rich and fair. Then fell all the ladies and damosels to praising Saintré, and to making vows and prayers that God might grant him to return with great honour.

And when the King desired to withdraw, he called Saintré unto him, and devising with him of divers matters, entered into his bedchamber, and thence into his wardrobe; and shortly sent him, by John de Suffle, his gentleman of the bedchamber, III thousand crowns in three satchels, to be employed for the needs of his jousting. And when the Queen heard that the King had given him three thousand crowns, she was passing glad thereof. Then called she My Lady and said unto her: "Fair Cousin, I am right glad that my lord hath given Saintré three thousand crowns, for the costs of his journey; verily I cannot give him less than a thousand, and I pray you that you give him

two or three hundred ". "Ah, Madam," said My
Lady unto the Queen, "you cut goodly ſtrips from
other folk's hide!" And she assented not without
much entreaty. And when My Lords of Anjou, of
Berry, and of Burgundy knew what the King and the
Queen had given him, they gave him every one a
thousand. In this wise he had seven thousand, beside
other gifts which divers more lords gave him. But
truly he never asked nor let any ask for him a penny,
wherefore he was held in much more eſteem; and
they said: "Ought not we indeed to help so young a
squire, that is yet but a child in years, and of his
great courage doth undertake such deeds of valiance?
Assuredly he ought to be well beloved!"

FIVE-AND-TWENTIETH CHAPTER

*How Saintré, when he was ready to depart, came to ask
leave of the King to pursue his enterprise; which the
King granted him, notwithſtanding that he was sore
grieved at his departing*

AND when the time drew near for his setting forth,
eight or ten days before, there came Saintré with his
three knights, his nine squires, his Kings-of-arms,
heralds, and all the reſt of his people, he and all of
them clad in raiment of his livery, and attended by
sundry other lords, knights and esquires, his friends;
and kneeled all before the King, in presence of My
Lords of Anjou, Berry and Burgundy, his brothers.
Then said Saintré moſt humbly unto the King:—
"Our Sovereign Lord, it hath pleased your grace to
grant me bear this bracelet as Emprise,[31] to perform
the jouſts, ahorse and afoot, that you have seen set

down in writing. Now am I come unto you most humbly to entreat that it be your good pleasure to grant us leave that on the fifteenth day of this month of July, with the help of God, Our Lady, and my lord Saint Michael, we may set forth, I and my gentle brethren and friends here present, who of their courtesy desire to bear me company".

The King, who had already given them leave, as hath been told, said: "How now, Saintré! Are you so soon made ready?" "Sire," said he, "I am." Then said the King unto him: "Saintré, you are of gentle blood; there have been valiant men of your house. God grant you grace to resemble them, as I hope that you may, for you have made a beginning full young. And whatsoever befall you, be not dismayed; for you are but an apprentice to arms, though I hope with God's help you shall in time be a master. But one thing remember: whatsoever deeds of arms you undertake, to win or to lose honourably and cheerfully". After these things, the King gave him leave to depart, wherefor Saintré thanked him right humbly and joyfully. And the King went thence; and Saintré, most humbly likewise, thanked the aforesaid lords for the gifts which they had given him.

SIX-AND-TWENTIETH CHAPTER

How Saintré went unto the Pleasance to take his leave of My Lady, who gave him more counsel for all his goings; and how at the last they parted, not without shedding of many tears on either part

Now when the tenth, the twelfth, and the fourteenth day of the month came, My Lady, because of her great dolour and heaviness at his departing, made each day her signal with the pin, whereto he answered. And when they were together in the Pleasance, with many a heavy sigh and many a tear, for that their parting drew near, My Lady said unto him : " Mine only Love and more than I can express : My Lord the King hath given you three thousand crowns, the Queen a thousand, my fair uncles each a thousand, which are seven thousand, beside the rest that other lords have given. And forasmuch as no man knoweth what may chance, I shall give you three thousand, which will be in all ten thousand at the least ; wherewith, without too great excess of prodigal spending, you may keep up good estate for long enow.

" One thing I pray you : that each day at the end of your Mass, being yet on your knees, you shall cause your priest, after he hath given the general benison, to give you that benison which Our Lord spake unto Moses out of His own mouth, as it is written in the Scriptures ; the which I have before told you and now again tell you for better remembrance :

' *Benedicat tibi Dominus et custodiat te.*
Ostendat faciem suam tibi, et misereatur tui.
Convertat Dominus vultum suum ad te, et det tibi pacem.'

" This same benison also I pray you to say yourself, with a good will, before the onset when you perform your jousts, whether afoot or on horseback ; making the sign of the Cross, and saying :

' *Benedicat mihi Dominus et custodiat me.*
Ostendat mihi faciem suam Dominus et misereatur mei,
Convertat Dominus vultum suum ad me, et det mihi pacem.'

" And thereafter set forward steadfastly, and do that you have to do with a good courage ; for in this wise you can do nothing, win or lose, but it shall be to your honour; and let come what may, I shall never fail you". And with these words the well of tears in her heart rushed forth at her eyes so that, to give them cease, she spake no more.

And Saintré, who by reason of the great benefits and honours which My Lady had done him accounted himself of all lovers in the world the best assured, and the more so that the benefits, the honours, and the most noble and chivalrous counsel that she gave him were every day increased more and more, said unto her, with passing great distress of heart: "Ah, my most high and sovereign peerless Goddess, you that ought most to comfort me in this most dolorous grief that my heart hath, by cause of my departing from you, that are my one desire, mine only joy and my sovereign weal: now do I perceive that your griefs leagued with mine own have so assailed and beset my heart that they have vanquished it and wounded it to the death; and so I go hence to die, and Lady, fare you well". And with these words he turned him to depart.

My Lady, whose river of tears was by now well-nigh dry, hearing Saintré's words said unto him, mingling with her speech a most piteous sigh: "O dear Love, turn again if you will! You know how that we women have tender and piteous hearts toward them that we love. Let not this thing vex you, for behold I am now quite comforted, trusting that God shall bring you back with great gladness. Now my most true Love, my weal, mine only thought, treasure of my life and death,—be of good cheer and go forth joyously; for, by my faith, I will abide joyful and merry for love of you. And as for your tidings, look to it that you write none unto me, as you hold your life dear; but write fully unto My Lady the Queen, and so shall I know all without any danger. And now must we kiss farewell, dear Love ". Then were given kisses and kisses given again, beyond number and beyond measure, with piteous sighs attended. And so long were they at this dolorous pleasure and unhappy joy, that it struck midnight, whereat they were much amazed. Then needs must their sad parting be fulfilled. And at leave-taking My Lady, kissing him, put him upon one of his fingers a passing fair rich diamond ; and so " Fare you well ".

SEVEN-AND-TWENTIETH CHAPTER

How Saintré took his leave of the King, the Queen, and the ladies, unto whom he gave each a ring of gold ; and how the Queen asked for one, which he gave her, asking her pardon and saying he had not thought she should have deigned to accept so simple a present

THE next morning, the fifteenth day of July, which was the term appointed for his setting forth, after Matins had been heard and the priest had given Saintré his benison, Saintré with all his company drest in his livery came to take leave of the King, who said unto him : " Saintré, God grant you to fare prosperously, to acquit you well, and to return with much honour. One thing have I besought you, and do beseech : that you be mindful to win or lose honourably ". " Sire ", said he, " with the grace of God you shall hear naught to the contrary." Then the King touched his hand. And after, he went thence unto the Queen, who said unto him : " Well, Saintré, sith you must leave us, we all do pray God to grant you the prize in arms and good success in love ". " Madam," answered he, " as for the prize in arms, may it be as you desire ; but my love is all of serving the King, and you also." And with that he took his leave of her, and then of My Lady, briefly enow, only saying unto her, sighing: "Of you have I taken leave already".

Then went he unto the other ladies and damosels, unto whom he gave each a little ring of gold, all enamelled with forget-me-not flowers; whereat there was not one could keep from weeping, so had they all loved and still did love him. And when the Queen heard it reported how these rings were given, she summoned Saintré and smiling said unto him: "What, Saintré, fair sir, are we not ladies like the rest, my Fair Cousin and I? Wherefore may we not wear your livery?" "Perdy, Madam," said Saintré, "may it be forgiven me! I had not hardihood enough, nor thought that such ladies should deign to wear so small a gift from me." "That will we," said the Queen, "though we would not from every man." So he gave them the choice of all that he had (though indeed all were alike); and after, they said unto him: "Gramercy, Saintré". And with that Saintré took his leave again. And at his departing, My Lady could not keep from weeping; but she said unto the Queen, for an excuse: "Whatsoever grief or affliction I might have, I shed never a tear, except only when I behold others weep". "Why in sooth, Madam," said the others, "what heart of woman might keep from weeping, to see this youth go forth to such great peril, that hath been bred up among us and hath ever done us so many pleasures?"

EIGHT-AND-TWENTIETH CHAPTER

*How Saintré, after that he had taken leave of the lords
and barons of the King's court, went thence to dine with
his companions ; and as he sat at meat the Queen sent
him a piece of cloth-of-silver, passing fine, and divers
lords other gifts and presents ; and how at his setting
forth he had heralds, trumpeters and minstrels to attend
him, and gave them supper at Bourg-la-Reine, where he
lodged*

Now when Saintré had taken leave of the ladies in
their hoſtel, he went to take leave of the aforesaid
lord dukes, who each spake him passing fair words.
And then he departed, with all his company, to dine
in his own hoſtel. And while they were at dinner, the
Queen sent unto him a piece of cloth-of-silver, passing
fine ; My Lord of Anjou sent him a fair courser in
right good point ; and My Lord of Berry, a great
cloak of six hundred skins of fine sable marten ; and
My Lord of Burgundy, fifty marks weight of plate.
And unto them that brought these presents he gave
to every one an hundred crowns, for the honour and
love of the Queen and of the Dukes. And when they
had all dined, and the horses were all bridled and girt,
there came knights and squires of the King's household,
of the Queen's, and of the Dukes' aforementioned,
and many more, to the number of near a thousand
horse, all come to set him on his way. Then bade he
set forth, firſt of all his two foragers, his cooks and his
chaplain, four trumpeters bearing banners of his arms,
and then his three heralds ; and after, his three knights
and IX squires, two and two, with all their people
following, clad in his liveries ; his five sumpter-horses,

129

trapped with cloths of his arms, led by two varlets on foot; and then his tabors; and next his four coursers, dight with caparisons of fine Florence taffetas, grey, green, and violet, with his device in great silver letters, and on their heads, each a fair head-piece of steel, all garnished with fair ostrich-feathers made out of broidery and all bespangled with silver; and on the coursers four gentle pages clad in his livery, all their sleeves charged with silver spangles, and on their heads each a passing fair cap with feathers of his colours; and after the coursers there followed the two grooms and then the marshal. There came next sundry taborers, and after them the minstrels that were come for to attend his going; and after the minstrels came the pursuivants; next, the Dukes' heralds and the King's, and then the royal Kings-of-arms; and after, there came all the trumpets and clarions; first the Dukes', and then the King's. And after the trumpeters came Saintré, in raiment bearing his device, like his pages, his sleeves all bespangled with gold, and on his head a like feathered cap, riding upon the fair courser which My Lord Duke of Anjou had given him for a present at his departing. And he rode in the midst of four lords, two before and two after; and then followed all the other lords, knights, and esquires, mingled together, and in such high honour attended him at his setting forth from the Court, a good league out of the city of Paris. And at their parting, he made go with him all the Kings-of-arms, heralds, pursuivants, trumpeters, minstrels, taborers and other merry-makers, to sup with him at Bourg-la-Reine, where he lodged that night: and he made them right good cheer, and in the morning gave unto them fifty crowns. And now make I an end of telling of his setting forth, and I shall speak of his journey and of the coming of Lusignan, the pursuivant.

NINE-AND-TWENTIETH CHAPTER

How, Saintré being in Avignon, the King-of-arms of Anjou brought unto him the sealed answer to his letter of challenge, and told him how he had spoken with Enguerrant and shewn him his letter, whereat he was passing glad

And when Saintré was in Avignon, upon news of his coming, the King-of-arms of Anjou, bearing the answer under seal, delivered it unto Saintré at his issuing forth from Mass. And when Saintré had well read and understood the said answer, in the presence of all men he straightway returned publicly unto the church, to give thanks devoutly unto God; and afterward publicly required the King-of-arms to tell him the whole manner of his deliverance, and who he was that had undertaken to deliver him.

Then said Lusignan: " I arrived first in Barcelona the third day of June, somewhat late, and rested that night. On the morrow, after Mass, I returned unto my lodging and put upon me your coat-of-arms, as was my right, and the box, wherein your letter was, in my bosom; then caused I a serving-man of the hostelry to bring me unto the King's palace, and by God's grace, I met at the gate with a knight most goodly of body and well attended, called Sir Enguerrant of Cervillon; whom I saluted courteously in passing. But when he saw me, clad in your coat-of-arms, he called suddenly unto me, saying: ' Herald that you be, as I suppose by the tabard which you wear, what is your name ? ' ' Messire,' said I, ' my name and style is King-of-arms of Anjou, Touraine, and Maine.' Then said he unto me: ' King-of-arms, you are welcome ! Methinketh you should be

131

come to this King's court for the sake of some deed
of arms. And if so it be, I pray you declare it unto
me'. 'Messire,' said I, 'true is it that I am sent
by a noble and worshipful esquire of the Kingdom of
France, called John of Saintré, who on the first day
of this last month of May, by vows made in the
presence of divers high and noble ladies and damosels,
lords, knights and squires, a great number, took upon
him as Emprise to bear on his left arm a rich bracelet
of gold and precious gems ; and this for the space of
a twelvemonth, unless he should first find some knight
or squire of gentle birth and of coat-armour, without
reproach, who should be willing to deliver him of his
vow by jousting on horseback and afoot, as in this
letter is set forth ; and indeed I am to bring unto him
the seal of him that will deliver him. And to this
intent he cometh first of all into this Kingdom, to
the Court of this most noble King, where he shall
abide a full month awaiting his deliverance by some
knight or esquire, as I have said. And if he find none,
he shall go likewise unto the King of Navarre's Court
and to the King of Castile's, and then the King of
Portugal's, tarrying at each court one month, if he
find none such as I have said.'

"'Now, King-of-arms, I pray you shew unto me
these letters, for I do promise you, on the faith of a
gentle knight, that if these be honourable combats,
with the grace of God, my lord Saint George, and my
sovereign lord the King, I shall be he that shall
accomplish them, to the best of my power.' And
when I heard him speak in such knightly fashion,
who was so handsome of body and so nobly attended,
and hearing the good faith that he promised me,
meseemed I had found that which I sought. Then
drew I your letters from my bosom and rendered them
unto him ; which having read with much joyfulness,

he said unto me : ' King-of-arms, come you with me '. Then turned he about and spake unto divers knights and gentlemen of the court, unto whom he shewed your letters. And afterward he said again unto me : ' King-of-arms, come with me ' ; and taking me by the hand, he brought me into the King's presence, who was but then come from Mass. Then, he holding me by the hand, we kneeled down, and all the others also, and in his own tongue he said : ' Sire, going out from this your palace, by good fortune I met with Anjou King-of-arms, who is here present ; and beholding the tabard wherein he was clad, I well knew that he would not wear it, in especial at the court of so high a Prince as you are, unless it were for the cause of some deed of arms. I called therefore unto him, and asked him whence he came, and the cause wherefore he wore a coat-of-arms in this your court, seeing that you are at peace with all the princes of Christendom.[32] And he made answer unto me as he shall himself tell you, an it please you to hear it '."

THIRTIETH CHAPTER

How the King-of-arms declared unto Saintré how that the King of Aragon had given Sir Enguerrant leave to deliver him of his Emprise, and had made him good cheer ; whereat Saintré and his companions were greatly rejoiced

" At these words, the King, who had bent his look strongly upon me, said unto me, touching my hand, that I was right welcome. He bade moreover that I should tell him all that I had told Sir Enguerrant of Cervillon. Then declared I unto him, word for word, all that I had said unto him. And, to be brief,

'Where are these letters ?' said the King. 'Sire,' said Sir Enguerrant, ' here are they.' Anon the King bade read them. And when they were read, Sir Enguerrant said unto the King : ' Sire, the noble privileges of true honour do require of noble hearts that each according to his ability shall strive to win the illustrious dower of honour in the worshipful profession of arms, whether in challenges to joust, whether in wars belligerous, or in any other honourable wise. And forasmuch as the favour of this adventure hath fallen first upon me, albeit there be many others in this your Court that are much valianter, more puissant, and more worthy than I am, yet Sire, for the fortune of my adventure, I that am the first do entreat and beg of you, as humbly as I may and ought to and am able, that if you grant the achievement of these jousts unto any one of your Court, it be unto me '.

" Now when the King had heard his petition, before making answer, like a wise prince he withdrew apart and called unto him sundry lords and other knights and esquires old in counsel, that were there present. And it was not long before he called him and said publicly unto him :—' Sir Enguerrant, We have heard your humble and worshipful petition, which, for the honour and love of you as well as of the noble squire that beareth the Emprise, We do grant you ; and We appoint a day for your jousts, the fifteenth day after his coming (now truly, God keep you both in good health !) and so shall you give much joy unto the ladies '. For this the King's most gracious answer, Sir Enguerrant and all his friends thanked him full humbly ; and so did I also on your behalf. Then departed the King and went to dinner. And Sir Enguerrant brought me to his lodging and sent fetch my horses and stabled them with his own ; then made he me to dine with him, right heartily, and

to do off your coat-of-arms and to sit in my doublet.
Afterward he gave me a passing fair rich gown of blue
figured velvet, richly broidered with gold, and furred
with sable marten, the which I have here in my
baggage. And he made me tarry all that day and
the next; and more also, an I had willed. And
whiles he was inditing his answer unto you, the King's
heralds came and greeted me and led me round about
the city. And when my letters were done, he brought
me to take leave of the King, who made me passing
good cheer; and for the love of our lord the King and
of you also, he bade give me a tabard of black figured
velvet, trimmed with sable marten, and an hundred
Aragon florins. And at leave-taking, he most graciously besought me to salute you on his behalf.

"And of these jousts of yours, as it was many times
told me, the Queen and the ladies and damosels,
knights and esquires also, with all the city and country,
are so glad, that there is everywhere talk thereof.
Moreover at my parting from Sir Enguerrant, he
said unto me: 'King-of-arms, commend me well
unto my brother, John of Saintré, and tell him that
with God's grace I shall be all in readiness on the day
which the King hath appointed for us: commend me
also unto all his following; and God be with you!'
And when I was about to get upon horse-back, he
sent me forty Aragon florins."

Now when Saintré and all his company heard this
report and good tidings, and how he was so speedily
to be delivered of his vow, marvellous was the rejoicing
among them. The which tidings were noised abroad
everywhere and borne unto the King and Queen, so
that My Lady knew of it and all the Court likewise;
and it was published throughout all the realm. Then
began ladies and damosels to fast and to make vows
and pilgrimages and prayers for Saintré's sake. But

at these good news, he like a true Christian ascribing to God his honours and his advancement, returned back again to the minster; and there on his knees, with head bared and hands joined, did devoutly make his prayers and oblations unto God and unto Our Lady. And afterward they went thence to dinner.

ONE-AND-THIRTIETH CHAPTER

How, Saintré being at Perpignan, the news of his coming was brought to the King of Aragon, who prepared then his lodging at Barcelona. And further, how Enguerrant came out to meet him the space of a league outside the city, and honourably received him; and of their converse and devising one with another

Whiles these things were doing and Sir Enguerrant was making him ready, it was not long before Saintré arrived in the town of Perpignan. Then was made known unto the King of Aragon his coming, his great state, and the goodly company that he brought. Then weened the King and every man that he must surely be a man of great worship; and forthwith bade prepare full honourably his lodging at Barcelona, which was delivered over unto his foragers two days before his coming. And at his entering into the city, Sir Enguerrant, who came out above a league to meet him, right nobly attended, and many other lords, knights, and esquires, that came out likewise for to meet him, marvelled greatly at two things: the one, Saintré's great youthfulness; and the other, the right fair array wherein he and his friends came, even as at their setting forth from Paris. And when Sir Enguerrant beheld how young Saintré was, he was wroth that

he muſt perform such jouſts with one that might have
been his son. And he looked hard upon Saintré and
oft, marvelling within himself at so high an enterprise
undertaken by so young a man as he was. And when
they were come unto Saintré's lodging, Sir Enguerrant,
ashamed at the jouſts he muſt perform with him, said
unto him privily: " John of Saintré, my brother ;
you are a young man and a squire ; I am an old man
and a knight ; if it were your pleasure to be willing
to quit me of the promise I have sealed you, I would
give you as adversary, to accomplish your jouſts, mine
own nephew that is much about your own age, and
is a knight as I am ; and this I do entreat you ". But
Saintré, very wisely and courteously, made answer
directly saying: " Messire Enguerrant, by the will
of God and my good fortune my Emprise hath fallen
firſt into your hands ; wherefore I thank you as
humbly as I may, that of your courtesy, like a chivalrous knight, you have consented and under your seal
have promised to deliver me of my vow. And though
Messire your nephew be a valiant knight and worthy
to have ado with the beſt knight in the kingdom of
France, yet forasmuch as my fortune hath addressed
me unto you, there will I hold faſt and abide, and I
pray you pardon me for thus doing. And if for any
cause such as I know not, nor cannot conceive of,
you should fail me of your promise, I should account
me honourably and worshipfully quit and delivered
of my vow ".

Now when Sir Enguerrant heard so young a man
speak thus chivalrously, he marvelled much, and
perceived in his heart how Saintré meant that an he
durſt not jouſt he should account himself quit of his
vow ; therefore he resolved to fulfil his promise, and
said unto him : " Saintré, my brother, I have heard
your right noble words ; what I have promised you

under my seal, that will I perform, with the grace of God, Our Lady, and my lord Saint George, at the day and hour which my lord the King hath appointed for us. And for to make an end of these matters the sooner and the more honourably, meseemeth that I ought to come and seek you when the King returneth from Vespers ; you shall be ready, and shall come to do your reverence to the King and the Queen, who will be right glad to see you ; and there, in the King's presence, I will deliver you of your bracelet ; then tomorrow I shall give it unto you again, as it is provided in your challenge ; and I truſt in my lord Saint George that it shall fall to my Lady's share ".

And with that he took his leave. And at firſt he would not ſtay to dinner, for any entreaties, but at the laſt Saintré prevailed upon him to ſtay, desiring to behold his countenance and his bearing.

TWO-AND-THIRTIETH CHAPTER

How Sir Enguerrant presented Saintré unto the King and Queen, who made him a right fair welcome and feaſted him in ſtate

THEN went Sir Enguerrant unto the King, to tell him of Saintré's marvellous seemly bearing and courteous words ; whereat the King, who had heard already some report of him, prized him greatly and had much desire to behold him ; the Queen also and all the ladies of the Court. And after Vespers, the King sent to summon him. Sir Enguerrant, right nobly attended, holding him by the arm, and both kneeling, presented him unto the King, the Queen being there present. And when the King firſt beheld him, he

came down two or three steps toward him, and then
said : " Welcome unto this fair young sapling of a
squire ! " Then bade he him arise. And when they
had arisen, Sir Enguerrant brought him and presented
him unto the Queen, who said unto him : " Master
John, you are right welcome ! " Then took she him
by the hand and made him to arise. Sir Enguerrant
brought him thither where the ladies were, and albeit
it was not customary, he made him to kiss them all,
for thus was he commanded. Anon they returned
again unto the King, and kneeled both before him.
Sir Enguerrant said unto the King : " Sire, you have
seen my brother Saintré's letter concerning the
conditions of his jousting ; and of your grace you have
granted me license and have appointed a day and a
place, to deliver him. Grant now your good leave
that I may accomplish that which is contained in his
vow ; that is, first of all, to take off the bracelet which
he weareth upon his left arm ". Thereupon the
King, like a wise prince, desired to know out of Saintré's
own mouth whether he did avow it ; and there
publicly caused his letter to be read, and asked him
whether he maintained it : and after, said unto him :
" John of Saintré, bear you this bracelet as Emprise,
in such manner as in your letter is set forth ? " " Sire,"
said Saintré, " I do."—" Well then," said the King
unto Sir Enguerrant, " I grant you leave to deliver
him." Then Sir Enguerrant took off the bracelet,
and when it was taken off he bore it all that day on a
fair cord of gold and silk around his neck, and then on
the morrow gave it again unto Saintré, with his own
hands.

And this done, they went unto the Queen and the
other ladies, who paid them high honour and made
them good cheer. Afterward they went thence unto
the ante-chamber, and there played at many games,

until it was time for supper. Then took Saintré his leave, and bade Sir Enguerrant to sup with him, and divers knights and esquires. And Sir Enguerrant, all that evening and many days after, ceased not from telling of the fair and gracious demeanour of Saintré and all his following. And on the fourth day, the King desired the Queen to bid him and all the gentlemen of his company to dinner; and after was dancing and singing, wherein Saintré, who sang exceeding well, and other of his companions, greatly pleased the King, the Queen, and all men. And thus were they feasted every day at that Court. And of this the history telleth no more, in the intent to be brief and to come unto the chief matter.

THREE-AND-THIRTIETH CHAPTER

How Saintré entered solemnly into the lists, with much fair company of princes and knights attending him; and of their array

Now when the fifteenth day was come after his arrival, the day appointed for the beginning of their jousts, on which day they were all arrayed and apparelled,—on the said day, at ten of the morning, the King, to do honour unto the strangers like a wise and honourable prince, sent unto Saintré, for to bear him company, the Count of Cardonne, Don Frederic de Lune, Sir Arnold de Pereillo and Sir Francis de Moncade, four most noble lords and knights of his Court, passing well attended; to honour him in his going unto the jousts. And this commanded, the King departed and went up into his stand, which was at one side the lists, full richly tapestried all about; and with him the princes, lords, and other knights and esquires of his council, a great many, and at his left hand the Queen, in her ſtand, attended by many princesses, ladies and damosels of her Court and out of all the realm, that were come thither to behold that jouſting. And when the King and the Queen were gone up into their places, then did the Kings-of-arms and heralds, by the King's ordinance, bear unto the two combatants the commandment to perform their devoirs. Anon Saintré, (who was already all arrayed) as mover and challenger in the enterprise, mounted upon horseback, he and all his company, and set out in the manner following:

Firſt there set forth from his lodging, on horseback, his own taborers and all the others that were come to bear him company; two and two.

After the taborers came his three sumpter-horses, bearing coffers with his harness, all overspread with tapeſtries and thereon his arms, done in broidery, each one led by his varlets; and after them came the two armourers, on foot.

After the armourers came all the pursuivants two and two, clad in their tabards, side by side.

After the pursuivants came Saintré's minſtrels.

After Saintré's minſtrels came the King's minſtrels.

After the King's minſtrels the trumpeters of Aragon.

After the trumpeters of Aragon the heralds of Aragon.

After the heralds of Aragon the French heralds.

After the French heralds came the two Kings-of-arms, Aragon and Anjou, each wearing his lord's tabard, and the French heralds with Saintré's arms very richly broidered.

After the Kings-of-arms came his four trumpets and clarions, and after them the knights and squires, bearing on their thighs twelve great spears, whereof six were pointed and all wrapped about in cloth of silver, of his colours, trimmed with marten, and the other six very richly painted in like manner.

After these twelve lances there came Don Bernard de Cardonne upon a moſt fair courser, bearing on his thigh a lance, whereon was a banner of fine crimson velvet, lined on the back side with the same and bordured with a passing rich gold fringe; and on either side of the banner were the four blazonings of Saintré's four principal lines of descent, in rich broidery.

After the banner came Don Frederic de Lune upon a moſt puissant courser, bearing the truncheon of a spear, swathed and trimmed with fur like the six pointed spears, and thereon Saintré's helm, which had for a creſt a great thiſtle with four great golden leaves, that quite covered the upper part of the helm; and from under the thiſtle there hung a long Pleasance scarf[33], flowing free, richly bordured with gold thread and great pearls, and the reſt thereof all sewn with letters of gold.

After the helm came Saintré upon a right fair frisking courser, that bore upon its head an head-piece of ſteel with three great feathers like an oſtrich's, and Saintré's three colours richly broidered thereon; he and his courser trapped in crimson satin, all sewn with hearts of ermine and edged with great fringes, of silver and of silk alternately, of his three colours; on his head a fair gay cap; and he armed with his vambraces, leg-harness and sollerets,[34] and no more; in his right hand his pennon whereon were the Virgin and Child, and at every ſtep, as he went, he signed himself therewith.

And after him came his four pages, attired and mounted on fair coursers trapped with caparisons, even as they had been at his departing and setting forth from Paris, as hath heretofore been rehearsed.

After Saintré came Sir Francis de Moncade and Sir Arnold de Pereillos, each upon his fair courser, side by side. And after them, all the other knights and squires, a great many, that at the King's command were come to attend him. And with all this array and goodly company, he came down unto his great pavilion, fairly dight, which the King had caused to be set up for each of them without the lists, at the two entrances; and there he lighted down off his horse, and with him his four lords counsellors, and such of his own people as he had bid attend him.

FOUR-AND-THIRTIETH CHAPTER

How Sir Enguerrant entered likewise into the lists in most triumphal array

WHEN Saintré was come down, the Kings-of-arms, heralds, pursuivants, trumpeters and minstrels went forthwith unto Sir Enguerrant, for to do him honour and bear him company; whom likewise they found all arrayed, ready to mount. And anon set forth, first of all, the taborers, and then the minstrels.

After the minstrels followed many lords, knights, and esquires that were come to attend him.

After the knights and esquires came his four coursers, all saddled, and their saddles covered over with the same cloth of gold wherewith they were caparisoned. Now the first courser was caparisoned with rich blue satin, figured and shot with gold, with broad edges of fine miniver[35]; the second courser was caparisoned with another blue figured satin, shot with gold, with broad edges of sable marten; and the third courser was caparisoned with another passing rich figured satin

143

of purple colour, shot with gold (these were his three colours) and trimmed with ermine; and they were led by three varlets on foot.

After the three coursers there came XII knights on fair steeds, bearing XII more spears, whereof six, two and two, were swathed with the same three cloths-of-gold and trimmed in like manner as his caparisons were.

After the XII spears came the King's trumpeters, and after them Aragon King-of-arms, who had on his passing rich coat-of-arms and bore at his neck a light and shining escutcheon of steel, bordured with cloth of gold, threefold, and in the four quarters of the shield were blazoned the arms of the four houses whereof he was issued, and in the midst of the four blazons, his own.

After the King-of-arms there came the Count of Orgel, on a fair puissant courser, bearing on a lance-butt Sir Enguerrant's helm, whereon was a demi-roebuck naissant[36] or, wearing a collar, and in the three parts thereof a fine ruby, a fine diamond and a fine balas, each one set between two passing great pearls.

After the helm came Sir Enguerrant, armed at all points saving his head, whereon he wore a fair chaplet of divers flowers and leaves, on a right fair and puissant courser, he and his courser trapped with rich figured velvet, crimson woven with gold upon gold, trimmed with wide bordures of ermine; and in his right hand a truncheon of a lance, whereon his arm rested.

After Sir Enguerrant there came the Count of Prades and the Count of Cardonne, his counsellors, and then the other lords, knights and esquires, past numbering, that were come to attend him. And so came he down into his pavilion, and there was armed with his helm and served with such things as he had need of.

FIVE-AND-THIRTIETH CHAPTER

How the King let measure the lances of the two champions, and how Saintré bore him honourably in his passing before the King and the Queen in their stand

Now when they were both arrived, the King straightway let measure their spears, which were to be XIII feet from point to rest. And when they were measured and delivered unto each party, the King sent word unto Saintré bidding him come forth the first; and so did he. But when he was mounted upon his courser, he asked for his pennon, and therewith made a great sign of the Cross, pronouncing his aforesaid benison which My Lady had taught him, as hath been told. And in this manner, signing himself with the Cross, he entered at a foot pace into the lists, unto his appointed station; and with him the four lords, his counsellors, and others on horseback and on foot in like number, as was ordained. And in this array he took a turn back and forth all the length of the lists, which were hung with fine scarlet cloth, and both in going and in returning, when he passed before the galleries where the King and Queen were, he bowed as low as he might, making his obeisance. Whereat the King said unto his companions : " Truly this squire, in all his deeds and words, sheweth plainly that he is gently born and bred in the Court that is the school of all honour ". The Queen and all the other ladies praised him no less; for there was not one among them but spake well of him, and her neighbour better ! And the most part of them prayed to God for him. Anon, at a foot-pace, he came down unto the end of his course, and there set his spear upon his thigh and rode full tilt forth and back unto the end of his course again. Thereafter the King bade Sir Enguerrant come forth; who, to be brief, did even as Saintré. And when each was at his own end of the lists, the King commanded that they should do that which they had to do.

SIX-AND-THIRTIETH CHAPTER

How Saintré made the sign of the Cross three times before couching his lance, and thereafter the two champions set on valiantly. And how on the first day the King commanded Sir Enguerrant to go forth first from the lists, declaring that Saintré had won the victory for that day

ANON Saintré, holding his pennon, began to make his great Sign of the Cross and to say his benison thrice. Then took each his spear and couched it in rest upon his thigh, and they hurtled together as fast as their coursers might run. But at the first running they did naught.

At the second running, Sir Enguerrant his spear-point glanced off from under Saintré's visor; and Saintré smote him beneath the greater arm-piece, and in breaking his lance, he swayed somewhat. And at the breaking of his lance, the trumpets began to sound with a great noise.

At the third running, Sir Enguerrant couched his lance over-low and brake it against the saddle-bow; and Saintré carried off the roebuck from upon Sir Enguerrant's helm. Then began the trumpets to sound, but forasmuch as the lance was not broke properly, the King bade them cease.

At the fourth running, Sir Enguerrant smote Saintré in the midst of his hauberk, and brake his lance exceeding well; and Saintré smote him on the under side of his helm, and the spear glancing off passed between his body-harness and the roundel of his spear, and the point entered in between the hand and the gauntlet, which it carried off, yet without piercing the flesh; but his hand was thereby all benumbed, so that they were not able to finish the joufts until the fourth day following. And in passing on, his spear brake at the casing of the point, but that was not counted.

Then the King bade read out the challenge, which provided that one muft wait upon the other for the space of eight days; and he commanded therefore that each should go forth by the gate and return unto his hoftel. And thus each returned, armed at all points excepting their heads. But the King was pleased to honour Saintré the more inasmuch as he bade Sir Enguerrant pass forth firft, declaring that the advantage remained with Saintré.

SEVEN-AND-THIRTIETH CHAPTER

How the King sent summon the two champions to sup with him. And how they returned the next day into the lifts and did marvels one againft the other

Now when they were both unarmed and refted a little, and Sir Enguerrant's hand dressed, the King sent summon them to sup with him; and set Saintré at his right hand, as a gueft, and Sir Enguerrant at his left, as a subject and one of his household; and he bore his hand bound with a scarf. And when the tables were cleared away, the King sent fetch thither the Queen, with all her gentlewomen. Then began

147

the dances, and the Queen took Saintré; the other ladies and damosels took likewise the other knights and squires that had come with him. There was Saintré mightily praised by every man and woman. Sir Enguerrant moreover, to the utmost of his power, honoured and feasted Saintré, who was feasted thus until Sir Enguerrant's hurt was quite amended.

And on the fourth day, the King commanded them to come down armed unto the lists, to finish their jousting. And they came in the same array as before, Saintré also armed at all points save his head; they and their coursers all trapped in new apparel.

And when they were all prepared, the King bade them do their devoirs. Then with lance in rest they urged their coursers each against other.

At this fifth running, Sir Enguerrant smote Saintré with his spear at the joint of his elbow-cop, and Saintré him on the under side of his helm; and each brake his lance well, so that the splinters flew in the air, and their coursers were like to have fallen. Then fell the trumpets to sounding and the cry of the people was so great that they could scarce be made to hold their peace. And thus had each now well broken two lances.

At the sixth running, Sir Enguerrant smote Saintré again upon the elbow-cop, and Saintré him under the beaver; and both well broke their lances. And thus had each now broke his three lances.

At the seventh running, at the meeting of the lances Sir Enguerrant's courser veered aside, and so they did naught.

At the eighth running, when that same courser beheld Saintré coming on, it turned about all suddenly; and but Saintré had speedily raised his spear, he had smitten Sir Enguerrant in the back; wherefore he was much praised by the King, the Queen, the lords

148

and ladies, and all the common folk also. And thereafter Sir Enguerrant departed and sent unto his pavilion to change coursers. And when he was returned again they dressed their lances and spurred on their coursers, but neither one of them touched other.

At the ninth running, Sir Enguerrant, from the furiousness of his fresh courser, couched his lance somewhat over-high, and Saintré smote him upon the under side of the roundel thereof, and glanced thence on to his body-armour, and then on to the lance-reſt,[37] which was torn wholly off, and in the tearing Sir Enguerrant ſtaggered sorely. Thus had Saintré four lances broken. And Sir Enguerrant was con-ſtrained to go seek him other harness. And when he was returned back into the liſts, and each had set his lance in reſt, they spurred on their coursers as faſt as they might, but passed by without touching.

At the tenth running, it fortuned that they crossed their two lances, and with the great hurtling of their coursers they ran one againſt other, despite the tilt[38] (which was of scarlet cloth, hung from a cord); and Sir Enguerrant's courser fell and Saintré's brake a shoulder. Then lit Saintré down and got upon a rouncy,[39] and so to his pavilion to change coursers; yet for aught any might say, he would not do off his helm. And when Sir Enguerrant had arisen, he returned back unto his end of the liſts, and there awaited Saintré.

At the eleventh running, Sir Enguerrant dressed his spear somewhat low, and smote him upon the lower plates of his body-mail; and Saintré him upon the roundel of his spear, the which he bent backward out of true. Now Sir Enguerrant, by cause of smiting thus low, did somewhat sway; yet each brake his lance fairly. And thus had Sir Enguerrant four lances well and fairly broken, and Saintré five; the splinters whereof lay in many pieces about the field. Then fell trumpets to sounding and the voice of the people to shouting, so lustily that it was long until they ceased. And now that Saintré's five spears were broke, as it was required in his challenge, Sir Enguerrant, perceiving well that Saintré's five spears were broke and that the honour of that day was fallen to him, besought of him to break a lance for the ladies, whereat Saintré was well pleased. But when the King heard how that they would have run a lance for the ladies, he sent and forbade that joust, because of the jousting on foot. And he commanded then that both of them should come before him even as they were. And when both were come, he bade unhelm them; and then, by the mouth of his King-of-arms, whom he had caused to come up into his gallery, he let say unto them the words which here follow :—

EIGHT-AND-THIRTIETH CHAPTER

The judgment of that jousting spoken by Aragon King-of-Arms ; and of the prizes and offerings given by one unto the other ; and of their going forth from the lists

" My two lords here present (I call neither by name) : my lord the King hath beheld your chivalrous jousting, so marvellous well done and performed by either, that no man living might do better, as hereafter followeth in writing." Then in the presence of all he read the tale of those jousts, every course and every stroke well set down in writing ; and afterward said : " Now, you both being then equal in lances broken, the noble squire John of Saintré hath at the last running fairly

broke his fifth lance, and so accomplished his jousts
on horseback; therefore unto you, gentle squire
John of Saintré, the lord King hath adjudged the
prize ". Anon Sir Enguerrant drew toward Saintré,
to have given him the ruby.[40] But Saintré, beholding
him approach, set spurs to his courser and advanced
to meet him as fast as he might. Then bowing low,
he took him by the hand and embraced him as heartily
as he might, saying unto him : " My lord and brother,
for the great honour that you have done me I do
thank you as well and as warmly as I may ". Then
said Sir Enguerrant unto him, like a wise knight and
a courteous : " Nay, brother, what say you ? 'Tis
I that ought to thank you for having so well vanquished
me ! Now I pray God and my lord Saint George
that he grant you to persevere from good to better,
and I pray also that your fair Lady may recompense
you. And unto her I humbly commend me, and in
witness of these my words I do deliver up unto her
this ruby, which for her sake you have rightfully won,
beseeching her that she be willing to accept it ".

Then Saintré, bowing, took that passing fine ruby,
and thanked him courteously; and said then unto
him : " Now, my lord and my brother, 'tis through
you I have won it, for you put not forth your full
strength. And that your well-beloved Lady may not
be the loser, I pray you be pleased to give unto her
this little diamond, commending me full humbly
unto her ". And when Sir Enguerrant beheld that
passing fair large diamond and Saintré's high courteousness, he turned him unto the other lords that
were by, and in his Castilian tongue said unto them :
" Truly this is the very flower of all young gentle men ".
Then said he unto Saintré : " Certes, brother, I
thank you, for my Lady and for myself, and we are
as much beholden to you as though I had taken it and'

she received it. But you shall excuse me this time : I will not take it ; but you shall give it unto her that hath indeed won it ". Saintré long besought him, and Sir Enguerrant would not, until the King asked what was the matter. And when it was told him, and the Queen also, no need to ask whether Saintré was mightily praised of the King, the Queen, lords, ladies, knights, damosels, esquires and all the commonalty. Nathless, the King seeing Saintré's great pleading, sent bid Sir Enguerrant take the diamond, sith such was Saintré's courteousness that he ought not to refuse it. Then Sir Enguerrant took it. And this done, trumpets began to sound and minstrels to play with a great clamour. And the King commanded them to go thence and unarm them. Sir Enguerrant and Saintré, in their great courteousness, each desired to accompany the other. Then was more pleading, but in the end Sir Enguerrant prevailed. And the better to shew his courtesy, he made Saintré to ride with him side by side, on his right hand, whether he would or no. Now when they were come unto Saintré's lodging, Saintré with all his might sought to accompany him back again, and would have so done, but that the lords of the Court, of either party, held him by force.

Saintré much entreated the lords his counsellors, and others, to sup with him that night, but for all his prayers there was not one would stay, but they all left him to take his repose for that night. And so also with Sir Enguerrant, for they thought to have achieved their jousts on foot on the day following. But the King, like a wise, gentle, and gracious lord, bethought him that night of the labour that they had that day had, and caused their jousting to be adjourned for that day, that each might well rest him at his ease.

NINE-AND-THIRTIETH CHAPTER

How Saintré, after he had heard Mass, sent unto Sir Enguerrant, by two heralds-of-arms, two axes, according to the terms of his challenge. Also, how the King sent his herald to make known unto Saintré the hour appointed for going down unto the lists

THE second day following, being the day assigned unto the jousting, Saintré before he did aught else heard the Mass of the Holy Ghost, whereat he caused his aforesaid benison to be given him. Then sent he two heralds and a varlet to bear unto Sir Enguerrant two axes, covered up, for him to take his choice between them, as in his challenge was set forth. And one of those axes being chosen and taken, the heralds met with Aragon King-of-arms as he came first unto Saintré to inform him, in the King's name, the hour when he must come down unto the lists to perform his jousting on foot, which was two o'clock of the afternoon. By the which King-of-arms Saintré sent unto the King most humble thanks, and gave the King-of-arms a passing fair cloak of crimson damask, shot with silver and trimmed with fine sable marten, for the sake of the good news which he brought. And he, afterward, made his report unto the King.

And when it had struck an hour after noon, the King and Queen went up into their galleries, as hath before been told. Then sent the King unto the champions to bid them come. Anon Saintré, as mover in the jousts (yet not as challenger, for he had not challenged him more than any other) mounted first upon horseback, making with his pennon the true Sign of the Cross, and pronouncing his benison aforesaid. And the rest followed in such array as here followeth :—

FORTIETH CHAPTER

*How the two champions entered solemnly into the lists
for the third time*

FIRST the tabors, and next the sumpter-horses charged
with his armour as aforesaid, and led by their varlets;
and after the sumpter-horses his two armourers, on
foot; and after the two armourers his four minstrels,
two and two. After the four minstrels came the
pursuivants and then the heralds of lords of that
country: all, both heralds and pursuivants, vested in
tabards in such manner as they ought to be. And
after the heralds came the French lords and knights of
his train, all clad alike; and after them came the
Kings-of-arms and heralds of the King, side by side
with those of France and at their left hand. And
after those heralds there came Saintré's trumpets and
clarions and then the King's. And after the King's
trumpets came the Count of Prades, on a right puissant
courser, bearing before him Saintré's axe. And on
either side the Count there rode Don Bernard de
Cardonne and Don Frederic de Lune. And after
them followed Saintré, all unarmed save for his
vambraces, his greaves, and his sollerets, on his passing
good and puissant courser, wearing on his head a fair
cap and thereon three fair plumes like ostriches', made
of rich broidery, ribbed with small diamonds, rubies,
balas rubies, and other precious gems, and springing
from a very rich and fair buckle whereon was a great
diamond, set amid three great balas rubies and three
great pearls; he and his courser trapped in crimson
satin all covered with spangles of fine gold enamelled
bright red, with a wide band of white satin sewn with

154

silver spangles enamelled white, and three labels in fine gold: which were his arms. And in his right hand he bore his banner, whereon was Our Lady and Child, and signed him therewith at every ſtep. And after him, side by side, there came the aforesaid Sir Arnold de Perillos and Sir Francis de Moncade. And after, all the knights and esquires that the King had sent to attend him. So in this array he came down into his tent, which was hard by the gate of the liſts, on his own side. And there was he armed at all points, saving only his head. And when Sir Enguerrant was come likewise down into his tent, then the King bade his King-of-arms to summon them. Then came Saintré on foot, attended by the lords his counsellors and others, as far as the gate of the liſts; and there the King's marshal asked him who he might be and what he was come thither to do. Unto whom, smiling, he humbly answered: " My lord marshal, I am John of Saintré, come at the day and hour appointed by the moſt excellent prince, the King here present (as true and competent judge between my lord and brother Sir Enguerrant de Cervillon and me) to perform the jouſting on foot for my Emprise, as in my letters of challenge is provided ". Anon, these words said, the marshal went unto the King to make his report.

Then bade the King open the gates of the liſts, that Saintré might draw unto his pavilion. And when the gates were opened, Saintré advanced to enter in; and with his banner, which he had in his right hand, he made a great sign of the Cross, then kissed it, and entered into his pavilion. Sir Enguerrant, to be brief, entered in like manner. Now when they were both in their pavilions, it was not long before the marshal came, attended by four men-at-arms, one behind the other; and he began firſt with Saintré and led him armed at all points, and his appointed counsellors following, and presented him unto the King, who was in his gallery. Now in his going, he passed before the gallery wherein were the Queen and the other ladies, and Saintré went down upon one knee, making his reverence. Then might you see ladies with hands joined praying God to preserve him from hurt. So came he before the King, unto whom he likewise did obeisance upon his knee. And while he was yet there, there came Sir Enguerrant. Then bowed Saintré low unto him (albeit it was not the custom) and afterward said unto him: "My lord and brother, without prejudice to either of us, I pray God that he grant you worship and honour". "And unto you likewise, brother", said Sir Enguerrant. Then kneeled they both before the King. And to be short, the King bade the marshal take of them such oaths as were proper to the occasion. Then the marshal made them to swear on the Holy Gospels, on the faith they had in God, on their lives and on their honour, that they bore not upon them nor had intent to bear nor would bear any such things as enchantments, spells, charms, herbs, necromancies nor other diabolical devices of evil artifice, wherewith one might assail the other or defend himself; but that they were without hatred, envy, or ill-will, being desirous only to win honour and renown and their fair Ladies' good favour. The which oaths being taken, each arose and went thence unto his pavilion; but at Saintré's arising he turned about as he departed and made again his reverence unto the King, unto the Queen also and unto the ladies, as he had done before. And thereafter he withdrew unto his pavilion and Sir Enguerrant likewise, for to let put on their basinets.[41]

156

ONE-AND-FORTIETH CHAPTER

*How they issued forth out of their pavilions to achieve
their jousting*

WHEN they were both arrayed (to be brief, I pass over
all the cries and challenges which appertain to such
occasions) the King bade let them sally forth out of
their pavilions. Now at Saintré's sallying forth, with
visor raised, he kissed his banner, pronouncing his
benison which My Lady had taught him, and making
a great Sign of the Cross; and then kissed it again
and gave it unto one of his counsellors. And this
done, taking his axe in his hands, he let down his visor
and fell to working his arms and his shoulders into his
armour, going down first on one knee and then upon
the other, with as much ease as though he had been
clad only in his doublet. And when both had come
out from their pavilions, and the pavilions were
removed out of the lists, then by the King's command,
the marshal cried out with a loud voice, standing in
the midst of the lists: " Fall on; fall on ! "

TWO-AND-FORTIETH CHAPTER

*How they set on one against the other and contended right
valiantly*

Now when the marshal had made his cry, they set on
one against the other, like to two lions unchained.
And Saintré as he came on cried with a loud voice :
" For my most honoured Lady, whose servant I am ! "
And with that they began to lash one at the other.

157

Sir Enguerrant, that was a full valiant knight, stout
and puissant, and taller of stature than Saintré was,
lifted up his axe and smote him such a buffet over the
hinge of his basinet that he made him all to stagger;
and Saintré with the point of his axe so smote him
upon the slot of his visor that he caused him to yield
a full pace back. Then lifted Sir Enguerrant up his
axe again, and with all his might brought it down, as
he had before; but Saintré, who had felt the first
stroke full sore, covered himself with his axe in such
wise that he was not touched. Then Sir Enguerrant
heaved up his axe to have struck at him again, but
Saintré, as he so did, smote him with the edge of his
axe upon the fingers of his right hand, so lustily that
notwithstanding the roundel it bruised and benumbed
all his fingers. Sir Enguerrant in the heat of the
combat not feeling the mischief that he had, sought
to lift up his axe, but could not. Now when he felt
the pain and could no more hold up his axe, like a
bold and valiant knight he took his axe in his left
hand, spreading out his arms to lay hold on Saintré.
But when Saintré perceived his intent (though he
knew not of his hurt) he hindered him to come nigh
him, by dealing many strokes with the point[42] of his
axe. And considering well, he addressed his stroke
on a sudden at Enguerrant's left hand, which held the
axe, making it to fall from his grasp. And when Sir
Enguerrant found himself without an axe, he advanced
all suddenly like one possessed, and came and laid
hold on Saintré by the body, and Saintré on him by
one arm, for with the other he held his axe. Now
when the King saw Sir Enguerrant's axe upon the
ground and their two bodies at grips, he straightway
threw down his wand, like a just prince and judge,
crying out: "Hold, hold!" Then were the combatants parted by the men-at-arms.

At that the King sent by the marshal to bid them come before him, and then caused him to say unto them: "You, Sir Enguerrant, and you, John of Saintré, the King hath bid me tell you that you both have so worshipfully and valiantly performed your jousts, your devoirs, and your honourable obligations, that there is no man might have done better. But according to the purport of your letter of challenge, John of Saintré, you must contend together with your axes until one of you were borne to the ground or had let go his axe with both hands. Therefore by virtue of the said letter, my lord the King, here present, hath unto you, John of Saintré, adjudged the prize".

Then the King commanded them both to rise up, for they were yet kneeling, and bade unarm them of their basinets. And when Saintré heard the King's judgment and sentence, he thanked him therefor as humbly as he might, saying: "O most excellent and mighty prince, for the honour which you have been pleased to do me, and for your sentence upon our jousting, which you do adjudge in my favour, I thank you as humbly as I may. But as for the prize which you adjudge me, as dutifully as I may I do entreat of you to bethink you further and consider how my lord and brother here hath with his axe well trounced me; and all that I have done, Sire, was but by good fortune; and that ought you well to consider". At these words of Saintré's the hearts of all his hearers were astonished, and every man's tongue was loosened, striving who might most praise him. And whatsoever love they had toward Sir Enguerrant, they could not but say of Saintré that truly he was the crown and the pattern of all honour and modesty. The King in his stand and all the lords that were there with him, marvelled greatly. The Queen, the Lady Eleanor of Cardonne, wife to Sir Enguerrant, and all the other

princesses, countesses, baronesses and ladies that were
in the great gallery with the Queen, fell all to praising
him mightily. And in like manner Sir Enguerrant
could not keep from saying unto the others that were
round about him : " Hearken now to these right noble
words of his ! Where is the man, or ever was before,
that sought to divest him of such honour for to clothe
his adversary therewith ? "

The King, well pleased to speak and to hear praise of
Saintré, (who heeded him not but abode yet upon
his knees) all at once commanded him to arise and
said unto him : " John of Saintré, as for that which
you ask me well to consider, I make answer that I have
considered it wholly ; and to the end that all men may
know what grace and honour God hath granted you
this day, it is my will that you shall keep them ".
Then the King commanded Sir Enguerrant courteously
to render up his axe and to perform the rest of his
devoir when he was unarmed. At that, Sir Enguerrant
caused the axe to be given him, and with his wounded
hand, as well as he might, with the help of his left
hand, he rendered it courteously unto Saintré, saying :
" Brother, I render you your axe, and I shall perform
the residue of that which in your letter of challenge
is prescribed, praying God and my lord Saint George
that they give you increase of all honour more and
more ".

Now when Saintré heard the King's commandment,
and Sir Enguerrant's gracious words, he asked for his
bracelet, which one of his servants held. Anon,
having received his axe, he bowed unto Sir Enguerrant,
and said : " My lord and brother, sith the King's
good pleasure is such, I do obey him ; but I would
acquit me toward you, and I give you here my bracelet,
which you have well deserved, heartily beseeching you
that you accept it ". Sir Enguerrant and all the rest

marvelled more at this thing than they had before, and
Sir Enguerrant answered him : " Ah, my brother John
of Saintré, is there no end to your courtesies ?   For
your bracelet, and for the honour you do me, I thank
you as heartily as I may ; but in sooth you shall give
back the bracelet unto your fair Lady ".   Now at this
the King asked what entreaties they made one another.
The marshal said unto him : " Sire, 'tis John of
Saintré who seeketh by all means to give unto Sir
Enguerrant his bracelet, as though 'twere he that won
the prize ".   " The bracelet ! " said the King.   Then
turned he toward the princes and other lords that were
with him, and said unto them : " What say you of this
honour and valiance in so young a squire ? never saw
I his like ".—" Truly, Sire," said they, " nor did we.
And in sooth it is evident that he muſt be of moſt
noble birth, and hath well observed and learned in
the noble Court wherein he was bred up ; and so are
also all his companions."   This said, the King bade
him keep his bracelet.   But when Saintré heard the
King, he kneeling said unto him : " Ah, Sire, for God's
love, suffer at leaſt that I may elsewhere beſtow it ".
" Elsewhere ? " quoth the King, " that do We grant ;
the bracelet is yours to beſtow where you will ; only
We would not have it said that it were through Us,
or by Our judgment, that you had beſtowed it."
" Sire," said Saintré, " gramercy ! "

Then called he the King-of-arms of Anjou, and
Touraine and Lusignan, the heralds that had come
with him ; and to the King-of-arms he gave the
bracelet, and sent them then all three unto the Lady
Eleanor de Cardonne, Sir Enguerrant's wife, who was
in the Queen's ſtand, saying : " Tell her I commend
me humbly unto her, and since 'tis she (as I muſt in
reason think and believe) that hath above all others
beſt deserved to have this bracelet, therefore I beseech

her and pray that, for my most dear Lady's sake that
gave it unto me, she may graciously please to accept it ;
and right sorry am I, in love's and honour's name, that
it is not fairer and fitter to be hers ".

The Queen, the Lady Eleanor, and the other
princesses and ladies that were with them, the King
also, who was in his gallery upon their right hand, and
all the lords in his company—it needeth not to say
how they all marvelled. Then answered the Lady
Eleanor to the King-of-arms and to the heralds :
" King-of-arms and heralds : friends, I do thank this
right courteous and valiant squire John of Saintré ;
but, by his leave, 'tis not I that have deserved this
bracelet, as he saith, but she through whom he hath
this day won so great worship and honour. Therefore
bear it again unto him, and pray him excuse me ".
The Queen, when she heard that answer, like a wise
lady and well-advised, said unto her : " Nay, truly,
Fair Cousin, you ought not to refuse this honour from
so perfect a gentleman as this is ; I pray you take it ".
At that the Lady Eleanor did as the Queen desired,
and the Queen herself was pleased to put the bracelet
upon her left arm. And when it was upon the Lady
Eleanor's arm, she took from the pendant of her
necklace a passing fair rich ornament of a great and
costly pearl of four or five carats, clustered about with
three great diamonds and three fair rubies ; the which
she gave unto the King-of-arms, and said unto him :
" Ye shall bear this little jewel, you and the heralds
that are here present, unto this most courteous squire
John of Saintré, commending me right heartily unto
him ; and ye shall say that though his bracelet
belongeth far more to his own fair Lady than to me,
yet at his request I have taken it. And because
meseemeth that his fair Lady ought to have some
token of the honour he hath this day won, therefore

I pray you give him on my behalf this little ornament, asking him that he please to present it unto her, commending me unto her well ".

The King was right glad when it was told him of these words and the jewels given and taken. And thereafter he bade unarm them both. Then withdrew each unto his own end of the lists, to mount on horseback. And when Saintré was mounted, he drew straightway toward Sir Enguerrant, who by reason of the hurt to his hand was constrained to be helped somewhat in his attiring; and perceiving Saintré, he quoth unto him : " What! brother, brother ; hath your Lady bid you serve your companions with such meats ? "—" Why, my lord and brother ! " quoth Saintré, " hath yours bid you feast them that joust with you upon such buffets ? " And when they were mounted upon horseback, there was much disputation between them, which should go forth last out of the lists, for the honour thereof. The King, who meant the honour to be Saintré's, sent word anon that they should go forth side by side ; but forasmuch as Saintré had won the prize, he bade him ride on the right hand ; and so they departed each unto his lodging, in like manner as they had come. But at their departing the controversy was great, for each was desirous to bear the other company. And when the King beheld their entreaties, he sent word again unto them bidding them make an end to these courtesies, and each to go his way. So they took leave one of the other and departed unto their lodging to unarm them and to take their ease all that day until supper-time, when the Queen sent to summon them. Now to be brief, there were they served abundantly with good wines and viands, meats and sweetmeats ; and thereafter most joyously beguiled with songs, dances, and morrisses, of sundry sorts.

And with that I will leave speaking of the high honours, the dinners and the suppers which the King and Queen and the other lords and ladies made Saintré, and Saintré them; and I shall speak of his leave-taking and of the gifts that they gave one unto another.

THREE-AND-FORTIETH CHAPTER

How Saintré took leave of the King, the Queen, and all the rest of the Court; and of the gifts that were given

AFTER Saintré had accomplished his jousting in such fashion as you have heard, he tarried yet two days at Barcelona, while they feasted one another. And on the third day he took his leave of the King, the Queen, the lords, ladies and damosels of the Court, and likewise of the other princes, princesses, and ladies of that country, that had come thither to behold those jousts: for men held such matters of more account than they do at this present time. And the King and Queen decreed that at that leave-taking the custom of the country should be broken in so far as concerned the persons of Saintré and the knights and squires of his company: to wit, that they should be every one kissed by the ladies. And the Queen was pleased first to begin, kissing first Saintré and afterward the knights and squires of his company; and all the others did the like, which because of the custom of the country they had never before done, nor did they ever again, save in great intimacy of friends. And alas! at this leave-taking, Love with his sweet ardent flames had on one side and on the other their tender hearts so kindled, that at this sad parting, though their mouths might make some semblance of smiling, they might

164

PLATE IV

SAINTRÉ'S DEPARTURE FROM BARCELONA

[face p. 164

not withhold the tears out of their piteous hearts from coursing from their eyes adown their cheeks.

Now after his leave was taken and his baggage departed, Saintré sent as a present unto the King the fairest and stoutest of his four coursers, caparisoned in the richest trappings he had; and thereon a fair gentle page, his nephew, in very goodly array. Moreover, he sent as a present unto the Queen an hundred ells of the finest brocade, and another hundred ells of the finest Rheims cloth that he had been able to procure in Paris, and a passing fair Book of Hours all adorned with precious stones and fine gold. And likewise unto all the ladies and damosels of the Court together he sent as a present other two hundred ells of the aforesaid cloth which he had sent the Queen; unto the King's and Queen's household, and unto the officers of the Court, an hundred crowns, half and half; unto the Kings-of-arms and heralds of Aragon and others, excepting his own, another hundred crowns; unto the trumpeters and all the minstrels, fifty crowns; unto the Lady Eleanor, a fair white hackney, saddled, with trappings all of full costly crimson velvet plush, broidered with great patterns in gold thread, all fringed with gold and party-coloured silks of his own colours. And unto Sir Enguerrant he sent another of his best coursers, saddled, and trapped in another of his richest caparisons, with a fair sword all incrusted with fine gold. And unto each of the four lords, his counsellors, he sent a good courser.

The King, who had before ordained it, sent him at his departing a right fair and puissant Apulian courser and two fair jennets of Andalusia, a goodly covered cup and beaker of gold, thirty marks weight of gilt cups, and fifty marks of kitchen pewter; unto his III knights, a piece of crimson velvet; and unto his IX squires, three pieces of crimson damask; unto

his heralds, trumpeters, and minstrels, two hundred
Aragon florins, and an hundred florins more. The
Queen sent him a passing rich cloth of purple velvet
broidered with silver, proper for a squire, and two
pieces of fine damask, the one crimson and the other
black ; and unto the three knights of his company,
each a piece of blue figured satin ; and unto all the
nine squires, each a piece of satin, plain blue.

The Lady Eleanor sent him a fair chain of gold of
four marks weight. Sir Enguerrant sent him a right
fair Spanish courser and a good Andalusia jennet ;
and upon each a page, a Moor, passing well attired
after the Moorish fashion ; and a piece of crimson
damask broidered with silver. The Count of Cardonne sent him fifty marks of silver plate. Don
Frederic de Lune sent him twelve passing good large
arbalests of steel, and twelve coats of mail whereof
four were covered with plain velvet, broidered and
purfled with gold, four more covered with blue velvet,
and the other four with damask of divers colours,
garnished with silver gilt. Sir Arnold de Perillos
gave him a Blackamoor, richly clad, on a fair goodly
jennet, all armed and attired in the Moorish fashion.
And Sir Francis de Moncade, two good suits of harness,
all complete : the one for war and the other for
jousting, very richly adorned, and a fair sword garnished
with gold and enamelled all in white ; and also a
Turk, his wife, and their two children, cunning workers
in gold and silk thread, whom Saintré afterward gave
unto the Queen, who was right glad thereof. Of the
other ladies and damosels of the Court, there was not
one but gave him shirts broidered with gold or silk,
tunics, broidered purses and gloves, all after the
fashion of the country ; musk, Cyprus birds,[43] and
so many more sweet-savoured odours that it were a
long matter to rehearse them all. Such was their

PLATE V

THE KNIGHT-ERRANT'S RETURN

[face p. 170

grief at parting from him and from them that were
with him, that it might scarce have been greater.
What shall I say more ?   I never read, saw, nor heard
tell, before nor after, of any that set forth with such
high favour and praise of all men, as this gentle squire
and his companions.

FOUR-AND-FORTIETH CHAPTER

*How Saintré, attended on his way by all the barons,
departed from Barcelona to return into France*

Now when Saintré was all ready to mount on horseback
and depart thence, he took leave of his host and of
many others.   Then came the Counts of Prades, or
Orgel, and of Cardonne, and the other lords knights
and esquires whereof I have told, to the number of a
thousand or twelve hundred horse, to bear him
company.   And furthermore, the King caused all
their costs to be paid, to the limit of his kingdom, by
a steward and a clerk of the Treasury.

And with that I will leave speaking of the honours
done Saintré and of the presents, and the leave-
taking; and I shall tell of his coming unto the King,
and of the vows and pilgrimages which My Lady had
made for love of him.

FIVE-AND-FORTIETH CHAPTER

*How Saintré and his companions came unto the Court ;
and of the good cheer that the King, the Queen, My
Lady and the other ladies and everyman made them*

WHEN Saintré was in his lodging, the next evening
after his departing from Barcelona, considering how
he might the most honourably make known unto My

167

Lady the issue of his jousting, his deeds, and his return, he bethought him that if he sent forward any of his heralds unto the King, men might suppose that he sought to glorify himself by his good news, which some in their hearts might think blame to him. And he resolved therefore to speak thereof unto Sir Peter de Pruilly, in whom he much trusted. And he answered him that truly it were more honourable if he should let some other bear the tidings and not one of his heralds, albeit it appertained to their office; and moreover that he should not write unto the King, nor unto the Queen, nor any other. " But ", said he, " if you desire, I shall send William my cousin, as though from me; and I shall write unto the King, the Queen, and the ladies, telling what honour you have won; and William, who hath understanding enough, shall declare it all unto them likewise; and indeed, I shall inform him what he shall say." And thus was it done. And when the King, the Queen, and the rest of the Court, and in especial My Lady, heard the tidings, there was everywhere such joy that for many days they spake but little of aught else; and looked eagerly for his return. My Lady, since his departing, had scarce ceased day or night from her prayers and orisons, performing every Friday and Saturday her sworn vow, not to wear any linen next her naked body, until his return, as hath heretofore been told. But when she afterward heard the news how that at the Court of Aragon he was to be delivered of his Emprise by a knight who had already the King's assent thereto, she increased her vow, swearing that every Wednesday she would cause Masses to be said and give alms to the sum of ten crowns, and moreover would make pilgrimages secretly about the City. And she was oft at great pains so to do, especially at the time of the jousting, which she knew.

Now while she was at her prayers, there arrived William de Pruilly, sent by Sir Peter, bearing such tidings as I have said. And when My Lady heard that right welcome news, which Ysabel came running to bring her, then, as soon as she was well assured of it, she straightway gave thanks in her heart unto Our Lord, lifting up her eyes to Heaven; then returned she into her chamber, and there all by herself on her bare knees and with hands joined she thanked Our Lord again. What shall I say more? On the one hand, so great was her gladness that she could scarce keep countenance; and on the other, such was her longing to behold him that day nor night she could not rest, and it well-nigh made as naught the joy she had at his good fortune.

And here will I leave to speak of the great joy that she had, turned to grievous melancholy by her ardent longing to behold him; and I shall tell of his coming into the King's presence, and of the high honour and good cheer that were made him.

SIX-AND-FORTIETH CHAPTER

How Saintré journeyed and came unto the King; of the honour and good cheer that were made him; and how My Lady's heart was made whole

Now when Saintré and his train had so far ridden on their journey that they were come within two leagues of Paris, they encountered many barons, knights, esquires, burgesses and others of the Court and of the City of Paris, all come out to do him honour and bear him company, so great love and good-will had they all toward him. Then was such joyful greeting between them that it was great gladness to see. And

169

when he had done his obeisance unto the King and after unto the Queen, who made him most joyous welcome, then went he unto My Lady, whose joy was such, that she might scarce contain herself; howbeit, like a prudent Lady that she was, she hid the full measure of her joy. Anon he went unto the other ladies, who made great joy of him, and after he had kissed them all, the Queen commanded that there should be dancing, because of his return.

And while they danced, My Lady, who sat by the Queen, said unto her: " Ah, Madam! Saintré, as you have heard, hath danced enow in Aragon, wherefore he is a-weary. Pray you, let call him, and make him to sit down here with us, and ask him concerning the states and fashions of the ladies of Aragon ".— " Truly, Fair Cousin," said the Queen, " you say well." Anon the Queen bade call Saintré, and three more ladies also; and said unto Saintré: " Friend Saintré, we desire you to take your ease ". Then said she unto the other three ladies: " Be seated all of you, and the most courteous among you shall give him the train of her gown whereon to sit ". But My Lady, desiring to behold him face to face, would not be the most courteous, and turned a deaf ear. Then the Queen questioned Saintré, first concerning his coming unto the Court of Aragon, what cheer the King, the Queen, the lords, and in especial the ladies made him; and then concerning his jousts, both on horseback and on foot; and of the beauty, the demeanour, and the raiment of the ladies. Of which matters, for the first, touching his jousting, Saintré passed lightly over it, and all that he said was more to Sir Enguerrant's honour than to his own; but as for the rest, he spake great praise of the ladies of Aragon, in all regards, and of the King also and all the lords, whom he could not too highly praise.

And now will I leave telling of the praises and the honours that he spake of them ; and I shall tell of the very perfect joy and good cheer which My Lady made him, and how from time to time, as often as she durst, she feasted her eyes upon him.

While they devised thus, My Lady looked this way and that, as though she paid no heed to aught in especial ; and then on a sudden turned her gentle gaze upon him ; and so doing, took from her raiment a pin, and fell to picking her teeth therewith, which was her signal. And when Saintré espied My Lady's signal, he straightway answered by rubbing his right eye a little. And thus did they spend that passing long and weary day, in joyous distress of heart, until the evening and the hour between them covenanted, when they should meet together in the garden ; and then began merry greeting between them, with many a kiss given and given again. There were their joys, their desires, their hearts healed of all their ills ; and in such delights they continued from eleven of the clock until two hours after midnight, when they needs must part one from the other. And here will I leave speaking of their perfect felicity, and I shall speak of Saintré's advancement and of his companion called Boucicault.[44]

SEVEN-AND-FORTIETH CHAPTER

How Saintré was made chamberlain to the King ; and of the fellowship between him and the squire Le Meingre, surnamed Boucicault

THE King's love for Saintré, which was before great, as you have heard, increased little by little until, not long after, he ordained him to sleep in his chamber, and then to be his first chamberlain. Saintré had

ever well remembered My Lady's teaching, how in his
tender youth she had exhorted him to be virtuous and
well-mannered, commending unto him the words of
Albertus, how he said :—

" *Non tua claudatur ad vocem pauperibus auris, etc.*"

and likewise the fair verse wherein Aristotle thus
saith :—

" *Vir bone, qui curas res villes, res perituras,*
Nil proffituras dampno, quandoque futuras.
Nemo diu manssit in crimine, sed cito transsit :
Et brevis atque levis in mundo gloria que vis."

and divers other admonishments also, touching them
that are raised to high estate. And therefore, whatsoever estate he had and whatsoever honour the King
did him, never was his heart swollen with pride nor
his bearing less humble, but he shewed himself daily
more gentle, more kind, and more courteous toward
every man.

In those days there was at the Court a passing
gracious young esquire of the Duchy of Touraine,
called Le Meingre, but men named him in sport
Boucicault, and he was grandsire to the Boucicaults
that are at this day living ; a most wise, subtle, and
courteous squire, and high in the King's favour. This
Boucicault, perceiving Saintré in such favour of the
King, and so high advanced above others, sought his
acquaintance. And the young Saintré, knowing him
a man of much worship, and from his own country,
was well pleased to be acquainted with him ; and they
so cherished and companioned each other that two
brothers could not have been better friends. Of this
fellowship between them the King was right glad,
for he already well loved Boucicault ; and he ordained
that he should sleep with Saintré on the little couch
in his bedchamber ; that is to say, when he lay not

with the Queen. What shall I say more? These two squires loved each the other as well as two brothers ever did, and were so loyal and true one to the other, that never was there any variance between them. And when either one of them went abroad upon his business, or for an enterprise or a voyage of adventure, as they oftentime did, then the other kept his place in such manner that none might enter in. And though Boucicault was afterward a right valiant knight, and moreover, more subtle and prudent than Saintré, yet in deeds of arms Saintré was accounted the more notable. And therefore the Kings-of-arms and heralds made a common proverb, which thus saith:

> " If it needeth an assault
> Saintré's more than Boucicault;
> If a treaty is to plan,
> Boucicault's the better man."[45]

That is to say, the one for arms and the other for counsel.

So in this wise, as long as they both lived, their love and fellowship endured. And now will I leave speaking of them; and I shall tell of the other new jousts which Saintré did against the Lord of Loysselench,[46] a baron of Poland, who bore *argent, an ox rampant gules, horned and hoofed sable*; the which jousts were held in Paris before the King, the Queen, My Lady, and other lords and ladies beyond number.

EIGHT-AND-FORTIETH CHAPTER

How My Lady bade Saintré take the gage of battle which the Lord of Loysselench bore

THE year after Saintré's jousting with Sir Enguerrant was accomplished, there came the Lord of Loysselench,

173

a baron of Poland, tall, strong, and a full puissant
knight, seeking to win worship and his fair Lady's
good favour, and with him four barons, of Poland
likewise : to wit, the Lord of Endach, who beareth
gules, a saltire[47] *pierced vert* ; the Lord of Nulz, who
beareth *or, an ox's head sable* ; the Lord of Morge,
who beareth *argent, three heads sable* ; and the Lord
of Terg, who beareth *or, a cross voided*[48] *gules* ; who
all four, when these jousts were done, purposed to go
upon pilgrimage to Saint James.[49] The same Lord of
Loysselench wore, as challenge to combats on horseback and on foot, two bracelets of gold, the one above
the elbow of his left arm, and the other above his
ankle, the two chained together with a middling long
chain of gold ; and this for the space of five years,
unless in the mean while he should find a knight or
squire of blood and coat-armour, without reproach,
to deliver him by arms, as hereafter followeth. And
the sooner and the more honourably to accomplish
these combats, he bethought him to come unto the
most noble Court of France, where all noble and
chivalrous men were wont to be honoured and well
entreated ; desiring also to get knowledge and acquaintance of them. He caused therefore Brunswick, the
herald that was with him, to read and construe out
of the Polish tongue into French his letter of challenge,
the which, to be brief, said thus :

That he who should deliver him of his vow, and he
himself, should undertake to run X courses of spears,
of such measure as the prince of that country should
decree ; and this in harness and war-saddles, without
other advantage ; unless during the said ten courses
there should be three lances well and properly broken,
by the prince's judgment. And if at the end of the
said ten courses, or three lances well broken, God had
preserved their bodies from scathe, the second day

following they should fight on foot ten bouts of
spears without respite ; and after, there should be a
breathing-space to take other weapons, to wit : axes
of like size, wherewith they should combat with point,
back, or blade, as they might please, ten more bouts,
without breathing-space ; and after respite, ten more
bouts with their swords, using the point ; and so
likewise with daggers. Of the aforesaid spears, both
ahorse and afoot, all pointed, and of the other weapons
also, he desired and bound himself to grant the choice
unto his adversary in the lifts. And if it fortuned in
the said joufts that either of them should be disarmed
of any part of his harness, he should be bound to
continue in such ftate, or deemed to have forfeited
the prize for that jouft.

And he unto whom God should give the advantage
in the five combats : for the combats on horseback
his adversary muft give him, then and there, a diamond
of the price of three hundred crowns or upward ; and
for the spear-bouts afoot, a ruby of like price ; and for
the axes, a fine pearl of four carats or more ; and for the
swords, a balas ruby of like price ; and for the daggers,
a sapphire of like price also. And if it should chance,
which God forfend ! that in accomplishing the said
joufts on horseback and afoot either of them should
be so hurt that he might not continue for that day, or
if either should be unhorsed or borne to the ground in
the combats afoot, or should be so disarmed as to head,
body, or arms that he should refuse to finish the said
combats in such case, then should that combat and
those that remained to be fought be accounted as
fought. And he should be bound to acquit the prizes
of the bouts that had remained to be fought, as though
he had loft them all, one after another. And in order
the sooner to acquit the prizes which should be loft,
each of them should be bound, before the beginning

175

of the jousting, to bestow them into the prince's hands, that he might dispose of them according to his good pleasure.

These challenges being thus made known, My Lady, without more ado, summoned Saintré unto her as soon as she might and said softly unto him : "Dear Love, now is come the day that God and fortune have granted you, to honour and raise you up, by the coming of this Polish knight whose challenge is published abroad. Therefore I pray you, as urgently as may be, that you be the first with My Lord the King, to make request to deliver this knight ; and have no care for the cost, for God and ourselves shall provide all. And though you be mine only Love, and all my weal, and more than I can express, wherefore I, more than any other, ought to dissuade you, nay rather forbid you, to put yourself in such jeopardy, yet such is the love I bear you, that I would have you in everything the most valiant and the worthiest, trusting that God shall give you the victory".

When Saintré heard My Lady speak thus nobly [albeit his heart was already resolved], he went down upon one knee and thanked her right humbly, saying : "My most honoured Lady, by the love and fealty I owe you, I was even now thinking the same, and how I might break it unto you ". "Go quickly," said she, "lest any other be before you." Then all hastily he went thence unto the King, and fell straightway upon his knees, and made his petition in such manner as was fitting. The King, who loved him well, looked on him smiling, and marvelling much that so young a man, and of no great stature, should be bold to undertake combats so perilous against a man so stout and tall as this Polish knight was. Anon he said unto him : "Saintré, have you well pondered this ? " "Pondered ? Sire," said he, "ay, truly, since first I

beheld him I have had none other desire." And
while they were in this converse, there came the
Viscount Beaumont, to make a like request of the
King. And as he did so, there came also the Seigneur
de Craon; and anon the Seigneur de Vergy; then
the Viscount des Quaisnes, the Seigneur de Saucourt,
the Seigneur de Hangest, and a many more, every one
to make his petition unto the King. And when the
King heard these many barons that vied one with
another in asking, he said unto them :—

" Friends, in such matters first come is first served :
ye see here Saintré, the foremost, kneeling yet upon
his knees. Certes, he is full young ; but Our Lord
is the God of the strong and the weak, of the young
and the old ; and since God is for the weak as well
as for the strong, and for the young as for the old,
therefore meseemeth that We should do injustice to
Saintré's good courage, did We refuse him." At that
every man rose up, praising the King's judgment, and
better content with Saintré than they had been with
any other. Then Saintré, as humbly as he might,
thanked the King. The next day, the King let
summon to dinner the Lord of Loysselench, the other
four barons, and the knights and squires of their
company, unto whom high honour was paid. And
after dinner there was dancing with the ladies, the
Queen being present : who full graciously bade them
all welcome, and then, by the interpretation of such
as knew both tongues, asked them somewhat concerning
the ladies and the estates of their land, saying it rued
her much that she could not understand their speech.
And when the dancing was done, before the coming
of the spices and the Parting-Cup, Monjoie, the
French King-of-arms, read again, by the King's
command, the letter of challenge, there being present
the Queen, with lords and ladies in plenty. And when

12

the letter was read, Monjoie demanded of the said
knight whether that seal were the seal of his arms,
and whether he did maintain all that in his letter
aforesaid was found. And when all this was inter-
preted unto the said knight, he answered that he did
avow it to be his seal and his letter. Anon Saintré
knelt before the King, who confirmed the leave given;
then arose he and said unto the knight: " Sir, you
are right welcome! With the help of God, Our
Lady, and my lord Saint Michael, I shall free you of
your vow and of the bands and chains wherewith you
are bound ". With that he drew near him to loose
the bands. But when that knight beheld Saintré so
young and small of stature, he drew back as though
ashamed, and said unto his people, in his Polish
tongue: " Is this he that shall deliver me ? Is there
none in this Court so hardy as he ? " Then was it
told him who Saintré was, and how beloved of the
King, and how that he had already jousted in Aragon
before the King, ahorse and afoot, and that of the
two that fought, he had had the advantage. So he
looked hard upon him, and then said: " If this be so,
I cannot refuse him; let him do according to his
good pleasure. I can well aver that such men be
sometimes more to be feared than them that are
stouter of body ".

Then said they unto Saintré, who was about to
question him further: " Saintré, accomplish that
which you have undertaken, for he doth thank you
right heartily therefor ". Anon Saintré loosed the
bands. And this done, the King appointed, for
the day of their jousting on horseback, the thirtieth
day after; and with that withdrew to his chamber. And then Saintré, bearing the two gold bands,
the one before and the other behind him, hung on
the chain which was around his neck, went with

many others to attend the said knight unto his
lodging.

And here will I leave speaking of the high honour
and good cheer that were made them, and I shall tell
of the great heaviness that My Lady had within her
heart, and the fair words that she spake unto Saintré.

NINE-AND-FORTIETH CHAPTER

*How My Lady made her plaint for Saintré ; and of the
gentle words that she spake unto him*

MY LADY (who never had beheld that knight until
the loosing of the bands) when she beheld him so tall,
so puissant, and so well accoutred, was mightily
dismayed, and it repented her so sore of the words
she had spoken unto Saintré, that she had now no joy ;
yet, sith the thing was thus far advanced, there was
no other counsel might prevail. Wherefore day and
night she ceased not from lamenting and sighing, and
said in her plaints : " Alas, unhappy I ! What haſt
thou done, and what waſt thou about, when by thy
counsel thou didſt put in the way of such perils him
that thou moſt loveſt in this world, and whom above
all others thou shouldeſt have dissuaded ? Alack !
and he muſt contend with so mighty a man, so ſtrong
and puissant, that there is none but would fear him.
Now, if any mischief should befall, to his person or
his honour, (which God forbid !), alack, wretched,
unhappy I, I shall never more know joy in mine heart ;
and what is more, he will perchance never love me
more. And verily he would have cause, albeit I
urged him to this thing only in the intent that he

179

might be among the good and worshipful knights of renown. And that do I call Thee to witness, O my true Lord, and likewise thy Blessed Mother, called Our Lady of Lesse in Laonnois, unto whom I vow a waxen image of him, armed in all his harness, upon a courser caparisoned with his arms, the whole of three thousand pounds weight: beseeching thee, Holy Virgin, upon my knees and with hands joined, that thou vouchsafe to send him back to me whole in honour and in person; and for the reſt, come what may! at leaſt he shall go forth well armed ".

And when My Lady had done saying these words, she came where the Queen was. And it was not long before she espied Saintré; then took she her tooth-pick and made him her signal. Saintré, who of his own accord was much desirous to have speech with her, answered her ſtraightway. And when the night and the appointed hour were come, and they were together, My Lady seeing him so passing joyful, her heart's complexion was changed and her great heaviness was turned to great joy, and anon she said unto him:

" Now, dear Love, ſtudy to do well and virtuously: lose or win honourably: for whatsoever befall you with such and so puissant an adversary, you cannot but win honour. And fear not the tallness nor the might of this man, that is a giant to you, for God is over all and helpeth his friends when they are in need; and this is the reason thereof: the ſtronger do despise the weaker and fight in their pride, but the weaker ask help of God, who suſtaineth them and is on their side. Therefore, man for man, and ſtrength for ſtrength, none is to be feared save God; and as for them that be equal in might or in numbers, and all with a good will ask help of God one againſt other, let him beware who is in the wrong; for God, who is a juſt judge, giveth unto every man his due. Now, dear Love, may you fare as it shall please God! If he grant you some small measure of honour, that little shall be more to you than much honour to another; and if this adversary overmatch you, being as a giant in comparison to you, he cannot so vanquish you but the world will the better esteem you than if you had not adventured yourself; for I have heard valiant men affirm that a gentleman that fighteth without quarrel and is overcome is more to be esteemed than he was before; for men strive together, but God giveth the victory unto whom he listeth. Therefore, dear Love, have no care but to do honourably. And as touching your expense and worthy arrayment, lo! here in this satchel are six thousand crowns: spend them honourably, and God be with you!"

Saintré, perceiving how My Lady's love toward him daily increased, thanked her as humbly as might be. Then, to be brief, he took leave of her, and all that night was so filled with joy that he could not sleep for thinking of this new matter. And when the morrow was come, Mass heard and his Hours said, he busied himself and rested not until with God's help, the King's and My Lady's, he was so well furnished with arms, with horses, and with passing rich horse-trappings and other apparel, that in sooth it would have sufficed a royal baron.

And now will I leave speaking of all these matters, and of the great noise that there was everywhere of his jousting, and the prayers that all men made for him, by cause that he was so young and so small in comparison to the Polish knight that it seemed to all men he must be overborne at every stroke; and I shall speak of the jousts, upon the day appointed.

FIFTIETH CHAPTER

How the Lord of Loysselench and Saintré came to the lists to perform their jousting a-horseback, in presence of the King, the Queen, and sundry other princes, lords, and ladies

WHEN the thirtieth day was come after Saintré had taken the Lord of Loysselench's Emprise, the day ordained for the beginning of their jousts, the Lord of Loysselench that morning caused to be borne unto the King's stand twenty great spears, all armed save for the points, and all alike, as in such cases is proper.

And when the King, the Queen, and the other royal lords and the ladies were in their galleries or at the windows of Great Saint Antony's Street in Paris, the Lord of Loysselench sent by a herald a leather box full of very fair lance-heads for the lances wherewith they were to joust, for the King to ordain the measure of them as it should seem good to him. And whiles the lances were being pointed, there arrived with a passing great and fair company of French lords, knights and esquires, ordained thereto by the King, the aforesaid Lord of Loysselench, and likewise the knights and esquires of his company, above an hundred and fifty horse, all clad alike and in new apparel ; and before him five very fair coursers, whereof four were trapped in velvet caparisons of divers colours and with divers sorts of golden ornaments. And the fifth was caparisoned with figured velvet, whereon were his armories, charged with golden ornaments ; to wit : *Argent, an ox rampant gules, horned and hoofed sable ;* and upon each one a fair gentle page of his, full richly arrayed. And after

182

this last courser there came the Count of Estampes, bearing his helm upon a lance-butt, and the crest on his helm was a demi-ox gules between two daggers[50] argent, naissant from a wreath of the same and of gules. And after him the aforesaid Lord of Loysselench, on a right puissant courser, armed at all points, save only his head, whereon he wore a fair chaplet of many violets; he and his courser trapped in passing rich crimson velvet plush, figured with gold upon gold, all trimmed with fine sable marten; and at his right hand there rode the Duke of Berry, who for the King's honour and by his ordinance did attend him, as was due unto a stranger knight. And when he was come as far as the entrance of the lists, the King, without any ceremonies, bade him enter in and pass under the covering of a great pavilion of tapestry, enclosed from one side unto the other with a great curtain on running rings, wherein stood a dresser for his arming, with wines, fruits, and spices a-plenty, to refresh them all.

And in the mean while that he was within his pavilion, there arrived Saintré, armed in like manner at all points, saving his head, which was covered with a passing fair beaver cap, wound about with a fair Pleasance scarf, flowing free, all broidered and fringed with fine gold; and upon the front thereof was a passing rich brooch with a great diamond, clustered about with three great balas rubies and three great pearls of four carats, the which My Lady had given him just as it was; he and his courser all trapped in fine ermine trimmed with sable marten, very fair to see. His other six coursers and his pages, most worthily arrayed, I pass them over, for any man may imagine them. After these six coursers came the Count of Alençon, who loved Saintré so well that he deigned to bear his helm upon the truncheon of a lance. And after him came Saintré, with at his right

183

hand the Duke of Anjou, who was pleased thus to honour him. And after them, lords, knights and esquires beyond number, who elected to bear him company. And when he came unto the entrance of the lists, like a good Christian he made a great sign of the Cross with his banner, whereon was a figure of Our Lady, and pronounced the benison which My Lady had taught him, as hath been told. And when My Lady beheld him, she thought him fairer by far than she had ever done. And as she sat with the Queen, in the gallery, because of the great love she bore him and the great jeopardy whereinto she deemed herself to have led him, it so repented her that little by little, with this great affliction, her heart failed her. And when the Queen and the other ladies saw her fall as dead, knowing not what ailed her and desiring not to affright the King and all his company, they made no alarm, but laved her face, her nose, her wrists and her hands with vinegar and with such remedies as could be found there, and so was she chafed and tended that little by little she came to herself. Then did she open her eyes and fall to looking now here now there, first at one, then at another ; anon she began to speak, saying : " Ah ! most blessed Virgin, comfort me ! " Anon they comforted her as far as they might. But she would not, for all the Queen's entreaties, turn and look upon the jousting.

Saintré, as he entered smiling into the lists, looked up in passing toward the King's stand, and then the ladies', and doffing his cap bowed as humbly and as low as might be. Now not seeing My Lady, he was somewhat disquieted; but supposed indeed what the cause thereof might be, misdoubting that My Lady had not courage enow to look upon his jousting ; for so had she told him already. And anon, all on horse-back, he entered into his great pavilion, curtained, arrayed, and furnished like unto the other, and with him my lords the Duke of Anjou and the Count of Alençon, and those that had been ordained to attend him, and no more.

When they were both arrived, and in such array as I have said, the King, who already had ordained the measure of the lances and caused them all to be pointed with steel, commanded that they should arm them at all points, and that the Lord of Loysselench, as challenger, should first come forth ; and this was done. And then he commanded that Saintré should come, wearing upon his helm his beaver cap, all adorned as he had worn it upon his head. And when both were come, the King sent unto the Lord of Loysselench ten knights, with ten lances all alike, bidding him choose five. The Lord of Loysselench, like a good and courteous knight, thanked the King full heartily, and sent then the lances unto Saintré that he might choose, as in the challenge was ordained. Saintré (to be brief) thanked him, and bade them keep the five biggest. Then my lord the Duke, who as aforesaid had deigned to serve Saintré, took one of them and set it upon his thigh, until it should be time for the onset. And when each had been given his lance, the King bade them set on, in the name of God. At these words each set spurs to his courser, one against the other, as though they should never encounter soon enough.

Now in that course, the Lord of Loysselench smote Saintré upon the left elbow-cop, glancing off ; and Saintré smote him at the joint of his body armour, breaking his lance in many pieces, and himself swayed somewhat, by cause that the stroke was a little low. Then was there so great noise of people and of trumpets that it continued a long space.

185

At the second running the Lord of Loysselench smote Saintré upon the cheek of his helm so ſtrongly that he well-nigh ſtunned him, and Saintré smote him on the brow of his helm, and so pierced his silver ox that in passing he turned it back to front; and after that course they reſted a space.

At the third running, the Lord of Loysselench smote Saintré even as Saintré had smitten him, and upon the point of his spear he carried off his beaver cap, all adorned as it was; and Saintré smote him at the top of his arm-piece, which he dinted, and the over-guard also, and brake the laces, and the arm-piece fell to earth. Then began such outcry of people and noise of trumpets that scarcely might they be made to cease.

And the Lord of Loysselench being thus disarmed, the King asked to see again the letter of challenge, to know what it contained. And he found therein three clauses, whereof the firſt was: that if it befell (which God forfend!) that in the performance of the said jouſts, ahorse or afoot, either one of them were so hurt that for that day he could not continue; or if he were smitten from the saddle, or borne to earth from his feet; or if he were so disarmed as to head, body, or arms, that he should refuse to continue the said combat in such case:—then that same combat and all others remaining to be performed should be accounted as done; and that knight muſt forfeit all the prizes, as though he had loſt them all, one after another. The King therefore caused them to cease their jouſting, and bade shew and signify unto the Lord of Loysselench the purport of his letter of challenge, by the four lords of Endach, of Nulz, of Morg, and of Terg, the Polish barons which had come thither in his company, as hath been said; and in their presence the letter was read. And the King besought them to say unto their Lord, that for his

186

part he desired not to put in so great peril his soul, his honour, and peradventure his life.

The Lord of Loysselench, when he heard these things aforesaid, thanked the King very dutifully; but being full wroth at his misadventure, he answered: Befall him what might, for he would surely finish the combats! Neither could the French lords, whom the King had given him to attend him, prevail to turn him from it. Anon the aforesaid Polish lords told him roundly that they would squire him no longer in such condition. Then said the Lord of Loysselench: "Ye do perceive better than I mine honour and my shame: into your hands I confide them". Then said they that they would be answerable for it, because of the great peril wherein they beheld him; adding, for his solace, that in the combats afoot he might amend his fortunes. And so in great pain and distress of heart, he consented. The tidings whereof being brought unto the King, he commanded them both to withdraw and to unarm their heads, and then to come before him on horseback, each bearing the prize which he was to give.

When the Queen and the other ladies beheld the Lord of Loysselench thus disarmed, they ran all unto My Lady, where she lay upon cushions of gold and of silk, making her prayer to God and Our Lady of Leesse, unto whom, as hath been said, she had commended him. "Come now, Fair Cousin," said the Queen, "rise up and come see a-many fair things, and how our good little Saintré hath disarmed the great Polack, so that my lord hath sent for them to come before him; I know not why, if it be not to give the prize." My Lady, whose heart knew not where it was, for joy at these news, feigned as though she cared but little. Then said the Queen unto her: "Why, Fair Cousin, we do perceive that verily you rejoice but little in the honour which this most valiant squire hath this day won, wherein also my lord the King and Ourselves have share. Come now, rise up briskly!" Then took she her by the hand, and the other ladies by the other hand and made her to rise up in sight of the galleries. My Lady, whose joy was in this wise restored, dissembled it under cover of the Queen's chiding, and said unto the Queen: "What! Madam, how hath this noble Polish knight his shoulder thus disarmed?" Then the Queen told her all the jousting, and how Saintré broke his first lance, how he pierced through the knight's silver ox and turned it hind before, and how he had disarmed him. Whiles she devised of these matters, My Lady in her gladness could not take her eyes from looking on Saintré, and Saintré, looking first here, now there, on a sudden his glance lit upon her. At that My Lady made him her signal, whereto he replied courteously.

And when they were come before the King, he bade Monjoie, the French King-of-arms, say unto them: "My Lord of Loysselench, and you, John of Saintré: the King my sovereign lord, here present, hath commanded me to tell you, that one and both of you have in so high and honourable fashion performed your jousts this day, that there is no man might better have performed them. But forasmuch as your arm-piece, My Lord of Loysselench, hath been smitten off by a spear-thrust, unto you, John of Saintré, hath the King adjudged the prize, according to the terms of the challenge; and he doth require of you, My Lord of Loysselench, that you render it up, and here is the wherewithal". Therewith he gave unto him the fair costly diamond which the King had held. And the same words were said after him, word for word, by Brunswick, the herald that was come with the Lord of Loysselench. Then the Lord

of Loysselench bowed to the King, and in his Polish
tongue thanked him for the honour which he had done
him, saying that in sooth Saintré had worshipfully
won the prize. And with those words he took the
diamond and drew near unto Saintré, and set him
the diamond upon his finger. Then the King commanded that they should go both twain and unarm
them; and so they did. But at their parting, one
company from the other, Saintré went with him a
piece of his way, riding side by side with him, upon
his right hand, with all ceremony. Then trumpets
and clarions and minstrels fell to playing, and there
was joy in the City more than can be told.

And now will I leave speaking of these twain, how
they went thence to unarm them; and I shall tell
how the knight supped with the King, who did him
great honour, and his companions; and how the
Queen bade Saintré to sup with her.

When the supper was prepared, the King sent seek
the Lord of Loysselench and all the other four barons,
with the Polish knights and squires; and Saintré,
right nobly attended, went to bid them come. And
when they were come into the King's presence, he
made them passing good cheer and high honour.
Then were the tables set and supper was spread. The
King made the Lord of Loysselench to sit at his right
hand, and at his left the other four barons, and the
rest at the next first table after the King's. Of the
wines and meats and the sundry ceremonies, it needeth
not to write, for any man may imagine them. Saintré,
after all were seated and served, went thence to sup
with the Queen, as she had bid him. Of the good
cheer that they made him, she and My Lady and the
other ladies and damosels, no need to ask, for there was
none among them could leave off therefrom. My
Lady, though of them all she made least of him, could

not keep from looking at the fair diamond, the prize, which he wore on a chain of gold around his neck; then the Queen also desired to see it, and divers other ladies. Anon My Lady said unto him: "Truly, Saintré, most happy is the Lady that hath won this!" The Queen, hearing those words, said unto him: "I pray God, Saintré, that you may fare from well to better, and win every other prize". Then answered he them, kneeling: "Gramercy, Ladies! But I have not deserved it of God; and what I have achieved cometh unto me from him, through your good prayers". Right so, the chief butler brought water for the Queen to wash her hands; and when she was seated, she made Saintré, whether he would or no, to sit at her right hand. What shall I say more? Such joy was there on either side, that it were beyond telling.

Now when the tables were cleared, the King from one side and the Queen from the other came into the Great Hall for the dancing. Then were there dances and morrises of divers sorts; but because of all the travail which the Lord of Loysselench had that day had, and Saintré likewise, the King called soon for the spices and the Parting-Cup, and thereafter withdrew him into his chamber, and every man took his leave. Saintré and all the rest, taking each a knight or a squire by the arm, attended Loysselench and his people back to their hostel, a right fair company. And now speak I no more of the honours, the wines, and the meats which the King sent them each day, nor of the business of the day following, with their combats on foot; but I shall tell of My Lady and of Saintré and of the passing perfect joy which they had together that night in the Pleasance.

That night, as My Lady had covenanted with Saintré, they met together in the Pleasance. Then were such kisses given and given again, that—what shall I say?—that they had never dreamed of any joy so perfect. And My Lady said unto him: "Alas, my Heart, alas my Joy, alas mine only and sovereign Desire: I saw yesterday an hour, wherein I thought never more to behold you alive; and when I beheld you enter into the lists, my heart so fainted with the great dread I had for you, that I fell like one dead; and had I not been right soon succoured, I had indeed given up the ghost. But when I heard your victorious tidings, my dead heart came straightway to life, and my lady the Queen, with the other ladies, came and raised me up and brought me with them into sight of the galleries".

"Alack, my most high, most perfect and mine only Lady, what is this you tell me? Ay me! an I had known it, what had mine unhappy heart done? Death had been more dear to me than life. Now God be praised and thanked that I knew naught thereof. When I entered into the lists, I did perceive you at the Queen's side; but when I came all armed for the jousting, I saw the Queen and all save only you; and I supposed you had not courage to watch the jousts, for so you had already told me; but I never thought you in worse case than that. Well now, my most honoured Lady, all that well endeth, is well. Praised be God, our Lady, and you for the honour I have this day won through you; and I hope, Lady, to fare from well to better. And I pray you, be of good cheer, and have no fear for the rest of the matter, for that same God that hath been at our combats to-day will be at the other combats, the day after tomorrow." And with that they took leave full tenderly of one another. And here will I pass over what business they did on the morrow, and I shall speak of their combats on foot, and how they fared.

ONE-AND-FIFTIETH CHAPTER

How the Lord of Loysselench and Saintré came down unto the lists, and how they performed their combats on foot

THE day whereon the jousting was to be, and at the hour appointed, the King, the Queen, the Lords, and the ladies were in their stands. The Lord of Loysselench sent unto the King, by the Lords of Endach and Morg, two jousting spears, both alike, pointed with steel, furnished each with a guard to defend the hand, and painted scarlet; and likewise two axes, two swords, and two daggers, every pair alike without any advantage to either, for the King to dispose of as he might please. And to be short, the King took four of the said weapons and sent unto Saintré, and the four other he gave to the aforesaid lords of Endach and of Morg, to bear them again unto the Lord of Loysselench. And this done, the Lord of Loysselench, armed at all points save for his head, came forth out of his hostel with like array as he had at the jousting a-horseback; and furthermore, the Counts of Nevers, of Boulogne, of Tancarville, and of Retel, rode before him bearing his four weapons; and after them came the Duke of Berry, bearing his helm; and then he himself, armed at all points and clad, he and his courser, in fine velvet of the colours of his own arms; and after him many barons and other noblemen; and for the rest, even as it had been at the former jousting; and in such array he came into the lists, and lit down in his own pavilion, which the King had let pitch for him, and with him those that were appointed for to attend him. And when he had come down, it was not long before Saintré came with a passing fair and great company; before him rode the Counts of Perche, of Saint Pol, of Clermont, and of La Marche, bearing his four weapons before; and after them the Duke of Anjou, bearing in like manner his helm; and with this moſt fair and great company he came down likewise into the other pavilion, which the King had caused to be set up for him also. Of the Kings-of-arms, heralds, pursuivants, trumpets, clarions, and minſtrels of divers sorts, I make no mention, to be brief. And when both twain were made ready, the King let bid them both to issue forth. Then the two lord Dukes gave unto each his jouſting-spear, and Saintré as he took his spear, kissed the pennon thereof, making the Sign of the Cross. Then at a great pace he advanced, and encountered the Lord of Loysselench near to his ſtarting-point; and at the firſt blow he ſtruck, he cried with a loud voice:—" For Our Lady, and for my moſt beloved Lady ".

At this onset that he made, the Lord of Loysselench thought no less than to have borne him to earth or smitten him down; and because of his ſtrength, which was mightier by far than Saintré's, I ween it might well so have fortuned him: but God, at Our Lady's requeſt, which are the ſtrength of the weaker when such do come unto them with a good will; though men ſtrive together, yet these give the victory unto whomsoever them liſteth. Then the Lord of Loysselench smote Saintré with all his might above the joint of his body-harness, and his spear glanced off a span beyond, without piercing; and Saintré's spear, at the firſt ſtroke, glanced aside likewise, and in thus glancing smote his adversary between his spear and his right hand, which he pierced through the middle, both hand and gauntlet, three good fingers' breadth. And when they sought to deal a second ſtroke, the Lord of Loysselench was not able to draw back his right hand, nor Saintré his spear, so firmly was it held. Therewith the Lord of Loysselench let fall his spear, to come at grips with Saintré, but could not, for Saintré seeing his spear thus held, thrust forward therewith with all his might. Now when the King beheld Loysselench's spear upon the ground, he declared that jousting at an end, and that God was for the younger. Then caused he them both to be led unto their pavilions and there unarmed of their helms, and Loysselench's hurt to be looked to, and then bade them come before him. And I could not tell you the half of the passing great dole that the Lord of Loysselench made, both for his ill-fortune, and also that so young a man should have put him to the worse, both ahorse and afoot; and with his hand all pierced through as it was, that for heat and anger the blood might not be staunched, he would yet have accomplished the rest of the combats; but the blood flowed so fast from him, that perforce he must desist. And when he was physicked, and his hand bound up, and his arm unarmed, Saintré came to condole with him as he issued forth from his pavilion. The Lord of Loysselench, his countenance restored, embraced him kindly, and said unto him, in his Polish tongue: "Saintré, my brother, an you continue in arms as you have begun, there shall be none that may withstand you". And Saintré, being informed what he had said, answered smiling: "Nay, my lord and brother, all you say is of your charity; if I take part in any combat, it is but to bear the weapon; for my beloved Lady doeth the rest".[51] Right so came my lords the Dukes, and brought them before the King. And now will I forbear for a space to speak of how the prizes were given, and I shall tell of the great joy that the Queen made, and My Lady, and all the other gentlewomen and damosels, and of My Lady's meditations.

The Queen and My Lady, with the other ladies, laughed and made merry unceasingly for Saintré's sake and for his victory. But when My Lady, who turned her eyes never away from Saintré, bethought her that verily, considering the evident grace that Our Lord had granted him, at Our Lady's request, she ought to render thanks to them, then made she semblance to have an head-ache, and said unto the Queen : " Madam, I pray you excuse me, for I must lie down a little ". " Fair Cousin," said the Queen, " do ever as it pleaseth you." And when My Lady had lain down in the little chamber beneath the galleries, she sent away her gentlewomen. Then arose she, and going down upon her bare knees, with hands joined and eyes lifted up to Heaven, she gave thanks unto God and Our Lady for the grace they had granted Saintré ; and she was long at this. And when her devotions were done, she returned joyously unto the Queen, as though quite restored. Saintré, who looked up ever and anon, and indeed full oft, toward the ladies, not seeing My Lady, weened it had befallen her as before. But when he espied her returned, his heart was an hundred thousand times more glad. And here will I make no further rehearsal of these matters, but I shall tell how the prizes were given.

TWO-AND-FIFTIETH CHAPTER

How the King commanded the prizes to be given

THE King, being provided with the VIII goodly jewels that were the prizes, four on either part, for to give them unto him to whom they should be due,

commanded the aforesaid Monjoie, the French King-
of-arms, who was in the gallery, that he should bear
the message that here followeth; and first, a herald
cried with a loud voice: "Silence, in the King's
name!", that all might hear.

Then said Monjoie:

"My Lord of Loysselench, and you, John of
Saintré, our sovereign lord the King, here present,
hath commanded and bid me to say unto you, that in
this your last combat ye both have done so well and
so valiantly that there is no man might have done
better. But, forasmuch as you, My Lord of Loysselench, are not fit nor able to continue it to an end,
the King, in pursuance of the terms of your challenge,
as sole and competent judge doth command you to
render up your four prizes, which by his commandment,
leave, and license I here do give you."

And when the Lord of Loysselench perceived that
Monjoie had done speaking, he asked what he had
said; which being told him, and the King's judgment
well understood (which was indeed none other than
he had foreseen), he kneeling said that he was most
humbly beholden unto the King; he lamented full
sore his evil chance, which had not suffered their
combats, neither afoot nor ahorse, to continue longer
for the pleasure of the ladies; but sith fortune thus
willed it, he was ready to acquit him as the King had
commanded and as right required. And these words
said, Monjoie came down and gave unto him those
four jewels, that he might acquit his debt. And when
he had received them, he drew nigh unto Saintré, to
render them up. Then was his heart so wrung with
anguish that no word could he utter. The other
four Polish barons, well perceiving what sore affliction
he had, sought each to make his excuses, as well as
they might. Anon Saintré advanced, led by My Lord

of Anjou, and bowing took the four jewels, and then smiling said unto him : " My Lord and Brother, for the honour which it hath pleased you to do me, I thank you to the utmost of mine ability and power ".

Then began trumpets and clarions to sound, so loud that they could scarce be made to cease. And these things accomplished, the King bade them withdraw to their pavilions, and mount on horseback, for to return unto their lodgings and unarm them. And when Saintré was mounted upon his courser, My Lord of Anjou said unto him : " We desire you, Saintré, to be honourably and nobly attended ". Then brought he him nigh unto the Lord of Loysselench, who was already mounted upon his courser. And he set them both together ; then he and My Lord of Berry put themselves in the forefront, and in this fashion bore him company as far as his lodging. The honours and requests which each made to other, and those things which they did afterward, until supper-time, I pass over ; but I shall tell of the great rejoicing and talk that the Queen made, and My Lady, and the other ladies and damosels, and the King likewise and all the Court, and all the Town also, all that day and night ; for there was neither man nor woman but spake praise of Saintré.

THREE-AND-FIFTIETH CHAPTER

How the Lord of Loysselench supped with the Queen

Now when the King and Queen were returned unto their palace of Saint-Pol, the King bade the Queen send the seneschal to summon the Lord of Loysselench and his company to supper ; and he desired that

Saintré should be there also. And when supper-time came, Saintré went with a goodly company to seek him. And when they were come unto the Queen and in converse with the ladies, the seneschal came to summon them to supper. Then took the Queen the Lord of Loysselench by her right hand, and made him to sit down; and said unto Saintré: "Saintré, sith this is for you a day of festival, I will sit betwixt you twain". And with much excusing and compliments and ceremony, needs must he obey. My Lady, full joyful at the great honour that was done her lover, said unto him as he sat down: "Saintré, Fair Sir, God increase your honours!" "Madam," quoth he, "you see how it is at the Queen's bidding and not because I have deserved it; and if I have achieved aught, 'tis through her whose servant God doth grant me to be." Then the Queen asked for the Lord of Morg, by reason that he spake French; and set him opposite Loysselench, that she might the better have converse with him. The other Polish barons, knights, and esquires she made to sit among the ladies and damosels, who feasted them with high honour. Of the wines and meats, of many sorts, it needeth not to write nor to ask.

And to be short, when the tables were cleared away, the minstrels began to play for dancing. And it was not long before the King came, with My Lords his brothers and others of the blood royal. Now after the dancing and many songs sung, by reason that the Lord of Loysselench was a-wearied and hurt also (though he strove to make merry cheer, yet the leeches said he suffered sore), the King called for wine and spices, and thereafter took his leave. Then Saintré, with a great and goodly company, set the Lord of Loysselench upon his way; and at their parting bade him to dinner the next day, and all his company. What more shall I tell you? At that dinner were lords, ladies, and damosels, knights and people of condition, so many that such a feast had long not been seen. And to be brief, when the tables were removed, the minstrels struck up for dancing. Then were country dances, songs and other new dances, and passing rich morrises; and verily on that day none could remember when so fair and so joyful a feast had been made, nor one so well ordered. But by reason of the pain which the Lord of Loysselench had from his hand, they agreed to cut short the feasting. And then took they every one leave of the other.

The fifth day after, the Lord of Loysselench, being somewhat more amended of his hurt, bade Saintré and divers lords and ladies to dine with him the next day, after the Polish fashion. With wines and with meats of marvellous kinds, even as our own custom is, they were full richly served. And the tables being removed, there was dancing and many songs sung; and moreover, after that right plenteous feast, whereat there was great good cheer, the Lord of Loysselench, at their arising from the tables, came bearing a great silver bason, wherein were many diamonds and rubies set in gold, all mingled together; and there was no lady nor damosel at the tables but received one. And this done, all took their leave one of another, and so farewell for that night.

FOUR-AND-FIFTIETH CHAPTER

How Loysselench took his leave

THE day following, the Lord of Loysselench with all the others of his company came to take leave of the King, the Queen, and of all My Lords the King's brothers, and others of the blood royal, and of the principal ladies, purposing to depart the day after and to perform their pilgrimage to Saint James. And that evening, the King sent moneys unto his guests in payment of all that they had there spent ; and in the morning he sent unto the aforesaid Lord of Loysselench a piece of velvet plush, coloured purple and very richly broidered with gold upon gold, twenty marks weight of gold plate and two hundred marks of silver gilt, and a passing goodly Apulian courser ; unto each of the other four barons a piece of figured velvet, crimson, and a fair courser also ; and unto all the other knights a piece of plain crimson velvet ; and also unto the squires, a piece of crimson satin ; unto Brunswick, the herald, one of his richest gowns and an hundred francs-à-cheval.[52] And the Queen gave unto the said Lord of Loysselench another piece of passing rich velvet plush, of azure figured with gold, and a costly buckle of a square diamond clustered about with three great pearls and three goodly rubies ; and unto the other four barons, each a piece of blue satin figured and shot with gold ; and unto the knights, each a piece of figured blue satin ; and unto the squires, each a piece of satin, plain blue. And My Lady sent unto him a passing rich diamond of five hundred francs. And there was not one of My Lords the King's four brothers but gave them : unto some, coursers ; unto others, silken cloths broidered with gold ; and unto others, vessels gilt and of silver, a-plenty. And when they beheld the high honours and rich gifts of the King, the Queen, and all the Dukes, and of My Lady also, they were desirous to return and thank them humbly, albeit they had already taken their leave. And at their departing from their hostelry, Saintré, who everywhere attended them, gave him as a present a right puissant courser, saddled and all

armed with a chamfer[53] and fair plume, and with a
most bright and shining barde[54] of fine silver-gilt,
with flaps of velvet plush, broidered and fringed with
gold and silk of his own colours, very fair to see. And
on the other hand, the Lord of Loysselench made him
a present of his goodly courser, whereon he had
jousted, caparisoned as it was with cloth of gold
trimmed with sable marten; which was all ready
prepared, for to be given unto him.

Then they mounted each upon his new-given
courser; and in this fair array Saintré bore them
company above a league. And with this will I leave
speaking of the Lord of Loysselench and of his company,
that go their way unto Saint James's loudly praising
the King, the Queen, the Princes, My Lady, and all the
Court of France, for the gifts and high honours
bestowed upon them, saying everywhere that verily
the Court of France was indeed the flower of all
largesse and the school of all honour.

After the departing of these lords of Poland, Saintré
was feasted at leisure by the King, the Queen, the
ladies, and all the Court. Of the passing gentle and
loving cheer that My Lady made him, no need to
write nor to ask more, for any man may well conceive
it. Now thus it continued for the space of about a
year, until My Lady bethought her that verily it was
time for him to achieve some new thing, to increase
yet more his fame; and that as a Frenchman, and so
forward in the King's service as he was, he ought to
undertake some deed of arms against the English.
And when they were together, she said unto him:
"My sole Desire and mine only Thought, day and
night I cease not from pondering the increase of your
honours. And I have bethought me that amongst
all the feats of arms you have performed, you have
never yet made yourself known unto these English.

Wherefore I pray you, whiles God, Our Lady, and
Fortune are for you, that with My Lord the King's
good leave and under assured safe-conduct from the
King of England, you hold, for three days in each week
of this coming month of May, a passage-at-arms
between Gravelines and Calais—which is but three
leagues and all a level road—for to receive and joust,
on each of those three days of the week, with one
knight or squire only, the first that shall offer himself
in the lists, horsed, armed, and with a saddle of war,
to run against you, and you against him, ten courses
of spears, all of like measure, unless indeed either one
of you shall first have broke three lances or shall be
disabled of body. And he unto whom God shall
give the mastery shall win a diamond or ruby of an
hundred nobles' worth or upwards; provided always
that the adventurer have letters from his King or
prince royal, with seal appended, declaring that he is a
gentleman of birth and coat-armour, without reproach.
And that you may have proficient judges, and to the
intent also that men may the more willingly come
thither, my lord the King and the King of England
must each for his own party, assign one of his Kings-of-
arms (which are public officers) the one French and
the other English. And when your passage-at-arms
shall have been accomplished, if God hath preserved
your person from scathe, as I devoutly beseech him
to do, and if there shall be any other nobleman that of
his own accord shall challenge you to perform other
honourable combats either ahorse or afoot, then I
pray, dear Love, that you grant him his desire, with
the help of God, Our Lady, and my lord Saint Michael,
either before the King in Paris, or in whatsoever place
he will, that your good renown may flourish ever
more ". And with these words My Lady ended
speaking.

Those moſt high and noble words so pleased Saintré, that he ſtraightway kneeled and thanked her as humbly as he could or knew how to. And after their departing one from the other, he secretly besought the King, night and day, to grant him his leave ; and this he had at length with much difficulty. And the King assigned him, for his French judge, the King-of-arms of Anjou, Touraine and Maine. And all that day and night Saintré busied himself with seeking out good coursers, and arming him, and purveying twelve caparisons for the twelve days, rich, gay, and well-looking. And whiles he thus made him ready, he sent unto the Duke of Normandy, herald to the King of England, informing him of his passage-at-arms, and beseeching him that he should not refuse him a truce of two months, that is to wit: from the fifteenth day of April until the fifteenth day of June, for the counties of Boulogne and of Guines, French and English, and the marches of Calais ; that all men might come thither. The which things being by both parties gladly granted, the news was spread everywhere abroad, and many came thither.

Now when the fifteenth day of April was paſt and the truce begun, Saintré sent maſter carpenters of Paris, to build him two towers, both alike, out of beams and planks, the one for himself and the other for the English lords and their company, that should come to jouſt at his passage-at-arms. In the said towers were fair halls, chambers, wardrobes, couches, dressers, ſtools, benches, and settles, all well garnished ; and one and both of the towers fairly beseen within and well tapeſtried ; at half a bow-shot one from the other and all fenced about with ſtout palings ; and within the palings, ſtalls for three hundred horses. And at the further end of the liſts, at the place of encounter, he caused to be set up a fair ſtand, well tapeſtried, wherein were to be the two judges and the heralds.

Now when the time drew near for the jouſting, and Saintré had taken his leave of the King, the Queen, My Lady, and all the lords, he drew with a goodly company of three hundred horse unto Gravelines, where he lodged that night. Of the gifts, the exhortations, and the gentle speeches that My Lady made him I make no mention, to be brief. And when he beheld the two towers so fairly bedight, he was well content. Then was it noised abroad at Guines and at Calais how that Saintré was come, and through all the marches; and when the Earl of Buckingham, who was already at Calais in readiness to begin the jouſting, heard tell of Saintré's coming, he was passing glad. Anon he sent unto Saintré the Garter King-of-arms, that was ordained judge for their party, and with him four more heralds, to see him and offer him their service, and to give warranty, in their King's name, that all the twelve which came to jouſt in his passage-at-arms, were peers of the blood royal and other barons chosen and ordained by the King's will, for to hold the field againſt all comers. The said King-of-arms and heralds, Saintré made them right good cheer, and after dinner took them to see their lodging, praying them that they should be pleased graciously to accept the same.

And the King-of-arms, when he returned, told the Earl all the good things that he had there found, and Saintré's nobleness and high eſtate, and he told also of the lodging so fairly tapeſtried and garnished, save only for linen and bedding, which it behoved the Earl to send thither and to guard, with whatsoever else he thought to use. At that, all fell to praising Saintré, in such fashion that they could scarce have praised him more. And so they continued until the third day after, which was the firſt day of the month and the opening of the passage-at-arms.

The Beginning of the Jouſting

On Sunday, which was the firſt day of the month and the opening of the jouſting, there came thither the aforesaid Lord Earl of Buckingham,[55] in the morning after matins, with a passing great and goodly company; and upon the high gable of his lodging set up his banner, which bore the arms of England with a bordure argent; and his cry was: England! Saint George!

Now when the hour was come for beginning the passage-at-arms, their two judges, Champagne and Garter Kings-of-arms, attended by their heralds, went up into their ſtand, the better to judge; and then began the jouſting, which was hard and fierce and full honourable to both twain. But notwithſtanding that the aforesaid Earl was at the laſt running hurt some-what in his hand, yet he won the diamond, for having the better broken his lance.

The second day, there came the Earl Marshal, who likewise set up his banner upon the gable; and he bore the arms of England with three labels argent; and his cry was: England! Saint George!; who bore him full worshipfully, but Saintré firſt breaking his lance, won the diamond.

The third day, there came the Lord Cobham, in right fair eſtate, bearing *gules, a chevron or, and three lions sable upon the chevron;* and he cried: Saint George! Cobham! and set up his banner upon the gable. And at the seventh running, he and his courser were borne to earth, and thus he loſt the ruby.

The firſt day of the second week, there came in passing goodly eſtate the Lord Dengorde, and set up his banner like the rest, which was *ermine, a chevron gules and thereon three bezants*[56] *or ;* and his cry was : Saint George ! Dengorde ! and he won the diamond.

The second day of the second week, there came the Earl of Warwick, in passing fair estate ; who likewise set up his banner, which was *gules, a fess or between crosses crosslet of the same ;* and he cried: Saint George ! Warwick ! ; and lost the diamond.

The third day of the second week, there came in right fair array the Lord Clifford, who likewise set up his banner, which was *chequey or and azure, within a bordure ermine ;* and his cry was : Saint George ! Clifford ! ; and lost the diamond.

The first day of the third week came the Earl of Huntingdon, in passing fair estate, and likewise set up his banner, which was *azure, semé with crosses crosslet or ; a chief or ;* and his cry was : Saint George ! Huntingdon ! ; and he lost the ruby.

The second day of the third week came in passing fair estate the Earl of Arundel, who did likewise with his banner, which was *gules, a lion argent, langued and armed of the same ;* and his cry was : Saint George ! Arundel ! ; and he lost the ruby.

The third day of the third week there came, fairly arrayed, the Lord Beauchamp, who likewise set up his banner, which was *gules, a fess or ;* and he cried : Saint George ! Beauchamp ! ; and lost the diamond.

The first day of the last week there came in passing fair and high estate the Earl of Norfolk, who in like manner set up his banner, which was *party per pale, or and sinople,*[57] *a lion gules, armed argent, and over all a fess or ;* and he cried : Saint George ! Norfolk ! ; and won the diamond.

The second day of the last week there came in passing fair estate the Lord Bruce, who likewise set up his banner, which was *gules, a lion or, with forked*

PLATE VI

SAINTRÉ JOUSTING

tail; and his cry was: Saint George! A Bruce!; and he lost the ruby.

The third and last day of the jousting, there came in full high estate and splendour the Earl of Cambridge, who set up his banner passing rich with broidery, whereon were the arms of England with three labels copony[58] argent and gules; and he cried: England! Saint George!

Concerning this combat there was great disputation between the judges, for both lances were so well broke that they wist not which were the better. And they were at first agreed that each should depart without prize; but yet they resolved at the last that neither ought to lose his pains nor his due; and so they commanded that each should pay other; and the Earl to begin, for Saintré had first broke his lance.

So in this wise, Saintré lost three jewels and won eight, which maketh eleven, and the twelfth was both lost and won.

As for these jousts and the strokes that were there given, I pass them over, for it were too long a matter; save to say that all did right worshipfully, and some better than others, and God be thanked! with no death nor any great shedding of blood. And at their parting, such honour and reverence paid they one another that had they been brothers, they could have done no more. And there was not one among them but gave unto the other (beside the prizes won) gifts of rings, cloths of gold or of silk, chamber-hangings of tapestry, coursers, hackneys, gold plate, and many things more; so in this fashion they parted well pleased one from another. And Saintré bade them every one to supper, after the jousting; and at their departing, he gave unto Garter King-of-arms his best surcoat and horse-trappings, which were of crimson satin, trimmed with gold, with wide bordures of sable marten, and two hundred francs-à-cheval; and unto the other heralds he gave their tower aforesaid, where they had lodged, and their stand, and an hundred francs; unto the English trumpeters, clarions and minstrels, all together, two hundred francs. And unto Champagne King-of-arms, one of his judges, he gave his second surcoat and his horse's trappings, which were of passing rich crimson satin, figured with silver braid, and all trimmed with fine sable marten, and three hundred francs-à-cheval; and unto the other French heralds and pursuivants he gave his own tower, and two hundred francs; unto the trumpeters and minstrels of his company, which were a great many, he gave three hundred francs. And there was no knight, squire, herald, nor any other of his company but had a gown of livery (beside the other gifts that he gave especially unto certain knights and squires that had attended him) such as would have befitted one of the high princes of the blood royal. And thus, full well content one with another, they departed from him.

And when Saintré came again into the King's presence, God knoweth what honour and good cheer he made him, and the Queen also, and to be short every man and woman. Of My Lady, as I have before said, no need to write nor to speak, for all may conceive it, both by reason of the love she bore him, and the high honour that all men did him. And here will I leave speaking of the honours and the loves of My Lady and Saintré, and I shall tell what passed between them about the space of fifteen months after, when Saintré was assailed in another assault-at-arms.

FIVE-AND-FIFTIETH CHAPTER

How Sir Nicolas des Malleſteſtes,[59] *Knight, and Gallias de Mantua, Esquire, came to jouſt at the Court*

THE fifteenth month after Saintré's return, there arrived in Paris two young and valiant gentlemen of the Italies, that we call Lombards ; the one knight and the other esquire ; who came with a passing fair and large company, having lately jouſted before the Emperor with the Lord of Wallemberghe, who bore *ermine, an escutcheon gules,* and with the Lord of Eſtandebourg, who bore *argent, three torteaux*[60] *gules,* for the sake of the Emprise which the aforesaid Lombards bore. The Emperor, seeing how well and fiercely their combat on foot was fought, to the honour of both parties, commanded that they be made to cease. And in this manner their challenge, wherein it was written that one party or the other muſt be overcome, remained open, and upon the same terms as before.

Now when they were arrived in Paris, and lodged at the sign of the Bear, by the Baudet gate, one of the King's heralds fell acquainted with one of theirs, and learned who they were and wherefore they were come ; ſtraightway went he and told it to the King, in the Queen's presence and My Lady's. Then sent My Lady in haſte to seek Saintré, and charged the herald not to make known the tidings unto any other. And when Saintré came unto her, she told him all haſtily of the coming of those Lombards, how they were come in great eſtate for to jouſt ; and asked him whether his courage were ſtout enough to be one of the twain that should undertake that jouſting.

"Stout enough?" said he, "alas, Lady, what new thing have you seen in me, that my courage seemeth to you less stout than aforetime?"—"Up, then," quoth she, "make haste, lest some other be before you; and meseemeth it were well to seek out your brother Boucicault, right soon and before any other, to know whether he be willing to make the second." And when Saintré heard this right welcome news, he thanked My Lady full humbly and unfeignedly.

Then went he thence unto Boucicault and said unto him: "Brother, praise God and Our Lady, I bring you good tidings; there are but now arrived at the sign of the Bear, by the Baudet gate, two gentlemen of Lombardy, in passing fair array, that bear Emprises-at-arms and are come hither to be delivered of them. What say you? Shall we give them deliverance?"— "Deliverance?" quoth Boucicault, "Brother, you and your good tidings are right welcome; and I do pray and beseech you with all my heart, that we go with all speed unto the King and ask this boon, that we may be first." And this the King deigned to grant them, after much difficulty and long asking; but he commanded that they should first inform them who were these Lombards and what Emprises they bore. Then sent they Guyenne King-of-arms, a wise and proficient herald, to inform himself fully thereof. The which herald brought word that the one was a knight called Sir Nicolo des Mallestestes, a very noble and puissant baron of the marches of Ancona, and the other a Lombard squire, a most noble man, called Gallias de Mantua, each of them wearing above the elbow of his left arm a great bracelet all of gold set with precious stones; the which they were vowed to bear through the Courts of VI Christian Kings (for unto the Saracens they durst not trust themselves) unless they first found two other knights or esquires of gentle blood and coat-armour, without reproach, as they were, to combat againſt them on foot with pole-axes and small-swords only, until the one party or the other should be borne to earth or disarmed of their weapons.

Parenthesis

This Gallias de Mantua, methinketh he was that same Sir Gallias de Mantua, a knight of great worship, who afterward fought *a l'outrance* with Sir John le Meingre,[61] Marshal of France, in presence of the laſt Lord of Padua,[62] not long before the Venetians overcame him by durance of long siege and after caused him to be ſtrangled in prison : which was great pity, and he was much bemoaned throughout all the Italies, as the father and refuge of all wandering knights.

SIX-AND-FIFTIETH CHAPTER

How Saintré and Boucicault went to seek out the two champions to bid them come and speak with the King of France ; and how they jouſted with them

Now to return to my purpose, when Saintré and Boucicault heard this very glad and joyful news, they betook them with all speed unto the King, like hearts moſt amorous and chivalrous, and told him all their tidings ; and he confirmed them their much desired leave. The which tidings, and the Lombards' coming, and the King's consent, were right soon spread abroad throughout all the Court; wherefore no man sought any more to ask the boon for himself. Anon went the two companions, right nobly attended, under semblance of visiting the ſtrangers to bid them welcome, and out of their own mouths were plainly informed as to their Emprise, even as hath been told. And when the time came when the King desired to see them, Saintré and Boucicault went with a goodly company to seek them; and the King, the Queen and all the lords made them passing good cheer. What shall I say more? There, in the presence of all, did Saintré loose the Emprise of Sir Nicolas, and Boucicault that of Gallias; and the King appointed a day.

And when the day was come, and the King, the Queen, the lords, My Lady, and the reſt, were gone up into the galleries and they themselves entered into their pavilions (to be brief, I say naught of the honours and pomps of their coming), the King, who at the former combats had offered to make Saintré knight, this time also desired so to do; but he ever excused himself, saying that he would never be made knight except it were under the King's banner, or in battle againſt the Saracens.

And when they were in their pavilions and had taken the oaths and then the pavilions were removed out of the liſts, and the Marshal had said his say, they all four, who had been seated upon their ſtools face to face, rushed together like lions unchained; and then was the battle hard and fierce, and endured a long while in such fashion that none might tell which had the advantage. Now as they fought, Saintré againſt Sir Nicolo, by misadventure Saintré let fall his pole-axe; and no need to ask if My Lady and all his party were affrighted. But he like a squire full of craft and hardihood, without yielding any foot of

ground, drew straightway his small-sword, and therewith covered himself, holding it with both hands;
and every time that Sir Nicolo lifted up his axe,
Saintré approached nigher, until he was enabled to
disarm him of his sword, which he threw a great way
off. But at the last, Sir Nicolo by reason of the great
advantage that he had from his axe, advanced him,
and thrusting with the point of his axe lodged it in
one of the slots of Saintré's visor, causing him somewhat to stagger. Then perceiving that his point was
fast held, in his ardent desire to make him give ground
he thrust with all his heart and body, bearing upon
Saintré with the whole strength of his arms; but
Saintré stood firm and defended him in such manner
that with his right foot he yielded a pace and thrust
against the pole-axe with his sword (which he held
shortened with both his hands), so that his parrying
the stroke and his stepping backward were all in one.[63]
And with the great force of his thrusting, Sir Nicolo
fell to the ground on his hands and knees. At that
Saintré lifted up his foot, for to have dealt him a
buffet in the side and borne him altogether to the
ground; but for his honour's sake he forbare. Then
turned he to aid his companion, who had won already
more than a spear's length of ground from Gallias.
And as Saintré was going, Sir Nicolo arose, yet holding
his axe in one hand, and made for to run upon Saintré;
but the King bade them withhold him. Anon
Gallias, who fought now against both twain, was
borne to earth and yielded him. And thus was their
Emprise-at-arms brought to a conclusion, having been
right valiantly disputed by either party.

As for the honours, the gifts, and the good cheer
that were made them, as much as any of the others, or
more, to be brief I pass them over, save to say that
they everywhere spake praise thereof, marvelling at

213

such honours, such nobleness, such riches, and such men of worship, whereof was more abundance in that Court than any man could write or tell. So they took leave of the King, the Queen, the lords, and the ladies, and departed, Saintré, Boucicault and many others right worshipfully attending them. And now will I leave speaking of them, and I shall tell what other things befell at the Court.

SEVEN-AND-FIFTIETH CHAPTER

How Saintré jousted against the Baron of Tresto, and how they were adjudged to be equal

THE news of that jousting was in brief space noised everywhere abroad, and in especial at the Court of England ; whereby the codicil of Saintré's Passage-at-arms was called again to mind : and it came to pass that the Baron of Tresto, a young and forward knight, heard how the challenge was so worded that if, after the Passage-at-arms, any knight or esquire of gentle blood and coat-armour, without reproach, should of his own accord require Saintré to do any jousting, ahorse or afoot, then he would perform the same before the King of France his sovereign lord, or his deputy, provided that God had preserved his body from honourable scathe. This knight therefore resolved that verily he would summon him to fight with four weapons, man to man, *a l'outrance*, or until all four weapons should have been lost ; and so it was done. Now to be brief, the combat, before the King, the Queen, the Dukes, and My Lady, was passing hard and fierce ; and it befell, that as they fought Saintré let fall his pole-axe; which proved all to his advantage. For he took ſtraightway his great war-sword, which hung on a hook at his right side, and therewith fought and guarded him right valiantly. Now as they combated thus fiercely one againſt the other, Fortune willed that the Baron of Treſto encountered the spike of the pole-axe where it lay upon the ground, in such manner that it pierced through the sole of his shoe, in front of the foot, and anon as he drew back, seeking to be free of the pole-axe, Saintré pursued him full fiercely, until the King, for the honour of both, caſt down his arrow, and the combat was ſtayed. And he bade them issue forth side by side out of the liſts, on horseback; and after, he made this aforesaid Baron fair gifts and right good cheer. Then took he his leave and returned again into England.

And with this will I leave speaking of all these jouſts and others which he afterward did, for it were too long a matter; and I shall tell of other things that befell.

Now was Saintré in favour of the King, the Queen, the Princes, My Lady, and all others, and in brief, the moſt loved and honoured squire of France, by reason of his great gentleness, humility, and largesse also (which greatly aideth); for never, for good success in love nor for any honour that he received at the hands of the King or any other, was there any semblance of pride in him. And about this time the news came to him of his father's death; wherefore he was from this time on called the Seigneur de Saintré.

EIGHT-AND-FIFTIETH CHAPTER

How My Lady exhorted Saintré to go upon the Crusade into Prussia, against the Saracens ; and how he promised her to go thither ; and how the King made him Captain of five hundred lances

Now it befell that in that same year was held the Crusade into Prussia. Then said My Lady unto Saintré: " Mine only Desire and whole Thought, such is the strong and perfect love that I do bear you, hoping to make of you the best and most valiant in all the world, that verily it banisheth out of my heart the timorous fears which I have and must have on your account ; but 'tis for this once and then nevermore that I would have you adventure yourself. In the combats which you have fought, at the bidding of My Lord the King, or of others, you never have consented to be made knight, saying in excuse that you would never be made such, unless it were in battle against the Saracens, or under the King's banner. Now would I fain have you do him this pleasure, for you might have been knight long since ; and thus shall your high deeds of arms be requited you. And for one cause I take comfort, which is that no good deed was ever thrown away ; wherefore methinketh that truly it behoveth you to do as your forefathers did. And in order so to do, meseemeth that you could not with more sanctity or honour be made knight than in this most sacred Crusade into Prussia, in the holy war which is to be, against the Saracens.[64] It is my desire that you go thither in great estate, for the honour of My Lord the King, who shall give you subsidy therefor, and so shall I also ".

When Saintré heard My Lady's high and noble desire, he straightway kneeled and said unto her : " O my most noble and sovereign Goddess, that can and should more command me than all the rest of the world, and whom I will and ought most to obey : with hands joined I do thank you as well and as humbly as I can and may, for all your good will, your counsel and your commands, which with the help of God, Our Lady, and the True Holy Cross, I will obey and fulfil with a right good courage, trusting that by their holy grace you shall hear such news thereof as shall content you ". These words said, and what more I know not, he took leave of her. Then went he thence unto the King, and unto him day and night sued unceasingly, until he was given leave. The King, who loved him, as I have told you, better than any other, save only the Princes of his own blood, gave him largely of his bounty ; and besides was pleased so to honour him that (for the service of God and the Holy Christian Faith in this most sacred Crusade into Prussia which was shortly to be made against the Saracens) he made him Captain of five hundred lances,[65] all gentlemen, each lance having two men-at-arms, and of three thousand bowmen, without counting such lords as came at their own costs or with more people, which were more than two hundred lances, with bowmen ; and to attend his banner he commanded that there should go fifty out of each of the twelve provinces of his kingdom. The tidings whereof being everywhere reported, there came both from his realms and from without them lords and gentlemen beyond number, and proffered themselves ; unto whom the King, constrained thereto by much asking, granted this much, that they should be an hundred and sixty banners, whereof, as hath been said, he gave the captaincy unto Saintré.

And when Saintré, who might not refuse, had thanked the King right humbly, he called all his knights together in a place apart, and smiling said unto them : " Sirs, ye have seen how the King, notwithstanding all that I could say, hath been graciously pleased so to honour me, as to lay on me this great charge, which would better become one of the royal princes ; and hath made me like as the little chorister said—thus runneth the tale :—

" There was once a lord who went all trapped and spurred, with all his servants, to hear Mass in an abbey that was nigh his dwelling. And when Mass was said, there came five or six of the youngest choir-children and fell to unbuckling his spurs. Now when he beheld how his two feet were assailed by these folk, he asked : ' What may this be ? ' His servants, laughing, told him : ' The custom in great churches is to buy back spurs, which are set in the choir of the church '. Then he asked for a crown piece, and calling the youngest and most innocent of them all, he said unto him : ' Tell me which among you is the wisest '. Whereunto the child answered, without more thought : ' My lord, 'tis whichsoever the Lord Abbot willeth '. And that answer was taken much note of, as being a true saying. Now likewise may ye well say the same of me, for howsoever simple I be, yet am I the wisest of us all, sith the King so willeth."

At this droll tale all fell to laughing, and they said that the King well knew what he was about. So both in obedience to him and for love of Saintré, who well deserved it, they were all passing glad and well content. And herewith will I leave speaking of these matters, and I shall tell of the lords, barons and knights banneret[66] that came thither, whose blazons here follow :—[67]

And first, they of the Province of Ile-de-France :—
The Seigneur de Montmorency, who beareth *or,
on a cross gules five eaglets azure,*[68] and cryeth : " God
aideth first the Christian ! " The Seigneur de Trye,
who beareth *or, a bend azure,* and cryeth: "Boulogne!"
The Seigneur de Rony, *or, two bars gules,* and he
cryeth : " Rony ! " The Seigneur de Forest, *gules,
six martlets*[69] *argent.* The Seigneur de Vieux-pont,
argent, ten annulets gules. The Vidame of Chartres,
or, three bars sable, an orle[70] *of six martlets of the second ;*
and he cryeth : " Merlo ! " The Seigneur de Beau-
mont, *gyronny*[71] *of twelve, argent and gules.* The
Seigneur de Saint-Brisson, *azure, fleurdelysé*[72] *argent.*
Le Bouteillier, *quarterly or and gules,* and cryeth :
" Les Granges ! " The Seigneur de Marolles, *bendy*[73]
of six, argent and gules.

They of Beauvoisis,[74] *of the aforesaid Province of
Ile-de-France :—*

They of the Province of Champagne :—

They of the Province of Flanders :—

They that were of the Province of Acquitaine :—

. . . The Seigneur de Cadillac, *gules, a lion
argent, with an orle of bezants of the same.* The
Seigneur de Barbesan, *azure, a cross or,* and he cryeth :
" Sau[75] a Barbesan!" The Seigneur de Montmirail, who beareth *barry argent and sable, a lion gules,*
and cryeth : " Montmirail ! " The Seigneur de la

Tremouille, *or, three eagles azure, a chevron gules.*
The Seigneur de La Salle, *onduly*[76] *of eight, argent and
gules,* and he cryeth : "Mars ! " And many more
knights and esquires of French Guyenne.[77]

*They that were of the same Province, but holding
with the English faction, who in order to go upon this
most holy Crusade, were pleased to pass under the King's
banners, and to obey him :—*

*They of the marches of Anjou wherein are Touraine
and Maine :—*

*They of Touraine in the marches aforesaid, which
were there :—*

. . . The Seigneur de Montbason, bearing *gules,
a lion or,* and crying : "Montbason ! " The Seigneur
de Sainte More, bearing *argent, a fess gules,* and
crying : "Sainte More ! " The Seigneur de Mer-
mande, bearing *or, two bars sable,* and crying : "Mer-
mande ! " The aforesaid Seigneur de Saintré, bearing
gules, a bend or between three labels of the same, and
crying : "Saintré ! "
And many more knights and esquires of the said
Duchy of Touraine and Marches of Anjou.
*They that were of the County of Maine in the aforesaid
Province of Anjou :—*

They of the Marches of Ponthieu,[78] *which is called
"Poyers" :—*

Of the Marches of Vermandois[79] *there were there :—*

They of the Marches of Corbie[80] *that were there :—*

They of the Province of Normandy :—

They of the Marches of Berry, of the Bourbonnais, and of Auvergne, that were there :—

They of the Province of Brittany that were there :—

Of the Province of Artois were there :—
Messire Louis d'Artois, who bore Artois, that is to say *gules, a lion or armed azure,* and he cried : " Artois ! " The Count de Saint-Pol, who was there made knight,[81] *argent, a lion gules crowned and armed or, with tail forked and crossed.* The Seigneur de Fiennes, who bore *argent, a lion sable,* and cried : " Fiennes ! "
. . . .
. . . And many more knights and esquires of the said Province of Artois.

Of the Marches of Burgundy, the Duchy and the County, there were there :—
The Count of Burgundy, who to honour the King offered to serve under his banner, albeit he was not his subject[82] ; and he bore *azure, a lion or,* and cried : " Chatillon ! " The Count of Auxerre, who bore *gules, a bend or,* and cried : " Auxerre ! " . . .
And many more knights and esquires of the said Duchy and County of Burgundy.

*They of Barrois, which is in the Marches of Champagne,
and they of Lorraine that proffered themselves of their
free will to do honour to the King's banner and to be
present in this most holy Crusade :—*

They of Lorraine and Barrois both :—

*They of Dauphiny that offered themselves unto the
King and were there :—*

. . . And many more knights and esquires, for
to serve the King and to be in the said host ; which
were in all more than an hundred and sixty banners.
Now will I leave speaking of this right puissant nobility,
and of the lords, barons, and banners ; and I shall tell
of the very piteous and lamentable departure of
Saintré and of all the French knights, when they
departed from the King and from the Court.

NINE-AND-FIFTIETH CHAPTER

*How, when the time came for going forth into Prussia,
the King gave his banner into Saintré's charge, appointing
him his deputy. Then how the said Saintré and the
other lords took their leave of the King, of the Queen,
and of the ladies, who made great dole for their departing,
and My Lady in especial*

Now when the time came for setting forth, and
Saintré and all his company were made ready, they
sent forward their harness and all their baggage in

wains, and their bowmen, clad every man in a scarlet jacket with the white cross thereon. Then as for Saintré and all the nobility, which were clad also in like coats as their retainers, most fair to see : after their solemn Mass which the bishop sung at Our Lady's church in Paris, where they were all confessed, he gave them papal absolution from punishment and guilt ; and there in the King's presence his banner and all the others were blessed.

Thereafter they attended the King back again, and then went all to dinner. And at two of the clock, when all were together assembled, they came to take their leave. And all kneeling on their knees, the King said unto Saintré : "Saintré, I give you charge of this host and of my banner, which is in place of myself, and of these lords and other gentlemen here present, whom I commend unto you as I would mine own person". And then turning unto the other lords, he said : "Friends, ye are all noble and come of noble houses, whereof there have been valiant men enow, unto whom ye have by your own valiance oftentime likened yourselves. And now that ye go forth in the service of our true Lord, Jesus Christ, in which service ye may acquire true salvation for your souls and honour for evermore, I do commend into your keeping all our holy Faith, my banner, and your own honour. Men strive together, but God giveth the victory unto them that are his friends. Therefore if ye and the other Christian princes and lords are in God's good grace, there is no doubt but it will be well with you, no matter how great the might of the Saracens, which will be such that their number will be beyond all reckoning. And as for me, if it were not for the great business of state which I have, I do assure you that I would be of your company. And I say no more ; only one thing I pray you all, from the greatest unto

223

the least :—that ye be friends and brothers, without enviousness, strife, nor broils ; for thereby have armies been oft rent asunder and brought to great dishonour and abasement ".

Then took he his banner and gave it unto the Baron of Chastel-Frémont to bear ; and thereafter said unto them :—" Now, friends, as your King and father of you all, I desire to give you my benison ". Then made he the Sign of the Cross, saying : " In the name of God the Father, our Creator, in the name of God the Son, our Redeemer, and in the name of God the Holy Ghost, our Light in darkness, one true God in three names and in three Persons, go ye all forth, those to remain whom it shall please Him to take unto Himself, and the rest to return safe in soul and in honour ; and I adjure you every one, wheresoever ye be, to lose or win honourably, and if any doth otherwise I desire that he return not ". And with those words, weeping and scarce able to say : " Farewell, Friends ", he touched all their hands. Then might you hear on every side tender hearts sighing and see every eye weeping, so that there was neither man nor woman could utter any word.

Anon they went unto the Queen, who because of her tears had withdrawn apart, with her gentlewomen. And Saintré, as well as he was able, spake for them all, saying : " Our sovereign Lady, is there any thing it may please you to command us ? " The Queen turned her toward them and touched all their hands, saying no word.

They went afterward unto the three Dukes, the King's brothers, and said likewise. Then quoth My Lord of Anjou : " Saintré, and ye our fair cousins and good friends, ye have heard what our Lord the King hath said : go now joyfully and perform it, and it cannot but be well with you ".

Then came they unto My Lady. And of her let us not speak, for howsoever she strove, yet because of her natural affections and passing sore grief of heart, beholding Saintré she was like to have swooned, and had fallen down an she had not hastily recovered herself.

Then came they unto the other ladies and damosels, who made every one as great dole as though all their lovers lay there dead, saying one to another: " Alas, unhappy we! never more shall we see so great and joyous a company together ". And the officers of the Household, all weeping aloud and making moan for Saintré, said one unto another: " Alas! now goeth hence he that counselled us in our business, that comforted us in adversity and that succoured us in necessity; and we know not whether we shall ever see him more ". And they laid hold on him on every side, weeping and making prayers and vows, so that he might scarce prevail on them to let him go. And thereafter they went all to their rest for that day.

Now when the next day came, in the morning, the trumpets began to sound to saddle. Then went they all unto the minster, and when their Mass was said every man mounted upon his horse and they began their departure. There present were the three Lords Dukes of Anjou, of Berry, and of Burgundy, with all their following, who were pleased to bear them company, for to attend the King's banner out of Paris; and other knights, esquires and burgesses of the Town, so many that scarce one remained behind.

The Departing of the Banners

First there went the trumpets and clarions, a great many, two and two.

And after went the pursuivants on horseback, two and two, clad in their tabards with blazons of arms upon their sleeves both front and back.

After them went the heralds, two and two, clad in tabards with their lords' arms upon the front side thereof.

Next went the Kings-of-arms of the several Marches, two and two, clad in tabards with the King's arms upon the front side thereof.

Next went Monjoye, the French King-of-arms, clad in a tabard of the royal arms, all alone.

Next went the Seigneur de Chastel-Frémont, bearing the King's banner, between the Dukes of Anjou and Berry.

Next went the Lord Duke of Burgundy, on the right hand, and on the left hand Saintré.

After Saintré went the three first banners of the kingdom, the most anciently raised at the King's command, according to the ancientest books of the Monjoyes, Kings-of-arms of the French, that were wont aforetime to have cognizance of such matters by their Visitations[83] of the several Marches of the realm, in company with the other Kings-of-arms of the said Marches, to confirm in honourable rank them to whom it rightfully appertained, and to preserve lords and ladies from all enviousness and dissension. And after the three banners aforesaid there went the three lords unto whom they belonged; and in such fashion, three by three, they went all through Paris. The which array and departure was a right sumptuous thing, very fair to behold.

And all that day, by reason of their departing, there was not a man that laboured, nor any shop open, no more than on Easter Day; but as they went thus through the City, a many ladies and damosels, burgesses and their wives, and folk of every condition,

were upon scaffolds or at windows to see that noble
company pass by. Then might you see them every
one sighing, lamenting, and weeping, for dolour and
pity, so that there was neither man nor woman but
muſt cry out aloud, and with hands clasped : " Ah !
gentle squire Saintré, the God of Gods grant thee and
thy company to go forth and return with great
rejoicing and honour ", and therewith promising unto
God masses, pilgrimages, alms, and vows. And when
they were gone some way out of Paris, they prayed
the Lords Dukes to return, and there took they leave
of them and of the reſt.

And now will I leave speaking of their departure
and of the great lamentations that the King, the
Queen, the lords, ladies and damosels and every man
made for them, and above all else My Lady, who
thenceforth ceased not from making pilgrimages,
saying Masses, giving alms, and secretly weeping and
making dole ; and I shall tell of Saintré and of his
company, how they arrived moſt joyfully at the town
of Thorn[84] in Prussia.

Saintré with all his company of men-at-arms and
bowmen went on their way journeying until they
came into Prussia, unto the town of Thorn, where
the assemblage was to be. And there they found all
the prelates, princes, and lords that here follow,
whereof the moſt part came out to meet them, to do
honour to the King's banner ; and they were right
glad when they beheld so many lords, so many banners,
and so much people well armed that for five or six
thousand of good fighting men they could not have
been bettered.

In regard to the King of England, by reason of
affairs which he had undertaken, he would neither go
nor send any of his men, but after much entreaty
he gave leave unto the lords that here follow ;

First, the Earl of March, who bore *azure, three bars or ; in chief an escutcheon argent ;* and his cry was: "March!"

The Earl of Northampton, who bore *azure, on a bend argent three mullets*[85] *gules ;* and his cry was: "Northampton!"

The Earl of Suffolk, who bore *sable, a cross or ;* and his cry was: "Suffolk!"

The Lord Cobham, who bore *gules ; on a chevron or three lions sable ;* and his cry was: "Haston!"

The Lord Clifford, who bore *chequy, or and azure ; a bend ermine ;* and his cry was: "Clifford!"

The Lord De Lisle, who bore *or, two chevrons sable ;* and his cry was: "Lisle!"

The Lord De Moleyns, who bore *sable, on a chief argent three lozenges gules ;* and his cry was: "Moleyns!"

The Lord of Rokeby, who bore *argent, a chevron sable ;* and his cry was: "Rokeby!"

These eight lords came all in one company, with an hundred lances and three hundred archers.

And to sunder and weaken the great might and assembly of the Saracens, the four Christian Kings of Spain (that is to wit, the Kings of Castile, of Aragon, of Portugal, and of Navarre) had allied them together for to assail by sea and by land the Kings of Grenada, of Morocco, and of Bellemarine, the Saracens that were nighest to them ; yet for all that, the Saracens' host was so great that it was a marvellous thing to see, as hereafter shall appear.

The Prelates, Princes, and other Lords that were there :
First, the Duke of Brunswick, for the Emperor, who by reason of sickness was not able to come ; and he had charge of his banner, which was *or, an eagle*

with two heads sable, crowned or, membered sable, and of all the princes and lords ordained to go in his company, to wit :

The Duke of Austria, the Duke of Bavaria, the Duke of Brabant, the Duke of Stettin, the Duke of Limbourg, the Duke of Luxembourg,[86] . . . . and many more lords, knights, and esquires, all Hain-aulters.

They of the County of Alost that were there :—

The Ruyters of the Duchies of Limbourg, of Luxemburg, and of Blankenburg, that were there :—

The Almains of Bavaria that were there :—

The Flemish Ruyters of Brabant that were there :—

The Ruyters of Holland and of Zealand that were there :—

. . . all come in very goodly array for the service of God and at the Emperor's behest ; and they were thirty thousand horse, and bowmen twelve thousand, and other fighting men on foot, twenty thousand.

The Prelates of the Almains that were there :—
First the Archbishop of Cologne, with three thousand horse, three thousand foot, and two thousand bowmen.
The Archbishop of Trèves, with three thousand horse, two thousand bowmen, and three thousand

other fighting men on foot; the Bishop of Mayence, the Bishop of Passau, the Bishop of Liege, the Master of the Teutonic Knights and all the Brethren, four thousand horse, five thousand foot, and two thousand bowmen.

And there present were the Dispost of Roumelia, for his brother the Emperor of Constantinople, with his banner, attended by three thousand horse and three thousand foot; the Count of Silich, for the Emperor of Trebizond,[87] with his banner; the Duke of Lesto, for the Emperor of Bulgaria, with his banner; all these three came in one company.

And there was also the King of Bohemia, in person, who bore *gules, a lion argent, with tail knotted, forked, and crossed, crowned and armed or;* and in his train the Duke of Saxony, the Marquis of Brandenburg, the Count Palatine, ... and divers other knights and esquires to the number of ten thousand horse, eight thousand foot, and six thousand bowmen.

And there was present also the Duke of Latvia, for the King of Poland, bearing *gules, a horse argent, and thereon an armed man or, having in his hand a sword argent, crossed and hilted or;* and with him

. . . . and many more knights and esquires, to the number of eleven thousand horse, ten thousand foot and eight thousand bowmen.

And there was present also the Duke of Misgrave, with the King of Hungary's banner, which was *barry of eight pieces, gules and argent,* and a great company of dukes, princes, marquesses, counts, viscounts, barons, bannerets, knights bachelor, and other knights and esquires, of whom, to be brief, I make no mention; to the number of twelve thousand fighting men on horse and two and twenty thousand on foot.

And in the whole hoſt there were fivescore or sixscore thousand horse, whereof thirty or forty thousand were knights and esquires well arrayed; and bowmen and others an hundred and forty or an hundred and fifty thousand good fighting men.

SIXTIETH CHAPTER

How that the Saracens were a great many, Turks and infidels, more than men had seen since the days of Mahomet

ON the part of the Saracens, there was the mightieſt army that they had ever gathered, since the days of Mahomet; for there were present all the Soldans, Kings, and Princes of the three regions, that is to say, Asia Major, wherein are six provinces : India, Persia, Syria, Egypt, Assyria, and Asia.[88] The province of India is bounded by the sea which is toward the South, which some call the Black Sea, and others the Beaten Sea, because of the great turmoil that it is in both day and night, by reason of the seven thousand five hundred eight and forty isles that are therein; whereof one is passing great and hath ten cities; the chiefeſt is called Gelbona, and in that city is great foison of gold and of precious ſtones, and there do oliphants multiply more than in any other part of the world; the which isle was converted aforetime by Saint Thomas the Apoſtle, albeit the moſt part of that country are unbelievers.

And they of the second region of the Saracens, that were there, were of Persia, that is to say of Turkey, which hath sundry provinces, to wit : Africa, Media, Persia, Mesopotamia, where is the great city of Ninevah, which is three days' journey across, and

now men call it Babylon, and therein is the beginning
of the marvellous Tower of Babel, which is four
thousand yards broad ; and there are the provinces
of Chaldea, of Arabia, of Saba, and of Tarsus ; and
there is Mount Sinai, whither the angels bore the
body of my lady Saint Catharine, which now lieth
in the church of Saint Mary of Rubo, not far from
the aforesaid Mount.[89]

They of the third region that were there, were of
the region of Assyria, wherein are the provinces of
Damascus, of Antioch, and the land of Phœnicia,
where are Tyre and Sidon ; and there is Mount
Lebanon, whence the River Jordan springeth ; and
there are the cities of Palestine, of Judea, of Jerusalem,
of Samaria, of Gabes, of Galilee, and of Nazareth ;
and in that land were the two cities of Sodom and
Gomorrha, which were swallowed up because of
their abominable sin. And from these three regions
there were in that host so many kings, lords and people
that all the land was covered with them ; and the rest
they thought to conquer, as I have said. And of
these Saracenish lords I shall hereafter name a part.

Now when the day fore-ordained for the battle
was come, and all the Christian lords were in the field
and had heard their high and solemn Mass, which the
Archbishop of Cologne sung early in the morning,
and all being in a state of grace, as befitteth all good
Christians, and after the Cardinal of Ostia, the Pope's
legate, had given them absolution, and they had made
their peace one with another ; then they that listed
broke their fast. And then, all being horsed, and each
in his appointed company, Saintré went unto the
King of Bohemia, and drawing his sword besought of
him the order of knighthood,[90] in the name of God,
Our Lady, and Saint Denis. The good king, who

well loved King John and all the French, right gladly
gave him the accolade and order, praying God that
he would grant him all such honour and joy as he
desired; and from that time on he was everywhere
called Sir John of Saintré. Then came forth from
the rest every one that sought to be made knight:
that day was many a banner raised and the tail of
many a pennon cleft.⁹¹ And when all was done,
and they were returned back into their companies,
then making every one the Sign of the Cross, they
rode forth.

The Order of Battle

God and Our Lady willing, it was ordained that
the vanguard should be the banner of France, with
that of the Teutonic Order, which was *argent, a cross
sable*, those of the five prelates, and of certain German
dukes, counts, princes, and barons, and those of the
English; to the number of thirteen thousand horse,
whereof four thousand were chosen knights and
esquires. The King of Bohemia and his company,
which were ten thousand horse, were to make one of
the wings, upon the right side. The Duke of Latvia,
with the King of Poland's banner, whereof he had
charge, and his company, which were eleven thousand
horse, were to be the other wing, upon the left. The
banner of Our Lady, which Sir Godfrey de La Salle⁹²
bore (who had once before borne it) and the banners
of the four Emperors, to wit: of Germany, of Constantinople, of Trebizond and of Bulgaria, with those
also of the other dukes, princes, barons, bannerets
and other gentlemen, five-and-twenty or thirty
thousand good fighting men on horseback: these
were to make the main host; and the Duke of Misgrave, who had charge of the King of Hungary's

banner, and all his chivalry, twelve thousand horsemen, were to be the rear-guard.

And of the sixty thousand footmen there were to be made two battalions, half and half, one upon the left wing and the other upon the right, on a like alignment and somewhat in advance of the rest, upon the two flanks of the vanguard; and they were to follow a standard, no man going before the same; and they that were not bowmen were to bear each, for their defence, a great buckler all painted with a great white cross; and they were to stand still whensoever the standard halted, to shield the bowmen.

Now when all were thus set in order, and had broke their fast, and by their leaders and princes had been so heartily exhorted that never were men more confident, then rode they in that fair array, at a foot-pace, over the great plain of Bellehoch. And it was not long before they beheld their outriders returning, bringing with them right welcome tidings of the enemy. And when they were within a mile of them, they bade the footmen halt and sent horsemen to spy out the Saracens; who reported that they had but three battalions, following close after one another, with no wings; but upon the flanks there was much light-armed people.

The Saracens had made six companies, that is to wit, three ahorse and three afoot, and those afoot were to follow after, to smite and slay all that had been stricken down, and to hew at the Christians' legs and at their horses'.

The Order and Array of the Saracens' Host

Now in the first company Abzin chose to be, which was at that time the Grand Turk of Persia and bore on his banner *gules, with a great Turkish sword, in bend*,[93] *argent, hilted azure, crossed and pommelled or*;

and in the great pride of his might, which was thirty
or two-score thousand horse and upwards of an
hundred thousand foot, he held the Christians as
naught.

In the second company rode Zizaach, that called
himself Emperor of Carthage, and bore on his banner
sable, two horses' heads endorsed[94] *or* ; and Almoch,
Soldan of Babylon,[95] who bore a banner all *or* with no
other charges ; and Azahul, Soldan of Mabaloch,
attended by sixty thousand horsemen ; and after
them, an hundred and sixty thousand foot.

In the third company were the Kings of Greater
Armenia, of Fez, and of Aleppo, and Bagazul, Lord
of Wallachia ; who had two-score thousand horse and
three hundred or four hundred thousand footmen,
out of Armenia, Barbary, Russia, Samara,[96] and
Tartary ; so many that all the face of the land was
covered with them.

ONE-AND-SIXTIETH CHAPTER

*How in the battle with the Saracens Saintré first slew
the Grand Turk, and did so valiantly his devoir that
all his enemies gave way before him. And then how the
Emperor of Carthage and the two Soldans of Babylon
and Mabaloch the Turk were all slain, and divers others
on both parties*

Now when they had drawn nigh to one another,
within a bow-shot, the Turk stayed his host that he
might behold the ordering of the Christians, and that
all his men and their horses might take breath.

Here Beginneth the Battle

But perceiving that their vanguard stirred not, and
that the great shooting from the wings of bombards

and of culverins, of long-bows and of arbalests, did so much mischief to his people, he resolved to bestir him; and he caused his footmen, which were behind, to be divided into two parts, and bade each assail the companies of artillery. But they suffered such exceeding great scathe from those missiles that there was none among them durst come near. Then, as in desperation, the Turk advanced his banners, and as fast as horses might go, they rode with great shouts toward the vanguard.

At that, the French crying out aloud: "Jesus! Our Lady! Monjoye! Saint Denis!", the King's banner advanced and all the rest followed after as fast as their coursers might go, and they hurtled each against other. And it befell that the Seigneur de Saintré (all armed upon his right puissant courser, both he and his courser richly caparisoned with cloth of gold painted with his arms, and upon his basinet a passing fair plume, shewing high above all others), as God willed, smote the Grand Turk with his spear through the slot of his beaver and the whole spear-head entered in; and with the force of the thrust laid him dead upon the ground, and the butt of the spear in him. Then began the battle, passing hard and fierce, for there were as yet but few of the Saracens that wist of their lord's death. And you might see men and horses stumbling one upon other, and on every side was great outcry, marvellous to hear.

Now when Saintré beheld himself bereft of his spear, he straightway set hand to sword, and smote right and left, so fiercely that there was no Turk but yielded place before him. And when he sought to come nigh the banner, he was assailed upon every side, so that except he had been holpen by God and right soon succoured, he had most surely been slain. And the King's banner everywhere followed him, with the help of valiant Frenchmen and others, that it would be too long a matter to name ; moreover, if I should relate all the great prowess of some, that they did, and not of others, it would seem that I sought to glorify them only ; and therefore their posterity, an it please them, must hold me excused ; but as for Sir John of Saintré, of whom this history telleth, I must speak of him more fully.

When Saintré was thus delivered, he set spurs to his horse, and drew nigh to the Turk that bore their banner, and gave him with his sword such a buffet on the hand that the banner fell. The other Turks that in the mean while fought and awaited succour, defended themselves as valiantly as any. And whiles this passing fierce battle continued, the two Soldans drew near. But seeing the Grand Turk's banner borne to earth, they stood still to take counsel how they might best assail the Christians. And the other Turks, being no more able to sustain the assault of horsemen and footmen, brake asunder. Then sent the two Soldans and their people, as fast as horses might go, to hasten the third host to their aid. And they gathered together ; but at that same moment it fortuned that, to succour the vanguard, who were passing weary, the King of Bohemia and his company (that were one of the wings) came from the one hand, and the Duke of Latvia (that had the other wing, and bore the banner of Poland) from the other hand ; and so assailed them that they attained even to the banners, whereof one was borne down. And when the Saracens' company of footmen, that followed after, beheld their lord's banner borne to earth, there was none among them durst advance him further.

Now when their third host, led by the Kings of Greater Armenia, of Fez, of Morocco and of Aleppo, and the Lord of Wallachia, saw the other two wholly discomfited, and how as yet, on the part of the Christians, neither the main host nor the rearguard, nor the two wings of foot-folk had joined battle, they were all dismayed. Nathless, forasmuch as they were come thither to fight, and were so passing mighty both in horse and in foot, they resolved to join battle as soon as might be. And when the main host of the Christians perceived the Saracens' last host coming on, then the princes that had the governance thereof (and had as yet seen no enemy wherewith they might join battle) sent word to the rearguard to advance hastily, as soon as they should have joined battle, and to strike at the flank; and the two wings of footmen they bade come in upon either flank in such order as they were already in; for in that great plain there were neither woods nor valleys where any might lie in ambushments. These commandments were well fulfilled, and forthwith all made ready to join issue. Then ensued a most fierce and cruel battle, which might have done mischief enow. But the rear-guard, crying upon Our Lady and the King of Hungary, Saint Lancelot, came as fast as spurs might urge, and smote against the flank, with lances in rest; and the two wings of bowmen and artillery smote upon the great rabble of foot-soldiers, who as soon as they felt the missiles, brake asunder and fled. Then was the slaughter as great as though they had been sheep, and with no more resistance.

But the battle between the horsemen endured yet a long space, and would have endured longer (by reason of the great multitude that they were) if the rear-guard had not come up, whereby the enemy were the sooner discomfited. And with that were their banners put to confusion, borne down, and overthrown, and they by the grace of God put to flight. Then was the slaughter among them so great that

PLATE VII

[face p. 238

THE BATTLE WITH THE SARACENS

never was the like before nor after, since the battle of Thessalia wherein Pompey was discomfited. And there were slain the Emperor of Carthage, the two Soldans of Babylon and Mabaloch, the Grand Turk Bazul, Lord of Wallachia; the Kings of Morocco and of Aleppo taken; and so many more great lords taken or slain that, to be brief, I pass them over. And they pursued after them more than six leagues, when by cause of nightfall, the Christians were constrained to draw off, and to encamp by the marshes of Lascan, at the edge of the forest, and there to refresh both themselves and their steeds, which were passing weary and travailed, and to physick those men and horses that were hurt, until the morrow, when all went out very early to seek for their dead; for that night, because of the great pursuit that many made, they knew not whether to suppose them slain or no; and in the night, by fire-light, many returned from pursuing.

And when the morning came, all they that had not their full number went seeking about the field where the battle had been, and found many Saracens stricken but not yet dead, lying beneath their horses and stretching out their hands for to yield them; but all were put to the sword. And after, they drew forth all the dead Christians, all wearing crosses of divers colours, as each captain had bid his men; and likewise many wounded Christians that lived long after. Then were all borne to the camp, and thence into the towns, to be physicked; and the dead were buried with high honours and lamentation and solemn Divine Service. And the French knights were an ensample unto all the others, for they clad them every one in black, and for this shewing of the love they bore one another, they were by all men mightily praised.

TWO-AND-SIXTIETH CHAPTER

How the tidings sped everywhere, and especially in France, that Saintré had done marvels ; and among other things, in especial how he had slain the Grand Turk and brought down his banner ; whereat the King was passing glad and gave thanks unto God and the Saints with great solemnity

THE tidings of this moſt holy victory flew everywhere in like fashion as Perseus did by Pegasus the Flying Horse. And each man wrote thereof unto his own country, telling how things had fallen out ; and among the deeds of valiance that all had done, those of a certain young and new-made knight of France, called Sir John of Saintré, were everywhere reported and told : how at the firſt joining of battle he bore the Grand Turk dead to earth with his spear ; and then how by his prowess beyond compare he did such feats of arms that he won even unto the Saracens' banner, which he bore to earth ; and so many more marvellous deeds that it were too long a matter to rehearse them all.

And when this moſt blessed news was thus published abroad, then haſted all true Chriſtians, of whatsoever region, ſtraightway unto the churches, with great ringing of bells, for to give thanks unto Our Lord. And among the other Chriſtian princes, the King of France mounted ſtraightway upon horseback, and rode unto the great church to thank God and Our Lady, and afterward unto Saint Denis. Moreover it was not long before Anjou King-of-arms, who had been in the battle, came unto the King and out of his own mouth told how things had befallen, and the deeds of valiance beyond all computation done by the nobles of his kingdom, living and dead, especially the Seigneur de Saintré, as all their letters had declared.

And when the King had heard the truth of the matter, he said: " Ah, Fair Lord God, be Thou praised! And grant Thy mercy on them that have perished in Thy service! " And for the good tidings, he gave unto the said King-of-arms his gown and three hundred crowns.

Then was such rejoicing as you may suppose, throughout the Court and the city, save among ladies and damosels and others that had lost their friends.

And now will I leave speaking of these matters; and I shall turn again unto Sir John of Saintré.

THREE-AND-SIXTIETH CHAPTER

How Saintré and all the noble company of French Crusaders, after the discomfiture of the infidels, returned to Paris, where they were joyfully received by the King, the Queen and all the people

WHEN the Seigneur de Saintré and all that noble and chivalrous company were come unto Saint Denis, and had performed their devotions in the church before entering into Paris, there came out to meet them the three lord dukes aforementioned and so many more that scarce any remained behind. And they returned in the selfsame array wherein they had set forth, and came unto the great court of the Palace of Saint Pol, excepting only the banners of the slain and of the Lord of Chastel-Frémont and others that were left behind hurt; and in his stead the Lord of Maulevrier, by the choice of all, bore the King's banner. Then was great honour and good cheer made them by the Dukes, and by the others also. And when they came before the King and Queen and My Lady and their company, who were in the Great Hall, and had at entering made unto the King their first reverences, then the King, who was seated, rose up (to do them honour and because of his great gladness) and came toward them a step or two, and then in great joyfulness touched all their hands.

And while all were touching him, Saintré and his companions went to do their obeisance unto the Queen, unto My Lady, and unto all the ladies there present, who were much rejoiced at their coming, save a few whose lovers and kinsmen had not returned. Now when all had made their obeisance, and kissed and embraced the ladies and damosels, the King sat again upon his throne and said unto them :—

"Friends, Our Lord be praised, and his most blessed Mother, that ye return with such honour and gladness, and may They be pleased to have mercy upon the souls of them that have not returned, whom we must, according to our holy Faith, believe to have attained salvation. But to the end that Our Lord may deliver their souls out of the pains of Purgatory and give them rest in his glorious Kingdom of Heaven, therefore We will and command that we go all to Vespers at Our Lady's church, where We shall cause to be said Vespers and Matins for the dead, and tomorrow requiems, and afterward a solemn Mass which the Bishop shall sing, and at all the altars of the church shall be said requiem Masses, as many as there shall be priests for; and I pray you all to be there. And this service, We will and ordain that it continue thirty days; and moreover We shall found a perpetual Mass, every day, with every year an *obit*, on the same day that these true martyrs did end their days in the service of God." And this did he do.

And with that I shall leave speaking of these matters; and I shall tell how My Lady, being much desirous to have speech with Saintré, made him her signal, and how he answered with his.

After all these things were accomplished, that evening whiles the King, the Queen, and all the lords and ladies strove which might make the most festivity for those knights, and especially for the Seigneur de Saintré, My Lady, who made not so great display as the rest, nevertheless in the great joy of her heart could not refrain from drawing near unto him before them all, and saying : " Messire de Saintré, when these ladies shall have done greeting you, let us at least see you in our turn ! We have known the days when you were held to be a right courteous squire. Are you perchance changed or altered because of your deeds of valiance and because you are called ' Messire ' and are newly made knight ? " And so saying, she took her pin and made her signal therewith, whereto Saintré straightway answered, and smiling said unto her : " Lady, whatsoever there be in me, or whatsoever I am become since last you did see me, I am even such as I was aforetime ". Then, all being present, they fell to other talk until supper-time. And there were some who when the tables were cleared, spake of dancing ; which the King hearing, and the Queen, they said that for the sake of the fallen there should be neither singing nor dancing ; and that all might be at Mass in the morning, the King called for the spices and his Parting-Cup.

FOUR-AND-SIXTIETH CHAPTER

*How Saintré besought of the King that in honour of his
return he should lie with the Queen, which he promised;
and how the Queen was very merry thereat, asking him
wherefore he had made such request. And then afterward
how he went to speak with My Lady privily, at midnight,
and how she made him the fairest welcome in the world,
not without sundry kisses and embraces*

Now when the King was in his bedchamber, Saintré
smiling said unto him: "Sire, because of our safe
return, I pray you, lie this night with the Queen".
The King, that was a full gracious prince and well
loved him, smiling answered him: "You ever were
and ever will be courteous and serviceable to ladies;
and for love of you, I will". Then came Saintré
all smiling unto the Queen, and said unto her: "Now,
Madam, say me thanks!" And the Queen, seeing
him thus joyous, quoth unto him: "Why, Saintré,
wherefore shall I say you thanks?"—"Madam, say
it; and I will tell you after!"—"That will I not,"
answered the Queen, "for you would make mock of
me."—"Madam, 'tis for something whereof the
King, yourself, and I also, shall have joy. Will you
not trust me?"—"I will", quoth she, "sith the
matter is thus, I say you Gramercy!" Then said
Saintré unto her: "Madam, be of good cheer, for
I have hope that this night (an 'tis not already done)
there shall be a goodly son begotten on you; for the
King, in honour of our safe return, hath promised
me that he will lie with you". "Now truly", said
the Queen, "you are kind! 'Tis but two days since
I lay last with him. But I pray you tell me what it is

244

hath moved you to make my lord such a request."
"Madam," quoth he, "I will tell you ; you know
how when some lord or lady cometh where children
are at school, by custom, at their request, the scholars
are given an holiday ? "—" Ah," quoth she, " Saintré,
Saintré, that is not the true gate whereby you seek
to enter in ! I conjure you, in the name of arms and
of love, tell me the truth ! " Therewith she caught
him by the sleeve, saying : " Until I know the truth,
you shall not escape ! " Then Saintré laughing
called unto My Lady and said : " Madam, I pray you
help me, for here is the Queen would do me violence ! "
And he told her of the request made to the King, and
all that he had said unto the Queen. Then said My
Lady unto the Queen : " Come, Madam, let him go,
for he hath told you the truth ". " Nay, he hath
not ", said the Queen, " there is more than that in
the wind,⁹⁷ for my lord told me but yesterday that he
greatly desired his coming, that he might talk with
him ; and he hath played this trick that he may be
free to go elsewhere."

My Lady, fearing, as well she might, lest their
laughter and the signals between them might betray
her, said unto Saintré (in order well to conceal their
enterprise) : " Ah, Sir, Sir, would you do thus ? If
the Queen will hearken to my counsel, you shall tell
her the truth ere you escape hence ! " Then said
he unto them : " Now by your faith, Ladies, will you
let me free if I tell you ? "—" Ay, forsooth ", said
the Queen.—" And you, My Lady, do you promise
me, as well as the Queen ? " Then said he : " Madam,
for a month or six weeks we have been continually
on horseback ; and because the King would have
kept me all night answering his questions, and I
desired to sleep and to rest me, therefore, Madam, have
I thus escaped him."—" Ah ", said the Queen, " this

245

time I do believe you!" Then said My Lady, making her signal again: "Truly, Ma'am, 'tis well devised!"

Now when the much desirèd hour was come, when My Lady and her lover might have speech together at their leisure, what need I to tell you? Then were kisses given and given again (yet had they never enow) and such questions and answers as love doth make and propose. And in this most comfortable joy they abode until they needs must part. Nor might they again return thither, save when the King lay with the Queen, the which they brought to pass so oft as the King was willing. What shall I say more? They continued thus for fifteen months. And now will I leave speaking of their love, which was so loyal and secret that never in this world was any covenant more loyal nor better kept.

FIVE-AND-SIXTIETH CHAPTER

How Saintré resolved to bear a golden basinet-visor for the space of three years, and how the king granted him leave, notwithstanding that it was much against his will

It befell in the fifteenth month after he had returned out of Prussia, that a new thought came many times into Saintré's mind; and he said oft within himself: "Alas, poor that thou art in sense, in mind, and in all good qualities! Never hast thou undertaken any deed of arms save at the bidding of thy most sweet and noble goddess! Now verily, I do conclude and resolve that for love of her I will do some deed of mine own accord". Then resolved he to seek out five knights, whereof he himself should be one, and five esquires, of the stoutest

and best in arms that he might find in the Kingdom
of France; and these would he entreat to be companions and brothers all together, and to bear for the
space of three years a basinet-visor, of gold for the
knights and of silver for the esquires; whereon there
should be, between the two eye-slots, a rich diamond;
until they should find a like number of knights and
esquires to combat with them *a l'outrance*, each one
giving as gage the aforesaid diamonds, and their
adversaries like ones; and that no man should know
aught thereof until the last day of April, when he
would make known his purpose unto such knights and
esquires as he should choose.

And when he had made all these resolutions, he
sent to Florence a pattern of painted cloth, in the
form of a figured satin, all white, and thereon were
to be gold visors, very richly broidered, for their gowns
and horse-trappings; and there were to be likewise
pieces of fine damask all white, broidered with like
visors in silver, for the esquires' gowns and horse-
trappings. Moreover he let seek out privily white
horses, the fairest and most mettlesome that were to
be found; the which were taken to a secret place and
there kept. And he caused also to be made ten caps
of the fairest and newest fashion, all with like broidery
in the semblance of ostrich feathers, and charged with
precious metals, gold for the knights and silver for
the esquires.

And when the silken cloth was come and the ten
horses found, he caused the gowns to be cut upon
persons of like bigness to them that he had in mind;
and furthermore, from the same cloth, he let make ten
caparisons, passing fair, with great fringes of white
silk interspersed with gold and silver tassels; and all
these were made ready in secret.

Now when the last day of April came, he bade to

sup with him the Seigneur de Pressigny, the Seigneur
de Bueil, the Seigneur de Mailly, Sir Hugh de Craon,—
five knights with himself,—the Seigneur de Moy,
the Seigneur de Herly, the Seigneur des Barres, and
the Seigneur de Clermont, esquires; whom he made
right good cheer, in his hostel. And when the cloths
were taken away, without rising up from the table,
they all said grace unto God. Then called Saintré
the varlet that had charge of his bedchamber, and
bade bring him a certain little coffer; and sent all his
servants out from the Hall, to get their supper. Then
quoth he unto them, smiling: "Sirs and brethren,
if I be too presumptuous, may I be pardoned for those
things which I purpose to say unto you; but on mine
oath I desire to be the least among all that are here;
and that which I have in mind, and would impart unto
you, is all for the increasing of our honour, which all
noble hearts are bound to seek. Therefore have I
chosen you out of all this realm, that we may be
brothers and companions together, to do some deed
of arms for the love of our Ladies and for our honour's
sake. Well now, sirs and brethren, what say ye?"

At that they looked with great joyfulness one at
another, to know which among them should first
answer, to do him honour; saying: "Answer!"
and "Nay, 'tis for you to answer!" Anon the
Seigneur de Genly first spake, and said: "Messire
de Saintré, let each say what he will, but so noble a
challenge, meseemeth, ought not long to tarry for
an answer. As for me, with God's help and Our
Lady's, for my part I do assent thereto, and I thank
you that you have chosen me to be of the number of
such a company". Nor was there one but proffered
himself as eagerly as might be, albeit there were some
among them that, blood for blood, deemed themselves
at the least Saintré's peers; but such was his valiance,

248

as you have heard, such his largesse, his gentleness,
his courtesy, passing all bounds and limits, that there
was not one there but would have put his body in
jeopardy for him; and all the more, because the King
loved him above all others, wherefore it was every
man's delight to do him pleasure. Anon he thanked
them all in the best fashion that he could, and opening
his coffer gave unto each his visor, with the diamonds;
all alike, saving that five were of gold, for the knights,
and the other five of silver, for the esquires; and said
then unto them: "Now, sirs and brethren, in the
name of God the Father, the Son, and the Holy
Spirit, likewise of the Blessed Virgin his daughter and
his mother, I give these unto you. And ye shall take
them upon this condition: that each among you shall
bear one upon his left shoulder for the space of three
years, unless before that term we do find a like number
of knights and esquires of gentle blood and coat-
armour, without reproach, to combat against us and
we against them, with spear, pole-axe, small-sword,
and dagger, until either party shall have lost four
weapons or have been borne to earth. And that
party which God shall suffer to be vanquished, if it
be ours each one of us shall be quit by rendering up
the diamond in his visor; and if it be theirs, they
shall be quit by giving each one a diamond like unto
ours. Now as for pursuing our enterprise, and as for
sending challenges unto the Court of the King of
the Romans and then unto England, and wheresoever
else shall seem good to us; that may ye commit
unto me. Moreover I will make request unto the
King that he help us bear our costs". (At that,
each thanked him yet more heartily.) "And that
we may the better acquit us and do our devoirs, I
counsel that each go hence unto his Lady, and beseech
her that she be pleased, with her own hand, to set

his visor upon his left shoulder, for the first time, without otherwise making it fast until the morning, when we shall put them on, all of us together. And for to make our enterprise more novel, I pray you be here in the morning at four of the clock, and we will go and awaken the King and Queen, who are to lie together this night; and if it be their pleasure, we will take them a-Maying."

And they were all so well content that they might scarce have been better. Only the Seigneur de Moy said: "Good lack! What shall any among us do, that hath not his Lady's leave?" Then quoth Saintré unto him: "Ha, my brother de Moy, he shall have all the more cause to ask boldly for her grace and favour, for unless she be crueller than all others, she shall never refuse it him for so worthy an enterprise".

Then took they leave one of another, and went every one whither they had been told. And with that will I leave speaking of these lords and their ladies, and I shall tell how it fared between the Seigneur de Saintré and My Lady.

SIX-AND-SIXTIETH CHAPTER

How Saintré went unto the Pleasance to have speech with My Lady, and told her of his Emprise, whereat she was sore grieved and vexed; howbeit Saintré so importuned her that at his request she set him his Emprise upon his shoulder

THAT night, which was the eve of the first day of May, in the evening, after the King had taken the spices and the Parting-Cup, Saintré drew nigh unto the

Queen, and then called My Lady and said smiling unto
the Queen : " What will you give me, Madam, if I
bring it to pass that you lie this night with the King ? "
—" Nay, Sir," answered the Queen, laughing, " I
shall be in no wise beholden to you ". And laughing
at these her words, he made My Lady their signal.
My Lady, well underſtanding his meaning, that it was
to inform her of the King's lying with the Queen, was
neither deaf nor dumb, and ſtraightway answered him
by her signal.

And when the King was in his bed, the Seigneur de
Saintré was there for the cuſtom that was observed of
old by princes and princesses, lords and ladies of
condition, that their chamberlains should give Holy
Water unto the lords and their gentlewomen unto the
great ladies, when they were in their beds, which
cuſtom at this present time many do think shame and
an ill thing to do, so well assured do they deem themselves againſt the Devil. And when he had given the
Holy Water and drawn the curtains and given them
Good-night, he went thence unto his own chamber,
where he abode until the much-desirèd hour came,
when My Lady and he might be together. Then to
kissing and kissing again, and playing and sporting
at such plays and disports as the god of love bade
them.

And when they had been a long time at such play,
Saintré fell upon his knees and said unto My Lady :
" O my moſt high and peerless Goddess, as humbly
as may be I do crave of you grace, mercy, forgiveness
and misericord ! "—" Now wherefore, Dear Love ? "
said My Lady.—" Lady," said he, " in the time that
I have been your moſt humble bondman and loyal
servitor, there had never been so much worth in me
an I had not, for love of you, undertaken sundry deeds
of arms. But all those deeds that I have done or

wherein I have shared have been at your bidding, by your counsel and by your suggestion. And forasmuch as I do perceive how greatly I have failed and fallen short, and yet, 'tis better late than never, therefore, Lady, I do most humbly pray and beseech you that it may please you with your own hand to set upon my left shoulder this Emprise which for your sake I with nine others have resolved and undertaken to wear; and all my companions have done the like, with their Ladies' good will; which are such and such and such . . . and he named all their names. And thus saying, he drew from his sleeve his Emprise, all wrapped in a dainty kerchief, and giving it to her sought to kiss her. But My Lady, when she had heard his words, was exceeding vexed, and would not have him come nigh her; and anon said unto him: "What, have you taken upon you Emprises and journeys, hither and thither, without my knowledge or my leave? Never, so long as I live, will I love you any more!" Who was astonied at those words? Certes, 'twas Saintré, for he wist not whether 'twas in disport or in anger she spake. And he looked long upon her; and when he saw that she relented not, anon he said unto her: "Alas, Lady, this is grievous news, that I must be punished for well-doing, I that so long and so faithfully have served you and given heart, body, honour and life, to obey you. And now when I thought to do my devoir in your service, to the increase of your favour and mine own honour, must I lose her to whom I am so bound? Ah! my most honoured peerless Lady, have mercy upon your servant, and may it please you to forgive me this once; and if ever I fall again into such error, may I be well punished".

Then said My Lady unto him: "Go quickly unto your companions and revoke this enterprise".

" Alas, Lady, how may this be ? It is already so far advanced that for my life or death I could not! Bethink you that, an it were possible, you are she whom above all others I muſt obey. And therefore, Lady, here upon my knees and with hands clasped I do moſt humbly entreat of you that you forgive me cheerfully and with a good will, and set my Emprise here. And have no fear for the reſt, for I truſt in God and Our Lady that they shall grant us good success."

At that My Lady took that Emprise full sorrowfully, and set it upon his left shoulder ; and then, half yea half nay, suffered him to kiss her. And thereafter, for the lateness of the hour, he took leave of her very humbly, and departed thence. And here will I leave speaking of My Lady ; and I shall tell of the coming of Saintré's nine companions.

SEVEN-AND-SIXTIETH CHAPTER

How the nine companions came in the morning

ON the morrow, which was the firſt day of May, when the nine companions came very early unto the Seigneur de Saintré's hoſtel, to be short, after they had there heard Matins, the Seigneur de Saintré made them all to enter into his bedchamber. Then gave he unto each one a gown of silken cloth, with the visors of gold and silver broidered thereon, as you have heard ; and afterward sent fetch thither the ten caps, fair and gay as they were ; and then unto each a belt of gold or of silver, to gird round their gowns ; whereat all were amazed. Then asked he for the visors, and with his own hands bound them for that occasion upon their left shoulders, and smiling asked each one whether he were well content with his Lady. Alas ! naught said he of his own, nor of the sore grief which his heavy heart must bear!

And when they were all ready to issue forth out of the house, there were the ten fair frisking coursers, all white, which he had secretly caused to be bought, caparisoned every one with the same cloth whereof their gowns were made, and at the end of the flaps, in the middle, and at the cross-seams, the caparisons were adorned with silver visors, gilded for the knights and plain for the esquires. And then he bade give him three dice, and said: "Each to his fortune! He that shall throw the most points shall have first choice at sight!" At that they thanked him, each one more than the last, saying one to another: "Never was such as he!" And at their mounting, each was furnished with new spurs, all alike, gilded for the knights and silvered for the esquires; the straps whereof were all of silk, like as men used to wear in the good times. And as they came forth from the hostel, you might have seen horses leaping and prancing, running hither and thither and turning in the air, and sparks of fire flying through the air, with crying and shouting and all men running thither; never was there greater joy at anything. And they went thus upon their way until they came unto the great court of Saint Pol. Then made they merrier than ever, for they well knew that the King was already awake.

Now when the King heard the noise, he bade the damosels that slept in the bedchamber to arise and see what it might be. Then ran they to the lattice and cried out straightway unto the King: "Ah, Sire, Sire! come and behold this great marvel; never was seen so fair a thing!" The Queen, who was not asleep, being desirous to see what it was, said unto the King: "Come, my lord, let us see what this is!" Therewith the damosels returned, so filled with joy

254

that they could scarce speak. Then asked the King
and Queen for their raiment and gowns, for to arise;
and the King, with his night-cap yet on his head,
went unto the great window, and the Queen unto
the lattice. And when the ten companions, who rode
back and forth, shouting and singing, perceived the
King, they hasted all towards him, and perceiving then
the Queen near him, they cried out aloud: "Sire,
Sire! and you also, Madam! Give you a right good
morrow and a merry May!" And the King answering
said unto them: "Good day, friends, good day!"
Then the King and the Queen withdrew, to get them
dressed; and the ten companions lighted down off
their horses and came into the King's chamber;
whom they found with his gentlemen of the bedchamber all about him, arraying him. Then all
kneeling, the Seigneur de Saintré began to speak, and
said :—

"Sovereign prince; these my lords and brethren
here present, and I in their company, have all vowed
this day that with your good leave, will, and license,
we will wear upon our left shoulders this Emprise-of-
arms which you here do see; and that for the space
of three years; and as for the rest, you may see it in
full in this letter of challenge; and most humbly do
we entreat you that you may graciously please to
grant us leave to pursue it."

Now when the King heard this news, and saw their
Emprises already upon their shoulders, he was but ill
pleased, and said unto them: "My friends, you do as
a man doth who first taketh his cousin to wife and
afterward asketh for dispensation! 'Tis ill done of
any man to undertake a thing, and worse to perform
it, without leave of his lord or of him that hath
authority over him. And strictly considering, whatsoever good might come of it, he ought to be well

punished ". Thus saying, he took their letter of challenge; and said then unto them: " I shall see what is here written! And as for you, Saintré, will your heart and you never cease from undertaking jousts and voyages? Meseemeth 'tis enough ".— " Ah, Sire ! " said Saintré, " 'tis not my heart nor I, but Honour, wherein you do share, that moveth us all to this enterprise."

By this, the King was ready, and went forth to Mass. Right so came the Lords Dukes his brothers, and saw the ten companions thus arrayed, and their new Emprises; who, having made their obeisance, commended their cause unto them. Whereto they answered: " In the matter of your Emprises, My Lord the King saith truth, even although ye have sought his good leave and license; if ye had done otherwise, 'twere a simple matter ! We go now unto him, and we will ask his favour for you ".

After the King and the Dukes, the Queen was not long in coming, and greeted them very joyfully; and after, there came My Lady, who made them but sorry cheer. Then went they all unto the service of High Mass, where you might see ladies, damosels, knights and esquires look with wonder upon the ten companions.

And when the King was in his chamber again, he called the three Dukes, his brothers, and shewed them the letter of challenge, and then asked counsel of them. And to be short, the conclusion was that for this once the King should give them leave, but under pain of for ever forfeiting his favour and receiving such punishment as he might decree, if they, or any others of his kingdom or subjects, should ever again undertake any enterprise without his leave.

Then came they all most humbly to thank him. And when the Feasts were past, they employed themselves every one incessantly, night and day, in putting them in good array; and they let make for them gowns for every day of the week, all of like ſtuff; and for all their retainers a like livery; and harness for their horses, moſt fair to behold. What shall I say more? The tidings thereof were noised through all the realm. And whiles they made ready their array, the Seigneur de Saintré and his companions did indite a right fair letter-of-arms, sealed with their seals and subscribed with their hands, addressed to the Emperor's Court, as the chiefeſt of all; and they forthwith sent it thither by the Duke-of-arms of Normandy. And now for a space will I leave speaking of these things, and I shall turn to what followed.

EIGHT-AND-SIXTIETH CHAPTER

How the King spake unto Saintré; and of the gifts which he made him and his companions

Whiles they prepared their habiliments, as you have heard, the King, who well loved Saintré, said unto him: " Saintré, who hath persuaded you to take upon you this Emprise without my leave? Hath Fortune sealed you her promise that because she hath so long been for you, she cannot forsake you? Fear you not, moreover, the wrath of Our Lord, who forbiddeth us such vanities? And if He hath so oft given you advancement thereby, you are so much the more beholden to Him, and ought to take heed not to offend Him more, if you are a good Chriſtian! Yet sith this thing hath so been made public that there is no turning back, for this once I am willing; but I forbid you ever again to do it ".—" Ah, Sire," said he,

" may I be forgiven ! "—" Well," said the King, " I
do forgive you right heartily. Where purpose you
to perform your joufts ? "—" Sire, we purpose to
publish them in the Emperor's Court ; and if we find
naught there, we shall make them known in the Court
of the King of England, hoping that in one of these
two we shall not fail of what we seek."

" That is well ", said the King. " What array have
you ? What number of people ? Intend you to
have one purse in common, or what ? " And when
the King had heard his answers to every queftion, he
said unto him : " I will give you four thousand
crowns, and unto each of the nine a thousand and
five hundred ". And the Queen gave unto him a
thousand and five hundred, with a piece of velvet
Cramoisy, dyed purple, and an hundred marks' weight
of silver plate ; and unto each of the others six hundred
crowns ; unto the Knights, each a piece of grey
velvet, and unto the esquires, a piece of damask, grey
likewise. And My Lords the Dukes gave him, every
one of them, a thousand and five hundred crowns,
and XL marks worth of plate ; and unto the others
six hundred crowns apiece.

Now it was not long before their setting forth.
And to be brief, when the day was come, they went
all together to take leave of the King, the Queen, the
Dukes, and the ladies ; but as for the fair speeches
that they made unto them and thanks for their gifts,
I pass them over, that I may come to the secret
lamentations, tears, and moft anxious sighs which My
Lady's heavy heart did make because of her lover's
departing, which was more than ever displeasing to
her ; yet could he not choose but go. And now will
I leave speaking of their farewells, and of their journey
whereon they fare ; and I shall tell of what grief My
Lady had, and of another new matter.

Of My Lady's Great Affliction, and what Resolve she took

My Lady bereft thus of her lover, found naught wherein her heart could take any pleasure ; tourneys nor jousts, dancing nor hunting nor any other pastimes ; and when she beheld lovers communing together side by side, her griefs were renewed again ; until she was so fallen into this melancholic way of life, that she had changed eating and drinking for fasting, and sleeping for waking, so that little by little her fair rosy countenance was turned to a pale sickly hue, whereat all marvelled.

The Queen beholding her thus mournful, pale, and pensive, many times asked of her what ailed her. "Madam," answered she, "'tis naught ; you know how we women are ill when we please." "That is sooth," said the Queen, "and oftentime, more than we please ; but in good earnest, Fair Cousin, tell Us what aileth you and where is the seat of this malady ; and if We are able to aid you, perdy, Fair Cousin, you may be assured that We shall thereto right willingly apply Ourselves." "Ah, my most gentle Lady, I do thank you as humbly as may be." And with that their converse ended. But the Queen, who loved her well, failed not to send unto her her physician, Master Hugh de Fisol, a passing good and sufficient physician and philosopher, who at the Queen's behest enquired into her malady so far as she would reveal it ; and he bade her keep her bed, saying he would come and see her in the morning ; and she did so. In the morning, after Master Hugh had well examined all her condition, he found her body sound and free of head-ache, of fevers of the reins, of gout, and of all other diseases ; save that in her heart she had such a pain hidden, that if it were not speedily amended she was dead beyond hope of remedy ; for by the oppression of this pain, all the natural spirits dependent upon her heart were perishing within her, and the most of them were already stifled. Nathless, he gave her such relief as he was able, and said then unto her : " Madam, as for your body, I find it very well disposed ; but your heart is not, for it hath within it some great secret dolour, which if it be not healed and that speedily, you will fall into some grievous decline, most hard to cure ; wherefore, Madam, cast from you this dolour, and I will answer for the rest ".

How My Lady answered Master Hugh, and how he Comforted her

When My Lady heard Master Hugh speak thus nearly of her disease, she said unto him : " Woe is me, Master Hugh, I have no pain in mine heart save one, wherein you can indeed help me, but only with words ; and on mine oath, if you were pleased so to do, I should be evermore beholden to you ; and moreover I would give you a good cloak of the finest Scarlet that is to be found ".

When Master Hugh heard speak of the Scarlet cloak, he said very cheerfully : " Madam, command : for there is naught in my power I would not do for you ". " Now truly, Master Hugh," said My Lady, " I thank you ; physicians are confessors, and that which I purpose to tell you is in no wise to your dishonour or damage ; but I pray you keep it to yourself."—" Madam, speak boldly, for there shall never word be said by me."—" Well, Master Hugh, I must tell you that this affliction of mine heart cometh solely from the longing that I have to go, for two months or three, to see mine estate, which hath great need thereof, for 'tis more than sixteen years past since I was there, and mine affairs are none the better therefor; but if the Queen knew that this came from me, I am sure she would not give her assent."—"Ho! Madam," quoth Master Hugh, " I will be answerable for that; and be of good cheer, for you shall go; and I wot well the way to bring it about; but you must keep your room for three days or four, and leave the rest unto me."

Then went Master Hugh unto the Queen, and said: " Madam, I have just now seen My Lady your cousin ". —"Alack," said the Queen, "why, how doth she, Master Hugh?"—"Madam," answered he, " truth to tell, but poorly; and I see but one remedy." " Good lack! What say you?"—" 'Tis so."—"And what remedy?" "Perdy, Ma'am, that she should go refresh her in her native air for the space of two or three months."—"Marry! an she were there, might she be cured?"—"Madam," said Master Hugh, " please God, ay; and I go now to look to her victuals and to prepare certain comforting electuaries."

The Queen went straightway to see My Lady, whom she found couched in her bed. And she comforted her as best she might, saying in especial that she should be soon healed an she were in her native air; and in God's name to be of good cheer and make haste to go thither. My Lady had need of no other physic to drive from her the affliction that her heart felt when she saw other lovers dancing, singing, and sporting one with another, whiles she might not so do until her true Love's return; and she took comfort at thought of departing. And to be short, as soon as she was able, she took leave of the King, the Queen, and the Dukes, and bade farewell unto all, and departed thence. But at her leave-taking, the Queen gave her leave for two months only, making her promise to return again if indeed she should be then in good health. And so took she her leave, and departed.

NINE-AND-SIXTIETH CHAPTER

*How My Lady came unto her Manor, and how she was
made welcome*

Now the name of that province, and of the estate,
and of her manor whither she went, we may not here
make mention thereof, for the history telleth them
not, and for certain causes and things which shall
hereafter follow, I desire to say naught thereof;
but I shall suppose that her principal manor was a
league distant from a fair city, and at another league
from her manor was an abbey which My Lady's
ancestors had founded aforetime; and from that
abbey unto the aforesaid city there was no more than
another league; so in this wise My Lady's manor,
the abbey, and that city were like to the feet of a
trivet.

*Of My Lady's Homecoming and what Cheer the Folk
of that Country made her*

Now when the news was spread abroad through
those parts, how that My Lady was returned unto her
manor, there came thither lords and ladies, damosels
and esquires, citizens and their wives, for to see her;
and by their coming, little by little, her grievous
melancholy began to abate. And here for a space
will I leave speaking of My Lady's sojourn; and I
shall tell of the Abbey and of the Lord Abbot.

Here it Telleth of the Lord Abbot and of his Abbey

As I have said, this Abbey (which shall be nameless)
was by My Lady's forefathers founded; and they did
every one of them so much for it, that it is even at

this present day one of the ten goodliest in France. The Lord Abbot of that time was son to a rich burgess of the city, who by gifts and petitions unto lords, and besides by friends at the Court of Rome, contrived that his son was made Abbot; who was of the age of five-and-twenty years, stout of body, strong and lusty; at wrestling, leaping, tossing the bar or the weight, or playing at tennis, in his leisure time, there was neither monk, knight, squire, nor townsman that could match him. What more shall I tell you? Lest he be thought idle, he employed his time in all manner of gaiety; and for the rest, he was free and bounteous of all his goods, wherefore he was well loved and esteemed of all good fellows.[98]

When the Lord Abbot was told of My Lady's coming, he was passing glad; and he let charge one of his wains with great quarters of bucks, with boars' heads and sides, with hares, conies, pheasants, part-ridges, fat capons, poultry and pigeons, and an hogshead of the best Beaune that he could find; and sent them as a present unto My Lady, craving that she would please to accept it. When My Lady beheld this fair present, no need to ask if she were joyful; and she bade give good entertainment unto him that came with it, and to thank My Lord Abbot.

At that time it was near the beginning of Lent, and because there were at the Abbey special pardons on Mondays, on Wednesdays, and on Fridays in Lent, My Lady taken with great devoutness, resolved to go thither, but to wait until the great press of people was past, and the first XV days. Then sent she word unto the Lord Abbot that she should be at Mass on the morrow, to acquire those pardons. The Lord Abbot, who had never yet beheld her, was full joyful. He bade garnish the altar whereon the relics were and the oratory, and the chapel wherein her ancestors lay

263

buried; he sent also to the town for lampreys and salmon and other of the best sea-fish and fresh-water fish that might there be found; and bade fill the stable-racks and mangers up to the brim with oats and hay and clean straw, against My Lady's coming. Then were made ready wines and meats of divers sorts, and fires in the chambers and halls to warm My Lady and her people, for the cold was not yet alto-gether past.

And when My Lady arrived and had lighted down at the Monastery gate, there were the sacrist and three of the principal monks, who in the Lord Abbot's name, upon their knees, offered unto her the Abbey, its possessions, and all the brethren; whom My Lady thanked right heartily, and passed on. And when she had made her oblation at the High Altar, she was led unto her chapel to hear Mass. Then her Hours being concluded and ended, there came the Lord Abbot, attended by the prior and all the brethren; who kneeling said unto her: "Our most honoured Lady, you are right welcome in this your House; most glad and joyful are we that God hath given us grace to see you here; and unto you, as our patroness and foundress, we do offer this Abbey, with our bodies and our goods".

Then said My Lady unto him: "Abbot, we thank you right heartily; moreover, if there be aught that we can do, or for you or for any of the brethren, we shall most gladly accomplish it".

Anon My Lady asked to see the relics. The Lord Abbot rose up (for he was yet upon his knees), and took the heads, arms, and other bones of Saints' bodies, that lay there in great plenty, saying: "Madam here lieth the most valiant prince our first Founder, who from the first conquests of the Holy Land did bring back this head, this hand, and these bones of

my lords Saint So-and-so, and Such-and-such ; and
my lord his brother gave us this finger, these jaw-bones,
and these arms of my lords Saint Such-and-such, and
my lady Saint So-and-so.   Thus, to be brief, have all
your noble forefathers given these great many relics
and builded this church and a great part of the rest
that you see ; and the rest have mine own predecessors
done and the lords and ladies of these parts that here
lie buried ".

When My Lady had kissed the relics, and given a
cope and two tunicles, with a cloth for the High Altar,
all of fine velvet plush, crimson and richly broidered
with gold, she bethought her to return thence.   And
whiles the carriage-horses and others were fed hastily,
that they might be harnessed, the Lord Abbot brought
My Lady into his own chamber, to warm her at the
fire.   The chamber was excellently well hung, tapestried, carpeted and glazed.   Then said he unto them
all, like a good fellow and a jovial :—" Go we forth,
and let us leave My Lady to warm her and take her
ease a little ".   And thus they did.

Now when My Lady and the gentlewomen and
damosels in her company were well warmed and rested,
My Lady sent to ask whether the carriages were ready.
Whereat the Lord Abbot, who already had told the
Cellarer that My Lady would dine there, praying him
look to it that all was prepared, entered in with the
rest.   And at My Lady's coming forth out of the
chamber, the Lord Abbot led her into his passing
seemly little hall, all hung and tapestried and carpeted
like to an antechamber, and the windows glazed,[99] and
a good fire ; wherein were three tables spread with
marvellous fine linen, and a dresser well furnished with
goodly plate.   And when My Lady saw the tables
thus laid, she quoth unto the Lord Abbot : " Abbot,
do you dine already ? "—" Dine ? " quoth the Lord

Abbot, " why, Madam, is it not time ? See here the clock ",—the which he had put forward an hour and an half, so that it was at the hour of noon. My Lady, seeing that it was noon, would have hastened her going. " Would you depart ? " said the Lord Abbot ; " nay Madam, by the faith I owe you, you shall not go until you have dined." " Dined ? " said My Lady, " truly I could not ; for I have much to do."—" Ho, Cellarer ! and ye, my ladies, will you suffer me to be refused my first request ? "

At that, the gentlewomen and damosels (and the Cellarer also) who were all fasting and had good appetite for dinner, bethinking them that they would fare better here than at the ordinary of the inn, nudging and winking one at another so importunately besought My Lady to grant the Lord Abbot his first request, that she consented. Then the Lord Abbot, ever joyous, gracious, and amiable, made haste to kneel and thank My Lady, and the other ladies and damosels also. Right so, the horses were put back in the stalls, whereat all the company, notwithstanding that they had well breakfasted, were exceeding glad. " Now, Madam," quoth the Lord Abbot, " you are in the holy time of penance and in a House vowed to penance ; and therefore it is no marvel if you must do penance here ; and the more so, Madam, because I knew not of your coming until yestere'en, very late."—" Abbot," said My Lady, " we cannot but fare well here."

Then called the Lord Abbot for water, for My Lady and the other ladies and damosels to wash their hands ; and they brought fine rose-water, warmed a little, whereat My Lady and the rest had great joy. My Lady desired the Lord Abbot, as a prelate, to wash him first, but this would the Lord Abbot by no means do ; and to put an end to My Lady's entreaties, he went and washed him at the side-board. By that, the table was

266

prepared, and My Lady prayed the Lord Abbot to be seated. "Madam," said the Lord Abbot, "you are Lady and Abbess here ; be you seated and give no heed to me." So My Lady sat down, and at the nether end of her table Dame Joan, Dame Katharine, and the Seigneur de Gency, who was with her ; and there sat at the second table one of the Priors of the Abbey, with Ysabel and the other damosels and two or three squires, and Sir Geoffrey de Saint Amant opposite Ysabel. Then went the Lord Abbot with a napkin at his neck unto the wine dresser, and caused My Lady to be served with sops in white hypocras,[100] and all the tables likewise, and after with Lenten figs roaſt in sugar. My Lady much besought him to be seated, yet would he not, saying : "Madam, with your good leave, I will bear the Cellarer company, and shew him the way for this once". And when the Lord Abbot and the Cellarer returned and the firſt mess was served, My Lady said unto the Lord Abbot : "Verily, Abbot, an you will not sit down, we shall arise ".—"Very well, Madam, I muſt and shall obey you." My Lady would have let draw back the table, that he might be seated ; but the Lord Abbot said : "Ah, Madam ! God forbid that ever the table be moved for me ! " And he bade bring a ſtool, and sat down opposite My Lady, a little lower down. Anon he caused white wine of Beaune to be served, and then red of three or four sorts, whereof they all drank. What more shall I say ? They were much besought to make merry and to drink one to another, so that it was long since My Lady had made such good cheer.

Now as they drank, My Lady unto the Lord Abbot and the Lord Abbot unto My Lady, their eyes, the heart's archers, little by little began to shoot at one heart and at the other ; until their feet, which were covered with the long table-cloth down to the ground, began little by little to touch one another, and then to tread one upon the other. Then pierced the fiery arrow of love through the heart of one and then of the other, so that they lost all lust for eating; but the Lord Abbot, who was more joyous than any at this new adventure, drank first to one and then to another. What more shall I tell you? Never was abbot so merry. First he ariseth and causeth his stool to be borne thither where the ladies sit and there sitteth a little, and then goeth toward the damosels and prayeth them to eat, then unto the tire-women and drinketh unto them, and returneth unto My Lady and sitteth down joyfully opposite her. Anon began their archers of love to shoot again yet faster, and their feet to tread one upon the other more than ever they had done.

As for the other good cheer of wine, meats, lampreys, salmons, and many more sea-fish and fresh-water fish, I pass them over, to come shortly to the relation of what things were said.

SEVENTIETH CHAPTER

How My Lady and the Lord Abbot communed together, and how she thanked him

WHEN the tables were cleared and the Cellarer and others gone to dine, My Lady gave the Lord Abbot thanks for the good dinner and good cheer that he had made them; and talking and walking together, they came to the further end of the hall, where they communed pleasantly until all had dined. And whiles the last were at dinner, the Lord Abbot let apparel his bed with fine linen sheets, for My Lady to rest. But when her steward had dined, My Lady

bade fetch the carriages. "How now, Madam!"
quoth the Lord Abbot, "Would you break the custom
of the House?"—"And what is the custom of the
House?"—"Madam, the custom is this: that if
any ladies of rank or damosels have dined here, they
and their company must lie here also, sleeping or
waking, winter or summer; and if they have supped
here, for that night I leave them my bedchamber
and go elsewhere to lodge; and therefore, Madam,
you ought not to deny the custom of this your Abbey."
Such were the entreaties of the Lord Abbot and of her
gentlewomen, that My Lady was gracious and denied
him not. And anon My Lady entered into her
chamber, where were wine and spices set out; the
door was shut; and My Lady took her rest until
Vespers.

ONE-AND-SEVENTIETH CHAPTER

How the Lord Abbot was praised

WHEN the ladies were by themselves apart, Ysabel fell
to speaking and said: "You say naught, Madam, nor
do you other witless ladies, of My Lord Abbot's
good cheer, and how he hath feasted us with all these
good wines, meats, and fish". "In truth", said
My Lady, "meseemeth 'tis a worthy man."—
"Worthy, say you?" quoth Dame Joan, "Ne'er
saw I so courteous a monk."—"And you, Madam,"
quoth Dame Katharine, "you could scarce be persuaded to stay."—"Ah," quoth Ysabel, "I well
knew by his entreaties that things were well prepared."
Then the damosels all together, as women are wont
to do, fell to praising the Lord Abbot's largesse, his
merry cheer, and his comely person. My Lady, who
was already so much smitten therewith that she had

quite forgot her former griefs, said briefly : " 'Tis a most worthy man ".

Now whiles they yet spake of the Lord Abbot, it rang to Vespers ; and to be there, they needs must arise without having slept. And when Vespers were said and My Lady thought to have ridden thence, the Lord Abbot took her by the hand and she said unto him : " Abbot, whither lead you us ? "—" Pray you, Madam," said the Lord Abbot, " I lead you to a trifling collation,[101] for 'tis time." Thus saying, the Lord Abbot taketh her under the arm, and pressing her hand bringeth her into the lower hall which was next the Abbey church, well tapestried and having a good fire ; wherein a dresser and tables were set, all bespread with salads, cress in vinegar, great platters whereon were roast lampreys in pasties or in their sauce ; great soles boiled, fried, and roast in orange-verjuice ; mullets,[102] barbels, salmons roasted boiled or in pasties, great plaice[103] and carp ; dishes of craw-fish, great fat eels reversed in galantine [104]; dishes of sundry sorts of corn covered with jelly, white and red and golden ; Bourbon tarts ; talmouses,[105] and almond cream flans, thickly sugared ; roast pears ; fresh apples and pears, almonds sugared and peeled, and walnuts in rose-water ; figs also, of Morocco,[106] of Algiers, and of Marseilles, and raisins of Corinth and of Orthes ; all set in order in the manner of a banquet.

TWO-AND-SEVENTIETH CHAPTER

How My Lady partook of her savoury collation

My Lady, who was fasting and thought to partake but of spices and wine, found the tables thus garnished, and though that the traitorous god of love had at dinner so fiercely assailed her that with his amorous darts he took from her all desire to eat, yet Nature will be served, and gave her such appetite that she needed but little persuading. And when the other ladies in her company beheld My Lady seated, and the Lord Abbot also, face to face in the middle of the table, they all, or the most part, hearkened to the Lord Abbot's entreaties (in obedience also to My Lady, to bear her company), and sat down every one at the two ends of the table or at either side ; and among them, to be the merrier, four or five of those courteous monks. Then might you see drinking and drinking again, and eating in like proportion. What more shall I tell you ? Such joy was there and gladness as had never before been made by a like number of people. But at length, with sore lamentation and sighs on My Lady's part, needs must they take their leave of the Lord Abbot for that time.

And at their mounting into the carriages, there were there the Lord Abbot and the Priors, to thank My Lady full humbly and to commend unto her bounty the church and the Abbey. Then said My Lady : "We shall see you more often henceforth, for we purpose to seek a larger share of your pardons " ; whereat all were well content. " But as for you, Abbot, we desire and charge you that you desist from your prodigalities in wines and meats, for verily we will have no more thereof ".—" Now, Madam, a sop in Duke's Powder,[107] in Hypocras, in Muscatel, in Grenache,[108] in Malvoisie,[109] or in Greek wine, to keep out the cold, . . . you forbid not that ? "— " Yea, I forbid it," quoth My Lady ; " for in these days we mean to fast."—" Fast, Madam ? That shall not hinder you from fasting : I will give you abso-lution." And with those words, the Lord Abbot got upon horseback and rode with My Lady a piece of the way ; and then took his leave.

THREE-AND-SEVENTIETH CHAPTER

How My Lady and her gentlewomen spake praise, one unto the other, of the Lord Abbot

WHEN the Lord Abbot was departed, there began as it were a strife who should speak most praise of him. Ysabel, that was the merriest, first began to speak, and said laughing unto My Lady : " Ah, Madam, how I did hate you when you refused those good dinners ! Madam, none ought to refuse good things when fortune bringeth them ". Then said Dame Joan : " Now in sooth, Ysabel, you do err ! My Lady meaneth to go oft thither : must she then dine there every time ? " Said Dame Katharine : " Ye err both twain : there is no cause why My Lady should every time dine there ; but I should not blame her an she took the offer sometimes in good part, for on my faith, he maketh it right heartily and willingly, and what is more, methinketh he lacketh not the means. And you, Madam, what say you ? Say I not well ? " My Lady, who had heard them all, answered : " It is enough to take wool from the sheep ; therefore I go no further than the sops in Duke's Powder, Hypocras, and other foreign wines, which ought to suffice us ; but truly, I mean to win all those pardons, or the most part, for we know not when we shall find them again ". And by that, they were come as far as the manor. My Lady, whose heart was thus afire with this new flame of love, all night did naught but moan and sigh and lament, such desire had she to see again the Lord Abbot and have more converse with him. And the Lord Abbot, assailed by that same desire, by cause of the gentle and amorous shew that they had made one another, had no rest that night, for sighs and longings of ardent love kept him all night from sleeping.

Now when the much desirèd morn was come, My Lady said unto her gentlewomen that verily, the better and the more worthily to gain the pardons, she purposed to be confessed by the Lord Abbot, who was a prelate, and as herseemed, a man of great piety. Then said Dame Joan : " Madam, 'twere well done ; as for me, I was yesterday confessed ". Then My Lady bade little Perkin, a page of her household, to mount upon horseback, and sent word unto the Lord Abbot that he should come unto her without delay. The Lord Abbot was not backward, and made haste to obey My Lady. And his reverence made, My Lady said unto him publicly, before all her gentlewomen : " Abbot : the more worthily to gain your pardons, I am minded to confess me to a priest ". —" Ah, Madam," said the Lord Abbot, " now are you well with God ! And who is your confessor, Madam, that I may give him some spiritual strengthening if need be ? " Then answered My Lady : " There is none here worthier than you, nor so competent ".—" Ah, Madam, 'tis then by reason of my crozier ; for else am I the most ignorant of all."

With that My Lady entered into her little tiring-chamber, which was fairly hung and tapestried, with a good fire, and the Lord Abbot devoutly followed ; then was the door shut, and for the space of two hours, she being full penitent and ashamed of her good deeds and loyal love, the Lord Abbot did well and heartily confess her, in gentle sport. And at their parting, My Lady went unto her jewel-chest, and took thence a passing fair great balas ruby set in gold, the which she put upon his middle finger, saying : " My Heart, my one Thought, and my true Desire, with this ring I wed you this day for mine only lover ". Then the

Lord Abbot thanked her as humbly as might be, and afterward bethought him of the common proverb which saith : " He that serveth, yet not to the end, no wage deserveth ".[110] So he gave My Lady absolution, and in charity kissed her moſt gently, and took his leave. And in his passing through the outer chamber, he said very devoutly unto the gentlewomen and damosels : " Until she call you, let none enter. My siſters and my friends, until I come again I commend you unto God ".

My Lady tarried a space to get again her colour, which she had loſt in the fervour of her penitence : her gentlewomen and damosels, and all her household, that were awaiting to hear Mass, abode there until the clock ſtruck eleven. Then My Lady called Jennet, and was arrayed in her plaineſt gown ; and the better to hide her face, put on her biggeſt kerchief ; and in this array, simply and quietly, went forth from the little chamber with eyes caſt down, and so to Mass very devoutly, and afterward to dinner. And so passed that day.

On the morrow, Wednesday, when there were pardons, My Lady returned again, to acquire them. The Lord Abbot, quite filled with joy, bade make ready great abundance of sops in wine, and prepare hypocras and foreign wines of divers sorts, roaſt herrings and soups for the varlets, with hay, oats, and litter a-plenty. When My Lady had heard Mass, the Lord Abbot taketh her under the arm and leadeth her into his chamber, where was a good fire and breakfaſt all set out. And when My Lady had well broken her faſt, the Lord Abbot taketh her and saith : " Madam, while your company make good cheer, I shall shew you my new building ". Then went they together from chamber to chamber, until the gentlewomen knew not where to find them. And at their coming forth from a certain secret chamber, the Lord Abbot gave unto My Lady a piece of fine velvet, plain black, which she afterward sent for secretly. Then returned My Lady again into the great guest-chamber, where they all were; and when her gentle-women drew nigh, she chid them as though she were exceeding angry: "Whence come ye? I bade you follow me and weened ye had so done; but ye love the fire and the good sops in wine better than ye do me!"—"Nay, Madam, by my faith, we could not go fast enough to find you!"—"Ah, Madam!" quoth the Lord Abbot, "let them be forgiven this once!" Then fell My Lady to praising the Lord Abbot's buildings mightily, and thereafter went to mount into her carriage; and there the Lord Abbot took leave of her. What need I say more? Not a week passed in Lent but she went in all piety to gain pardons, and oftentime with small company, privily to dine, feast, and sup; and after her sleep, went oft a-hunting foxes and badgers in the woods, or other disports. And thus, all that Lent, she passed the time merrily.

FOUR-AND-SEVENTIETH CHAPTER

How the Queen wrote unto My Lady the first time

Now the two months, whereafter My Lady had promised to return again unto the Queen, were past without any news of her by letters or in other wise; wherefore the Queen, greatly marvelling thereat, wrote unto her in the manner following:—

Unto Our most dear and beloved Cousin:—

Most dear and beloved Cousin, in regard to the promise which you did make unto Us, the two months

are now paſt and an half month and more, and never
since your going had We any word from you, whereat
We marvel much ; and We do require you to fulfil
your promise during this present month, so great
desire have We to see you ; and if you have need of
aught that We are able to do, We shall right gladly
perform it ; and that shall Our truſty secretary
Julian de Broy certify unto you, in whom for this
matter We pray you to have confidence as in Ourselves. Moſt dear and beloved Cousin, Our Lord
keep you. Writ in Our City of Paris, this eighth day
of April.

BONNE.

FIVE-AND-SEVENTIETH CHAPTER

*How My Lady, having read the letter, writ her answer
unto the Queen without hearing the message*

WHILES that My Lady was at the Abbey acquiring
pardons, there arrived the aforesaid Maſter Julian de
Broy, secretary to the Queen, who found her at table,
dining ; and unto her presented the Queen's letter,
frankly and joyfully, thinking (as one of her especial
friends at Court) to have a right good welcome. My
Lady, who had naught but displeasure at his coming,
took the letter with few words and read it ; and to
be the sooner rid of him, she made haſte to finish
dinner and to let clear the tables : then ſtraightway
departed she unto her manor, for to write an answer,
saying unto Maſter Julian : " Dine, and come unto
me forthwith ".

The Lord Abbot, ever courteous, made Maſter
Julian right good cheer, and sat opposite him, to talk
with him. And whiles he dined, there came unto the

Lord Abbot one of his huntsmen, who told how he had
found a passing great hart and with him ten or XII
goodly hinds. "'Tis pity My Lady is not here",
said the Lord Abbot, "to see marvellous fine sport;
but at all costs we will wait until tomorrow."—
"What?" said Master Julian unto the Lord Abbot,
"doth My Lady take any pleasure in hunting?"—
"Pleasure?" quoth the Lord Abbot without thinking,
"pleasure, say you? Why, 'tis but two or three days
a week that we are not at one chase or another, ahorse
or afoot."—"Why, My Lord Abbot," quoth Master
Julian, "are you furnished with good dogs and grey-
hounds?"—"Ay, that am I," said the Lord Abbot,
"as well, I wot,—and with good hawks also—as any
prelate in France, be he who he may."—"Holy
Mary!" said Master Julian, "this doth you much
honour."

Now as he talked with the Lord Abbot, he espied
on his finger the passing fair large balas ruby which he
had seen My Lady wear aforetime; he said no word,
but thought none the less. And when he had dined
and understood as much as he chose, from the Lord
Abbot's talk, he took his leave, thanking the Lord
Abbot full heartily; and then got upon horseback
and went unto My Lady, as she had bid him, and told
her his message, confirming the letter. My Lady,
who was in haste to be rid of him, gave him her letter
for the Queen, which she had prepared already with
her own hand, and which was as hereafter followeth:—

Unto my most honoured sovereign Lady, the Queen:—

Most honoured sovereign Lady, as humbly as may
be I do commend me unto your good grace, by Master
Julian de Broy your secretary, here present. I have
received your letter and well marked the purport
thereof; and most humbly I beseech you that you

please to grant me pardon for failing of my promise, through the necessity of my sickness, which hath up to this present time kept me here; howbeit, God be thanked, I begin to be much amended. And after a little business that I have among my dependants, I will be with you ſtraightway, to acquit me of mine oath; and for the reſt, may it please you to send unto me your commandments which I shall gladly obey unto the moſt of my power. And of that I call to witness the Holy Spirit, whom I pray grant you, my moſt honoured sovereign Lady, such joy as you desire. Writ with my hand at my manor of . . . . this eleventh day of April.

Your very humble and obedient, &c.

SIX-AND-SEVENTIETH CHAPTER

How My Lady gave her letter unto Maſter Julian and told him his message, according to the purport of the letter

THEN My Lady, in her great eagerness to be soon rid of Maſter Julian, gave him forthwith her letter and told him his message, such as she chose, and by way of good cheer gave him to drink of her wine, and no more, though at the Court he was one of her moſt faithful friends, (wherefore the Queen had sent him unto her); but with the great desire that My Lady had of his departing, she asked him naught of the King, nor of any lord, lady, nor anyone of the Court; and with that, " Fare you well, Maſter Julian ". Maſter Julian, who had heard how the Lord Abbot and My Lady delighted in the chase, lacked not comprehension of My Lady's eagerness. And he took his leave of My Lady toward nightfall, none too well pleased, and found such lodging as he could for the night; and so went his way until he came again unto the Queen. The Queen, as soon as she beheld him, cried out: "Cometh my Fair Cousin, Master Julian?"— "Madam," said he coldly, "she doth commend her very dutifully unto your good grace, and saith that you shall shortly have your desire." Then he delivered unto her the letter, and told his message; and prudently said no more at that time.

The Queen, who was but ill content with the answer and message, asked Master Julian, saying: "Is she in good health?"—"In good health?" said Master Julian; "Madam, ne'er saw I her in better." —"What doth she?" asked she, "how employeth she her time?"—"Now by my faith, Madam," answered Master Julian, "I know not; for I was not an hour with her before I was dismissed; nor was I once able to speak with Dame Joan, Dame Katharine, Ysabel, nor any man nor woman of her household, save: 'Bid you welcome!' and at departing 'Fare you well!'"—"Why how may this be, seeing that you are one of her chiefest friends?" Then he declared unto her how his way took him unto the Abbey, for to gain a pardon; where he found My Lady at table opposite the Lord Abbot, with but few others; and how he delivered unto her his letter, which having read she soon rose up, with heavy cheer, and bade remove the tables and bridle her hackneys, and forthwith departed unto her manor; and sith he had neither eaten nor drunken all that day, My Lady bade him dine speedily and come unto her; and how the Lord Abbot, who was a full courteous lord, after his hands were washed made him to sit down and himself sat before him to keep him company; and how the huntsman came, bringing news of the hinds and the great hart, where My Lady was to go

279

hunting; and then he told how he found her answer already writ, and what she said unto him shortly; but of the balas ruby, whereof he was not certain, he prudently kept his own counsel.

The Queen having heard his tale, said no more at that time, and charged him that he should say naught thereof unto any persons whatsoever; saying in My Lady's defence that it was well sometimes to take solace now with one and now with another. And with those words the Queen went thence, all pensive, yet not able to believe that My Lady had done thus ill; and she resolved that all that month and half the next, or yet more, she would tarry ere she wrote again unto her.

That month passed and the next, yet came not My Lady unto the Queen, nor sent word, nor writ. Then the Queen, thereat marvelling, bade write unto her more or less as she had before writ, and the more urgently because two more months were now past; desiring to know whether it were her intent ever to return. The outrider of her stables, that bore the letter, being in haste to return speedily, sought My Lady so diligently that he found her in the fields with the Lord Abbot, and delivered his letter. My Lady, who was to sup with the Lord Abbot, made there in the fields her answer in writing, affirming that she would be with the Queen very shortly. Then took the outrider his leave without eating nor drinking, nor scarce saying aught else unto her, and made great haste to return. The Queen, having received and well read the letter, and being told likewise how he had found her in the fields with the Lord Abbot, was sorrowful, and thought what she well might; and resolved within herself that she would no more write unto her, but that she might come when she pleased or stay as long as she chose.

But My Lady, unto whom it were mortal affliction
to leave her good Father Confessor, said unto him :
" Mine only Love, so long as I am able to abide in
your most beloved company, be sure that never shall
I forsake you ". What shall I say more ? In hunting,
in hawking, in fowling, and in many more delights
they spent a great part of the summer.

And here will I leave speaking of the good solace
they had together, and I shall turn again unto the
Seigneur de Saintré and his companions.

SEVEN-AND-SEVENTIETH CHAPTER

*How the Seigneur de Saintré and his companions came
unto the Emperor's Court ; and how to their great
honour they were delivered of their Emprises by ten
knights, all gentlemen of blood and coat-armour, without
reproach, and all Almains, ruyters of the host¹¹¹ ; to wit :—*

THE Count of Estainbourg, who bore *gules, a chief
argent*. The Count of Espenehem, who bore *chequey,
or and gules*. The Lord of Estonnenosse, who bore
argent, torteaux gules. The Lord of Flouraille, who
bore *argent, a saltire gules*. The Lord of Semalle,
who bore *or, a cross sinople*. The Lord of Huffalize,
who bore *azure, a cross or*. The Lord of Wassebech,
who bore *or, an escutcheon sinople*. The Lord of
Huppain, who bore *gules, three lozenges argent*. The
Lord of Tongre, who bore *vair, a fess gules*. The
Lord of Seulp, who bore *gules, a cross argent*.

When the news reached the Emperor's court that
ten barons of France were coming thither bearing an
Emprise-at-arms, there was great talk of who should

deliver them. Anon the ten lords and barons afore-
named went all together unto the Emperor, to entreat
that it might please him to grant them leave to
deliver them; and the Emperor granted it them with
a good will.[112] Then made each provision of all
things needful; all ten together sent courteous
answer unto the French; and there was not one but
gave unto the King-of-arms gowns, rings, or silver
plate. And it was not long before their foragers
came to seek lodging for them; and within eight days
afterward, themselves. The Emperor, like a wise
prince, summoned the aforesaid lords before him,
desiring to know whether they were agreed which
adversary they should choose; and he sent to know
the names of the French, in writing, as they were set
forth in the challenge; and lest there be any dissension, he caused them to draw lots for their adversaries, whereat every one was well content.

EIGHT-AND-SEVENTIETH CHAPTER

*How the French came and the high honour that was done
them*

WHEN the Seigneur de Saintré and his passing fair
company were within an half-day's journey from the
city of Cologne, the place appointed, whither the
Emperor and Empress were come to view the jousting,
they sent word unto their servants that they were nigh
and would be there for supper. And their coming
being made known unto the Emperor, he sent out to
meet them his cousin the Duke of Brunswick, for to
bear the Seigneur de Saintré company, and nine
Counts, one for each of the others, and with them many
barons, bannerets, knights, and esquires, all noble men,

with a very goodly following; and thus it was. And when they drew near unto the city, the Emperor had commanded that the two counts and eight barons who were to deliver them, all clad alike, even as the French were, should meet them, with a goodly company; and thus did they, and made them great joy and honour. Then, as the Emperor had commanded, each put himself at his adversary's left side (whether the French knights would or no), and the counts that had firſt met them, on their right side. And in this fair array and company were they led through the city and before the palace where the Emperor and Empress were, until they came unto their hoſtel. Of the other ceremonies and array of heralds, trumpeters, and minſtrels, I speak not, that I may be brief; nor of the honours and good cheer that they made one another, for the space of fifteen days whiles they there abode.

NINE-AND-SEVENTIETH CHAPTER

Of the Combat, and of the Emperor's judgment

THE eighth day after their coming, which was the day appointed for the combat, the liſts being made and the Emperor in his ſtand, attended by the princes of his Court and other princes and barons that were come thither to see those jouſts, and the Empress in her ſtand upon his left hand, attended by many princesses and other ladies of high degree, the Emperor bade summon firſt by name the Seigneur de Saintré and his nine companions, who came at the second summons. And so was it also with the Almains, who (to be short) came with passing large and goodly companies.

283

And when both companies were in their pavilions, and had taken the customary oaths, the Emperor bade them issue forth from one side and from the other, clad in their coats-of-arms, passing fair to behold ; and Saintré in the midst of his companions. Then were cried the challenges. And each of the French, holding in his hand his banner, made therewith a great sign of the Cross, and then kissed it and delivered it up. Then every one, armed as he ought to be, took in his left hand his shield, and lowered his visor, and took his casting-spear in his right hand ; and so abode with good and joyful countenance each facing his adversary, until the Emperor commanded them to set on and do their devoirs.

At that, from one side and the other, they rushed together like lions, and in the first encounter and casting of spears two of the French were hurt, but not so that they must give up the combat, and three of the Almains, whereof one had his foot pierced through. Then began the combat so fierce and hard that never before was such between like numbers of knights, and endured a full long time, but ever upon the Almains' ground ; wherein the Seigneur de Saintré made his adversary to yield much space. Now when the Emperor perceived the valiance of those knights and how neither one party nor the other brake, he cried out, saying : " Nay, how could mine heart endure such a mishappening ? " With that he cast down his arrow hastily, saying : " Hold ". Then were they all made to cease, and withdrew every man unto his own side. And anon the Emperor caused them all to come before him and unarm them of their helms and gauntlets, and bade look to the wounded, and afterward asked all twenty for their prizes which they must yield up if they had lost ; the which were brought unto him. And he gave them unto the

King-of-arms of the Empire, bidding him render unto each his own and to speak unto them in his name the words which hereafter follow.

EIGHTIETH CHAPTER

How the King-of-arms of the Empire spake the sentence and delivered the prizes

WHEN the Emperor had done speaking, the King-of-arms went down; and drawing nigh unto the XX knights, he said unto them : " My Lords Counts and other Lords; both Almain and French, all ye that are here : the moſt Chriſtian and victorious prince our sovereign Lord the Emperor and King of the Romans, here present, hath bid me tell you that ye have every one, Almains and French, as much upon one side as upon the other, this day so nobly contended and honourably performed your combats and your devoirs, that there are none living could have done better; so that when you were made to cease, men might hardly judge which among you all, nor which party, had the advantage. Wherefore he doth will, judge, and ordain that ye give in exchange unto one another, courteously and amicably, your prizes, each man to his adversary; but forasmuch as ye, My Lords the French, did by your valiance suſtain the combat upon the side and ground of my lords the Almains, the Emperor doth will, judge, and ordain that they shall therefore acquit themselves and pay you firſt, and afterward ye shall pay them, leſt your fair ladies lose any honour; and furthermore, that at your issuing forth out of the liſts, ye shall go two and two, side by side, and ye, my lords the French,

285

for the credit of your arms and of you, shall go forth
upon the right hand ".

Then all kneeling thanked the Emperor, and afterward rendered up their prizes one unto another, with
great ceremony; and anon went forth as it was
ordained. Then took they leave each of other and
departed thence unto their lodgings to unarm them,
and there abode until the evening, when they supped
with the Emperor; and on the morrow dined with
the Empress, who made them great honour and good
cheer; and every day dined and supped one with
the other until the fifteenth day after their coming,
when they dined a second time with the Emperor.
And then took they leave of him and of the Empress
and of the other lords and ladies, who gave them
cloths of gold and of silk, silver plate, and fair coursers,
and many more goodly presents; their adversaries
likewise, and they them. Anon, after their leave-
taking, they mounted upon horseback, right nobly
attended by many lords, a good league. Then with
much ceremony and courtesies they took leave one
of another.

And for many days after, all men and ladies that
were there praised their high honour and valiance,
the fair array and company also, that they had brought;
saying openly one unto another, that if the Emperor
had tarried but a little to make an end to the combat,
the Almains had surely been put to the worse, for one
was thrust right through the foot, so that he could do
no more, and two more had lost already so much blood
that they well-nigh swooned; and they had besides
lost much ground; so that the French had won
the day.

And now will I leave speaking of their combats
and their right joyful return; and I shall tell of their
coming into the King's presence.

ONE-AND-EIGHTIETH CHAPTER

*How the Seigneur de Saintré and his companions came to
Paris and into the King's presence*

WHEN the Seigneur de Saintré and the other knights,
his companions, were come by Luzarches to Saint
Côme and Saint Damien,[113] as pilgrims, and then in
the evening unto Saint Denis, the tidings sped everywhere of their right joyful and desired return, whereat
the King, the Queen, lords, ladies and all men were
passing glad. And there went out to meet them, by
the King's command, the Lords Dukes of Berry and
Burgundy, his brothers, who set the Seigneur de
Saintré between them. And there were there the
Counts of La Marche, of Flanders, of Clermont, of
Retel, of Brienne, of Perche, of Beaumont, of Armig-
nac, and the Count Dauphin of Auvergne, each being
commanded to attend one of the companions. And
they came before the King, who made them great
good cheer ; the Queen also and the other lords,
ladies, and damosels, and all the Court.

Now, to be short, when all had made their obeisance
and good cheer, and were a little rested from their
journey, Saintré all dismayed and astonied not to
behold My Lady, whom most in the world he desired
to see, doubted lest she were sick. He went therefore
unto the Lady de Sainte-More, his cousin, and amid
other talk, as though he thought naught of it, said
unto her : " Why, i'faith, Cousin, now that I bethink
me, is My Lady sick, that she is not here ? "—
" Sick ? " said My Lady de Sainte-More, " she is
sick indeed ; as for the Queen's favour, she hath
befouled her silk jacket there, truly ; for about three

287

weeks or a month after your departing, such a malady took her that she withered before our eyes, and according to the Queen's physician, she must shortly be in a consumption, or dead, unless her native air might amend her. And so the Queen gave her leave for two months; and at the end of two months and an half, seeing that she came not the Queen sent to require of her her promise, and sent a letter by Master Julian de Broy, and after other two months writ again; and she saith ever: ' I come, I come ', . . . and is yet to come."

When the Seigneur de Saintré heard how she was thus sick, he thought on that which she had said unto him, that is, that never would her heart have any solace until he should return; and him thought (as was truth) that she had gone thence to forget her amorous distress. Now was he more joyous by far than he had been, supposing that she would straightway return so soon as she should hear of his coming; but yet it beseemed him rather to go visit her before her returning, that he might commune with her more at leisure. And in such meditation he passed X or XII days; and said then unto the King: " Sire, an it were your good pleasure to give me leave for eight or ten days to go visit my lady mother, who hath sent to ask me, I would most humbly pray you do so ". The King said unto him: " What, Saintré, can you not tarry? Yet sith it is your mother that hath sent for you, We do grant you leave for a month ".

Now when Saintré had given him thanks, he rested not day or night from arraying himself, his men, and his horses, the more amorously to please her that was mistress of all his heart. Then took he leave of the King, the Queen, and the Dukes, and stayed not until he came unto the good city, a league from the manor where My Lady was; and there dined. Then put he

on a doublet of crimson broidered with fine gold, a
cloak of figured velvet, broidered with gold upon gold,
scarlet hose broidered with passing fine large pearls
and with My Lady's colours and badge, and a cap of
fine scarlet, such as men wore in those days,'⁴ whereon
was a fair costly brooch ; and attended by two knights
and twelve esquires of his household, in very seemly
array, clad all in like raiment, with My Lady's device,
came to see her at her manor. And when he came
unto the gate, which he found shut and the drawbridge
raised, he bade ask for her ; then came one of the
porters, whom they bade tell My Lady that Messire
de Saintré was there. "Truly," said the porter,
"My Lady is this morning gone to the Abbey, to
hear Mass and afterward to dine."

Then went he thence and came unto the Abbey,
and found that My Lady and the Lord Abbot, after
dining and sleeping, were gone a-fowling with hawks.
Then he bade shew him in what place they were
flying their hawks ; and when he was a little distance
away, he called IV or V of his people and said unto
them : "Set spurs to your horses, and go you this
way, you that, and you another ; and if ye see ladies
a-horseback, come unto me". Then went each about
the fields, and it was not long before one came again
all in haste and said : "Messire, I have seen XX or
XXV horses, and with them VI or VIII ladies or
damosels fairly attired".

Then made haste the good knight (who as yet knew
nor imagined naught of My Lady's false love) as fast
as horse might gallop, and himseemed as though the
hour would never come when he should behold his
fair Lady. And when he espied her, his heart ravished
with joy, he set spurs to his fair frisking courser, and
pricked straight toward her, he and all his train very
goodly to behold. Now one of the Lord Abbot's

monks, perceiving them, drew nigh unto the Lord Abbot and told him thereof. When the Lord Abbot, who rode at My Lady's side, saw those horses hasting thitherward, if any man felt assured, 'twas not he; for he weened it had been some kinsmen of My Lady, that were avised of their amours, and were come to dust his jacket for him. He turned therefore to the side, and with a kick of his heel very speedily made his mule to draw away from My Lady; and with hawk on wrist and the three monks that bore the great bottles and basket of victuals for their refreshment, he withdrew him apart as far as he could, as though he durst not approach nigh unto My Lady. And My Lady, on her tall hackney, hawk on wrist, awaited all quietly with her attendants to see what people these might be. And when her attendants perceived that it was the Seigneur de Saintré, then both men and women made great joy, for he was well beloved of them all.

My Lady, when she was told and herself perceived that it was Saintré, "God send you all mischance," said she, "must ye make such ado for the sake of a man?" And as she thus spake, the Seigneur de Saintré, his heart full of joy, hastily lighted down from his horse; and when My Lady beheld him on foot, she said loud enough for many to hear: "Ah, Sir, you are right ill-come!" The Seigneur de Saintré, who heard not those words, kneeled very joyfully upon one knee, and touched her hand saying: "Ah, my most honoured Lady, how do you?"—"How do I?" quoth she, "wherefore must I tell you what you can see for yourself? See you not that I am upon my hackney, holding my hawk?" With that she turned her hackney and called her hounds for fowling, as though she held him of no account.

The Seigneur de Saintré, hearing My Lady's most cruel answer, knew not what to think; but as the gentlewomen and damosels passed by, he touched each her hand, and embraced and kissed them ; then mounted he upon his horse and rode after My Lady ; and each came to do him reverence and to salute him. And when he had drawn nigh unto My Lady, he said unto her all sorrowfully : "Alas, Lady ! is it in good earneſt, or but to make trial of me, that you have made me so ungracious an answer, that so long have loved you and never yet did disobey you ? What, Lady ! Hath some one told you otherwise ? If any hath, you shall soon know the truth ! " My Lady, who took no pleasure in his company nor in any of his converse, said unto him : "Can you sing no other song but this ? An you know none, pray you hold your peace".

Now whiles they thus talked, the Lord Abbot, feeling more assured, sent one of his monks unto the ſteward[115] to know who this knight might be. And when he knew that it was the Seigneur de Saintré, he turned his mule and came in haſte to greet him, saying : "Moſt honoured Sire de Saintré, you and your fair company are·right welcome, for upon mine oath, I had more desire to see you than any knight in the world ". The Seigneur de Saintré, who perceived by these words, and by the three monks that were behind him, that this was the Abbot, answered him : "My Lord Abbot, give you good day, and your companions also ".

"My Lord," said the Lord Abbot, who was now wholly assured, " what think you of my moſt honoured Lady, who hath been pleased so far to ſtoop as to take some refeſtion with her poor monk, and afterward to come a-hawking ? "—"My Lady", said Saintré, " doeth like a lady of honour and dignity, that hath ever loved Holy Church." At that, the Lord Abbot drew away ſtep by ſtep, and left My Lady and the

291

Seigneur de Saintré together ; and by cause it had already rung to vespers, he drew toward the manor"[16] ; and sent then one of his monks unto the steward, to ask of My Lady whether they should bid the Seigneur de Saintré to supper. The steward came nigh unto My Lady and told her what the Lord Abbot desired. My Lady not hearing him well, asked him what he said, and he said it a second time, so loud that the Seigneur de Saintré, albeit he was a little way distant, plainly heard it. And when My Lady heard, she considered a little, and then said unto him : "Bid him do as he please, but not to rend his gown with overmuch asking!" Saintré, who heard all this and well perceived how matters were, pondered and said within himself that they should not need to rend his gown, for he would consent at the first asking, that he might see the farce. My Lady, who found her first love mightily irksome, said that she was a-weary and bade ride toward the manor. The Lord Abbot, ever courteous, had gone on before and made all ready.

The Seigneur de Saintré, having alit down off his horse, would have helped My Lady to alight, but she asked one of her servants. And when all had alit, Saintré would have taken leave of My Lady, but as she gave him her hand, the Lord Abbot, to shew his courteousness, said unto her : "Will you let him go thus ? "—"That I leave to you and to him", said she. Then said the Lord Abbot unto him : "What, My Lord Saintré, will you not take some refection with My Lady ? I pray you stay". And the Seigneur de Saintré answered the Lord Abbot : "My Lord Abbot, I would not deny you your first request". Then the Seigneur de Saintré kept two squires, a varlet, and a page, and no more, and sent all his train to sup in the city ; and bade his seneschal bring them soon again unto My Lady's manor.

Then were the tables set and the supper all made ready. My Lady firſt washed her hands alone, and the Lord Abbot and Saintré after. Then the Lord Abbot, by virtue of his high eſtate and dignity, sat down at the head of the table, with his face toward My Lady, and his back leant againſt the bench-end; and next him My Lady; and then the Seigneur de Saintré, Dame Joan, and after her Dame Katharine. And they were served firſt of all with relishes[117] and salad, whereof My Lady and the Lord Abbot had a great liking; then great platters piled with young conies, with partridges, and fat house-pigeons; and excellent good wine of Beaune, of Tournus[118] and of Saint-Pourcain.[119] And when bellies were well filled, at the hour when tongues begin to wag, the Lord Abbot waxed lively, and said: "Ho! My Lord Saintré, rouse you, awake! I drink to your thoughts! And what be they?—You do naught but think!" Then answered the Seigneur de Saintré: "My Lord Abbot, I do battle with all these good meats and good wines that I see before me".—"Wot you, My Lord Saintré," quoth the Lord Abbot, "I have many times marvelled how it cometh about that of you noble knights and squires, who so oft go forth to jouſt, all when they return again do say that they have won." Then turned he him unto My Lady, and said unto her: "Madam, is't not so?"— "Verily, Abbot," said My Lady, "you say sooth. Now whence cometh this, Fair Sir? Tell us your opinion."—"Shall I tell you, Madam?" said the Lord Abbot. "'Tis by your leave then: I know not whether My Lord Saintré will take it ill; but sith you would know, Madam, to my mind 'tis thus: there be divers knights and esquires in the King's court, the Queen's, and other great lords' and ladies', and about this kingdom, who say they are moſt loyal

lovers of you ladies ; and to win your favour, an they
have it not, they weep and sigh and groan before you,
and so play the dolorous that perforce ye poor ladies,
that have tender and piteous hearts, muſt be by them
deceived and fall into their snares : then fare they
from one unto another, taking for Emprises a garter,
a bracelet, a ring, . . . or a turnip for aught I
know, Madam, . . . and say then unto you,
each one unto ten or a dozen : ' Ah, Madam, 'tis
for love of you I bear this Emprise '. Alas, poor
ladies, how are ye abused by your lovers ! Then the
King, the Queen, and all the Dukes do praise and
eſteem them highly, and give them of their bounty,
wherewith they array them fairly. Is't not true,
Madam ? How say you ? "

My Lady, who was well pleased at this, answered
smiling : " Why, who hath told you, Abbot ? For
my part, I do believe that it may be so ". And thus
saying, she trod upon the Lord Abbot's foot.

" Nay, Madam, I will tell you yet more : when
these knights or squires go to perform their jouſts and
have taken leave of the King, if it be cold, they go
thence unto those German ſtoves and sport with the
wenches all winter ; and if it be warm, they go unto
the pleasant realm of Sicily, with its good wines, its
good and deleƈtable viands, its fountains, its goodly
fruits and its fair gardens,[120] and all the summer
feaſt their eyes upon the fair ladies and gentlemen
also, who make them good cheer and honour enow;
then they have an old minſtrel or trumpeter that
beareth an old ancient tabard of arms, and give him one
of their old gowns, and he cryeth at the Court :
' My Lord hath won ! My Lord hath won ! My
Lord hath won ! ' Ah, poor ladies, how are ye
abused ! I' faith, I do pity you."

My Lady, who was as well content as she could be

at these words, turned her head a little, and said unto the Seigneur de Saintré: "What say you to this, Messire de Saintré?" The Seigneur de Saintré, passing wroth at the charges and disparagements which the good Abbot spake againſt gentlemen, answered My Lady: "An it pleased you to take the part of the gentlemen, Madam, you know well 'tis false!" Then said My Lady: "I have seen some, indeed, that have not done thus; but what know I of the reſt? For my part, I am of the Abbot's opinion". And thus saying she trod back and forth, smiling and grimacing at the Lord Abbot.

"Ah, Madam," said Saintré, "you speak now very wilfully: I pray that God give you knowledge."—"Knowledge?" quoth the Lord Abbot, "what knowledge would you have My Lady to have, more than the truth."—"The truth!" said Saintré, "My Lord Abbot, unto My Lady's words I say naught; she may say what she pleaseth: but unto your words in disparagement of knights and esquires, I do answer that were you a man unto whom I might make reply, you should find an adversary to debate the matter; but considering your dignity and who that you are, I say no more; and peradventure you shall at some time learn better."

The Lord Abbot, who was all afire with the flames of love, said as in mockery unto My Lady: "Madam, 'tis for your sake I am menaced here in your house". And as he thus spake, the play betwixt their feet was unceasing. And when he saw My Lady smile and wink, he wiſt well that the sport was pleasing unto her; and said: "Ho! My Lord Saintré, I am no warrior nor man-at-arms, to combat with you, but a poor simple monk, living on what is given us for the love of God; yet if any man, whatsoever warrior he might be, would gainsay me in this disputation,

295

I would wrestle a fall with him ".—" Would you so ? "
quoth My Lady straightway, " have you such hardihood ? "—"Hardihood, Madam ? I can but fall;
but I trust in God and in my good and holy cause that
I should win the mastery. Come now! Is there
none here to answer for all these warriors ? "

The Seigneur de Saintré, hearing the Lord Abbot's
outrageous words, which pierced as it were his heart
from side to side, and all the more by reason of My
Lady's plain approval, was pale as dead. My Lady,
seeing how he said naught, quoth unto him : " What,
Messire de Saintré, you that are so valiant and have,
so men say, achieved so many fair feats of arms, dare
you not wrestle with the Abbot ? Certes, an you
will not, I shall say even as he doth ".—" Why,
Madam," said he, " you know that I was never a
wrestler ; and these worthy monks be masters thereof,
likewise of playing at tennis, of tossing bars, stones,
and iron weights, and all manner of exercises, in their
leisure time ; wherefore I know well, Madam, that
against him I could do naught."—" Now pray you ! "
said My Lady, " we shall see whether you will deny
me ! By my faith, an you do not this thing, I will
hold you up everywhere to reproof as a most craven-
hearted knight ! "—" Nay, Madam, what say you ?
I have done much more than this for a certain Lady,
whom God pardon ; but sith the thing standeth
thus, I will do your pleasure."—" What saith he ? "
asked the Lord Abbot of My Lady. Said My Lady :
" That he feareth you no whit, and will speedily
overmatch you ".—" Doth he say thus, Madam ?
Well, we shall see ! "

With that, without more ado nor removing of
platters, bread, cups, nor victuals, the Lord Abbot
all filled with joy thrust back his table and leapt up
first ; then arose My Lady, the Seigneur de Saintré,

and all the reſt likewise, marvelling at all this. Then
the Lord Abbot taketh My Lady and bringeth her
unto a fair pleasance, whence the sun had departed,
and saith unto her : " Madam, sit you down beneath
this fair flowering hawthorn, and be our judge ".
And there sat My Lady down as joyous as could be,
saying unto her gentlewomen : " Sit ye all here ".
And as for them, albeit that they dissembled, what
they perceived pleased but few among them.

Then the Lord Abbot did off his gown and ſtood
up in his doublet, with hose unlaced (which in those
days were not all of a piece, nor had long feet)[121], and
well rolled up below his knees, and came firſt of all
before My Lady. And after he had made her a great
bow, he cut a caper in the air, shewing his great white
thighs, all hairy and shaggy like a bear's. Then came
Saintré, who had unclad him at the other end of the
sward ; and in his hose, richly broidered with great
pearls, he made his bow unto My Lady, dissembling
the bitter grief wherein his heart did dwell.

Now were they face to face ; but afore the match
was begun, the Lord Abbot turned him toward My
Lady, and in mockery said unto her, kneeling upon
his knee : " Madam, with hands joined I pray you
that you commend me unto My Lord Saintré ".
My Lady, well liking the Lord Abbot's jeſt, said
smiling unto Saintré : " Ah, Messire de Saintré ! I
commend unto you our good Abbot, and beseech you
that you spare him ". The Seigneur de Saintré,
who underſtood this mockery, answered : " Ah,
Lady ! 'Tis I that have more need to be commended
unto him ! "

These words said, the Lord Abbot and Saintré
laid hold one upon the other and made a turn or two.
Then the Lord Abbot put forth his leg and crooked
it within Saintré's and anon brake loose from him all

suddenly, and seized and lifted him up in such fashion
that the Seigneur de Saintré's feet were some-deal
higher than his head, and laid him upon the ground;
and holding him beneath him, with his breast upon
his, the Lord Abbot cried out and said unto My Lady:
"Madam, Madam, commend me unto the Seigneur
de Saintré!" At that, My Lady laughing heartily
said unto him: "Ah! Messire de Saintré, deal
gently with the Abbot"; but she could scarce speak
for joy and mirth.

Then the Lord Abbot arose upon his feet, and when
he came smiling unto My Lady, she cried out unto
him: "Again! Again!" Then quoth the Lord
Abbot unto My Lady, so loud that Saintré and all
that were there heard him: "Madam, what I have
done was for the sake of our disputation, wherein
God and Love have borne me witness: but now, an
the Seigneur de Saintré were pleased to maintain
that he loveth his Lady more loyally than I do mine,
you see here a weak and simple monk who will strive
with him in such a combat".—"Would you so?"
said My Lady.—"Would I so? Ay, by God, Madam,
against all comers."

Then said My Lady all laughing, unto the Seigneur
de Saintré: "What say you unto this, Fair Sir?
Is there any heart of gentleman that would not
answer?"—"Lady," said Saintré, "there is no heart
of gentleman but would answer, so it were unto his
peer, and in such manner as befitteth such a case."—
"These are excuses," quoth My Lady, "and you
sought likewise to be excused from the other bout.
He hath well done to blame the courage of a gentleman that dare not uphold his loyalty for dread of a
wrestling-match; and I'faith, I ween that men might
seek well and find in you but little valour."—"Alas,
Lady!" said Saintré, "wherefore say you thus?"—

" I say thus ", said My Lady, " because you well know your blame, and that it is truth." Then quoth the Seigneur de Saintré : " Now perceive I indeed, Lady, that I muſt wreſtle again, sith there is no argument, howsoever reasonable, that may turn you therefrom ; and because it so pleaseth you, I am content ".

The Lord Abbot, who heard all these words, said by way of jeſt : " Ah, Madam ! I am afeared ; for but that right had been upon my side, he had over-borne me, such ſtrength found I in him ; which is no marvel, if he hath discomfited so many folk ; yet sith I have undertaken the combat, I am content to perform it ". Then cried he : " Back ! Back ! " and every one drew back. And the Lord Abbot cried out : " Now, Loyalty, guard thy right ! " And thus saying, he came and tripped up Saintré by a certain cunning device, so that he well-nigh bore him from his feet ; and they turned and swayed until with another throw he laid low the poor Seigneur de Saintré, and said then : " Madam our judge, have I well done my devoir ? Which of us both is the more loyal ? "—" Which ? " said My Lady, " why you, that have won ! " Saintré, who with the wreſtling and My Lady's rejoicing thereat had loſt all coun-tenance, could no word say. Anon went each to do on his raiment. His two squires that had abode there to serve him, were ready to die for despite, and said unto him : " You will not be a man, if you take no vengeance for this ". But he said unto them : " Fret not, and let me be ".

The Seigneur de Saintré, who had thus by treason loſt his Lady, whom he so long and so loyally had served, bore himself in such manner as though none of all this had befallen. Anon with great guise of merry cheer he increased My Lady's joyfulness and the Lord Abbot's, saying unto them : " Marry, Lady,

'tis great pity that so goodly and puissant a body as
My Lord Abbot's hath never been trained to arms ;
for I wot not of any two nor three, howsoever puissant,
that he would not have overthrown ". The Lord
Abbot, hearing such praise from such a man, sprung
in the air and cut another caper all round about ; and
after, called for wine and cherries, for refreshment.

Of the Embassy from the Brethren

Now whiles these things were said, divers of the
priors and elder monks of the Abbey, whom the Lord
Abbot's way of life mightily displeased, (and all the
more by reason that they had heard now of the
wrestling and of My Lady's and the Lord Abbot's
mockeries), ordained two of their number to go unto
the Lord Abbot and privily, in the name of all the
Brethren, to say unto him the words which here
follow :—

"Reverend Father in God and our right worshipful
Lord, the priors and officers of your Abbey, *una voce
dicentes*, with their humble and proper salutations, do
send us unto you. It hath been told them how you
have offered unto our most honoured Lady sundry
dinners, suppers, and other delectations, whereat all
the Brethren are well pleased, forasmuch as she is
our Patroness and principal Foundress ; and all the
more, when you brought this day to sup a certain
lord of whom is such good report and who is so near a
familiar of our lord the King. But inasmuch as you
have put yourself forward and made bold to defy him
to a wrestling-bout, and have divers times overthrown
him and made mock of him, which is in propriety a
thing forbidden to a prelate, abbot, or other monk
thus publicly to do, therefore are all the Brethren
passing ill pleased and wroth. And for this cause
send they us unto you, praying and beseeching you

so to contrive, before his departing, that he shall have no cause to make complaint either of you or of the Brethren; if otherwise, the Brethren do hereby certify unto you that if any ill thing come thereof, they will hold themselves excused and lay upon you the whole blame; and may it please you to pardon them every one".

The Lord Abbot's Answer and what Remedy he gave

The Lord Abbot, having heard this rigorous Embassy of the Brethren, answered them: "Priors, go unto the Brethren and say unto them that all that I have done hath been but in sport; and let them not fret themselves, for ere he go hence I will make all good".

TWO-AND-EIGHTIETH CHAPTER

How the Lord Abbot sought to appease the Seigneur de Saintré

IN the mean while that this Embassy was being made, the wine and cherries were brought; then drank they one unto another with as good cheer as any folk might. And when all had drunken, the Lord Abbot took the Seigneur de Saintré apart and said unto him these words :—

"My Lord Saintré, it hath pleased God to grant me such grace as to see you here in mine house, which is yours if you will; now I pray you that you do me the honour to come again to-morrow with My Lady, and take dinner in our humble fashion, and not to deny me this".

The Seigneur de Saintré's Answer, and the Lord Abbot's Entreaties

"My Lord Abbot, for your supper and for the excellent good cheer which you have made me this first time, I do thank you as heartily as I may ; likewise for the offer of your dinner to-morrow, the which in verity I cannot grant you, by cause of business that I have in the town".

How the Lord Abbot made his Excuses, and what Offers he made unto Saintré

"Alas, no ? " said the Lord Abbot. " My Lord, if in sport I have done aught to your displeasure, I pray you pardon me. My Lord, I have the fairest and best mule in all the kingdom, that wot I well, and I have one of the best falcons for heron and for the river that may be found, and I have three thousand crowns as good as the Pope or the King, and no more. Now I pray, beseech, and entreat of you, as earnestly as may be, that you be pleased to accept my offerings, one, two, and three, and pardon me, and let me abide in your good grace."

The Seigneur de Saintré, who had no need of his crowns, nor of hawks, having a sufficiency of all, thanked him very courteously, and said for his contentment :

"My Lord Abbot, I ride not upon mules ; your three thousand crowns I would employ, an I had need ; and as for your goodly falcon, for your sake I will accept it, on condition that you keep it for me, and if any ask you, you may tell him 'tis mine. But one thing I pray you—that you deny me not my first request."—" And what ? " asked the Lord Abbot : " My Lord, command ; for on mine oath, if it be possible, I will gladly accomplish it."—" Will you so ? " said Saintré. " Ay, upon mine oath ! " Then said he : " It is that you and My Lady come and dine with me to-morrow ".—" That I promise you ", said the Lord Abbot, " both for her and for me ; on condition that it be a dinner for simple folk."

Then came they both twain with right merry cheer unto My Lady, and the Seigneur de Saintré besought her. And when My Lady had heard him, she refused very shortly, saying that she had much to do ; nor did Saintré's prayers avail aught. Then the Lord Abbot drew her apart and said unto her : " Lady, you shall come, for I have promised for both, and you would put me to great shame an you made me thus a liar ; moreover, Lady, he might suppose you did him despite, and guess how things are about our love ; and you know how you muſt beware, as of fire, of these frisking gallants of the Court. Wherefore, Lady, you muſt come ". Then said My Lady, who could refuse the Lord Abbot naught : " Sith you desire it, I am willing ".

At that, the Lord Abbot called joyously unto the Seigneur de Saintré, saying : " My Lord, my moſt honoured Lady, whom you here see, hath denied you, fearing leſt you might wish to make great ceremony, and a great feaſt and solemnity ; but I have given her assurance that you will not ". Then said Saintré unto them : " Madam, and you My Lord Abbot, we of the Court leave the making of great feaſts unto you Lords Prelates ; we do without them well enow ; we like indeed some share of good meat and good wine, if they are to be had ; but with whatsoever ye shall find, My Lady and you muſt be content ". And by the time that these words were said, the hackneys and horses were all ready ; then My Lady and Saintré thanked the Lord Abbot and took their leave until the morrow.

Now when My Lady was in the meadows, she went riding as fast as her hackney might go ; the Seigneur de Saintré, galloping his courser, said unto her time and again : "Ah, my most dear Lady, wherein have I offended against you ? Is there any man in the world that dare say and maintain that I have not right loyally loved and served you ? "—"O Sir," said My Lady, "how you prate thereof ! You shewed it, forsooth, in your wrestling-bout ! Come, speak we no more of these matters, and leave me in peace." The Seigneur de Saintré, who saw plainly how things were, neither desired to win again her favour, nor would he at her request ever have deigned to love her more ; but he was desirous to cause her to feel what unworthy wrong she did him, yet without saying aught, nor seeming to perceive aught, of her new love. And when they were come unto My Lady's manor, before lighting down My Lady said unto him : "Get you gone, Messire de Saintré, for I have business which I must be about ", and so gave him his dismissal, with "Fare you well until to-morrow ".

The Seigneur de Saintré, pondering all these new matters, went his way with the few that he had with him, straight unto the town, where his people were ; and he had not long to seek ere he found all his company assembled as he had bid them. Then called he his steward and told him how My Lady and the Lord Abbot were to come on the morrow to dine at his lodging, and bade him use all diligence in finding good meats and good wines to serve every one of them, and for their company the same meats and wines wherewith themselves should be served ; and that liberally. Moreover he charged him that he should make the whole reckoning and well pay the host, both for the horses and for the cheer, and beyond all the rest, when he was paid, to give him X crowns to make him well content, and two crowns for the service of the varlets and maids of the inn. And he bade also that early in the morning his coursers, his chest, and the most part of his following should take their departure, and that twelve only of his retainers should abide; and thus was it done.

And when he was in his lodging, he let call the host and said unto him privily: "Fair Host, is there in this town any gentleman or burgess of the bigness of that tall squire that you see yonder?"—and he shewed him one of his people. "Ay, my lord," answered the Host, "a plenty."—"But wot you whether any hath a full suit of harness, and a fair one?"—"Full armour have they, and passing fair." Then asked he the name of him that was the best armed, and prayed him send for him, and he did so. And when the burgess was come, he made his reverence unto Saintré, who greeted him courteously and after said unto him: "Jacques, who is the burgess of this town that is the best armed?"—"My Lord," answered Jacques, "there be many; but though I be unworthy, I am as well armed, with five or six pair of full harness, as any burgess of this town or yet any gentleman of these parts."—"Are you so?" said Saintré, "by my lord Saint James, you are the better to be esteemed therefor! You have harness for your own body; could you find me another which would serve for that knight you see yonder?"—and he shewed him a knight of his own size. "My Lord," said he, "I will furnish you withal, and so fair and good as you shall be well content with; but would you have basinets, salets with beavers, or helms?"[122]— "Friend Jacques, I would have basinets; and also two axes, both alike; and have no fear, you shall lose naught by it."—"Lose?" said Jacques, who was full joyful to be acquainted with the Seigneur de Saintré;

" My lord, all that I have is yours and at your service. And when may it please you to have them ? "— " Jacques, I would fain have them now ; but let it be in a chest or in a bag, that none may espy them."

Jacques went straightway unto his house, and caused the two fair bright suits of harness to be brought secretly, with the axes ; whereat the Seigneur de Saintré was well pleased. And when the night was past and the day come, and Saintré had heard Matins, and all his baggage and all his men departed, save the XII that he kept, and the meats near ready and the tables set, he mounted upon horseback with all his company, and they went to meet My Lady. And when they had fared about half the way, he found My Lady and the Lord Abbot in the meadows. Then greeted they courteously, and the Lord Abbot first speaking said : " Ho ! Speak of the wolf,[123] and ye see his tail ! Were not your ears burning,[124] My Lord Saintré ? "—" I know not," said Saintré, " for I was thinking what poor fare ye will have. Have you not broken your fast, Madam ? and you, My Lord Abbot?" —" Yea," said My Lady, " being doubtful of your brewets,[125] we have broke our fast upon sops in hypocras and Duke's Powder."—" That shall well profit you, Madam, and My Lord Abbot also ! "

Now as they thus devised all three together, My Lady addressed herself ever unto the Abbot. The Seigneur de Saintré, perceiving that he wasted his words, drew rein, and would have talked with Dame Joan, but she bade him ride behind her ; then went he unto Dame Katharine, unto Ysabel, and all told him likewise ; for all were forbidden to speak with him. Then returned he unto My Lady and the Lord Abbot, and it was not long before they came where he lodged. Then Saintré took My Lady by the arm and brought her and her gentlewomen into his chamber, and the Lord Abbot into another. And whiles they took their ease in their chambers, he said unto his steward : "So soon as we go to table, let the horses be saddled, bridled, and in the stable all ready to mount ! "

Now to be short, the dinner was ready. And when My Lady and the Lord Abbot had washed their hands, the Lord Abbot, as a prelate, took his seat at the head of the table, and a little lower My Lady, who would not go far from him ; and Saintré would not be seated, for any entreaty, but took a napkin upon his shoulder and went hither and thither serving them all ; and there were wines and meats in plenty and of many sorts. What shall I say more ? The Lord Abbot was as well content with the Seigneur de Saintré as could scarce be told.

And when bellies were well filled and thirsts well quenched, the Seigneur de Saintré asked the Lord Abbot whether he had ever borne armour. "Armour ! " said the Lord Abbot ; " nay, I never bore armour."—" Why, perdy ! " said Saintré, " how fair a thing it were to see you armed ! What say you, Madam ; is't not so ? "—" Truly ", said My Lady, " I do think and am very sure that an he were armed, some who now do make mock of him would fare the worse ! "—" Madam, I know none that maketh mock of him ; but I say that never was a man that would look better in mail " : and he told Perkin, one of his household, to do as he had bid him. Then Perkin set up a table at the end of the hall, and afterward laid thereon the bigger suit of harness, without axe nor sword.

When the Lord Abbot beheld that passing fair and shining armour and heard himself so mightily praised, he bethought him that this knight was passing liberal and open-handed, and sith that he had no harness nor ever had been armed, he might for a jest give him it ; and he resolved that if he besought him to put it on, he would in no wise refuse. And to shew how well it pleased him, he began to speak great praise of the harness. " Why, sith it so liketh you, you shall have it, an it well fit you ! "—" Verily, my lord ? "— " Ay, My Lord Abbot, an you will."—" Now by my faith ! For love of My Lady, I will neither eat nor drink more until I am armed ! " Then cried he out : " Away with these tables, away ! We have eaten and drunk too much already ! "

The Lord Abbot, full of joy, did off his girdle and his gown and stood in his doublet ; the Seigneur de Saintré took the bodkin and laces, which he had all ready at hand ; then was the Lord Abbot speedily armed in full armour, with a basinet upon his head, well clamped ; and then gauntlets upon his hands. And when he was all armed, the Lord Abbot turned him this way and that. " What think you, Madam, of your monk armed thus ? "—" Monk ? " quoth My Lady ; " such monks are rare indeed ! "—" Perdy, why have I not an axe and one who would combat with me ! " Then said he, jesting : " Well, Madam, truly this harness doth weigh more than mine own ; but sith I have won it, it doth content me ". At those words, the Seigneur de Saintré said unto him : " Nay, you have not yet won it ; but you shall, and that shortly ". Then he bade bring the second harness, and was soon armed therewith.

When My Lady heard those words and saw Saintré armed, she said unto him : " Messire de Saintré, what mean you to do ? "—" Madam, you shall soon see."— " I shall see ? " cried My Lady : " what, Sir Jacka- napes, would you fight with an Abbot ? " Then the Seigneur de Saintré, being fully armed, commanded the door to be guarded and that none should go in

TO APPEASE THE SEIGNEUR DE SAINTRÉ

nor out; and said unto the ladies and damosels, monks and squires: "Abide ye there by the door; and if any, man or woman, ſtir thence or say any word, I will cleave his head to the teeth!" Then might you behold women and monks trembling with fear and weeping and cursing the hour that they ever saw him. Anon he came unto My Lady and said unto her: "Madam, you were pleased, of your good grace, to be judge of the combat betwixt the Lord Abbot and me; now I pray you right humbly that you deign to be judge of such a combat as I have learned to fight; and that you join with me in fulfilling the Lord Abbot's requeſt".—"I know not what requeſt you mean," said My Lady; "if you do him any despite, I deem it as done unto me."

The Seigneur de Saintré came then unto the Lord Abbot and said unto him: "My Lord Abbot, at My Lady's requeſt and at yours, I wreſtled two falls with you (which I yet do feel) nor might any excuse avail, but I muſt go through with it. Now do I challenge and pray you, likewise for the sake of the Lady whom you so loyally do love, that we combat in such fashion as I have learnt to do".—"Nay, My Lord Saintré," said the Lord Abbot, "I could not fight in mail!" Then said Saintré: "You shall go through with this or else through the window".[126] My Lady, perceiving that Saintré was fully resolved to fight, said unto him full wrathfully: "Messire de Saintré, We will and command that upon pain of Our indignation, you unarm, both twain; and if not, We will put you in peril of body and life, as a felon and a malapert".

When the Seigneur de Saintré heard himself thus reviled and threatened, he said unto her: "Now false, faithless, and such, and such, and such, that you are! I have served you as loyally as ever any Lady was served; and now for the sake of a ribald monk, thus falsely and traitorously, you have forsaken me! And to the end that you may remember this, and as an ensample to all others . . .". With that, he took her by the top of her wimple, and lifted up his hand for to have dealt her a box or two on the ears; but all at once forbore, remembering what great favours she had shewn him aforetime; and made her to sit down upon the settle, all weeping and nigh swooning with grief.

Then bade he bring the two pole-axes, two swords, and two daggers, which he caused to be girded on the Lord Abbot and given into his hands; and said then unto him: "My Lord Abbot, My Lord Abbot, be you mindful of all the disparagements that you spake of knights and esquires who do seek honour by the feats of arms that they go forth to do about the world; for you shall now pay for them. Now, My Lord Abbot, guard you!" With that he lowered his visor and bade lower the Lord Abbot's; and set on against him. And when the Lord Abbot perceived that he needs must fight, he lifted up his axe and smote with such strength that if he had stricken Saintré (having such might, and being moreover the taller) he had borne him to earth, failing God's aid and protection; and God knoweth how My Lady would have commended him! But with God's help and the skill that he had in arms, Saintré when he beheld that mighty stroke coming, guarded himself with his axe, and fixing him suddenly with the point, thrust him back as far as a bench; and there the Lord Abbot, under My Lady's eyes, took such a fall upon his back that it seemed as though the whole world were falling asunder; crying "Mercy, mercy! Mercy Madam! Ah, My Lord Saintré, in God's name, Mercy!"

PLATE VIII

SAINTRÉ'S DUEL WITH THE ABBOT

[face p. 310

The Seigneur de Saintré, being filled with vexation
and choler by reason of the mockeries and contumely
which the Lord Abbot had said and done unto him
without his deserving, and likewise unto so many
knights and esquires, whereof he had lied, was resolved
to put an end to him.   But as he lifted up his axe
there came into his remembrance the holy verse
which Our Lord spake in the Old Testament, in
Deuteronomy the fifth book of the Bible, which
saith :—

> "*Quicumque fuderit sanguinem humanum, fundetur sanguis illius.*"

He saith moreover in his passion :—

> "*Qui gladio percussit, gladio peribit.*"

He saith also unto **David** :—

> "*Non edificabis mihi domum, quia vir sanguinum es.*"

He saith also by the mouth of **David** :—

> "*Viri sanguinum et dolosi non dimidiabunt dies suos.*"

And he saith again by the same :—

> "*Si occideris, Deus, peccatores, viri sanguinum, declinate a me.*"

And so many more commandments of pity, mercy,
and forbearance hath He given us and by His own acts
commended and shewn unto us, that the Seigneur
de Saintré forbore to put him to death.   Howbeit,
whether in vengeance, or by divine Will (which by
reason of their very evident and manifest sin, would
assuredly have suffered him thus to punish them) he
cast aside his axe and his sword, and took his dagger in
his hand ;   then raised he up the Lord Abbot's visor,
and said : "Now, My Lord Abbot, you know that
God is a just judge, forasmuch as your strength and
your false mischievous and injurious words have not
availed you to escape chastisement ;   and that in the

presence of her by cause of whom you held yourself so proud, and for whose sake you did lie and speak so disworshipfully of knights and esquires who to win honour and their fair Ladies' most desired favour do go forth through the world and unto the courts of Princes to perform deeds of arms; and for that shall this false tongue of yours pay dear ". Then with his dagger he pierced through his tongue and both his cheeks, and left him thus: and as he arose, said unto him: " My Lord Abbot, now have you honourably won the harness ".

Then bade he unarm him; and when he was stripped of his harness and beheld My Lady with her hair and wimple all disordered, he said unto her: " Fare you well, Lady, the falsest that ever was! " And as he took his leave of her, he perceived that she was girt with a girdle of blue silk tipped with gold; and he came and ungirded her, saying: " How have you the heart, Lady, to wear a blue girdle? The colour blue doth signify loyalty,[127] and you are the most unloyal: verily you shall wear it no more ". With that he took from her her girdle, and folded it and put it in his bosom.

Then came he unto the ladies and damosels, monks, and the rest, that were all together like sheep in the corners of the hall, weeping, and said unto them: " Ladies and damosels and ye all, ye are witnesses of the things before said and done, which to my great displeasure are the causes wherefore I have done what I have done; as for any despite that I have done you, I was thereto enforced, and am right sorry, and ye must pardon me; and God be with you! "

Then went he down and said unto the host: " If the Lord Abbot desire to keep the big suit of mail leave it him; but the lesser one and the two axes you shall give again to Jacques, and tell him that I retain him all this month in my service. Fair Host, are you well content?" By that, the horses were ready and he mounted, with: "Fare you well, Fair Host!"

And now will I leave speaking of him, as he goeth thence unto the Court; and I shall tell of My Lady and of the Lord Abbot and their people.

THREE-AND-EIGHTIETH CHAPTER

How My Lady and the Lord Abbot abode with their following

WHEN My Lady had amended her disarray, and all had wept enow, and the Lord Abbot was unarmed, they sent in haste to fetch a chirurgeon by cause of the blood that flowed from his tongue and his cheeks. Then might you see them weeping and cursing their life that ever he had put on harness. Anon the Lord Abbot, who was not able to speak, was unclad and put to bed and his hurts dressed; and then must My Lady depart. But any that had heard her plaints, her weeping, and her moans for the Lord Abbot, and her menaces against the Seigneur de Saintré, would have thought that he must straightway die by her words alone. Her gentlewomen said: "Ah, Madam, we thought as much when he put on armour, or at least that some mischief would come of his having thus impugned the honour of gentlemen!"—"Ay, truly," said another, "and for treating him thus!"—"Fret you not," said My Lady, "he shall be well avenged, so soon as he be healed. . . . . and to have thought to strike me, and then to have borne away my girdle, murderer and thief that he is!"

And with that will I leave speaking of My Lady and of the healing of the Lord Abbot, who for the space of two months more took their pleasure together, as well as ever they had done, or better.

FOUR-AND-EIGHTIETH CHAPTER

How My Lady returned unto the Court

In the mean while that My Lady and the Lord Abbot thus disported themselves, both the King and also the Lords Dukes many times marvelled how their Fair Cousin so long tarried, and at one time or another spake unto the Queen thereof. The Queen, passing ill pleased with that which she guessed, for My Lady's honour said naught. Then besought they her to write again, in such fashion that she could not choose but come. The Queen told them how a long time afore she had done so, and sent by Master Julian de Broy, her secretary, and then a month and an half after by an outrider of her stables, and still she came not ; and that verily she might come when she chose, but she would never write unto her more for the sake of her coming. The Dukes, who well perceived by the Queen's words that she was very ill content with My Lady, wrote themselves unto her and sent one of their good priests. Then was My Lady cruelly constrained to forsake her gentle Abbot, and to name a day when she would be with the Queen, without fail ; and so took the good priest his leave of her, and returned thence.

Ah ! false, wicked, and traitorous Love, must you be ever like unto Hell, that was never yet surfeited with swallowing-up of souls ? Will you likewise be never sated with tormenting and wounding of hearts ?

Have God and Nature given unto you such might
that you take in your snares the hearts of Popes, of
emperors and empresses, hearts of cardinals, of kings
and queens, hearts of archbishops, of dukes and
duchesses, hearts of patriarchs, of marquesses and mar-
chionesses, hearts of abbots, abbesses, counts and
countesses, and of all other orders spiritual and temporal ? and that you have taken captive the hearts of
some (as it is found writ in many histories) and have
dealt full falsely and evilly therewith, and then at the
last left them all confounded, so that you are answerable
for the loss of their souls and their lives (unless God
have mercy upon them), and their honour ; witness
all these, whom I now leave to return unto my tale,
which thus saith :—

When My Lady was thus constrained perforce to
take her departure, such was the affliction that their
hearts must suffer that I could not tell nor write it.
Howbeit, she was contented with the Lord Abbot's
promise that he would come oft privily to see her.
And with this sweet hope in their sore distress of
heart, they had good pleasure together, save at
parting.

FIVE-AND-EIGHTIETH CHAPTER

*How My Lady came to the Court, and the good cheer
that everyman made her*

MY LADY all pensive and sorrowful by cause of her
love, came unto the Court, attended by many lords,
counts and barons, knights and esquires that had gone
out to meet her ; she made her obeisance unto the
King who received her well enow ; and went afterward unto the Queen, who said unto her : " You have

been long in coming; meseemeth the country air liketh you well". Then went she unto My Lords the Dukes, who greeted her courteously, saying unto her: "You have us to thank for your returning!" Afterward there came all the other ladies and damosels, knights and esquires, to do her reverence and to greet her: and thus passed XXV or XXX days.

It befell one evening, after supper, the King and Queen being in a fair meadow, and with them great plenty of ladies and lords, that the Seigneur de Saintré said unto the Queen and unto the other ladies: "Sit ye all here, and I will tell you a true tale and a marvellous history, which one hath writ unto me from afar".—"Come," said the Queen, "let us hear it, perdy! Be seated, Madam",—and she called My Lady her Fair Cousin; "and all ye ladies, let us sit down and hearken to this tale of the Seigneur de Saintré's."

Then sat the Queen down, My Lady beside her, and then the other ladies and damosels, mingled with the lords, knights, and esquires, that were there present. And the Queen, smiling, said unto Saintré: "Master Chronicler, begin!"

SIX-AND-EIGHTIETH CHAPTER

How the Seigneur de Saintré, naming no name, told the story of My Lady, the Lord Abbot, and himself; and how he gave My Lady back her girdle, lest he be deemed discourteous

The Seigneur de Saintré began anon his tale, as well as he could, saying:—

"Madam, I read of late a letter concerning a true history lately befallen which none hath yet heard tell. It befell, in Germany, that a very noble and puissant

lady was pleased to take into her favour a gentle
youth ; and she gave him such bounty, such honours
and such love that in a certain space of time she made
of him a worshipful knight ; and they loved one
another so loyally (so the letter doth say) that never
were truer lovers.

> " But Fortùne, the traitress maid,
> As good Boethius hath sayd,[128]
> With her right hand proud and high
> Doth her wooers sorely try ;
> Surpriseth them more suddenly
> Than a tempest of the sea,
> And doth so soon them overthrow
> That he is highest that was low
> And he that high was, is in need ;
> Nor of their wailing taketh heed,
> But when they most do rail and mourn
> She laugheth loudest in her scorn ;
> 'Tis her delight, in little space
> To raise the meanest to high place.

" Thus was it, Madam, with this poor wretch, who
was in such favour with his Lady that never was any
lover in better. It came to pass that by the will of
Fortune, for love of her, and to increase his honour,
he journeyed into France to perform deeds of arms,
out of which he came forth with honour. But
whiles these things were being done, his Lady fell
acquainted with a monk, tall, stout, and puissant of
body, who was a Lord Abbot : and they cast such
love unto each other that it was over-much."

" And then ", said the Queen, " she made such evil
joy as to forsake, for a monk, him that so loved her ? "

" Madam, it was so ; for I have it by a letter that
would not lie. Now hearken, Madam, and you shall
hear what came of it."

" Say on then," said the Queen, " and finish the tale."

Then word by word he told the story : first, how

317

the lover found them hawking; how the Abbot sent
to ask My Lady whether they should bid him to sup,
and the answer that she made; how the lover, to see
the farce, soon assented; how the Abbot and My Lady
disparaged knights and squires that went about the
world to do deeds of arms; and then how they
wrestled, and the two goodly falls that the Abbot gave
him, their laughter and merriment, the embassy that
the brethren made; and to be brief, the combat, and
how he dealt with the Abbot; likewise the words that
the lover spake unto his Lady, and how by cause of her
blue girdle, she being unworthy to wear that colour,
he ungirded her and bore it away.

For this matter, which was yet hid and supposed
to be in Germany, the Lady was much blamed by all
that were there, and the lover much praised for the
combat. And their pleasure at the tale was so great,
that they scarce could cease from praising it. But My
Lady listened to all simply and quietly, saying no word.

Then said the Seigneur de Saintré unto the Queen
and unto all the ladies there present :—

" Madam, and ye, ladies, the tale biddeth us say of
this Lady whether she did well or no; and you,
Madam, I ask first."

The Queen, when she had heard tell of the love
between a Lord Abbot and a lady, misdoubted somewhat that it might be her Fair Cousin; but sith she
wist naught of the love between her and Saintré, she
knew not what to think for certain; so, to see what
My Lady would say, she put upon her the task to
speak first of that Lady. Then answered she:
" Madam, may't please you to excuse me, for I paid
no heed to his tale. But, if you please, say yourself or
let the others say; and when you and all the rest
have spoken (though 'tis a thing whereof we ought to
be silent) I will say what I think, if I must ".

318

Then quoth the Queen : " Sith that We, as Queen, must first begin, verily Saintré, if it be as you have said, We say that such a Lady is false and evil ; and We will say no more ".—" And you, My Lady de Retel, what say you ? "—" I say as the Queen saith ; and moreover, that she ought to be banned from all gentle company that she was in."—" Now, My Lady de Vendôme, what do you say ? "—" I say, Messire Saintré, that she ought to be tied hind before upon an ass, and fiddled through the town."—" And you, My Lady du Perche, what is your opinion ? "—" I say that the Queen and all these ladies have so well said, that none could say better ; but furthermore, I would say that such a Lady as you tell of, if it be true, ought to be stripped naked and the girdle put upon her hind to fore, and to be all shaven and then besmeared with honey and led through the town for the flies to eat,—false Lady that she is (if indeed she liveth) to have forsaken her true servant, knight or squire, for a monk ! And blest be the lover that shall thus punish them ! " At that there was no lady nor damosel there but laughed.

Then asked he again the other ladies : " My Ladies de Beaumont, de Craon, de Graville, de Maulevrier, d'Yvry, and ye all : your verdict ? "— for as for the men, it was not meet that they should say aught. And there was none among them all but gave sentence before her.

Now when the Seigneur de Saintré had asked them all, he turned him unto My Lady and kneeling asked her opinion, as he had the rest. My Lady, who knew not what to say, being she whom the tale concerned, was so besought by the Queen and other ladies to speak, as they had done, that she said at length : " Sith that I must speak, I say that this lover, be he knight or squire, was passing discourteous to have

ungirded the Lady and borne away her girdle, as you
did say ".

" Forsooth, Madam ! " said Saintré ; " have you
naught else to say, save that for having ungirded that
false Lady of her blue girdle, and borne it away
by reason that she was not worthy to wear such
a colour, you say that he was therefore passing discourteous ? "

Then drew he from his sleeve the girdle all tipped
with gold, saying unto her : " Madam, I would not
be so discourteous ". And before the Queen and all,
kneeling full courteously upon his knee, he laid it in
her lap. And when the Queen and all that were there
saw and heard this wonderly thing, they looked one
at another, marvelling ; and they were all mightily
amazed at My Lady, as any man may suppose ; and
no need to ask if she was shamed : certes she would
fain have been far away over-seas ; and there loſt she
all joy and honour.

And here will I begin the end of this tale, praying,
beseeching and adjuring all ladies and damosels,
goodwives and others, of whatsoever eſtate they be, all
to take ensample by this noble lady who by her amorous
dalliance was undone ; and to be mindful of the
common saying which saith : " There was never
smoke without fire, howsoever deep it were under
ground " ; that is to wit, that never was there good
nor ill, howsoever secret, privy, and hidden, but in
the end all was revealed ; for thus hath the true and
almighty Judge of all things ordained, from Whom
naught may be hid, that He may reward the juſt and
good and punish the sinners and evil-doers, either in
soul, or in honour, or in body : as He did unto this
aforesaid Lady and unto many more men and women,
punished for their inordinate luſts.

There be indeed smokes without fire ; that is to wit, that there be many false deceitful tongues loosened to give forth smoke without fire, that is to say, to bear and report false lying tales about men and women, without cause or foundation; but these cannot kindle fire, which is the veritable proof whereby they are undone and damned in soul, in honour, and oftentime in body, and are reviled and mocked behind their back.

Yet another marvellous valiant deed would I record of this good knight, how he and fifteen more knights and squires fought with XXII renegade Christians at Cairo, before the Soldan, and discomfited them. And now will I make an end of this book concerning this most valiant knight, who beside the combats whereof I have told was in many more battles both by land and sea, and fought many more combats hand to hand, and journeyed so far abroad that it were a full long matter to rehearse all ; I say only, that when it was God's pleasure to take unto Him his spirit, by death, which spareth no man,—the day that Death shut his door upon the light of his eyes, he was held the most valiant knight of the kingdom of France. And he ended the days of his natural life in the town of Saint-Esprit on the Rhône, having received all the Holy Sacraments, as beseemeth every true Christian ; and was buried in that same church ; and for the sake of his valiant deeds I took pleasure to behold where his body lyeth, and laid to remembrance the letters graven upon the slab over him, which thus say, in Latin :—

ḃic jacet dominus Jobannes de Saintre, miles, senescalus Andegavensis et Senomanensis, camerariusque domini Ducis Andegavensis, qui obiit anno Domini MCCCLXVIII, die XXV Octobris, cujus anima in pace requiescat.[129] Amen.

And please God it may be so.

Concerning this most valiant knight, I have heard divers other valiant and ancient knights and squires record how that they who made his tomb found there a little casket wherein was a parchment which said :—

> " Here shall lie the body of the valiantest knight of his time, in France and beyond."

Concerning which word *beyond*, they say that thereby is meant the valiantest in the world, as indeed he was in his days.

Now most high, excellent, and mighty Prince, and my most redoubted lord, if in any wise, by writing too much or too little, I have erred, which I might well do, seeing that I am neither wise nor learnèd, may it please you (and all others likewise) to grant me pardon ; for many a man doeth the best he can yet doeth but ill ; therefore is it no marvel in me, that am and ever have been rude and simple of mind, in conduct, in deeds and in speech.

But to fulfil your desires, which above all other lords' are to me as absolute commandments, I have made this book, called Saintré, the which I send unto you after the fashion of a letter, praying that you accept the same. And beyond this, my most honoured Lord, I write you no more at this present time, save to commend me, as humbly as may be, unto your right good and worshipful grace, wheresoever I may be ; and I pray the God of Gods that he grant you full joy of all your desires.

Writ at Châtelet-sur-Oise, the sixth day of March in the year of Our Lord one thousand four hundred fifty and five.

Your very humble and obedient servant,
ANTHOINE DE LA SALE.

NOTE I

HISTORICAL BASIS OF THE PETIT JEHAN DE SAINTRÉ

THE scene is laid in the reign of Jean le Bon of France, the gallant but unlucky monarch who was captured at Poitiers, paraded in triumph through the streets of London, and ransomed for a prodigious sum. There is, however, little doubt that La Sale is describing the manners of his own, not of an earlier generation. It has long been a subject for speculation whether My Lady "des Belles Cousines" can be identified with any historical person, and various candidates have been proposed for the doubtful honour. None of their claims is convincing.

John of Saintré himself had a quite genuine corporeal existence (c. 1320-1368). In the reign of Jean le Bon he was Seneschal of Anjou and Maine, and Chamberlain to the Duke of Anjou. Taken with his king at Poitiers, but ransomed before him, he was appointed by the Regent—the Duke of Normandy—as commissioner to accompany Edward III's ambassadors, and afterwards filled other high offices. We have it on Froissart's authority that "men accounted him the best and most valiant knight in France". La Sale, as a young man, may easily have talked with people who remembered Jean de Saintré.

NOTE II

LA SALE'S FAMILY

BERNARD DE LA SALE is supposed to have come from
Agen, a town on the borders of Guyenne and Armag-
nac, about half-way between Toulouse and Bordeaux.
The family was evidently of knightly rank.

M. Joseph Nève, Antoine de la Sale's Belgian
biographer, devotes several pages to a genealogical
notice on the family of La Sale, extracted from an
eighteenth century *Histoire de la Noblesse du Comté
Venaissin.* This genealogy (derived in part from the
quack astronomer Nostradamus, the soi-disant historian
of Provence) seeks, without a shred of evidence, to
connect Bernard and Antoine with a Provençal family
of La Sales which flourished in the sixteenth and
seventeenth centuries. The arms of this family were
" lozengy argent and gules, on a chief argent a lozenge
azure between two lizards affronted vert ".

One almost suspects M. Nève of having skipped the
heraldic parts of *Saintré* ; at any rate he overlooked—
in common with all the other commentators—two
pertinent references to the name La Sale. The first
occurs in the long catalogue of French Knights who
went crusading with Saintré. Modestly placed at the
end of the contingent from the marches of Acquitaine
is " the lord de la Salle, who bore onduly of eight
argent and gules ; and his battle-cry was : *Mars* ".
It is significant that for almost every other knight the
battle-cry given is simply his name. The second
reference is to be found just before the battle with the

324

Saracens, in the description of the Crusaders' array. " The banner of Our Lady, which Sir Godfrey de la Salle bore, who had once before borne it ". This sounds like some family tradition, and it is fairly clear that in both passages the author is alluding to his own kin. The arms of these La Sales prove that the Provençal family referred to by M. Nève was not descended from them.

NOTES TO THE TEXT

[1] *Page* 31. Three " hiſtories " were actually written : *Saintré, Floridam et Eluide* (a romance by Nicolas de Clamanges, translated from Provençal into French by Rasse de Brunhamel and by him dedicated to La Sale) and *l'Addition des chroniques de Flandre*, a more or less hiſtorical work borrowed practically in its entirety from some unknown author. These three formed one book ; the second was to have been the romance of *Paris et Vienne*. La Sale, having evidently abandoned his intention of writing, or rather, rewriting this laſt work, crossed out a reference to it at the end of his dedication but forgot to alter the reference to four hiſtories and two books.

[2] *Page* 31. " *Une dame des Belles Cousines de France.*" She is never called anything else, but the ſtory seems to represent her as a lady of the higheſt rank, evidently a near relative of the King or Queen. There is no proof that she is not fictitious, but it has been suggeſted that she might be intended for one of the daughters of Jeanne, Queen of Navarre—the elder of whom was the widow of Alphonse I of Aragon and the younger the widow of Jean, Duke of Brittany. She afterwards married Henry IV of England.

[3] *Page* 33. Jean II, le Bon (the Valiant) of France is the King who was captured at Poitiers and a prisoner in England from 1456 until the Peace of Bretigny in 1460. He then left as hoſtage one of his sons, who escaped, whereupon the King surrendered himself again, pronouncing his famous dictum : " Si la bonne foi était bannie du reſte de la terre, elle devrait se retrouver dans le cœur et dans la bouche des rois ".

[4] *Page* 33. Horsemanship was greatly cultivated. " But the moſt honorable exercise in myne opinion, and that besemeth the aſtate of every noble persone, is to ryde suerly and clene on a great horse and a roughe, whiche . . . is no litle socour, as well in pursuete of enemies and counfoundyng them, as in escapyng imminent daunger, whan wisdome therto exhorteth." Sir Thomas Elyot : *The Governour* (1531).

[5] *Page* 38. " Real tennis " of course ; and originally played with the hand, not with a racquet, so that it was more like Fives—which was an old slang term for " hands " and may be compared with the French name " *jeu de paume* " (palm).

6 *Page* 43. The Parting-Cup (*Vin de Congé*)—wine and spices at the end of dinner—is frequently alluded to in *Saintré*. It seems to have been known in less exalted society as the "*Boute-hors*"; see Eileen Power, *The Goodman of Paris* (translation of *Le Ménagier de Paris*), Introduction, p. 37.

7 *Page* 47. C'est tout que d'aimer loyaulment,
En ung tout seul lieu c'est assez ;
Quiconcques le fait aultrement,
Il est de bien faire lassez
Et tous ses beaulx faitz sont passez.
Car ung cueur qui par tout s'espart
Et requert dames de tous lez
En doit avoir petite part.

Se part en a, c'est meschamment,
Et vient de lieux mal renommés,
Et ne se peult faire aultrement ;
Et puis quant il s'y est boutté
Et s'est après bien advisez,
Dieu scet s'il congnoist lors à par
Comment des riches bien cellez
En doit avoir petite part.

Celle part ne vaut pas gramment,
Quant plusieurs s'y sont ahurtez ;
N'amours n'accorde nullement
Que telles gens soient aimez,
Ains soient par tout diffamez ;
Car ung cueur qui par tout s'espart
Et requiert dames de tous lez,
En doit avoir petite part.

I have not been able to trace the author of this ballade. The absence of an *Envoi* suggests that it is an early one.

8 *Page* 48. Medieval literature, sacred and profane, is full of the Seven Deadly Sins. It is interesting to compare this courtly version with the bourgeois version in the *Ménagier de Paris* (see note 6 above) and with the allegorical description in Spenser's *Faerie Queene* Book I.

9 *Page* 49. "Fair son." Madame addresses Saintré as "mon ami" both as his instructress and afterwards as his Lady *par amours*. In translation I have used "fair son" and later "dear love" for this elusive expression which (still in modern French) can be anything from a half-patronizing form of address (or used by a grown-up person to a child) to an endearment between lovers.

[10] *Page* 54. Barratry=vexatious litigation, and is also still found, with the meaning of "fraud", in the standard wording of Marine Insurance Policies.

[11] *Page* 60. This amusing piece of casuistry seems to indicate that the chivalrous Code of Love was less platonic in practice than in theory.

[12] *Page* 61. Cf. Eileen Power, *The Goodman of Paris*, p. 92.

[13] *Page* 62. The Church, supported at times by the Crown, waged a long war against the "*duel judiciaire*", "trial by battle", which was legal until Louis IX (Saint Louis) altered the law, and continued to be practised long afterwards. Richelieu, in suppressing duelling, was only doing what many of his predecessors had tried and failed to do. In England it was actually not made illegal until about a century ago (though of course it had long fallen into desuetude) when a relative of a murdered person, dissatisfied with the acquittal of the suspected murderer, summoned him to trial by battle and caused a considerable legal sensation.

La Sale, quite reasonably, is trying to show the distinction between jousting, which was merely a rather dangerous form of sport, and duelling.

[14] *Page* 64. *De Re Militari*, translated into French as *l'Art de Chevalerie* by Jean de Meung, the author of the second part of the *Roman de la Rose*.

[15] *Page* 69. There follow here, in the original, a few pages of theological doctrine, beginning with the Creed.

[16] *Page* 78. Scarlet (from a Persian word) was a kind of fine cloth, varying in colour; the present meaning is a secondary one.

[17] *Page* 78. Brunet was a dark brown cloth. Saint-Lô is a small town in Normandy, still manufacturing woollens.

[18] *Page* 83. The French, *cuers*, may possibly be the modern *chœurs*—choirs and not *cœurs*—hearts.

[19] *Page* 90. Romany—Roumelian.

[20] *Page* 92. Carving was an important part of a Squire's duties:

"Curteys he was, lowly and servisable
And carf beforn his fader at the table"

(Chaucer's Prologue).

[21] *Page* 95. "*Qui bien et mal ne puet souffrir
A grant honneur ne puet venir.*"

[22] *Page* 98. Whether his father or his patron the Seigneur de Pouilly is not clear.

[23] *Page* 100. Emprise—first of all "enterprise" and then the token which the knight-errant vowed to wear until his enterprise

329

was accomplished, or until someone delivered him of the Emprise by jousting with him.   Cf. page 123.

²⁴ *Page* 101.   "*A petit mercier, petit panier.*"   The proverb is still current.

²⁵ *Page* 103.   See Introduction, page 21.

²⁶ *Page* 108.   The roundel was the guard protecting the hand. See Plate VI.

²⁷ *Page* 109.   Pole-axes were something like the more modern halberd.   Plate VIII shows two very clearly.   Each was three weapons in one : an axe-blade, a point at the back, and a spear-head at the end.

²⁸ *Page* 117.   " They without against them within " :   more usually *tenants* (i.e. the challengers who held the lists) versus "*assaillants* ".

²⁹ *Page* 119.   In the elaborately staged tournaments of the period the horses were trapped in magnificent caparisons : a good specimen can be seen in Plate VI.

³⁰ *Page* 120.   In Chapter LVIII, Saintré's arms are given as : " gules a bend *or* ; three labels of the same ".   It is curious that such a " wise and proficient herald " as La Sale should have stumbled over the blazoning of his hero's arms.   The label in heraldry, shaped thus ∽∽∽ is generally used for " differencing " an eldest son's arms during his father's life-time.

³¹ *Page* 123.   See Note 23 to *Page* 100.

³² *Page* 133.   In time of war, a herald enjoyed " diplomatic immunity " and his tabard was the mark of his office.

³³ *Page* 142.   *Plaisance* is Piacenza in Italy.

    " . . . the crest of parchment or leather towering above a helm whose mantle, from the ribbon-like strip of the early thirteenth century, had grown into a fluttering cloak with wildly slittered edge streaming out behind the charging knight."   *Encyclopædia Britannica, Article on Armour.*   Cf. also Plate VI which, by the way, is reproduced as an illustration of the *Encycl. Britannica* article.

³⁴ *Page* 142.   Vambraces (French *avant-bras*) were the pieces covering the forearms.   Sollerets were steel shoes.

³⁵ *Page* 143.   Miniver is the fur of the Siberian squirrel.   Miniver, sable and ermine were all much esteemed in the Middle Ages.

³⁶ *Page* 144.   *Naissant*, in heraldry=showing only the upper part of the body.   The *demi-* is therefore superfluous.

³⁷ *Page* 149.   The *rest* was the check holding the butt of the lance.

³⁸ *Page* 149.   As tournaments became more of a spectacle and less of a combat the *tilt* was introduced—a cloth stretched along the lists

Notes to the Text

so that the horses, charging along either side of it, could not collide though their riders might be unhorsed by a well-aimed lance above the tilt. Later in the fifteenth century, by the date of the MS from which Plate VI is taken, the tilt had become a barrier of wood. However, tournaments never became altogether a safe sport : Henri II of France was killed in one in 1559.

39 *Page* 149. *A rouncy* was an ordinary saddle-horse or pack-horse as distinct from the Knight's charger or rather *courser*, and the lady's *hackney*. Chaucer's Shipman " rode upon a rouncy, as he couthe ". The English surname Runciman is derived from the rouncy-man who looked after the rouncies.

40 *Page* 151. A jewel (for the winner's Lady) was the usual forfeit paid by the loser in a tournament. At the Tourney of Saumur (see Introduction, page 8) the vanquished jousters each had to give a diamond, a ruby, or a horse. A contemporary description of the Tourney says that fifty-four diamonds and thirty-six rubies were forfeited.

41 *Page* 156. Basinets—see Note 122 *Page* 336.

42 *Page* 158. See Note 27 *Page* 330.

43 *Page* 166. Cyprus birds (*oysellets de Chippre*) seem to have been bags filled with perfumed powder, shaped like birds.

44 *Page* 171. Jean le Meingre, called *Boucicault*, a famous French captain in the Hundred Years' War, was Marshal of France, fought against the Turks at the battle of Nicopolis (1396) and against the English at Agincourt, where he was taken prisoner, dying in England in 1421. He was Governor of Genoa 1401-1409, and La Sale, who was in Italy at the time, very likely met him.

45 *Page* 173.   " *Quant vient en ung assault*
      Mieulx vault Saintré que Boucicault ;
      Mais quant vient en ung traictié,
      Mieulx vault Boucicault que Saintré."

Boucicault, however, was born only two years before Saintré's death. It looks as though La Sale made up the jingle himself.

46 *Page* 173. " Loysselench " is perhaps meant for Leczinski, a noble Polish family.

47 *Page* 174. A *saltire* is a St Andrew's Cross.

48 *Page* 174 *Voided* is an heraldic term (French *vidé*) meaning that the inner part of the cross is removed so that the " field " can be seen through it.

49 *Page* 174. No doubt Saint James of Compostella, a very favourite objective for pilgrimages.

50 *Page* 183. The French is *penarts*, which the Glossary to the Champion-Desonay edition of *Saintré* gives as (*double*) *wings*, but I

331

prefer to follow Godefroy's *Lexique de l'Ancien Francais* in translating the word by " daggers ".

[51] *Page* 194. This was axiomatic. Cf. page 17 and Malory's *Morte d'Arthur* Bk. 10, Chapter LV :—" Such a foolish Knight as ye are ", said Sir Dinadan, " I saw but late this day lying by a well ; and there he lay like a fool grinning, and would not speak, and his shield lay by him, and his horse stood by him ; and well I wot he was a lover ". " Ah, Fair Sir ", said Sir Tristram, " Are ye not a lover ? " " Marry, fie on that craft," said Sir Dinadan. " That is evil said," said Sir Tristram " for a knight may never be of prowess but if he be a lover."

[52] *Page* 200. *Francs à cheval.* " Coin of King Jean II, on which he is depicted on horseback, in full armour " (Glossary to Champion-Desonay edition).

[53] *Page* 201. Chamfer, O.F. *Chanfrain* (literally "break-corner" from its shape) was a piece of head-armour for a horse. The horses in Plate VI are wearing them.

[54] *Page* 201. The *barde* was the horse's breast- and flank-armour Again see Plate VI.

[55] *Page* 205. The spelling of English names was rather too much for La Sale. Buckingham is *Bouquincan*, Cobham is *Gobehen*, Huntingdon is *Hostindon*, and Dengorde I have been unable to identify.

[56] *Page* 206. *Bezants*, in heraldry, are golden discs, from the *Byzantine* coin of that name.

[57] *Page* 206. *Sinople*, usually *vert* in English heraldry, was originally the colour of a species of oxydized iron which came from Sinope in Asia Minor.

[58] *Page* 207. *Copony :* an heraldic term meaning " with a bordure of alternate colours ".

[59] *Page* 209. *Mallestestes*—Malatesta.

[60] *Page* 209. *Torteaux* or *roundlets* are coloured discs used in heraldry.

[61] *Page* 211. See Note 44, *Page* 171.

[62] *Page* 211. *Francesco II*, who was despoiled of his possessions and strangled with his two sons, by the Venetians in 1406. La Sale was in Italy or Sicily during that year.

[63] *Page* 213. The sentence is very involved, but this seems to be approximately the meaning.

[64] *Page* 216. *Saracens* served as a generic term for infidels of any kind—in this case the heathen of East Prussia and Lithuania, against whom the Teutonic Knights waged war. But La Sale and his contemporaries did not worry much about geography or racial distinctions and, as will be seen presently, he arrays in battle

> " All who since, baptized or infidel
> Jousted in Aspramont or Montalban,
> Damasco or Morocco or Trebizond,
> Or whom Biserta sent from Afric's shore . . ."

65 *Page 217.* The *lance*, used in this sense, was a military unit composed of two or three men-at-arms, each with several archers and unarmoured followers.

66 *Page 218.* A *Knight banneret* was one having vassals under his banner.

67 *Page 218.* Moſt of the names and arms, which are very numerous, have been omitted.

68 *Page 219.* This is heraldically wrong; a colour should never be on another colour but only on a metal.

69 *Page 219.* *Martlets*, Fr. *Merlettes*, are little heraldic birds with no feet and no beak.

70 *Page 219.* An *orle* is a bordure round a shield, with the martlets diſtributed round it.

71 *Page 219.* *Gyronny* is (a shield) divided into triangles of alternate colours : the moſt famous example in British heraldry is the arms of Campbell.

72 *Page 219.* *Fleurdelysé*—sprinkled with fleurs-de-lis.

73 *Page 219.* *Bendy* is said of a shield divided into diagonal ſtrips.

74 *Page 219.* *Beauvoisis* : the diſtrict round Beauvais.

75 *Page 219.* *Sau*—perhaps a Provençal pronunciation of *Salut*.

76 *Page 220.* *Onduly*—divided into wavy ſtrips. See also Note II *Page 324.*

77 *Page 220.* At this period part of Guyenne was English.

78 *Page 220.* *Ponthieu* was the neighbourhood of Abbeville.

79 *Page 221.* *Vermandois* : the neighbourhood of St Quentin.

80 *Page 221.* *Corbie* : a small town near Amiens.

81 *Page 221.* A compliment from La Sale to his employer's family—see Introduction, p. 8.

82 *Page 221.* Perhaps a piece of flattery intended to catch the eye of Philip the Good, who was technically a vassal of the French King, but being actually more powerful and wealthy than his Suzerain, was trying to assert his independence.

83 *Page 226.* The pedigrees of gentle families drawn up by the English heralds in their periodic visitations of the counties, and preserved in the College of Heralds, are an invaluable help to modern genealogiſts.

84 *Page 227.* *Thorn* : in Weſt Prussia, on the Viſtula.

NOTES TO THE TEXT

[65] *Page* 228. The *mullet*, in heraldry, is a five-pointed pierced star, and really represents the rowel of a spur (Fr. *molette*). A well known English coat bearing a mullet is that of the De Veres.

[86] *Page* 229. A great many names, evidently very misspelt, of German and Dutch nobles have been left out here.

[87] *Page* 230. The Greek Empire of Trebizond, founded by Alexis Comnenus, ceased to exist in 1261 ; so this is rather a serious ana-chronism.

[88] *Page* 231. This very fanciful geography lesson was taken bodily by La Sale out of his earlier work *La Salade*.

[89] *Page* 232. The still existing monastery near the Gebel Katerin, in Sinai. Saint Catherine of Alexandria, martyred on the " Catharine wheel " was, like St George, one of the Saints popularised in the West by ex-Crusaders.

[90] *Page* 232. It was usual to create a number of new Knights before going into action.

[91] *Page* 233. The swallow-tailed pennon (see Plate VII) was the mark of a Knight, and the sentence means that many Knights were created.

[92] *Page* 233. See Note II, p. 324.

[93] *Page* 234. *In bend*—i.e. diagonally across the shield.

[94] *Page* 235. *Endorsed* is a heraldic term meaning " back to back ".

[95] *Page* 235. Probably Cairo, known in the Middle Ages as *Babylone d'Egypte*.

[96] *Page* 235. *Samara* in Russia ; unless it is meant for Samarkand.

[97] *Page* 245. Literally : " under the cap ".

[98] *Page* 263. Because La Sale pokes fun at the notorious short-comings of the late medieval Church, there is no need to jump to the conclusion that he was by way of being an early Protestant. But the state of this nameless Abbey is worth comparing with the description (almost contemporary) of life at the Abbey of Peterborough, in Volume III of the Lincoln Record Society's " Visitations of Religious Houses ".

[99] *Page* 265. Glass was still a great luxury at this date.

[100] *Page* 267. *Hypocras :* sweet spiced wine "which took its name from the particular sort of bag, termed Hippocrates's sleeve, through which it was strained " (Eileen Power, *The Goodman of Paris*, p. 324). The *Goodman* gives a receipt for making it (p. 299).

[101] *Page* 270. *Collation* is here used in its proper sense of " a light repast in the evening of a fast-day ". The derivation is from the *collationes patrum* (Lives of the Fathers) which were read aloud during the meal in Benedictine Houses.

[102] *Page* 270. The French *rouget* may be either the red mullet or the gurnard.

103 *Page 270.* Or perhaps lemon-sole.

104 *Page 270.* *Galantine* was usually a kind of fish-sauce. The method of preparing Eel Reversed (Anguille Renversée) is described by the *Ménagier de Paris* (p. 271 in the translation). It was split lengthwise, turned inside-out, and boiled in red wine.

105 *Page 270.* *Talmouse*—" a piece of sweet pastry, the ingredients of which included cream, cheese and eggs " (Godefroy, *op. cit.*). Cf. also *The Goodman of Paris*, p. 326.

106 *Page 270.* This is a guess. The French is " *Melicque* ".

107 *Page 271.* For *Duke's Powder*, a mixture of sugar and spices, see *The Goodman of Paris*, p. 299.

108 *Page 271.* *Grenache.* " A sweet Greek wine " (*The Goodman of Paris*. Notes, p. 323). But Larousse gives the term as still in use for a wine made in Languedoc and Roussillon.

109 *Page 271.* *Malvoisie* came from the peninsula of that name in Greece.

110 *Page 274.* " *Cellui qui sert, et ne parsert, son loyer pert.*"

111 *Page 281.* i.e. Knights (*Reiter*) of the Imperial Army.

112 *Page 282.* In point of fact, knights-errant were more often than not considered rather a nuisance. Jacques de Lalaing (see Introduction) visited most of the Courts of Europe and in only two—Spain and Scotland—did he find an adversary to joust with. In England he met with a very chilly reception from the virtuous but unromantic Henry VI, and was not allowed to publish his challenge.

113 *Page 287.* Evidently a shrine near Paris. St Côme and St Damien are the patron saints of surgeons.

114 *Page 289.* By the time *Saintré* was written, the high-crowned hat, worn by the man on the extreme left of Plate VI, had come into fashion.

115 *Page 291.* It is not clear whether this " maistre d'ostel " is the Abbey cellarer or My Lady's steward.

116 *Page 292.* " L'ostel "—but later on they appear to be at the Abbey.

117 *Page 293.* The French has " presust ", which M. Champion (Glossary to *Le Petit Jehan de Saintré*) suggests may have been meant for " pregust "—" a foretaste " : hors d'œuvre, if you like.

118 *Page 293.* *Tournus*, on the Saône.

119 *Page 293.* *St Pourçain*, in the modern *département* of Allier (Central France).

120 *Page 294.* La Sale knew Sicily well (see Introduction).

121 *Page 297.* The sentence is very difficult but I think this is the sense of it. Hose were still long stockings, not joined after the fashion of pants, as they were later.

NOTES TO THE TEXT

¹²² *Page* 305. *Basinets, salets with beavers, or helms.* "The desire for a better defence than a ſteel cap and camail and a less cumbrous one than the great helm, in which the knight rode half ſtifled and half blind, brought in as a fighting head-piece the basinet with a movable visor. This is found throughout the fourteenth century, disappearing in the next when the salet and its varieties displaced it. But there were many knights who ſtill fought with the great helm covering basinet and camail" (chain-mail neck-guard) (*Encyclopædia Britannica*, Article on *Arms and Armour*).

The salet was "a large ſteel cap, whose edge is carried out from the brows and ſtill more boldly at the back of the neck" (*ibid*). Not unlike the "tin hats" worn by the German army during the War.

¹²³ *Page* 306. Doubtless a euphemism for the Devil. In modern French, "*on parle du loup, et il sort des bois*".

¹²⁴ *Page* 306. Quite literally the French is "Was there not a buzzing in your ears?"

¹²⁵ *Page* 306. Brewets (broths with pieces of meat in them) are described in *The Goodman of Paris*, passim.

¹²⁶ *Page* 309. "*Par là ou par la feneſtre passerez.*"

¹²⁷ *Page* 312. "True blue."

¹²⁸ *Page* 317. Boethius, philosopher, poet and ſtatesman (Miniſter of Theodoric and put to death by him A.D. 525) was the author of the celebrated *De Consolatione Philosophiæ*, a popular work in the Middle Ages. Chaucer translated it into English, and La Sale perhaps borrowed this passage from the French verse translation by Jean de Meung. I have not had an opportunity of verifying this.

¹²⁹ *Page* 321. "Here lyeth Sir John de Saintré, Kt. Seneschal of Anjou and Maine and Chamberlaine to the Lord Duke of Anjou, who dyed in the year of our Lord MCCCLXVIII on the twenty-fifth daye of October, maye his soule reſt in peace."

ADDENDUM

¹³⁰ *Page* 113. For another instance of the custom of making vows when the peacock or other bird was brought in, see p. 53 of Miss Joan Evans's translation of *El Vitorial* ("*The Unconquered Knight*," Broadway Translations).

INDEX

The notes referred to are on pp. 327-336

Andalusian horses, 165-6
Anger, sin of, 49-51
Apulian horses, 165
Arming a Knight, 183, 308
Armour, descriptions of, 142, 157, 305, 308 ; owned by townsfolk, 305 ; for horses, 201
Avarice, sin of, 53-5

Badges, 78, 83-4, 87, 100
Barratry, 54 and note 10
Basinets, 305 and note 122
Basinet-visors, 247
Black Sea, 231
Blue, colour of loyalty, 312
Boethius (*De Consolatione Philosophiae*), 317 and note 128
Boucicault, 171-2, 210-14 and note 44
Bourbon tarts, 270
Brewets, 306 and note 125

Caparisons (for horses), 119, 143-4, 182, 254 and *passim*
Carving Squire, 92-4, 96
Choler, sin of, 49-51
Clothes, descriptions and cost of, 72, 78, 80-81, 85-6, 89-91, 97, 100, 119, 130, 142-4, 153-4, 247
Collation, 270 and note 101
Cross, Sign of the, 72
" Cyprus birds ", 166 and note 43

Dancing, 163, 190, 199, 243 ; -competitions, 112
Devices—*see* Badges
Doctor and patient, 259-261
Duke's Powder, 271-2 and note 107

Eels reversed, 270 and note 104
Emprises, 107-116, 123, 132-3, 139, 174-6, 210-12, 246-50, 252-3, 294 and note 23
" English faction " in Guyenne, 220
English nobles, names of, 205-7, 228
Envy, sin of, 51-3

Flattery, 75-6
Francs-à-cheval, 200 and note 52

Galantine, 270 and note 104
Garter King-of-Arms, 204-5
Gawain, 41
Gelbona, 231
Geography, 231-2
Giron the courteous, 41
Glass windows, 265
Gluttony, sin of, 57-8, 73
Grenache (wine), 271 and note 108

Hawks and hawking, 289-90, 302
Helms, 305 and note 122
Herald, duties of, 110, 131-5 ; visitations, 226

337

INDEX

338